Meg

Getting Away
With It

By Julie Cohen

Julie Cohen

Getting Away With It

headline
review

First published in Great Britain in 2010
by HEADLINE REVIEW
An imprint of HEADLINE PUBLISHING GROUP

1

Cataloguing in Publication Data is available from the British Library

ISBN 978 0 7553 5060 5 (Hardback)
ISBN 978 0 7553 5061 2 (Trade paperback)

Typeset in Sabon by Avon DataSet Ltd,
Bidford-on-Avon, Warwickshire

Printed and bound in Great Britain by
Clays Ltd, St Ives plc

HEADLINE PUBLISHING GROUP
An Hachette UK Company
338 Euston Road
London NW1 3BH

www.headline.co.uk
www.hachette.co.uk

To my mother

The Birthday

I sat on the cliff edge with my legs dangling over the drop, in a gold lamé dress barely long enough to cover my arse. My bare thighs crawled with goose bumps. I'd wrapped a winter coat around my shoulders and my blond wig was perched beside me on the cliff edge like a small, extraordinarily long-haired animal, maybe a mutant guinea pig.

I never took care of wigs because I hated them. They itched and got in my way and I thanked my lucky stars whenever I got hired to double for a brunette actress or one who wore a hat. Usually if the hair people knew me, they'd hang on to my wigs until the last minute so I wouldn't lose them in a bush or something. But last night Joanne-from-hair had been in the Purple Armadillo club with us, drinking Car Bombs, and therefore this morning she'd done my hair as quickly as possible before disappearing off to the back of the trailer to nurse her hangover.

Below me, the yellows and browns of the desert stretched out in a wide arid sea. Cactuses and rocks cast long blue shadows. It looked cold, but not as cold as me. The sun had only just come up over the peak of the mountain and the film crew, bussed in from Barstow at this god-awful early hour, huddled over their equipment. They were swaddled in jumpers

1

and anoraks, clutching paper cups of coffee and wreathed in halos of steam.

I yawned and kicked my feet in my driving shoes. It was a long way down to the sand and rocks. People thought that making a film was all glamour and excitement, even if you were a stunt woman, but mostly it was a lot of waiting around at inhospitable hours until it was time to do something. I could have done with an hour or two more of sleep. I rummaged in my coat pocket, found my tube of extra-strong mints and was about to pop one into my mouth when I heard the crunch of gravel behind me.

'Nice dress,' said Allen.

'I'd rather be wearing a snowsuit.'

'Got any chicken in there? I could do with some more breakfast.'

I glanced down at my cleavage, unenhanced by any inserts, of the poultry variety or otherwise. I hated those more than the wigs; there was nothing quite like being in the middle of a fight sequence and having half your tits fly out of your bra into your opponent's face. 'Thank God, the chicken is off the menu today. She's only a B cup.'

I heard him climbing over the guard rail behind me. 'Sure it's safe out here?'

'No. But that's the fun bit.'

His big, familiar body sat down next to mine on the cliff edge, on the other side of me than the wig. 'Brought you some more coffee.'

'Thanks. I can use it.' I took the steaming paper cup from him. He made sure our fingers touched.

'Nice view.'

I shrugged. 'It's a desert.'

'I was talking about your legs.'

I laughed. Allen could leap off skyscrapers without

flinching, he could trash me in a fair fight and he could always make me laugh even when I didn't feel like it – last night, for example. He rubbed his hand through his cropped black hair and then across the stubble on his chin.

'Fun night last night,' he said.

'Yeah, it was.'

'I'm feeling a little worse for wear, though. You?'

'I'm fine.'

'You seem on edge, if you don't mind me saying.'

'Well, I am half-dangling off a cliff.'

He chuckled in his big Texan way. 'I wasn't talking so literal.'

'I'm just waiting for the car to get here,' I said, which was at least one-third of the truth. 'I can't wait to see it.'

'Yep, she'll be a beauty, all right. Liza, I really did have fun last night.'

I knew from the way he said it, the way the tips of his fingers touched the bare goose-fleshy part of my thigh, that he wasn't talking about the drinking session at the Purple Armadillo with the crew, but about what had happened afterwards in his hotel room.

'It was lots of fun,' I said, and that was the whole truth. 'Thanks.'

I smiled over at him. He'd broken his nose too many times to be handsome, but I liked the way his skin crinkled around his eyes when he smiled, and I liked his hands, and I liked how he'd stopped me from feeling lonely last night. He was one of the good guys, though more often than not he doubled for a villain onscreen. Affable and laid-back and far too nice for me.

'So, are you a fool or not?' he asked.

'What?'

'It's the first of April. Is it your birthday today, or was it

3

yesterday? I couldn't quite tell with all the celebrating last night.'

'Oh. No, today's my thirtieth birthday. Yesterday was my sister's.' You'd think that with the cold and the hangover and the muscles pleasantly aching from a night of strenuous and athletic sex, I'd be numb to the little stab of pain and guilt when I mentioned Lee.

'That's cool. You were born a day apart?'

'We were born ten minutes apart, either side of midnight. Her birthday's the thirty-first of March and I'm the first of April.'

'Twins? Do you look exactly alike?' He raised an eyebrow in a comic impersonation of a leer.

'Don't even think about it. We're completely different, and we don't share men.'

'Twins with different birthdays. So you always got two parties, huh?'

'One was more than enough.'

'Too bad you're working this year. You must miss her, right?'

'She's busy. And I – haven't seen her for a while.' I picked up a rock and tossed it over the side of the cliff. I watched it fall downwards, bounce off a tussock and fly out of sight. 'I wish that Enzo would hurry up and get here. We're going to lose the light if we wait too much longer, and I don't want to get up this early tomorrow.'

'Did you have a fight?'

'I don't want to talk about it, to be honest, Al.'

'I've got four brothers and we always used to fight. But we'd wrestle it out and then go out for a few beers. Girls are different, I guess.'

'My sister isn't big on wrestling or beer. Hey, look, that's the truck.' I pointed to a silver vehicle in the distance, kicking

4

up a pillow of dust behind it on the desert road. I began to get up, but Allen stopped me with a hand on my wrist.

'I've been thinking, Liza.'

Oh no. My stomach sank.

'Seems silly you and me both live in LA and we never see each other except on a job. We should get together sometime.'

'Al, I like you. And last night *was* fun, but that's all it was. We were drinking, I was a bit lonely, we hooked up. Let's leave it there, okay?'

He shrugged. 'Seems like you shouldn't have to be lonely. We got a lot in common, we live in the same town, we're good in the sack. We could probably give it a shot.'

I took a deep breath. 'Al, you know that's not my thing.'

'It seemed to be your thing when we were in bed together last night.' He ran his thumb up my arm, bare under the coat. 'Think about it for a few minutes.'

'I don't need to. You're a stunt man, I'm a stunt woman, we work on the same films – it's so cosy, isn't it? It's very lovely and all that, but it's too safe. I know all your moves and you know all of mine. It's like pretending to fight.'

'It doesn't have to be that way. I think we could really build something, Liza. We could be a good team.'

I shook my head. 'I'm not a team person. I like being alone.'

'I thought you said you were lonely.'

'Well, you know, nobody likes to be alone on their birthday. But I'm not in the market for a relationship, not with you or anybody. I'm not a settling-down person.'

'In other words, it's not me, it's you.' Al's face and voice were as laid-back and friendly as ever, but I saw a dull glint of pain in his blue eyes. He shrugged. 'Sure. I've heard that before. I get it. No hard feelings. So you think you might want to celebrate your real birthday with me tonight? We can get cake and ice cream or something.'

I really did stand up this time, snagging my wig on the way. 'I'm sorry. I don't like ice cream.' I dropped my hand onto his broad shoulder. 'Let's leave it with good memories, all right?'

'Sure. Okay.' He stood up, too, brushing down his clothes. Bits of dirt and gravel fell off his trousers and bounced off the edge of the cliff. We both stepped over the guard rail and walked towards the circus of vehicles and trailers and tents, where the rest of the crew were suddenly active, getting ready for the truck that was about to pull up.

I finished off my coffee and crushed the cup in my hand. I really could have done without that conversation this morning. Or not the conversation so much as the obvious fact that Al was putting a bright face on it. Not when I was already thinking about the birthday card, probably pink, that was doubtless lying on the doormat of my apartment back in LA. Lee always sent a card. No matter what happened, what had gone between us, she always remembered. She'd feel good that she'd sent a card, that she'd fulfilled a duty, done the right thing.

And I remembered our birthdays too. I couldn't help remembering them. But not the same way. It was only one of the many aspects in which we were different. She sent cards, made phone calls, and I went out partying and got laid and thought about what she was doing without me. It was already lunchtime in Stoneguard; she was at work at Ice Cream Heaven, a bunch of fresh flowers on her desk. She'd have plenty of cards, lined up in a neat row.

I'd bought one for her. It was still sitting on my table in my apartment in Los Angeles, because I'd forgotten to send it before I left. Maybe I should call her. Yes, I should definitely call her. It was past time.

The problem was, I so rarely wanted to do what I should do. Just look at Al, walking beside me.

'So you're feeling all right?' he said.

'Fine. Great. Why?'

'I was thinking –' I made to interrupt him, and he continued over me – 'it wasn't about us, it was that I'm not sure I'd want to do a stunt with a hangover like the one you've probably got on you.'

'I'm not hungover.'

'Nobody will mind playing it safe, you know. It's an expensive car. And this is a dangerous road. We can do it tomorrow. I'll say it's my fault, if you want.'

I stopped walking. 'I am fine, Al. I'm doing the stunt.'

'If you're sure.'

'I'm one hundred per cent, totally sure. Are you giving me a hard time because I won't go out with you?'

For as long as I'd known him, Al had always been smiling. Always Texan good-natured, even in the middle of a stunt. Suddenly, he wasn't. His mouth straightened and his face looked grim, the broken nose a sign of violence.

'No,' he said. 'I'm asking you a couple of questions because I'm a professional. I saw you were drinking last night and I'm concerned about your safety. I'd ask anyone else the same thing.'

'You can go ahead and ask anyone else, then, because I'm also a professional and I know perfectly well when I'm safe to drive.'

I jammed my wig on my head and stalked away from him, tossing my winter coat aside. I hardly noticed the cold air hitting my bare arms and upper chest.

Todd, the second unit director, met me on my way to the

others. He was a tall and geeky guy, wearing a woolly hat and rubbing his thin hands together in excitement and cold. 'It'll be here in five minutes,' he told me.

'I know, I can't wait.'

'The Pipe King's coming, too; Gloria's going to try to get him out of the way so we can start shooting. Apparently he needed a haircut this morning, that's why it's late getting here.'

I rolled my eyes, but said, 'I guess you want to look your best to see your car being the star of a major motion picture.'

'Something like that. You going to be ready to roll?'

'No problem.'

We joined the entire second unit, who had assembled along the side of the road waiting for the truck. I sensed rather than saw Allen join us, a few metres away. The usual early-morning griping faded into murmurs as the silver vehicle and its long trailer pulled up with a rumble and a whoosh of hydraulic brakes. 'Seems like it would have got here a bit quicker if he'd driven the Enzo himself,' I muttered. 'The thing does happen to go over two hundred miles an hour.'

'Doesn't want desert dust on the paintwork,' Todd murmured back. 'I'm not sure the owner drives it, anyway. I think it's a trophy thing.'

'It is a crime to own a car like that and never drive it.'

'Maybe he's a lousy driver.' Hogan, the stunt coordinator, was standing behind us. 'How you feeling today, Liza?'

'I'm great.'

'Should be smooth sailing this morning anyway; you just have to make the car look good, which isn't hard with a vehicle like this. No need to book it, just go on the edge of caution.'

I nodded. I'd worked with Hogan plenty before and he

knew what I could do. The stunt business is built on trust and contacts, knowing the right people and doing a good job for them so that you'll get called to work again. We watched as the truck driver opened the trailer and extended the ramp. And then there was the car, being unbuckled from its tethers and set free.

Redder than sin and glossier than temptation, low to the ground, like a predator. It looked fast even when it was standing still. It came to life with a roar and rolled down the ramp to the road and I licked my lips in anticipation. The driver's side door opened like a wing.

Of course, then the bloody Pipe King had to go and spoil it.

He leaped out of the car, a short guy with thinning hair and rimless glasses, and shouted, 'Hey, guys! How about it, huh? You likee?'

'It's a pity that all the really expensive supercars have to be owned by rich people,' I said quietly to Hogan. Todd hurried up to shake the Pipe King's hand.

'All you have to do is make a fortune out of pipes, and this too could be yours,' he answered.

'You know, right now that's looking like a viable career ambition.' I walked up to the car. Up close, it was even more gorgeous, glorious low-slung high-tech speed, crouched on wide tyres. I touched the rear spoiler and slid my fingertips up the sleek red surface.

'The car's the star,' the Pipe King was telling everyone who would listen, in a hammering voice. 'The car's the star. You know, I had to be personally invited to purchase this baby: there were less than four hundred made, for special customers only. I went to the factory and saw it come off the line myself. I fell in love right there and then.'

I peered down into the engine compartment. Six-litre,

aluminium-block V12 engine, every part pristine, emblazoned with the Ferrari stallion. I shuddered with lust. The Pipe King might be a tosser, but he had a point. This car was a star.

'Six-sixty horsepower, top speed two-nineteen. Zero to one-oh-oh in six point six. Purrs like a lion kitten. I'm telling you, once you've driven one of these, you never look back.'

'Have you got it up to full speed?' I asked. The Pipe King looked at me with surprise that anyone else could do any talking.

'Not exactly, not that fast, no. I like it too much to risk it. Every time someone crashes one of these, the value of mine goes up another few hundred thou!' He chuckled. 'It's enough to feel all that power behind you, and the looks when you drive this baby out on the roads.'

I caressed it, walked around to the bonnet and followed the long line of it with my eyes. Imagine having a car like this, one of the fastest on the planet, and never driving it full speed. Imagine caring more about how people looked at you in it and what the figures were, than feeling the rush, the adrenaline, the power. Imagine calling it *baby*.

This car was most definitely adult.

'I can't wait to get behind the wheel,' I said.

'Of course, we'll be going nowhere near the full speed today,' Todd jumped in quickly to reassure the Pipe King.

'Sure, sure, I can't wait to tell everyone that's my car up there on the screen. I thought Carmen Clare was driving it, though?' The Pipe King craned his neck, peering around for a genuine honest-to-goodness movie star.

'I'm her stunt double,' I told him, holding out my hand for a shake. 'Liza Haven.'

'Oh. Oh, nice to meet you, I thought I'd be meeting Carmen today.'

'She'll be on set tomorrow to do the pick-ups in the car,' Todd told him.

'Oh, okay. I just thought—'

I knew what he'd thought. His fancy car would get him in with one of the most beautiful and famous women on the planet. Instead, he had me in a blond wig. 'If we're ready, we can get going,' I said to Todd.

'Sure, we're all set up, and I don't want the sun too high. Nice if we could get it in one take, otherwise we'll have to do it again tomorrow.'

'Shouldn't be a problem.' The hair and make-up crews descended upon me, tutting about my wig, and while they were faffing I reached for my walkie-talkie.

'Practice run first at halfspeed,' Hogan told me.

'I can do it without, we're pressed for time.'

Hogan frowned. 'You driven one of these before?'

'It's a car, Hogan. I can drive it.'

I heard a subtle sound behind me, like a cough. I glanced back: Allen.

'Will you be shooting the practice run?' I asked Todd. He nodded. 'Then I'm good to go.' I screwed up my eyes for a last powder-puff assault and then headed for the open door of the car.

The interior was stripped-down, stunning in its simple functionality. I slipped into the carbon-fibre racing seat and adjusted everything for my size. I was slightly taller than the owner. The edge of the seat was warm from the Pipe King's backside, especially compared with the chilled bare skin of my legs.

'You beauty,' I said to the car.

'Practice run first,' Hogan said to me, leaning in through the door. 'And remember, we're not testing the car, merely making it look good. Go on the edge –'

11

'– of caution. Got it.' I closed the door, turned the key in the ignition and pressed the start button on the dash.

Oh, heaven. The engine growled into life behind me, thrumming through the seat into my spine. Oh, *yes*. I touched the throttle, the merest touch with the tip of my toe, and it roared.

The way cleared in front of me and I drove the car, all restrained sleek power, to the starting point. The tracking vehicle was already waiting, cameras mounted. I couldn't hear anything above the engine, but I knew that Todd was shouting orders, alerting the camera crews along the road that we were ready to begin. Film sets: hours of waiting, and then everything happens at once.

I sat and looked at the car, felt it alive around me. Found the controls, learned its tricks. Of course a car like this could only show you its true identity once you had it on the road, at speed. I glanced at the road ahead of me; it was a curved course down the mountain, with a sheer drop on the left beyond the guard rail. For a moment I pictured hitting the accelerator without warning, jumping from nought to sixty within a heartbeat, scattering the crew waiting for Hogan's signal. I could roar past the cameras, forgetting 'the edge of caution', and once I got down the mountain to that glorious, long straight stretch of desert, opening up the engine and seeing what she could do. Just me, and the car, and a long fast ride to nowhere.

Of course, I wouldn't do that. Making off on a joyride with the fabulously expensive principal car was a one-way ticket to unemployability – if not a jail sentence. But for an instant I closed my eyes and imagined it. Then I opened them again, and waited for the signal.

The walkie crackled. 'All ready, Liza,' said Hogan's voice. The car leaped forward, pressing me back into the seat, and I began to smile.

The waiting crew passed by in a blur. The rising sun gilded the rocks of the cliff edge on my right.

'Practice run,' Hogan's voice said. 'Take it easy, get used to the car.'

I shifted gears with the paddles on the wheel, enjoying the sequential transmission. The steering was tight. Nice. It would be nicer in race mode; I hit the button and the engine instantly kicked up a notch and the steering got sharper. The car ate up the first few bends like a bead rolling over a ribbon – smooth, fast, frictionless.

It was too easy. A car such as this liked to be pushed; it probably never had been pushed, with an owner like the Pipe King. I had quite a way to go before I was teetering on the edge of caution, and Todd was shooting already; if I was lucky I could get this right on the rehearsal, and we could all go home.

I leaned harder on the throttle and let it rip. Not all the way, no.

But more. Always a little bit more.

Maybe a lot more.

'Slower, Liza,' said Hogan.

The Ferrari arched gracefully around the curves. Below me, the shadows were disappearing from the desert. I was mid-descent, but still high enough so that it felt as if I pressed the throttle a little harder, I could fly. Right up into the lightening sky, among the effortless clouds.

'Happy birthday to me,' I said, my voice lost in the thunder of the engine, and I edged it faster. The car growled in appreciation. The road straightened for a short stretch, dipping downward, and I used the straight to pick up some more speed.

What had Allen been talking about, anyway? I knew my limits, I knew my abilities. I knew who I was, and I had never felt better in my life.

'Slow down, Liza,' crackled Hogan. '*Now.*'

'Yeah, right,' I said, though he wouldn't be able to hear me.

A camera and crew were perched near the guard rail on the bend ahead, waiting to pick up the wide shot as I passed. I'd cut it fine, kick up some gravel for them. I smiled, reached for the handbrake for the turn, and it was at that exact moment that I realised I was going faster than I'd thought.

'Shit,' I muttered, maybe I yelled it, I don't know because the car was so loud, and I turned the wheel and engaged the handbrake and the car began its sideways slide, gravel spitting exactly as I wanted it to. All I had to do was power out and away – it would be fine. Fine.

Shit.

At times like these, everything slows. I saw Rory, that was the cameraman's name though I didn't know I'd known it, and Wanda beside him wound in a yellow scarf. Rory's face was obscured by the camera but Wanda was focused on the car, smiling with her eyes screwed up. She had no idea anything was wrong. *Don't take a camera out*, that's the first rule, but the rule should be *Don't take the camera crew out.*

I needed the throttle or I'd plough sideways into both of them and carry them over the cliff. I punched it and the car, the amazingly responsive car, shouted and sprang as more petrol fed into its hungry engine. The front tyres gripped the tarmac and sped me away from the crew and I held tight, tried to keep it on the road but I was going too fast.

'Fuck, Liza, what the fuck are you doing?' yelled the radio.

The back end of the car slid and I steered into it, but there was a cliff wall ahead of me and a drop-off behind me, not quite sheer at this point, no, but enough to tumble me into the desert, and I felt the moment when the car decides it's going to spin and there's not a bloody thing you can do about it, nothing but ride it out and hope there's enough room.

There wasn't. I braced my body against the back of the seat.

I saw every last rock and scrubby bit of brush on the side of the road. A small weed, spitting pink flowers. I heard gravel flying from the tyres. I got a glimpse of Wanda's yellow scarf far off to the left, safely out of the way, and then I felt the crunch of the guard rail against the side of the car and a sickening tilt.

April Fool, I had time to say, or maybe only to think, and then the car was flying.

An endless now. No past and no idea of the future. Gravity gone, and control.

My insides contracted with something that could be fear. Could be joy.

The noise of the engine seemed to have disappeared and all I heard was the rush of air. A strangely empty sound. Outside, the world should have been a blur but I saw tree branches scraping against the nearside window like skeleton fingers and then a jolt as if someone had unexpectedly kicked me. Then a crack. Then a long endless shivering squealing. Something snapped, I felt it snap inside me. The side of the bonnet crumpled in slow motion, the windscreen starred and the side of the hill was unnaturally close and getting closer. Just outside lay a crushed Diet Coke can. If not for the windscreen, I could have reached out and touched it. In a minute I would be it.

The airbag exhaled into instant huge life around me. I didn't feel any pain, and at that moment, while I was feeling nothing, my breath stopped itself in panic and the car rolled over, hit something and then stopped, the right way up.

I should feel it. I should feel pain. I looked down at my legs

15

and I couldn't see them, only the white airbag, and then I made myself breathe and smelled the fire.

'That's another few hundred thou on the value of the Enzos that are left,' I said, my voice flat against the airbag, and I reached down and unbuckled my seatbelt. I could do that, at least. Then I braced my hands, which seemed to be unhurt, and my arms unhurt too – at least, I couldn't see any blood – I braced them on the seat and pushed myself up as hard as I could, because if the car was on fire I needed to get out sharpish.

I couldn't move.

Something warm trickled into my eye. I blinked and it rolled downward. When I tasted it with the tip of my tongue it was blood. I'd hit something with my head, but that was the least of my worries, if I couldn't feel from the waist down. It must be a rib that had snapped. It had to be a rib. Not my spine. Please.

But it had been further back than my ribs.

I tried to twist my legs, tried to brace them against the car floor, while I grabbed a hand hold and pulled. It was getting hotter and I smelled petrol, smelled burning plastic and hot metal, and I could see the flames now, to my left beyond the suffocating embrace of the airbag. I pulled, gained half an inch. Pulled harder.

There was shouting now in the distance, and sirens. I pictured the Pipe King tearing out what little hair he had left. The loudest voices, though, were those inside my head as I struggled against the car.

The edge of caution, said Hogan.

We could probably give it a shot, said Al.

These are my lists, said my mother.

Loudest of all was that pink card, lying on my mat inside my door in Los Angeles.

I pulled. And gasped as the fire reached my leg, the skin of my bare right leg, but I didn't scream because the pain was good. It meant I was still there from the waist down, and if I could get out I'd be okay, if I could only pull harder and push with my toes . . . Agony shot up both my legs, as if the fire had reminded me how to feel again. Black spots grew in front of my eyes, merging together, blotting out the flames from my vision.

'Liza!' I heard, coming from the opposite direction than I'd expected, and then through the blossoming blackness I saw Al very close, grabbing me under my arms. He heaved backwards and I slipped out of the crushed car, from underneath the airbag, as easily and as reluctantly as a baby leaving her mother's womb.

Real Life

Four and a half months later

The phone rang as I was unlocking my apartment door, and I dropped my shopping so I could get in more quickly. Which wasn't quite as quick as it used to be, not these days, but at the moment I was far too distracted by the ring of the phone to mind my limp. It was a sound I hadn't heard for an unfeasibly long time.

I snapped up the receiver. 'Hello?' I practically yelled. There was a pause, and I repeated, only slightly more desperately, 'Hello?'

'Oh, good afternoon. I am calling on behalf of Laurel Leaf Insurance and I was wondering if you could spare a few minutes to talk to me. Do you happen to have a dog or a cat or other pet in your home?'

I slumped. Junk phone call. 'I don't have any pets and I've spent enough of my life talking to insurance companies lately,' I said, more politely than I felt, and hung up.

'Damn.' I wiped a film of sweat off my forehead and checked my answering machine. The display said *No messages* but I pressed play anyway, in case it was malfunctioning. There were no messages, not even from the insurance companies who'd been hassling me for actual good reasons.

'Double damn.'

Three weeks now I'd been making phone calls, letting people know that I was all healed up, as good as new – nearly – and looking for work. Before the accident, I would only have needed to ring a couple of people and word of mouth would have landed me enough offers so I could take my pick. This time, several people hadn't even bothered to hide the fact that they were laughing at me.

And the phone hadn't rung, though I'd had my mobile with me twenty-four-seven, even beside me on the pillow when I slept, in case someone in a different time zone wanted to ring. I'd trashed that Ferrari and my career in one fell swoop.

I wiped my forehead again, and the top of my lip. It was way too hot inside this apartment. I listened. It was also suspiciously quiet. I went to the nearest AC vent, put my hand in front of it, and felt no cold air. Los Angeles, in August, with no air conditioning.

There was no point in swearing again, but I did it anyway. Then I went out to the corridor to pick up my groceries and bring them into the kitchen. I threw away the dried-out cheese and wilted lettuce from the fridge, before I replaced it with fresh lettuce that would wilt and new cheese that would dry. I mostly went grocery shopping to use up some time; I'd been eating not much other than cold cereal, bananas, peanut-butter sandwiches and takeaway sushi for the past few weeks. Enough to keep me fuelled up. I'd never been a foodie, and certainly never a cook.

I stuck my head in the refrigerator for a few moments to feel the cool. I'd have to go out again in a few minutes and buy a fan to keep me sane until I could harass the super into fixing the AC. I grabbed a bottle of water and went into my living room to stretch out while I was on the phone.

Physical therapy is a bitch, but she's a generous one if you respect her. After the shattered bones in my legs and foot and spine had healed, she'd given me back the ability to walk and even run, if I didn't mind going a little crooked. My once-constant pain had reduced to a level that I could kill with a couple of ibuprofen. Marv, my bald and muscle-bound PT, who was the toughest person I'd ever met and who sang in a cabaret every night after our hydrotherapy sessions dressed as Marlene Dietrich, said I was his success story of the year. Of course, I'd been very fit before the accident, which helped, but mostly it was Marv and the generous bitch who made me work so hard to get me back to something close to myself. Despite my scars, my missing spleen, and the memories of the crash that haunted my dreams more than they should.

Pity I couldn't get any work.

My living room, like the rest of my one-bed apartment, was spartan and bare. I had only what furniture I needed: a small couch, a wide-screen telly, a futon in the bedroom. I ate my meals usually perched on a stool at the breakfast bar, or standing up in the kitchen. There was a mat on the rug and a rack of weights for working out, and a table with some files on it where I could put my laptop. I'd stayed in more lavishly decorated Holiday Inns. I had lots of stuff I could put up if I wanted to – certificates, photographs, stills from stunts, autographs, things like that – but it all seemed like too much trouble. Normally, I hardly spent any time here; I was on the road, on set, and the apartment was my stopping-off place between jobs. A little pause in my real life.

Except lately, it was my real life. I hadn't left it for any amount of time since April, aside from my PT sessions, and those had finished weeks ago. There was only so much time you could hang out in the gym, even in LA. Of course, now I didn't have air conditioning, and the place was stifling. I called the building's super and left a blistering message, and then considered what to do. I'd already worked out, I'd already done my shopping, I didn't feel like going to see a movie, and it was too hot to stay in here. Days like this, I used to go for a ride on my Triumph Bonneville, up Route 1 to Malibu and beyond, as fast as I could go.

My hands dampened. Not today. Maybe some other time.

What I'd really like to have done was go sit in a cool bar somewhere and have a beer and shoot the shit, the sort of thing I used to do with the other second unit crew on our days off. The problem was, of course, who to do it with. I scrolled through the contacts on my mobile, ruling out names as I went. She was working; he was out of the country; she was a bitch; he was an alcoholic; she hadn't called me in over a year; she had this thing where she believed I'd stolen her gig just because it was offered to me first. When Allen's name came up on the screen, I scrolled forward quickly. He'd visited me in the hospital after I'd come to, but as the second sentence out of his mouth after 'How are you?' was 'I told you so', I hadn't given him the warmest of welcomes. Well, okay, I'd thrown his bouquet after him.

I had nobody to call, nobody to hang out with. LA was my pause-place. I lived my real life while I was working. I saw Marv's number, and shrugged and called him. Maybe he'd finished torturing people for the day and wanted a beer before he got dressed up in his gown and diamonds.

'Hi, it's Marv, I'm crunching someone's bones, so leave a message and I'll get back to you, unless it's you, Mom, in which case, please don't, or you, Tyler, because I'm never giving those Jimmy Choos back to you and you can just twist in the wind and wait. Byesie!'

I hung up without leaving a message. What was I thinking? He was my physical therapist, not my friend. I hadn't even known that he had a mom to ignore. Let alone a shoe freak called Tyler. He had a whole life beyond the time he spent encouraging people to get better, and I had . . . this.

I stretched out on the mat on the floor, with no friends and no work and nothing to do but sweat.

I liked being alone. I chose to be alone. I'd spent most of my formative years, including all those months in the womb, being connected to another person, and that was enough. And then there was growing up in Stoneguard; that was enough to make anyone run screaming for privacy.

A little bit of loneliness was a small price to pay.

I got up and checked my email. I had two pieces of spam offering me sex-enhancing drugs and college degrees, and one email from my sister.

To: Liza <willcrash4food@ymail.com>
From: Lee Haven <emilyhaven@icecreamheaven.co.uk>
Date: 14 August, 11.34.56 PM
Subject: I bet I know . . .

. . . What you had for breakfast. Scrambled eggs on toast? That's what I had. It was delicious.
Love,
Lee xx

I smiled. It was a long-running joke: my sister would try to prove that we had a psychic link by showing that, for example, we'd had the same thing to eat on any given day, despite the five thousand miles, eight time zones and an ocean between us. It never worked. I wasn't sure if she actually believed that it would one day, or if it was her excuse to stay in touch. A game we could play by email and text and phone, without having to scrape ourselves on the deeper differences between us. I leaned down and typed.

To: Lee Haven <emilyhaven@icecreamheaven.co.uk>
From: Liza <willcrash4food@ymail.com>
Date: 14 August, 12.42.08 PM
Subject: RE: I bet I know . . .

I had two blueberry Pop-Tarts and a can of Diet Coke.
Wrong again. Nice try, though.
L xx

I laughed to myself as I typed it, picturing her dismayed reaction to my junk-food diet, but as soon as it disappeared into the ether my smile disappeared too.

Sharing genes didn't mean that my sister and I shared thoughts, or dreams, or even tastes in lunch. A fact that had only been proved by what happened in April. Any psychic twin worth her salt should know when her sister got into a life-threatening accident – and on her birthday, no less – but Lee hadn't rushed to my bedside. Nor had she sent me a Get Well card out of the blue. She would have done these things, I had no doubt, if she'd known about my accident, but she didn't because I hadn't told her.

It was enough that I was the laughing stock of the entire Hollywood stunt industry. I didn't need her pity, too.

Texts and emails and even phone calls could hide a lot, if you wanted them to.

I lay back down on the floor, stretched for a bit, and then gave up and lay there looking at my ceiling. It had a crack in it. One day there was going to be an earthquake and the whole thing would come down on my head, because if I didn't get

23

some work very soon, I could end up spending my entire life right here.

From the corner of my eye I saw movement, and turned my head in time to see a shiny brown cockroach scuttling across the blue carpet. I reached out my arm for something to throw at it, but only found last week's *TV Guide*, which was too fluttery a missile to do any good.

'There's some yummy dried-out cheese for you in the kitchen bin,' I told it instead as it disappeared into a tiny hole under the skirting board, en route no doubt to join its millions of cockroach friends and spread the joyous news about the desiccated Velveeta.

I got up on all fours and crawled to the phone. This way, I was at eye-level with it. I crouched there, about a foot away, and stared at it as hard as I could.

Ring, I told it, deep inside my mind. *Ring*.

It was a silver digital phone in a silver cradle. I bulged my eyes at it. I thought, Ring-ring-ring-you-bastard-ring-ring-ring-before-I-chuck-you-across-the-room-and-break-your-smug-little-buttons.

It didn't ring. This was pathetic.

I had to do something new. I'd never been one to save for a rainy day, and what I had wouldn't last forever. I needed work. And I had to get away from this apartment, get away from this town, before it drove me mad. I was healthy and fit, and if work wasn't chasing after me, I could chase after it.

London was as good a place as any to start.

Stealing Beauty

She's not sure why she does it, and that in itself is a scary gift, because she knows why she does everything these days. Walking through the bright showcase of a department store, her canvas bag of purchases over her arm – nothing exciting, sheets and some scented lotion – she sees the sweet-shop display of make-up and she stops. Her eyes are drawn not to the pinks, but the reds and purples. A single bottle of nail varnish in an unnatural turquoise, something a teenager would wear with a T-shirt and ripped jeans.

She reaches out and picks it up. It's small, rounded, hard and cool – definitely real, and fits in the palm of her hand. Quickly, she moves her hand over her bag and drops the bottle in. It lands amongst the plastic-wrapped sheets and doesn't make a sound.

Her breath's coming faster, her heart's beating loud. She doesn't look around, starts walking for the door, trying to keep her gait normal, but she can feel the stiff expression on her face and she knows that people must be looking at her. Nudging each other, whispering, 'Did you see that?' She keeps her eyes trained forward and tries to think about nothing, certainly not the security guards or the strange column things on either side of the exit, designed to catch shoplifters.

Then she's through, getting away with it and walking fast, an incredulous gasp of laughter escaping her lips as she heads for the lift to the car park. She can't believe she's just done that.

By the time she's halfway home, she's swearing she'll never do it again, and trying to forget that she's done it before.

The Reunion

Lee was waiting in the lobby of my hotel when I came down, sitting in one of the armchairs with a newspaper in her lap and a cup of tea on the table next to her. Her handbag was beside her chair, heedless of London thieves. She had her back to me, but I recognised her from behind. She'd tucked her straight dark brown hair behind her ears and she wore our grandmother's pearl stud earrings.

Identical twins are amongst the few people in the world who know what the back of their own head looks like. I stood near the lift, impulses warring. I wanted to run to Lee and hold her. I wanted to walk out of the door again.

She lifted her head, turned it, and saw me. For a split second I thought I saw the same feelings on her face that I had inside, but then she smiled, a big warm Lee-smile, and I couldn't believe that she'd ever had any doubts about anything.

'Liza,' she said, and came round and hugged me. Our heads rested on each other's shoulders and our hands touched the same spot on each other's backs. I hadn't touched my sister in over a year and a half. She smelled of vanilla and tea, and her cardigan was soft. Then we both retreated to arm's length and looked at each other.

'You've grown your hair,' she said. 'I was expecting it short.'

I touched it. 'Yeah, I couldn't be bothered to cut it. You've got a fringe.'

'So do you. They're the same.' She laughed and pointed to our reflection in the mirror on the wall by the check-in desk. 'Oh my God. That's hilarious, we have the same haircut. And look at your nails, you've grown them too!'

'They sort of did it themselves.' More likely, I hadn't done anything to break them. And filing them used up some time. I took her in. She was wearing a white sleeveless top, a pink-and-white striped flared skirt, and pink kitten heels. She looked like a bowl of strawberry ice cream.

I remembered comparing my sister's body to my own, in those expectant awkward days when we were both waiting for adolescence. Afterwards, too. I didn't know then, but learned, later, that every woman makes this surreptitious comparison. But sameness creates a microscope that lets you see the smallest of differences. It exaggerates advantages and magnifies faults.

'You look great,' I told Lee. 'Have you been working out?'

She shrugged self-consciously. 'Oh, Candace has got me doing yoga.'

'It's working. You've got a lot more muscle definition in your arms.'

'It helps me relax. I'm obviously not as fit as you are – I mean, I taste ice cream for a living, and you do all that physical stuff.'

Like pacing my apartment, and going on pointless errands. 'Well, you're probably a hell of a lot more flexible.'

'And relaxed?' She twisted her mouth up in half a rueful smile.

'That goes without saying.' Though there were small lines around her eyes that hadn't been there the last time I'd seen her. Her skin didn't glow quite as much. She looked tired.

Maybe she'd been as anxious about meeting up again as I was.

'This is hilarious,' she repeated, gazing at our reflections in the mirror again. 'Last time I saw you, we looked nothing alike. And now, if you took our heads off our bodies, you wouldn't be able to tell who's who.'

'I think anyone could tell the minute we opened our mouths.'

She took my hand in hers. 'Liza, I'm so glad to see you. It's great that you've come to London. I've missed you.'

I squeezed her hand in reply. 'Fancy a drink?' I asked quickly, before the topic got dangerous.

'Oh no, I've got a cup of tea, thanks. Do you want me to order one for you?'

'I mean a drink drink. I've got the mother of all jetlag, I need a pick-me-up. Come on, let's go into the bar.' I led the way; Lee picked up her bag and her cup and saucer before following me.

'How was your flight?'

'Wretched. It's always wretched. Fourteen hours of no leg room and breathing other people's air.'

'You got in yesterday?'

'At the crack of dawn this morning.'

'Well, I hope the trip is worth it for you. Is this new film exciting?'

I focused my eyes on the row of gleaming bottles behind the bar. 'Extremely. What do you want to drink?'

'I'm fine with tea, thanks. So what's the film about?'

I ordered a rum and Diet Coke for me and another cup of

tea for her. 'Oh, it's an action flick,' I said breezily. 'Nothing you'd like to watch, I'm sure.'

'I rented *The Sucker Punch* a few months ago. I couldn't recognise you in it, though.'

'Bloody wig and boob inserts.' I paid the barman for our drinks. 'There's a table in the corner over there.'

'So are you here in England for long?'

'I'm not sure,' I said truthfully. 'I flew over on a one-way ticket. It depends how long it takes.'

She shook her head. 'I don't know how you do it, living so unpredictably.'

'I don't know how you can stay in the same place all the time, doing the same job.' As soon as I said it, I saw her bite the inside of her lip. I'd touched a raw spot, too soon. 'Anyway,' I said, 'I'm glad you could get down from Stoneguard at short notice.'

'Of course I would.' She dropped her gaze to her tea cup. 'It's been too long.'

I swallowed my drink. For a moment neither of us spoke or looked at each other.

The trouble was, there were too many raw spots. Too many things we'd avoided talking about in careful phone calls and frivolous emails.

'So, the Haven sisters hit the town at last,' I said finally, making my voice cheerful. 'What are we going to do?'

'Well, I don't know what you wanted to do, but I assumed that we'd need to eat, so I made us reservations for dinner. I hope that's okay.'

'That's fine,' I said, though quite frankly I'd have preferred a noisy bar somewhere, a club with thumping music. Less opportunity to talk.

'We can have a good chat and catch up,' Lee said. 'Actually it's quite exciting. I've got us into Jett, in Chelsea.'

'Where?'

'Jett. It's hugely popular, you can't get in for love nor money, apparently, but the owner and chef is a customer of ours, so I pulled a few strings. I think you'll like it. But if you'd rather go somewhere else . . .'

I shrugged. 'You know what I'm like with food. As long as there's wine, we'll be okay.'

'If you want to do something else, just say so. I'm really easy, it's all about spending time with you.'

'No, dinner's fine. You're right, we need to eat anyway. Will I have to wear a skirt or something? Because I haven't got one.'

'I think you'll be all right in those jeans, but have you got a dressier top?'

Of course what I was wearing wouldn't be good enough. I swallowed back my reply and said, 'I might have something upstairs.'

'That's great. I could do with freshening up.'

'So, are you staying tonight? I have an extra bed in my room. You're welcome to it.'

Lee shook her head quickly. 'Oh, I'd love to, Liza, but I've got to catch the last train.'

'The last train to Stoneguard is at something like half past ten; the night won't even have started yet.'

'No, I couldn't possibly leave Mum overnight.'

'I thought she had someone with her all the time.'

'She does, but—' She bit her lip. 'I'd just prefer not to. Anyway, I've got to work in the morning, and I'm assuming you do too?'

'Well.' I shifted in my seat. 'Actually this is more of a fact-finding mission. I'm meeting with some people, talking about the film.'

'And then you'll be shooting it later?'

'Yeah.' The lie came out without any effort or thought. But with any luck, it would be the truth eventually anyway. If not this film, then something else, soon. Maybe some television, or an advert or two. Surely one of my old contacts in England would be willing to give me a chance. I was considering this hotel bill as an investment, until I could recoup the spent money. And the peak-season plane ticket, purchased at great cost at the last minute. It was the principle of risking a little money to make a lot. Probably safer than the stock market, these days.

If I got work, that was. And why was I worrying about lying? I was practically a professional at it.

I downed the rest of my drink. 'Well, are you ready to get going? We can nip upstairs and I'll get changed.'

'All right. The reservation's for half seven, anyway. Jett's not far from here, we can walk across the park.'

'We can take a cab, nature girl.' I stood up. 'I'll never understand your preference to get everywhere as slowly as possible.'

'I suppose I don't see the need for speed.' She stood up too, and smoothed her skirt down.

'And that, my dear sister, is why nobody would mistake us for each other. Come on, I think there's still some gin left in the mini-bar.' I started off for the lift, only stopping when I realised she wasn't following me. When I looked, she was still standing next to the table, watching me.

'What?' I said.

'What's wrong with your back?'

I put my hand in the small of my back, and then took it away. 'Nothing. Why?'

'You're walking oddly.'

'Oh. I'm just stiff from the flight. I'll stretch out a bit and it'll be fine.'

I must have been convincing, because she nodded slightly and joined me as we walked to the lift. Paying attention to every step, I didn't limp at all, and fortunately within a few steps it became second nature. I hit the lift button and smiled at my sister, the everything's-fine-everything's-perfect smile that I'd learned from seeing it on her face so many times.

'I worry about you,' she said quietly. 'You've got such a dangerous job. One day you're going to hurt yourself badly.'

'Nonsense. I'm a pro. My job is one hundred per cent about safety, or else I wouldn't be doing it.' I was grateful for the lift arriving at that exact moment.

'I don't understand how you enjoy risking your life like that, every day.'

'It makes you feel more alive.' I punched the button for my floor. 'Anyway, like I said, I know how to do these things, and I've got all the safety precautions. I'm safer in a burning building than you are crossing the road.'

'Ah, but remember, the roads I cross are in Stoneguard.'

'My point exactly. You're constantly in danger of marauding tourists or wandering tractors. Let alone Derek Hunter's Boston terriers. Does he still have them?'

'Yes. Cheeky died, but Derek got two more to replace her.'

'See? If I ever hear a news story about beasts savaging a small Wiltshire community, I'll know it wasn't werewolves. It was Derek Hunter's Boston terriers, and their thirst for human blood.'

The doors slid open and I walked, again paying attention, to my room. I was sure I'd been walking fine in LA. Damned wet British weather. I slid the key into the slot and let us both in.

'This is nice,' Lee said, putting her bag on one of the beds, the one where I hadn't pulled back the bedclothes, and going to the window. 'It must be so much fun to stay in London.'

'It's only London. You make it sound like it's an exotic thing to do. You've done it plenty of times.' I went to my suitcase and flipped it open.

'Not for a while. I'm so busy. Haven't you had time to unpack yet?'

'I'm not a big unpacker.' I drew a black silk top out of the bag. 'How's this?'

'It's pretty. Here, I'll unpack for you while you get changed.'

'There's no need, I don't have anything that can't be worn wrinkled.' I snagged a better bra out of the top of the case, and then reached for the hem of my T-shirt to pull it over my head.

Then I hesitated. 'I'll change in the bathroom for a minute, you can use it after.'

I thought for a second that Lee would question me, since whatever our desires for privacy might have been growing up, we'd never been modest around each other. What would be the point, when we were exactly the same? But she didn't say anything, just put my case on the bed and opened the wardrobe to take out hangers.

In the bathroom, I shut the door behind me and leaned against the counter while I popped out two ibuprofen from the stack of blister packs in my toiletries bag. *Pain is your body's way of telling you to take it easy*, I heard one of my early martial arts instructors telling me; but I'd as soon not listen to my body at the moment. The ache wasn't bad, nagging in my lower back, but if Lee had noticed a limp I'd do as well to get rid of it. I swallowed both tablets at once, without bothering with water. For some reason, the bitter chalky taste always seemed to make them work faster.

I changed quickly into the bra and shirt without looking in

the mirror, ran a comb through my hair, and grabbed my makeup bag before Lee could arrange all my socks and underwear into perfectly-folded, colour-coordinated order. Though when I got out, it was too late. She was surveying her work in the open drawers, looking pleased with herself.

'There,' she said. 'Now you can find everything.'

'Chance would be a fine thing. I could never find any of my stuff after you tidied up our room in Stoneguard.'

'And I could never find any of my stuff before I tidied it.' She closed the drawers with a soft, satisfied bump. 'Oh good, is that your make-up bag? I forgot my lipstick.'

'The perfect twin forgot her lipstick?'

'I'm not always so perfect,' Lee said, her voice quiet, her gaze on the bedspread. Immediately I felt sorry about sniping at her. She'd been trying to help me, in her organised, tidy Lee Haven way.

'You can borrow mine, no problem,' I said to her.

She straightened, as if she'd just woken up, and smiled at me. 'Thanks, Liza.'

'What are sisters for?' I said, handing her my make-up case.

She didn't answer, and we fell into silence, again. I sat on the bed, pretending to examine my boot, hearing the small plastic sounds of her looking through my makeup. I tried to think of some crack to make so that Lee would laugh. I'd usually been able to make her laugh, even when she was angry or disappointed, even when I was wrong.

But not always.

'Actually,' she said, and then she cleared her throat and started again. 'Actually, you know what would be fun? Remember when we used to do each other's make-up?'

It was a peace-offering. I nodded. 'I remember teaching you how to put liquid eyeliner on properly.'

35

'You had a head start on me.'

'Only about four years.'

We scooted around on the bed so we were both sitting cross-legged on it, facing each other with the make-up case between us. 'Remember the first time Miss Hanson sent me home?'

'She said you looked like a prostitute clown.'

I laughed. 'She was being cruel with the clown part.'

'Whatever happened to you that time? Mum was not keen on the make-up.'

'Nothing. I never told her. I took the train to Swindon and spent the day playing fruit machines.'

'In your school uniform? Where'd you get the money for the train?'

'Lee, as far as I can remember, I never paid for a train ticket until I was at least twenty years old.' I looked into her face, examining each of her features. Taken in bits, the resemblance between us wasn't so obvious. 'You need a bit more eye-shadow and some foundation – do you mind?'

'No. You can do what you like if I can, too.'

'Sure.' I put some foundation on the back of my hand, dabbed a sponge in it and began applying it to her face.

'You've got some great make-up here,' she said, picking through the tubes and brushes and compacts.

'The make-up girls give me tips. No, I knew you'd go for that one, but don't use it. It's too pink.'

'Too pink for me or for you?'

'For either of us.' I held up a tube of deep scarlet. 'This would look great on you.'

She raised her eyebrows. 'Do you really think I could get away with that?'

'I do, so you can.'

She selected another lipstick, thankfully not the pink one,

and laid it out next to the other cosmetics she'd chosen. 'Remember that time you convinced me to go to the dentist instead of you and I ended up having my teeth cleaned twice in two weeks?' she asked.

'And the time you did my geography project for me. It was the only time I ever got an A.' I knew what was happening – we were making a safe little blanket of reminiscence to smooth over the rough spots.

'And that tourist boy, remember – who sat outside the Heavenly Scoop all day waiting for me because he thought I was you? What was his name?'

'I don't remember any of their names.'

We sat facing each other, our knees touching. Our hands danced around each other, our eyes focused on each other. She paused to shut her eyes while I brushed on eye-shadow. She blinked her eyes in sympathy with me as she applied mascara to my lashes. For a moment, when we were both colouring in each other's lips, it felt as if I were looking in a mirror, putting the lipstick on myself.

This was what I missed, when I missed Lee the most. The rare moments of effortless harmony, where we worked as two halves of the same person. Times we didn't need to compete, where we filled in each other's gaps instead of emphasising them. We shaped each other's faces and when we were done, we went to the mirror together to see.

'We're going to have such a *nice night* together,' Lee said.

Our eyes met in the mirror and we both looked away.

A Sister Bonding Thing

The food at Jett was weird. It was one of those places where every ingredient had been made to look like something else or have a different texture or something, lots of foams and jellies and little fiddly bits arranged in precise mini-artworks. Personally, I was more interested in the wine. I reached for the bottle in the ice bucket and filled our glasses before our too-attentive waiter could get a chance.

'Don't you think you should take it easy?' said Lee. 'You're working tomorrow, aren't you?'

'And you could use a drink or two to loosen up.' I held up my glass to hers. 'Cheers.'

'Cheers.' She drank, a delicate little sip which she immediately diluted by taking a drink from her water glass.

'So how's Stoneguard?'

'I don't suppose you'd say it's changed that much,' Lee answered, poking at one of the things on her plate. 'This watermelon comfit is amazing – would you like to try?'

'No, thanks. So, still full of tourists and busybodies?'

'You're so dismissive, Liza. People in Stoneguard are nice. And tourists are our lifeblood.'

'I like that image. The people of Stoneguard battening onto

all the tourists, sucking the blood out of them, like a giant leech of quaintness.'

'You are so cynical.'

'Well, you know I never liked it there. It's not a surprise.'

She shook her head. 'So how's Los Angeles, then?'

'Hot. And exciting. There's always something going on there, you know?'

'There's always something going on in Stoneguard, too.'

I snorted. 'Yeah, like Morris dancing and meetings of the Ley Line Preservation Society.'

'You can't compare it to a big city, Liza.'

'You're right. It doesn't compare in any way to LA.'

'Do you even know your neighbours in California?'

'No. And that's the way I like it. I had enough curtain-twitching growing up to last me a lifetime.'

She sighed. 'Well, I keep busy there. And people are always looking out for you, in a small town. They know who you are.'

I knew we'd never agree about Stoneguard, so I changed the subject. 'How about your love life? Are there any decent men to date in Stoneguard – or in all of Wiltshire, come to think of it?'

'There are plenty of decent men. And my love life is fine, thank you. That looks incredible, can I have a taste?' I pushed my plate towards her, and she took a forkful of my food. She put it in her mouth, closing her eyes as she savoured it. 'Mmm. That's really, really good.' She wiped her mouth with her napkin.

'You were always the one who was keen on falling in love and getting married and having babies. Remember when we were growing up you had a massive crush on Lord Naughton's son? Whatever happened to him, anyway?'

39

'He's back in town now, doing a big restoration project on the Hall.'

'What a twat he was. And weren't you going out with some bloke the last time I saw you? What was he, some furniture restorer or something?'

'An antiques dealer. I don't see him any more. Do you like your dinner?'

'It's fine.'

'The chef, Edmund Jett, has two Michelin stars.'

'Well, you know, there's only so much you can say about an Eiffel Tower made out of crab.' I poured myself some wine. 'Maybe we'd better get another bottle.'

'Are you sure that's a good idea?'

'No, but when did that ever stop me?' I caught the waiter's eye.

'I don't want to—'

'You don't have to drink any, don't worry.'

'No, what I meant was I don't want to argue. Not tonight. We haven't seen each other in so long, I just want it to be nice. *Please*.'

Anger boiled up inside me. It had been my companion nearly as long as Lee.

'What you mean is that it was my fault we argued last time, and my fault that we haven't seen each other.'

'No, what I meant was—'

The waiter reached our table. 'Another bottle, please,' I said to him, and he went away. Across the table, my sister's cheeks were pink. Arguing in a public place. How embarrassing for her.

'We're sisters,' she said quietly. 'Is it so hard for us to get on with each other for one night?'

I sighed. And drank the last of the wine in my glass. 'No. Okay. Don't worry.' Though I noticed she wasn't contradicting my statement that it was my fault we'd argued, she had a point. I'd missed her, although I wouldn't admit it. 'I'll finish up my dinner like a good girl and then we can talk about whatever you want.' I loaded the remains of my food onto my fork, put it all in my mouth together, and chewed.

When I looked up, Lee was staring into her water glass, her knife and fork laid neatly across her unfinished food.

'Aren't you hungry?' I asked her. She blinked.

'I'm saving myself for dessert.'

'That's right,' I said, 'this place serves your product. How's it going at Ice Cream Heaven, anyway?'

'Fine. It's busy – you know.'

I didn't, nor did I want to, particularly, but I nodded, because this was another of those raw areas and I was happy to skim over it as quickly as possible. The waiter came back to take our plates and leave dessert menus. I didn't glance at mine, but poured more wine from the new bottle while she ran her finger down the menu, her face the picture of absorption. Lee took her sweets seriously.

'What are you having?' she asked me.

'I'll stick with the wine.'

'I'm going for the Knickerbocker Glory. I've heard he does really interesting things with it.'

Ice cream. Of course. Lee smiled at the waiter and placed her order.

'So one of the things I've been busy with is organising a charity ball,' she said, with the air of a woman bringing up the most interesting topic in the world.

'That so?'

'Well, really it's more like a disco. It's not black tie or anything, and it's in the school hall, but everyone's pitched together and lots of people are coming. It's this coming weekend.'

'Mmm.'

'You wouldn't think such a little thing would take so much planning, but it's taken weeks! There's so much to think about, all the food and the music and the lighting, and of course the invitations and getting the word out. But I really hope it'll be a success. It's a bit different from the usual barn dances that get put on all the time – you know, a little bit more up to date.'

'You mean you'll be playing music that's less than three hundred years old?'

'Yes. Nigel Peach is doing the music, he had a stint on Radio Wiltshire a few years ago. He's doing oldies right up to the present day. It should be lots of fun. Everyone's been talking about it constantly. And it's all to benefit Alzheimer's research. Because of—'

'Right.'

'I wanted to do my bit, and it seemed like something I could do.'

'You want to be careful, you'll be turning into Ma Gamble next.'

'Don't worry about that, there's only room for one Ma Gamble in Stoneguard. Can I tell you something awful? I purposely scheduled it for next weekend because I knew she'd be in Bristol for her great-niece's christening.'

'Shock and horror! An event without Ma Gamble, what is the world coming to?'

'I know,' she said, 'but she does tend to take over things, so I thought it would be easier. She's insisted on doing the catering and she donated the food so we couldn't say no, but at least we get to set it out ourselves. Anyway, maybe – maybe you'd think about coming too, if you're free this weekend.'

I nearly choked on my mouthful of wine. 'What?'

'I've got a spare ticket you can have. It could be like a sister bonding thing – you could stay at mine for the weekend. You'd have fun, and see all kinds of people you haven't seen in ages.'

'Lee,' I said, putting down my glass, 'I couldn't wait to get away from all those people. That's why I left Stoneguard in the first place. I'd rather fling myself under a bus than go back there. In fact I have, several times, and it's much more enjoyable.'

Her smile, which had been the widest I'd seen it since we'd got to the restaurant, froze.

'I don't mean you,' I said quickly.

'Right.'

'Really I don't, and I'm not fighting, I'm being honest. I'm enjoying being with you tonight, and it's been too long, I'll admit it. But don't ask me to go back to Stoneguard for fun. You wouldn't want me to be there, anyway. I'd be completely miserable and sulky and spoil your good time.'

'You'd have fun if you let yourself.'

'Honestly, Lee, I'd poison myself with gin and end up sleeping with old One-Eyed Pete the caretaker. You know I would.'

'Fine.'

Her dessert came, a series of cubes and swirls on a vast white plate, and she beamed at the waiter. 'This looks amazing, thank you.'

'Don't be like that,' I said, as soon as he'd stepped away. 'It's not about you. I don't like Stoneguard, that's all. Besides, I'm bound to be completely busy the whole time I'm here.'

'Of course you are. Forget I even asked – I should have known you wouldn't fancy it.' She put one of the little cubes in her mouth. 'Mmm, this is gorgeous.'

It must be great to be a twin, people used to say. *It must be so much fun to have another person exactly like you, to be so special, to never be lonely.*

Bollocks.

I drank some more wine and watched her eat. I wasn't going to argue. So there.

'So,' she said, her voice still light and lovely, sweet as dessert, 'you haven't asked about Mum yet.'

I sighed. It was going to come to this sooner or later, and I could only be thankful that it was happening now, when I had a substantial amount of white Burgundy inside me to cushion it. 'How's Mum, then?'

'She's more or less the same.'

'Right.' What exactly is 'the same'? I thought of asking, but I knew I should have asked that question long ago, and therefore I should have known the answer already. 'So she's . . .'

'She's got good days and bad days. And of course she's healthy as a horse. There's nothing wrong with her body, or nothing more than any other seventy year old's. It's just her brain.'

'Right.'

'Did you read all the material I sent you?'

'I – haven't had time.'

'Well, generally the course of the disease is quite predictable. They say the most recent memories go first, and that's what's happened with Mum. She forgets I'm in charge of Ice Cream Heaven now, even though that was her decision, and then she does things like insist I leave the books with her overnight so she can go over them, and she comes up with all these completely imaginary objections to things she thinks I have or haven't done. Last week she kept on asking about Peachy Keen, which was a summer limited-edition flavour back in 2001. I couldn't convince her we didn't sell it any more.'

'Right.'

'And it's scary for her. She gets very angry, sometimes. And she's taken to wandering in the night.' Lee put another cube of ice cream in her mouth, and waited until it had melted until she spoke. 'She asks for Dad.'

'A bit late for that,' I said. 'He's been in Australia for over twenty years. I can't recall her ever making much noise about wanting him back.'

'And when I tell her, she looks so . . . puzzled. Helpless.' Lee twisted her spoon in her hand. 'Anyway.'

'But she's got full-time care, right? I mean, you're not actually looking after her yourself, are you?'

'Well, she has someone in for a few hours every day, and someone for the night times. But it's still a lot of work. And a lot of . . .' She sighed. 'You're right, we shouldn't talk about it. It's fine, everything's fine, I'm handling it. There's nothing you can do. Let's talk about something else.'

'Okay.'

'You'd see her if you came home for the dance.'

'Lee . . .'

'We don't know how much time there is, and you should see her while she still remembers who you are.'

'I thought you said you didn't want to argue tonight.'

'Emily Haven!'

We both looked up. A blond man in chef's whites was approaching us across the crowded monochromatic dining room. He looked vaguely familiar, like someone I might have seen on late-night TV once, when I'd been desperate enough to watch cookery programmes. He got to the side of our table and stopped, looking from one of us to the other, the familiar, comical surprise on his face. 'There are two of you?' he said. 'Which one's Emily?'

Lee stood up quickly. 'I'm Emily Haven. How are you, Edmund?'

His surprise dissolved into a white smile. 'Excellent. Lovely to see you.' They exchanged air kisses and he held his hand out to me. 'You must be Lee's sister, then. I'm Edmund Jett.'

'Liza Haven.' I gave him a firm handshake.

'I'm sorry about confusing you. It took me by surprise and the likeness is extraordinary.'

'We've been enjoying our meal very much,' Lee said. 'Thank you for fitting us in at such short notice.'

'I'm always happy to accommodate my favourite suppliers. You had the Knickerbocker Glory, didn't you? What did you think?'

'It's different from the way we serve it in our own ice-cream parlour.' Lee laughed, charmingly breathless, as if she were dazzled by the chef.

'I love your product, simply brilliant stuff. And you're twins. How fascinating. Does a love of ice cream run in the family?'

'I hate it,' I said.

'It skipped Liza,' Lee said, 'but of course our mother was the one who founded Ice Cream Heaven, on the site of her father's dairy farm.'

'Fantastic, fantastic. I remember your mother, brilliant woman, she's the one who sold me your product in the first place. These small family-run businesses are the heart and soul of good British food. I'll let you into a secret.' He leaned closer to me, close enough so I could smell the odour of spices and butter. 'I hate cuttlefish. Can't stand the stuff, never could. Yet the cuttlefish risotto is one of the most popular dishes in this restaurant. And do you know why?'

'I really have no idea,' I said.

'Because I can *understand the ingredient*. I'm not blinded by my own personal taste. I can examine it, and dissect it, and draw out the fullest flavour of it, precisely because I would never choose to eat it myself.'

Okay, you're weird, I thought. 'Ah,' I said.

'That's really interesting,' said Lee.

'Isn't it?' He smiled at us both. The chef was very good-looking, blond and floppy-haired and utterly full of himself, with the over-groomed look that I recognised from the entertainment industry. 'What are you working on now?' he asked. 'Some incredible flavour, no doubt.'

'Well, um, we, that is to say . . .'

If I didn't rescue us, we'd be here talking to this windbag all night.

'Beetroot and horseradish flavour,' I said. 'Yum yum yum.'

His eyebrows drew together, and he appeared to be giving my random selection the most serious of consideration. 'Beetroot . . . and horseradish. How original.'

'Isn't it?'

'And of course,' said Lee quickly, 'we offer all the traditional favourites. Those are the backbone of our business, after all.'

'Of course you do. And that's why I so dearly love your product. It's so nostalgic, ice cream, isn't it? Listen, I've got to get back to the kitchen, but it's great to see you again, Lee, and lovely to meet you, Liza. Enjoy the rest of your evening. *Ciao*!' He exchanged more air kisses with both of us and left, pausing to speak with several more patrons on his way back to the kitchen.

Lee sank into her chair. 'Oh my God, isn't he amazing?'

'Pretty unbelievable, all right.'

'What was that about beetroot and horseradish?'

'It was a joke. He thought it was pretty funny, I think.'

She frowned at me. 'Do you?'

47

The waiter appeared at our table with two coffees and two liqueur glasses. 'From Mr Jett.'

'Oh. How nice.'

'Do you fancy him?'

'No. Anyway, he's married.'

'Never stopped me.' I drank the liqueur, which was sweet and spicy. 'Do you want yours?'

She shook her head. 'I've got to go in a minute.'

'You really could stay overnight,' I said. Though I was becoming less convinced that I wanted her to. All of this avoiding tricky subjects and swallowing down what I really thought was getting pretty tiring.

'I really can't. Listen, before I go, I've got something for you.' She reached into her handbag and pulled out a small package wrapped in silver foil, trailing a curly ribbon. 'It's because I missed your birthday.'

'Oh.' I paused with my glass halfway to my lips. 'I–I didn't get you anything.'

'That's fine, I wasn't expecting anything. I saw this and it was so pretty, I thought of you. Go on – open it.'

I took the package. 'You weren't supposed to get me a present, I don't want anything.' I looked down at the silver wrapping, the pretty ribbon. A little shiny stab of guilt. Had she done it on purpose? To remind me of my failings? Of all the annoyances I'd been hoarding up all evening?

'I just wanted to give you something,' Lee said. 'You don't have to take it if you don't want to, but I'd like it if you did. If it makes you feel any better, I bought one exactly like it for myself at the same time. So it's hardly a present at all, only a little fairness thing, so we're even.'

Of course she hadn't given me a present to make a point. She'd given me a present because that was the sort of thing Lee Haven did. She was always getting little things for people, thinking of small ways to brighten their days, to bring them closer together. Something I would never think of doing in a million years.

And of course that didn't make me feel any less guilty about it.

But I opened the package. I even opened it carefully, not tearing the paper or breaking the ribbon, putting them aside on the tablecloth in a careful offering to the semblance of sisterly harmony. Inside was a slender bangle made out of hammered silver. Lee held up her own wrist, to show me she wore the same thing.

'That's pretty.' I slipped it on my wrist. 'Thank you.'

'You're welcome. Happy birthday.'

'To you, too.'

She got up from her chair and hugged me, her standing up, me sitting down. She was a hugger, Lee. She knew exactly how to do it so you felt warm and cared-for, and I'm not sure where she learned it from, because hugs were not everyday commodities in our house while we were growing up. Maybe from Nana; maybe she'd inherited that easy affection along with her pearls. But if that was so, why hadn't I?

'Well, I'll get dinner, anyway,' I said.

'No no no, this was all my choice. I know you don't really care about eating out, and it was good of you to go along with it. Besides, Edmund Jett and I have worked it out between us already.'

She let me go, looked at her watch, and took a last standing sip of her coffee. 'I've got to catch my train.'

'I'll help you get a cab.' I got up, took a wild guess at how much the meal must have cost and took out several notes from my purse and put them on the table for a tip. Then we left our cosy table for two with its orchids and its empty plates and glasses and went into the shining damp of a London night.

I touched the silver bangle. Thirty seconds before she'd given me her gift, I'd been thinking about how I wanted her to leave. I was a crap sister.

I remembered a time when we were about six, when I'd upset Lee by taking her favourite doll and putting 'make-up' on it with permanent markers I'd found in our mother's office. My little-girl hands weren't all that skilled, and by the time I was done, Priscilla looked like the Joker in *Batman*. Then I thought she might look edgier, cooler, if I gave her honey-blond hair a short cut with our mother's scissors. That didn't work at all, so I hid Punk Priscilla at the bottom of my closet.

When Lee found her, she was so upset she refused to speak to me and her silence made me so upset that I couldn't speak at all. We moved through the big house on the hill like identical ghosts in separate rooms. We lasted all afternoon until we broke down and flew apologising into each other's arms.

Even then, I knew that what I had done was so much worse, that the pain quotient was nowhere near equal. Lee and I were supposed to be the same, but I'd always known that I had much more capacity for doing damage.

A cab approached, the orange light on its top glowing like the eye of an animal. Lee raised her hand to hail it.

'Did you say that Ma Gamble definitely isn't going to be at your disco thing?' I asked.

'No, she's not, but Liza, look, here's my cab.'

'I'll try to come, then.'

She grabbed my arm as the cab pulled up. 'Really? Do you think you can? That's wonderful!'

It felt good to make my sister smile. I could understand why everyone wanted to do it. 'I'm not sure if I'll be able to make it. I might end up having to work.' *If I'm lucky.* 'And I'm not going to spend the weekend hanging around reliving old times with the rest of the village. But if you want me to come to the disco, and you want me to stay with you for the weekend, I'll try to do it.'

'That is so great! Thank you so much.' She gave me another hug, this one swifter but warmer, and kissed me on the cheek. 'Call me and tell me what time you're coming on Saturday, or you can come on Friday if you want. Whenever you like.'

'All right. Don't miss your train.'

She got into the cab, but didn't shut the door. 'Oh, I'm so pleased you can come. Maybe this means we can put all of this behind us.'

I shut the door behind her, and stepped back onto the wet pavement. She waved at me from the back of the cab as it pulled away, taking her back to where she belonged, and I didn't.

'Maybe,' I said.

The Horrid Christmas

When we were in school, Lee used to read these paperbacks called *Sweet Valley High*. She got through them as if they were sweeties, sometimes rereading them if she couldn't find the next one in the series fast enough. The central characters were blonde, beautiful American identical twins, one good and one bad. I picked one up once and threw it down in boredom about twenty minutes later. I wasn't a huge reader anyway, but when I did read, I preferred to read about action and adventure rather than silly girls gossiping about silly boyfriends.

Every now and then, though, I thought about those twins. Was Lee so involved with the books because she saw parallels with our real life? She was dutiful, kind, responsible, happy. I was restless, risk-taking, rebellious, smart-arsed.

If I had the choice, I'd always choose to be the evil twin. Evil twins had much more fun, got to drive fast cars and blow up things and jump off burning buildings, while good twins stayed in the small English village where they'd been born and looked after the family business and their mum. They rang their sister every Sunday, even if she didn't answer the phone, and organised charity balls for awful diseases.

But surely evil twins never felt guilt, did they? Not real, proper evil twins. They wouldn't tell their sister they'd come home because they'd thought it would make her happy. They wouldn't, just for a minute or two, wonder what it would be like to be the sort of person who would be welcome home.

No, proper evil twins were strong and didn't care about what they said or who they hurt or whether their mother would recognise them any more. They went happily along their merry evil way.

I should probably get hold of one of those *Sweet Valley High* books. I could use a few evil-twin pointers.

I didn't want to go to Lee's stupid disco. I'd left home at eighteen and had managed to spend most of the twelve years since completely avoiding Stoneguard, Wiltshire. I worked at a succession of menial jobs. In my spare time I studied acting and martial arts in London. I dyed my hair platinum blond, went to Hong Kong and got some bit-part roles as a fighter in low-budget action movies. I then went to New Zealand and worked for a bungee-jumping company. I drove in stockcar rallies and learned how to fly a plane in Australia and then, when I had a killer tan and had broken several ribs and an arm and was brunette again, I went back to London and got my Equity card and began working my way up the stuntwoman food chain. And then I went to Hollywood.

I'd been back to Stoneguard three times in those twelve years and the place had never changed. The last time was Christmas a year and a half ago. The Horrid Christmas. And that had been a major mistake.

That Christmas eighteen months ago, two birthdays ago, I was in a lull between filming a sci-fi flick called *Blaster* and a vampire romcom called *Thicker than Water*. Everyone I knew was out of town; my latest shag, a very good-looking waiter at a Mexican restaurant that served the best enchiladas in town, was starting to get a bit too keen; and Lee said she missed me. She wasn't living in Stoneguard full time at this point. She was staying in Bath half the week, working for some auction house or antique dealer or something, and spending the other two days doing marketing for my mother's company, Ice Cream Heaven. But she was going to be at home for Christmas, and she'd love to see me.

She also said – and this was a shock – that our mother wanted to see me, after having expressed no interest in my doings or whereabouts for the previous ten years.

So I figured I might as well go for a couple of days; it might turn out to be marginally better than trying to find another restaurant that did enchiladas the way I liked them. Maybe my mother would make an effort to be friendly to me, since she'd asked to see me and all. I got a flight from LAX to Heathrow on Christmas Eve. At the duty-free shop, I bought Lee the biggest box of chocolates I could find and a Mulberry handbag. My mother invariably wore Chanel No. 5, so I bought her some Jean-Paul Gaultier perfume, the one with the pink bottle shaped like the woman's torso. I rented an Audi TT and drove to the village where I'd grown up.

Christmas had never been my favourite time of year anyway. The good citizens of Stoneguard, Wiltshire loved it. They went at Christmas like the non-Scrooge characters in a Dickens novel, draping holly and mistletoe over everything, mulling wine and putting up lights and whistling carols. The whole village became excruciatingly quaint and jolly – even more so than the rest of the year. Any sensible person would throw up into the nearest bin, that is if you could reach it through the forest of proffered mince pies. There was the Annual Christmas Carol Concert on the green, the Annual Christmas Fayre in the church hall, the Annual Christmas Eve Barn Dance and the Annual Christmas Day Toy Rally, to say nothing of the Annual Boxing Day Outside Bowls Tournament and Vegetarian Feast.

People in Stoneguard have this real thing for togetherness. Sometimes it reminded me of a bad science-fiction movie where all the humans have had their brains injected with the hormones of bees obeying their queen. *Must do everything for the good of the hive. Must do everything for the good of the hive.*

Ugh.

I arrived in Stoneguard in the lull between the Christmas Fayre and the Barn Dance. I went to my sister's house first, but she wasn't there, so I left my car with my bag still inside in front of her house, and walked to my mother's. When I got to the tall brick Victorian detached house where I grew up, Lee met me at the door with a full-fledged hug and a squeal. She grabbed me by both of my arms and danced me around the entrance hall. 'I'm so happy you're here, I'm so happy you're here for Christmas Eve and you're going to be with us for three whole days! This is going to be the best Christmas ever, the best the best the best! I am so excited!'

'Hold on,' I said, laughing, 'it's just you and me and Mum in a house.'

'No, it's Christmas! It even looks like snow, don't you think? A white Christmas, can you imagine?' Her eyes were shining. I'd seen her in the summer, but she had something extra now, a sparkle, a glow, something that made it look as if her feet weren't quite touching the ground.

'Why are you so happy?' I asked her. 'Did Mum start making morphine ice cream and let you be the first to try it?'

'Elizabeth. You've come.'

We stopped spinning around, but didn't drop hands. Our mother was standing in the door to the corridor that led to the kitchen, wearing a long black skirt, a dark green cardigan, a muted Paisley scarf. Her dark hair was pulled up, as ever, and fastened tight on the back of her head.

'Hi, Mum,' I said.

Neither of us made a move towards the other one. I let go of Lee's hands, and waited for her to come to me. I'd travelled five and a half thousand miles to get here; it was her turn now.

'You must be tired after your flight,' she said. 'I'll get some refreshments, which we can have in the parlour. I've got something to discuss with both of you.'

She disappeared back through the door. Lee and I exchanged a look.

'What's the big important thing, do you think?' I asked.

'She probably wants to plan Christmas lunch.' We went into the parlour, because a suggestion from our mother was as good as an order. 'So you're going to stay with me?'

'No, I thought I'd stay with good old Mum, reminiscing about happy times.' Even my sister looked surprised at that. 'Of course I'm staying with you, have you got the guest bedroom ready?'

'I've cleared all the work stuff out of it, and I wallpapered it last week – I hope you like it. I've been doing quite a bit of redecorating, thinking vaguely about getting an estate agent in to have a look round, maybe.'

'Trading up?'

'Something like that.'

Our mother's parlour was the same as it had always been: patterned carpet, patterned wallpaper, both in dark colours; heavy velvet drapes and lace curtains at the tall windows. The furniture was heavy mahogany, a long-ago generation's idea of elegance. The marble fireplace was cold and a vase of faded silk flowers sat on the mantelpiece.

'It's freezing in here.' I rubbed my hands together. 'Big surprise.'

'Mum said something about mulled wine. So you're really staying until the twenty-seventh?'

'My flight's in the evening.' I sat on one of the chintz armchairs, which was about as uncomfortable as it looked.

Lee did another little dance, though it was muffled by the carpet and the drapes. Sound was swallowed up in this room; our mother had had parties in here which never seemed to get any louder than a murmur. Though likely that was the nature of her parties, rather than the acoustics.

'Hooray!' she said, and kissed me on the cheek and squeezed my hand again. 'That means you'll be here for Boxing Day.'

'I'm assuming that you're not getting all excited about the bowls tournament.'

'No, it's even better than that. I've got someone I'd really like you to meet.'

'Oh? Who's that, then?'

'Here we are,' Mum said, arriving with a tray. Lee reached out to help her carry it but she shook her head and put it down on the highly-polished table between the chairs. 'Wine, Elizabeth?'

'Never said no before.'

She gave us each a glass of warmed wine and a small plate with a mince pie on it. I tasted the wine; it had been cooking long enough to kill off all the alcohol. And I recognised the mince pies as Ma Gamble's best. Organic, fair-trade, wholemeal and like rocks. I could hardly believe they were as bad as I'd remembered them, but they were. Lee sat on the other chintz chair, taking an obedient bite out of her pie.

Mum sat in her green leather chair, which had belonged to her father and grandfather before her. She crossed her legs at the ankles and put her hands neatly folded in her lap.

'Thank you both for coming,' she said. 'It is a long time since both of my daughters were in this house together.'

I bounced my mince pie on my plate. I felt about eight

years old, lined up in the parlour to be given instructions. In some ways I liked to think I'd grown up, but not when I was here. Not when I was with her. And I was expected to behave this way, anyway; I'd hate to disappoint anybody.

'No ice cream?' I said. 'Not even the special holiday flavour? What is it this year, Ravishing Roast Turkey Ripple?'

My mother looked at the pie on my plate. 'It seems that I neglected to bring any over from the factory.'

'How shocking. A Haven family gathering without ice cream. You're losing your grip, Mum.'

'Liza,' Lee whispered. She was right; I was only here for a few days, no sense starting another war. If I kept quiet, this would probably be over sooner, and I'd be able to escape for a spin in the Audi.

'I have something to discuss, something that concerns you to greater or lesser extents, and therefore I thought it best for both of you to be fully aware of the circumstances before I take action in the New Year.'

My mother always talked like this. It drove me crazy. It wasn't as if she were especially well educated, or had grown up rich; her parents were farmers, and so were her grandparents, and her great-grandparents, back into the mists of time. She grew up hearing broad Wiltshire country accents. But she spoke in written language, every vowel and consonant carefully and correctly pronounced. Lee said it was necessary, because our mother had set up her business in the 1960s when things like accent and class were still all-important. Even though all her marketing literature emphasised words like 'local' and 'fresh' and 'natural', she wouldn't have been given loans, she wouldn't have convinced suppliers to give her a try, if she sounded like what she was, the country-bumpkin daughter of a dairy farmer. It was bad enough she was a woman.

I thought it also might have had something to do with trying to impress the in-laws long ago. They were, to the last chit, City bankers. Though that never worked, as our father had taken flight just before our fifth birthday and was now living in Australia with his second wife and third daughter, never to be heard from except for the rare card at Christmas. Lee and I used to fantasise about what it would be like if he suddenly claimed us and took us to the wild-open country Down Under, but we knew it was never going to happen. He was gone for good, and we barely remembered him. I didn't try to find him when I lived in Australia. We didn't even have his name any more; Mum had kept her maiden name because she'd founded the business with it, and when the divorce came through she changed our names back to Haven to match hers.

I also thought she liked the air of distance her diction gave her. It was of a piece with her straight posture, her tailored clothes, her immovable hairstyle.

Of course the effect of this was always to make me more slangy, to exaggerate any little Americanisms I might have picked up.

'All right, we get it,' I said. 'What do you want to talk about?'

She hesitated, and that was the first thing I noticed that was any different from any of a thousand times our mother had gathered her twins together to talk to us. Usually, she launched straight in, with perfect grammar and oratory style, as if she'd rehearsed her every word about the week's chores or whatever.

'It's probably best if I show you first,' she said. She carefully put her glass on a coaster and reached down. Her briefcase was beside her chair, and she put it on her lap. Again, something felt different as she snapped open the clasps. She laid the case on the table beside the plate of mince pies, so we could see into it. It was full of papers and files and diaries; nothing extraordinary at all.

'These,' she said, 'are my lists.'

We gazed at her open briefcase. She didn't say anything else, just stood beside it, as if she were imparting some great and grave wisdom to her daughters. After a few minutes I spoke up.

'So?'

The corners of her mouth compressed and she reached into her case. She took out a pile of papers with one hand, and a notebook with the other, and held them out to us. Lee took the papers and I took the notebook. It was a black notebook, the kind with an elastic band around it to keep it shut, of a size easy to slip into a pocket or a small bag.

I opened it. It was lists, all right, written in my mother's neat spiky handwriting. Most items had ticks next to them. It looked like a list of errands and tasks: *Bread. Milk. Pick up cleaning. Ring bank re. payroll. Tissues and Paracetamol. Boiler servicing – ring Gerald, 255478, before 17.00.*

I looked up at my mother. Was this some sort of message, something she was showing me to try to make me feel guilty about my lack of involvement in her day-to-day life? Which was a joke, quite honestly, I thought. There was surely no other woman alive more capable of looking after herself than my mother. She could do errands and tasks with her eyes shut; she'd been running her own business for a lifetime. Giving affection, on the other hand, or praise to her younger twin daughter, or keeping hold of a husband, or ever admitting she'd been wrong . . .

She was watching us, her mouth still in a firm straight line. 'Keep looking, Elizabeth,' she told me, and though my instinct was, as ever, to challenge her giving me a direct order, the small differences in her tonight and the fact that she'd even asked me to be here made me play along to find out why. I flipped a few pages and read some more lists. Some were done in pencil, some in biro, some in ink, always with those ticks beside them, done heavily enough to dent the paper. *Go to Residents' Association meeting. Leave at 19.45 for 20.00, in school hall. School Street. Put out recycling in green bin. Two tablets in the dishwasher. Turn on the dishwasher. Lock the door. Pin morning list on door.*

I paused. Two tablets in the dishwasher? Pin morning list on door?

'Mum, what are these?' Lee asked beside me. 'Why do you need a list telling you to check that the gas isn't on?'

I turned over the page, and there it was on mine, too, before *9.15 train to Swindon, 9.45 Dr Rowe, Dentist, 45 Ivy Road. Take cab from station. Ask receptionist to book a cab to station afterwards. 11.25 train to Stoneguard.* Everything had big thick ticks next to it, as if my mother was angry at the dentist and the train.

'I need them,' Mum said calmly.

'But why? You'd know if the gas was on, wouldn't you? You'd smell it. And why would you need to write down directions to the garage?'

'So I won't get lost.'

'But the garage belongs to Stone Hamlin,' said Lee. 'It's right next to their farm. Why would you get lost going there?'

'It isn't only the garage, Emily.'

I'd put down the notebook and was rooting through the briefcase. There were three other notebooks like the one I'd read. Some more detailed; some with times for getting up, for going to bed, some with reminders of what to wear. And sheets of A4 and A5, some folded or crumpled and smoothed out; Post-It notes; scraps of paper. I picked out one that said *I sold my parents' house in 1987 when my mother died.* No tick next to this one.

'Mum,' I said, the bizarre note in my hand, 'what are you trying to tell us?'

Our mother sat back down in her chair. She smoothed her skirt across her knees. 'I'm not certain how long it has been happening. Of course, that's one of the symptoms in itself. I first noticed when I found it difficult to find a correct word for something. I would often walk into a room and realise I didn't know why I was there.'

'These things happen all the time to everyone,' Lee said.

'Not to me. When I forgot a meeting with a supplier, I began to make more use of writing things down. I acquired a diary, of which I had never had need before, and I began carrying around a small notebook, as you see there.' She took another one out of her pocket, identical to the others I'd looked at. This one had a pencil attached to the elastic. 'Of course, these strategies only worked when I could find a pen, and then there were the times when I forgot I was meant to be writing things down. I discovered that when my mind was not entirely focused on the task, my handwriting became illegible. But for the most part I found that in this way, I could carry on without a noticeable disruption in my daily life and business. As long as I remembered to look at my lists, I could be as normal.'

'How long have you been doing this?' I asked.

She paused to think. 'I cannot recall. Perhaps in the spring? I may not have written it down.'

'I've never seen you with any of these lists,' Lee said. 'I work with you and everything, and I've never seen it.'

'I didn't want you to.'

'But Mum—'

She held up her hand. 'This was, as you can imagine, a

distressing development for me. It is difficult to feel that, at any moment, you may lose grip of your life, your business, your very existence. I have been – worried. Despite the lists, I have begun to make mistakes.'

'If you're talking about that order for Praline Perfection, it wasn't any problem, was it? It wouldn't have even slowed us down if Doris hadn't started making chocolate already that morning.'

'Orders are our business, Emily. One can't misplace them. I had to disrupt the entire production schedule, have all the equipment cleaned and set up again, and keep everyone at work until nearly eleven at night to get the order filled in time.'

'These things happen.'

'Not to me. Never to me. I went to see Dr Percy the next day and demanded a brain scan.'

'You had a *brain scan*?' My sister's face went white and rigid.

'I told you I was going to a marketing conference in London. I was, in fact, in London, but in hospital rather than at a conference. I'm sorry about the deception, but it was necessary. I was subjected to a variety of physical and neuro-logical tests. I received the diagnosis late last week. I have Alzheimer's disease.'

We stared at her. She gazed back at us. She opened her notebook on her lap and held on to it carefully, as if it held any answers she might need.

'Do you have any questions?' she asked. 'Are you familiar with the disease?'

'You can't have Alzheimer's,' Lee said. 'You're too young.'

'I am very nearly seventy years old. You forget, Emily, that I had you girls very late in my life.'

'But you're not – you're not *old* old.'

'I am old enough to retire as Director of Ice Cream Heaven. And that is what I intend to do.'

'Oh, Mum.' Lee got out of her chair. She went to our mother and put her arms around her. My mother put her own hand on my sister's back.

I sat alone. Their circle of arms locked them in an embrace that excluded me. I should be used to it. 'Let me get this right,' I said. 'You have Alzheimer's. Isn't that the thing where you go gradually crazy until you die?'

'It's a forgetting disease,' my mother said over my sister's shoulder. 'It strips away your memories. Then it strips away your self. And then you may live on for as long as your body wants to live. That is what will happen to me.'

My sister leaned back so she could see my mother's face, though her arms were still around her. Tears had begun flowing down Lee's face. 'There's got to be some mistake,' she said.

'No. I researched the disease as soon as I'd seen Dr Percy, and my symptoms fit. I am in an early stage, but the decline is inevitable.'

'Is there some medication you can take? A special diet?'

'I have refused medication. I am not prepared to put up with the side effects. My brain is scrambled enough without adding to it.'

'Oh no, Mum.' Lee's voice was muffled.

'So you're quitting?' I said. 'You've got this horrible disease and you're just going to quit and let it ruin your life?'

I felt like punching something. It was taking every bit of my strength not to get up and walk out; the only thing that was keeping me there was my sister's face, streaked with tears.

'I am not quitting,' my mother told me. 'I have made every provision for care of myself and the business.'

'Except for taking medication to help yourself get better.'

64

'I told you, I'm not prepared to put up with the side effects.'

I got up out of my chair, but I didn't leave. I paced instead. 'Going crazy is easier, huh? Maybe for you, it will be. You won't know what's happening, right? But what about us? How are we supposed to feel about you refusing to help yourself to get better?'

'I will not get better. You don't recover from this disease. The medication can only slow the onset. It doesn't always work.'

Lee put her fist up to her mouth, as if holding in a sob.

'Then how are we supposed to feel about taking care of you?' I asked. 'You could do something to slow down the disease, but you won't. Doesn't that mean you're going to be helpless for longer? Look at Lee! Can you see what this news is doing to her? It's completely selfish to refuse to take the drugs.'

'Don't worry,' Mum said. 'You won't be expected to look after me. I wouldn't ask it of you.'

'But Mum, we want to look after you,' Lee said. 'Of course we do. What are you talking about?'

'Please sit down, Emily. You too, Elizabeth.'

Reluctantly, my sister left my mother, and I left my pacing. We sat in the twin chairs, side by side. Lee was sniffing, wiping her eyes with the back of her hand. I was tense, my fists clenched, my legs bouncing up and down with energy.

Mum glanced down at her notebook. 'I will retire from the company in the New Year.' Lee made a noise as if to protest, but Mum held up her hand to silence her. 'I absolutely refuse to have my frailty affect the business I spent my life building. The time will come, perhaps soon, when I will no longer be able to make effective decisions, and the most dangerous aspect of that is that I may not be aware I am making mistakes

65

until it is too late. The Directorship of Ice Cream Heaven will proceed to you, Emily.'

'But Mum— I'm not—'

'You have worked there faithfully for nearly your entire life, even if only part time. You know Ice Cream Heaven nearly as well as I do, Emily. And as you take charge, you will learn more. I have trust in you. How could I not?'

'So much for the business,' I said. 'What about you?'

'I will continue to live here in my home for as long as I can. I have substantial savings, a generous pension, and a lump sum payout from my life assurance. It should cover private nursing care for as long as is necessary. I have already made all the arrangements.'

'What will you do? I can't take over your business, your business is your life. You'll be lost without it, Mum, you know you will. How will you spend your time before you—' Lee couldn't say it, but I thought it: Before you get too crazy to notice time at all.

'I have no desire to make myself a fool of myself; I would rather retire gracefully from sight. Of course, I shall see you, Emily, on a regular basis. There will be a transition period with Ice Cream Heaven, and I know you will visit me regularly. In the meantime, we should carry on as normal during the holiday.'

'Right. Right.' I couldn't sit still; I stood up again. 'So basically you called us together here on the day before Christmas to tell us you're dying, that you won't do anything to stop it, and that you intend to shut yourself away from the world until you do actually croak. Oh, and Happy Christmas.'

'Liza!' Lee said. 'Don't make it worse, *please*.'

'I hadn't yet come to the Happy Christmas part,' my mother replied dryly, 'but yes, you have summed it up charmingly, Elizabeth.'

'She doesn't mean it, Mum,' said Lee.

'Yes, I do mean it, Mum. Why did you even want me to come here? Obviously I can't do anything to convince you to take care of yourself.'

'This is not the sort of thing one writes in a postcard. I wanted to tell you in person.'

'And now that I know, what now? Lee's going to take care of the ice cream, you've hired nurses to look after you. You've got it all sorted, as usual. What's my part in all this?'

'Nothing,' said my mother. 'I merely wanted you to know. As I said before, you won't be expected to look after me. I wouldn't ask it of you.'

There's a problem with the English language. 'You' can mean you plural, as in you and your identical twin sister, both of you, a unit. Or it can mean you, just you, you alone, the only one who isn't wanted.

This time, I heard the 'you' my mother really meant.

'All right. I get it. As I'm not needed, I'll take myself out of your way.' I walked out of the parlour.

'Liza!' my sister called behind me. I grabbed my jacket from where it hung on the coat tree, shoved on my boots and left the house, slamming the door.

The sky outside was even lower and greyer than it had been when I was driving into the town. All the Christmas lights were on, blinking and winking like a thousand happy stars, hanging from streetlights and buildings and cosy inside windows. As I approached the High Street I could hear children singing 'Hark, The Herald Angels Sing'.

'Fucking village,' I muttered and walked faster, pulling the hood of my coat up.

'Liza!' shouted my sister behind me. I thought about not turning around. I thought about sprinting away. I was faster than she was.

I stopped and waited for her to catch up. She'd come out without her coat on; she was wearing a cardigan, but the wind was blowing down the street and she couldn't possibly be warm enough.

'Where are you going?' she asked me.

'Back to your house. I'm going to drive to Heathrow and get a flight to LA.'

'You can't go! How can you go after what Mum's just told us?'

'I'm going *because* of what Mum's just told us. She doesn't want me here. Not now, not for the rest of her life. If she wants to sit and lose her mind in peace, I'll go away and let her.'

'But it's Christmas Eve!'

'So I'll buy a Santa hat at the airport.'

'Please don't leave. We need some time to get used to this – some time together. Please.'

'I don't need anything. Didn't you hear her? I have nothing to do with it. You're taking care of the business, the hired help is taking care of Mum, and of course you'll go and visit her and play the dutiful daughter. Meanwhile, I have other places to be, like anywhere but this hellish place.'

She grabbed my arm. 'Liza, stop it. There are people.'

There were people; people in hats and coats and scarves, people with packages and bottles and bags, milling around on their holiday business, between the Fayre and the Barn Dance, gazing at us standing here on the pavement arguing with each other. I hadn't even noticed them, but the fact that Lee did sent my anger up another notch. Of course she'd want me to shut up. Mouthy, inconvenient twin.

'I don't care about other people. I'm going to LA.'

'Why are you being like this?' She wrapped her arms around herself; her mascara was smeared. 'You're ruining everything.'

'*I'm* ruining everything?' I laughed, without any humour.

'Where have you been for the past half an hour? Haven't you noticed that it's not exactly the happy family occasion here?'

'Liza, be reasonable, please.' She said it quietly, putting her hand on my arm, trying to draw me away. 'Mum needs your understanding.'

'Oh, I understood her perfectly well. Especially when she said she didn't want me near her or her precious business.'

'She didn't tell you because she wanted to argue with you, she told you because she wanted you to know.'

'Why are you defending her? No, I think the real question here is why didn't you argue, too? She's an old woman who refuses to help herself get any better, and you're prepared to just sit down and go along with what she's decided?'

'She's *sick*.'

'And you're doing what you've always done, which is exactly what she tells you to.' I turned around to walk away and bumped straight into Jasbir Singh, who appeared to be carrying a boxful of aubergines.

'Sorry,' he said, avoiding my eyes.

'Did you hear that?' I asked him. 'Or would you like us to repeat the argument a little bit louder for you?'

'Well, I . . .'

'I'm sorry, Jas,' said Lee. 'My sister's a little bit upset, she doesn't mean to be rude.'

I rounded on her. 'Don't you apologise for me. Don't you *dare*.'

'Then don't be like this! Calm down, and act more like—'

'More like you, you mean? Jesus Christ, Lee, I can't imagine anything worse. I'm glad I'm not stuck here in this place at our mother's beck and call.'

'What are you angry about, then? If you don't even want to be here anyway, why do you care what she does with the business? Did you want it for yourself?'

I stepped backwards, feeling as if I'd been slapped. 'You think I'm that selfish?'

'I can't understand why you feel like you're the injured person here, when you're the one who gets to walk away!'

I put my hands on my hips. 'Tell me one thing, Lee: if I asked you, would you give me half the business? It's half mine by inheritance anyway. Would you share?'

She hesitated. That was enough for me.

'I get it,' I said. 'Don't worry, I reckon she did me a favour by giving you the company. I can get the hell out of here and never look back.'

'All right,' she said. 'Go ahead and leave like you always do. If you wonder why I belong here and you don't, that's why. Because *I don't run away*.' I'd so rarely seen anger on my sister's face that I barely recognised her: white-cheeked, thin-lipped, her eyes narrowed.

'And I bet you feel great about yourself, too. Congratulations.'

This time I really did walk away. Around Jasbir, who was still standing transfixed holding his box of vegetables. There were fat snowflakes in his hair and, I noticed for the first time, blowing in the air around us. Light and delicate, pure and picturesque. I left my sister behind me on the pavement, in the snow, under the coloured lights. I couldn't hear whether the children were singing any more, because my blood was pounding too hard in my ears.

When I rounded the corner to where I'd parked my car, Derek Hunter was walking towards me, his three white terriers straining on their leads. I stepped aside to give them a wide berth. 'Merry Christmas L— which one are you?'

'I'm the evil twin,' I told him. 'Merry Christmas.'

Plan A

Just over nineteen months after the Horrid Christmas, and two days after I'd successfully spent an entire evening at Jett with my sister without arguing with her, I was up bright and early and riding a train out of London towards the seaside. I'd spent the day before making phone calls from my hotel room, without much luck. Today I was in the mood for grabbing the bull by the horns. Or, more accurately, Ken Yamada.

I tried to read a newspaper on the train, but I couldn't concentrate that much so I gazed out at the suburbs as they petered out into innocuous fields and hills. I hadn't seen Ken for five years. He'd disapproved of my going to America. But he'd also been one of my favourite stunt coordinators when I was working in the British industry, and he'd always been glad to see me.

I hoped he'd be glad to see me today, especially as I was arriving unannounced. The phone calls were part of the problem, I'd decided. Over the phone, I was easy to dismiss. I couldn't show that I was fit, that I could still work despite the crash. In the flesh, Ken was bound to see that I was as good as I'd ever been. I didn't expect him to hire me right away – he was bound to have everyone he needed for his current production – but you never knew. He'd keep me in mind for

71

his next job, or the next. Sometimes these things took a little while to bear fruit.

If he hired me right away, though, I wouldn't have to go to Wiltshire this weekend. I was regretting my foolish promise to Lee. I didn't want to see my mother. I didn't want to go to Stoneguard. And I didn't want to have to sidestep around the things we'd argued about last time I was there. I'd never been good at being tactful and discreet, and though Lee might think that time and distance and nice little presents might smooth over the differences between us, I knew better.

We'd said what we'd really felt that Christmas Eve, things that had been bubbling under the surface for a very long time. Saying them didn't make them go away, and not saying them didn't, either. And there were worse things still bubbling down there, more dangerous things.

Things like *You were loved and I wasn't. And even though I love you too, I hate you for what you took from me.*

I wasn't sure I could trust myself, if I went to Stoneguard. By instinct, I was a fighter, but with my sister, peace was much safer. Because if we got down to the truth between us, we might destroy any chance of peace forever.

Overall, I'd prefer to be working.

Though the station was a small one, there were several taxis waiting there, no doubt because of the proximity of a film crew. I hopped into one and didn't even have to say anything. 'You going to where they're filming, love?' the driver asked me, pulling away.

'Yup.'

'Nice day for it. What do you do, are you an actress?'

'Stunt woman.'

'Nice one. You ever do a zombie film? I'm a big zombie fan, me.'

'No zombies, just vampires and werewolves and aliens.'

72

'Ah, pity. Still, they're the new big thing, eh, vampires. You can't go to the cinema without tripping over some vampire or other. Telly, too. It's all those young girls, they love the vampires. Give me a good zombie any day of the week, though, and I'm happy. Zombies or those movies where the whole town is evil. You see *Invasion of the Body Snatchers*?'

I nodded, stared out of the window, and let him babble. It wasn't a nice day for it; it was threatening rain. Typical British summer. I'd better get used to it again if I was going to work here. I wasn't really one to lie on a beach and tan myself, anyway. Most of the sun I got was on the job, or from riding the Triumph, and consequently I was nearly British fish-belly pale.

They were filming on an airstrip near a beach, close enough so that when I got out of the taxi and paid the driver I could smell the sea. I recognised the scenario, the trucks and trailers and the clumps of people talking and doing nothing while they waited, and I scanned the second unit crew for Ken's spiky black hair. I didn't see it, but lots of people were clustered around the far end of the field, and several were wearing hats.

A security guard approached me and I gave him my name and waited. Eventually, a runner appeared, a teenage-looking girl with spots and a ponytail and the ever-present earpiece and walkie talkie. 'Can I help you?'

I smiled at her. 'I'm looking for Ken Yamada, he's expecting me.' Which he wasn't, but a tiny white lie never hurt, especially to a runner. They had so little power they liked to wield it any way they could.

'Who?'

Argh, not only officious, but clueless. 'The stunt coordinator, Ken Yamada.'

'I'm sorry, I'm not quite sure what you're talking about.'

I resisted sighing and rolling my eyes. 'You know, the person who's in charge of the stunts? Who tells the stunt people what to do? Stunt coordinator?'

'Yes, I know that, but—'

'What the hell are you doing here?'

I recognised the voice right away, and with a sick drop of my stomach, I turned around and saw Allen standing behind me, wearing jeans, a sweatshirt, a Texas Rangers baseball cap and a scowl.

'I didn't know you were working here, Al,' I said.

'And I know that you're not. Why are you here?'

'I'm looking for Ken. He's expecting me.'

'He didn't tell me you were coming here.'

I put my hands on my hips. The runner had frozen, glancing at both of us like a frightened animal. 'I don't imagine Ken has to tell you every single thing about his job.'

'I imagine he does, since I'm doing it for him.'

For the first time, even my assumed confidence faltered. 'What?'

Allen cocked his head. 'Obviously you're not as tight with Ken Yamada as you think you are, if you don't know that his wife's just had triplets.'

'What?' I didn't even know he was married.

'And I've taken his place. So if you wanted to see the stunt coordinator, I'm it.'

Oh no.

I turned to the runner. 'Do you mind giving us a few minutes?' She glanced at Al, who nodded, and scurried away.

'So you didn't answer my question,' he said. 'What are you doing here?'

Right. I had two choices now: pretend everything was fine, stick it out and state my case, or skulk away. Even if I'd been tempted to do the latter, it was impossible as the taxi had left. 'Hi, Allen, long time no see. How are you?'

'Don't give me that. You gave up the right to small talk with me when you kicked me out of your hospital room after I saved your life.'

'Thank you for saving my life. But I was in traction. I didn't feel like being lectured.'

'You deserved the lecture. Nice of you to call me, by the way, to let me know you'd healed up all right.'

'I didn't call you.'

'Exactly.' He began walking, long strides across the tarmac. I walked alongside him, trying not to think about the last time I'd walked with him. On my way to fire and pain.

'I've been busy getting better, basically,' I said. 'But I'm fighting fit now, which is why I'm here.'

'You're also looking for work and can't find it anywhere, so you thought you'd try with Ken, either 'cause you thought he hadn't heard what everyone else in the industry already knows, or 'cause you thought he liked you too much to care. Too bad that's not true.'

'What's not true?'

'Neither of them. I'm sorry to be the bearer of bad news, Liza, but in case you can't figure it out yourself: if you can't find work, it's 'cause you screwed up so bad nobody wants to work with you any more.'

I stopped. 'Allen, you were there. You know I did the best I could in a spin like that.'

He stopped too. I'd forgotten quite how big he was. 'You're right, I was there, and that's bullshit. You were going too fast, and you were in no state to be driving. I tried to tell you before you got in the Enzo, but you reared up and wouldn't listen.'

'They took a blood alcohol test at the hospital, and I was clean.'

'You don't have to be drunk from the night before to be in no state.'

'If you thought that, why didn't you stop me?'

'You've got to be kidding me. It's easier to stop a freight train than to stop you, darlin'. That's only one of a hell of a lot of reasons you shouldn't be working on anything remotely dangerous right now.'

'So what are you saying – that as far as you're concerned, my career is stone dead? After one freaking accident?'

'It was one mother of an accident. And no, I'm not saying that. There's plenty of other stuff you could be doing that's not on the front line.'

A plane flew low overhead. I raised my voice. 'Like selling Girl Scout cookies?'

'Like teaching technique. Doing corporate events, team-building experiences. Stuff like that.'

I snorted. 'Team-building? Teaching? Me? You must be mad.'

'I'd be happy to put in a few calls for you if you want, for old time's sake.'

'I don't want a few pity jobs for old time's sake. I want a proper job, because I'm good and I deserve it.'

Allen narrowed his eyes, as if he were assessing me. I'd always thought he was easygoing, too nice. Now I wondered if I'd underestimated him.

'All right,' he said. 'You can have a job with me. Right now, starting today. You just got to do one thing first.'

'Whatever you can throw at me, I can take it.'

'Good. Come over here.'

He walked quickly away, and I kept up with him. The sun broke through the clouds for a moment; on the tarmac in front of us his shadow looked big and solid, and mine slight and straight. He took me to the far end of the airfield and stopped in front of the car that was crouched there.

It was a Porsche 911 Turbo. New, black and gleaming. 'Driven one of these before?' he asked.

'It's a 911, Allen, of course I've driven one.'

'Good. Then you won't need a practice loop. Get in.'

'You're going to let me drive it?'

'You drive down this airstrip to the other end, as fast as you can push it safely. You don't crash, you've got a job. That's it.' He thumbed his walkie talkie. 'Jack? Clear the strip, we're coming down,' he said, and then hung up and looked at me expectantly.

'You're kidding me.'

'I'm deadly serious, Liza.'

'Then you'd better call and tell them to send over the contracts.' I threw my handbag on the ground, shrugged off my jacket next to it, and got in the car. The interior was red leather, the colour of sun through closed eyelids. I adjusted my seat and fastened the belt. My heart thudded, fast and loud in my ears.

It was excitement. I'd been given a chance to prove myself. I put my hands on the wheel to get used to the car. My palms were wet. I glanced outside; Al had stepped back, but he was watching me, so I couldn't wipe them on my jeans.

One run down the airstrip, as fast as I could make it. Easy-peasy. I turned on the ignition and the car started with a lovely throaty purr. I put the 911 into gear.

My throat closed up.

I swallowed, hard. The wheel was slippery. My foot hovered on the accelerator, the clutch waiting to bite. Somewhere back in my throat I tasted blood.

Turning over in the air, falling, the smell of smoke and burning flesh. Al's hands underneath my arms. An empty can of Diet Coke.

77

'Just do it, Liza,' I tried to tell myself, I tried to say aloud, but I couldn't.

I couldn't. I held on to the steering wheel and I couldn't. A single trickle of sweat ran down between my breasts. I fought for breath.

The car door opened and Al's arm went across me. He turned off the engine. The silence was like a punch.

'You can't do it, can you?' he said quietly.

'Just – give me a minute.' It came out like a gasp.

'You've lost your nerve. I'm not surprised. And I don't think it's a bad thing either, because you had too much nerve to begin with. Way too much for your own good.'

'I can do this,' I said. But even more alarming than the fear and the paralysis, I felt the prickle of tears in my eyes.

'No, you can't. Maybe one day you'll get some of your nerve back, not all of it, but some of it. Then you'll be good at the job again. But right now, you might as well get out of the car.'

I got out. I couldn't look at Allen; instead I looked out, far out past the crew and the airstrip to the grey sea. As soon as the air hit my face my eyes stopped prickling and I wasn't in danger of crying, so it wasn't that; I couldn't look at him because I would remember him pulling me out of the burning Ferrari again. And I couldn't think about that right now, everything it had lost me, without throwing up.

'I'll call you a taxi,' Al said. I looked out to sea and I nodded. I felt something near my shoulder that might have been his hand, reaching for me, but then it was gone.

Plan B

'So when does this disco thing start?'

'Liza? I've been calling you like crazy, where have you been?'

I lay back on my bed, in the litter of my hotel room, and rubbed my eyes. 'I turned off my phone for a while.'

'I've been ringing every day since Tuesday.'

'What day is it today?'

A pause, where I could hear my sister tamping down her irritation. 'It's Friday, Liza.'

'Really?' I rubbed my eyes again, and rubbed my head. 'That went fast.'

Amazing how easy it was to lose yourself in London for three days, especially when you didn't want to think and there was a pub pretty much on every street. I could even walk everywhere, so I didn't have to worry about getting into a car.

I swallowed. Getting into a car. Had Allen known I'd choke behind the wheel of the 911? Had I known it?

I didn't own a car in LA; I owned my beloved Triumph T140 Bonneville motorcycle, which was fast and gorgeous and had the bonus of not getting stuck in traffic. I'd hardly ridden it in the past few months. At first that was because it was too painful, and I'd been telling myself lately that the riding posture was still too awkward for my back.

But was it really because I was too scared? Had the accident destroyed all my confidence?

'We ordered green,' my sister was saying. 'These are teal.'

'What?'

'Oh, don't worry, I'll sort it out. – Sorry, Liza, I was talking to Annabelle about the balloons – they've turned up in the wrong colour. Anyway, yes. The charity ball is tomorrow night at half past seven. Are you free?'

'It looks like I am, as a matter of fact, yes.' Plus my hotel reservation ran out tomorrow, anyway. I'd only reserved it for a week, figuring that when I got work I'd make other plans.

'So are you coming?'

My head really did hurt. I closed my eyes and ran through the other options than keeping my promise to my sister. I couldn't go back to LA, not right now. I had no job, but still had some money in my bank account. In theory, I could do whatever I wanted. Llama trekking in Bolivia. Hang gliding in New Zealand. Pot-holing in Utah. Anything, anywhere.

But what if I got on a llama and I got the shaking heebie-jeebies? Let alone a hang glider.

And I'd promised.

'Sure, I'll come,' I said.

'Okay. Great. That's excellent.'

She said 'excellent' in the same tone that she'd said 'teal'.

'Unless you don't want me to come any more,' I said.

'Of course I do!'

'It's just that you didn't sound quite as enthusiastic as when I first said I'd be coming.'

'Don't I? – No, those streamers aren't right either. I'm going to have to go to Swindon this afternoon, and the car is . . .'

She sighed. 'I thought you'd be ringing me before this to tell me, that's all.'

'Are you talking to me this time?'

'Yes. Anyway, that's great, when will you be getting in? Will you rent a car?'

'N-no, I'll take the train.'

'Okay, I'll meet you at the station.'

'Don't worry, I can find my own way to your house. I don't know the train times anyway.'

'They're at—'

'Honestly, don't tell me, I won't remember. I'll roll up at Paddington and see what happens. It's not fancy dress, is it? I'm not dressing up as a New Romantic or whatever.'

'No. It is quite dressy, though. I think most people want to make a nice night of it.'

'I might have to borrow something to wear. Actually,' I added, surveying the clothes crumpled and tossed all over the floor, 'I might need to borrow underwear and stuff too, until I can do some laundry.'

'That's fine, you can wear whatever you like of mine, and I've got a few dresses you might like. Listen, Liza, I have to go right now because the decorations aren't what I ordered and I've got to and sort those out, and Ma Gamble keeps on ringing me about the food even though she's in Bristol. Anyway, I'll see you tomorrow. You'll let me know when you're arriving, so I can be there? I'll be back and forth between my house and the school all day.'

'Yeah, yeah.'

'That's fantastic. I can't wait to see you. And everyone else is going to be so pleased to see you, too.'

'Hmph,' I said. 'See you soon.' I hung up and buried my aching head in the pillow.

I should probably have chosen the llama trekking. Because

Lee was absolutely wrong: everyone in Stoneguard was *not* going to be pleased to see me. I couldn't think of a single person who would. As a matter of fact, I couldn't think of a single person anywhere who would be pleased to see me at the moment.

Except for my sister. And that was why I was going: to make her happy.

But she hadn't sounded happy on the phone. She'd sounded flat, frustrated, irritated. And there was something in her voice, too, something more than annoyance at decorations. A very slight quiver, something that probably nobody else but her twin sister would be able to detect. It sounded a little bit as if she were on some sort of edge.

Which was silly. My sister didn't live on any edge. She lived solidly in the middle of a safe circle, surrounded by neighbours and countryside. A charity ball was so exactly her style that she must practically be exploding with contentment.

I got up to search for more ibuprofen. I'd find out soon enough, anyway. And I had enough to think about myself, what with being the prodigal twin.

Return to Stoneguard

The Wiltshire fields curved like voluptuous women. Rain and the rare sun had fed the trees into lushness, and ripened the crops into amber and green. The road meandered around stone farm buildings, twisted past ancient earthworks, dipped up and down sheep-studded hills. My suitcase and I were both in the back of a taxi that smelled strongly of socks and rubber.

Being in the back of a cab didn't seem to bother me, but being in the back of this one did. Engineering works meant that my train from Paddington had been delayed nearly an hour, and by the time I'd got to Swindon I'd just missed the train to Stoneguard and would have had to have waited another hour for the next one. So I'd got a cab instead, driven by a bloke with a grizzled beard and nicotine-stained fingers. I should have known when the boot wouldn't open that I'd chosen the wrong cab, but no, I got in it anyway because it was nearly six o'clock and I didn't want to be late for my sister's precious dance.

We were tootling along the road at an erratic thirty miles an hour, despite the speed limit being fifty. I craned my neck to look past the shabby seat backs and through the windscreen. 'What's going on?' I asked.

'Tourists.' The driver nodded at the people-carrier ahead of us, which had its brake-lights on. 'They like the horses.'

I frowned, because I couldn't see any animals except for sheep, but then I realised. Bloody white horses carved in the hillside by God knows who into the bloody Wiltshire chalk. There were about a million of the things around here.

'Can't we pass them? I'm in a bit of a hurry.'

'No passing here, love.'

'That depends on your driving skills,' I muttered, and sat back in my seat.

'You from around here?'

'No.'

The people-carrier sped up slightly and we followed, at forty. 'Bound to slow down again in a minute,' my driver said. 'There's another 'un after the turn-off to Devizes.'

' *"There once was a man from Devizes"*,' I quoted, ' *"whose balls were of two different sizes. One was so small it was no ball at all, and the other one won several prizes"*.'

The driver gave a wheezy laugh. 'That's a good 'un.'

'Only poem I know.' I looked out of the window again. I'd learned to drive on these twisty dippy roads, or rather I'd taught myself, mostly during the hours of darkness when I wouldn't be spotted, in someone else's car. You could get away with a lot after dark, much more so than during the day when people were watching your every move.

It was, of course, raining. My back ached, and I dug in my handbag for ibuprofen. I hadn't seen the sun for more than about five minutes since I'd got to England.

The taxi slowed right down. I sat up again. 'What's going on?'

'Tractor.'

'Ugh.'

I suddenly remembered I hadn't told Lee when I was

coming. Though at this rate, who knew when I would. *B there in 10, poss 20 depending on tractor*, I texted her and watched the landscape undulate around me. Slowly.

Lee would want to be early to the ball as she was in charge of it, and she'd want us to arrive together. I'd have to find something of hers to wear – God knows what, as we didn't exactly share taste in clothing – slap on some borrowed make-up and rush out the door again to see a bunch of people I didn't give a rat's arse about.

At least there would be alcohol. Alcohol and, with any luck, some decent food. I hoped Lee had arranged for something more sustaining than ice cream. There hadn't been a buffet on the train from Paddington, so whatever I drank was going to go straight to my head and I really would end up snogging One-Eyed Pete.

Then again, that might liven things up a bit. Why was I going to, of all things, a disco? I shuddered. I didn't dance. And the music was bound to be awful. And the conversation, too. Everyone lived in each other's pockets in Stoneguard; they knew everything about each other already.

When I thought about it rationally, I was probably having a more enjoyable time here in this taxi, breathing in socks and looking at the back end of a tractor.

I'd just decided this when the tractor made a sudden turn off to a muddy lane, and the driver sped up to the dizzying speed of forty-five. By now we were close enough to Stoneguard that I could close my eyes and see it just as well. Here was the incongruous mound of Ashes Barrow and its associated tourist car park on the right. Across the road, the rye in the facing field had been flattened in swirls forming the shape of a hydrogen molecule. Crop circles of one form or another were always appearing in the fields around here; whatever or whoever made them, I imagined it cheesed off the farmers.

The road bent to the left and before it dipped, the view opened out to the village slightly below: the grey stone spire of the church, the blue slate or thatch of the house roofs, and behind and above everything, up on Stoneguard Hill, the jagged stone circle that gave the town its name.

The stones jutted into the grey sky like rocky fingers grasping at the rain. A few brightly-coloured specks moved amongst them. Tourists in anoraks, the only industry of Stoneguard except for dodgy homeopathic remedies and, of course, ice cream.

We passed the stone and iron gates of Naughton Hall, set on higher ground than the village to remind the peasants of their place in the scheme of things, and then descended into the village. First, past the whitewashed Druid's Arms with its hanging baskets and tourists enjoying the local brew, and then along the High Street with its shops all sensitively selected and designed so as not to spoil the olde worlde charme of the place. Ahead, Ma Gamble's Wholefood Emporium had its doors open despite the rain to catch whatever was going on, as usual. The taxi crawled along.

'Nice place,' said the driver.

'You obviously never lived here. Turn right here, please.'

'After the ice-cream parlour?' The driver smacked his lips. 'Clotted Cream flavour, that's my favourite. Lovely on a bit of apple crumble.'

'We all scream for ice cream,' I said, looking away from the Heavenly Scoop, the ice-cream parlour owned by my family which was the scene of so many tedious teenage memories. My sister lived up Church Lane in a former almshouse which had been converted into three adjoining cottages, pebble-dashed and painted in pastel shades. Lee's was primrose yellow.

'It's here,' I said to the driver, checking my watch. It was gone half past six already. Lee, of course, would be dressed and ready, and probably pacing the floor waiting for me to get here. Fortunately, I wasn't the sort of female who required hours of preparation to be seen in public.

I paid the driver and got my suitcase out of the back seat myself. I pulled it behind me as I hurried up the short gravel path through the teensy cute front garden to my sister's green-painted wooden door. I turned the doorknob and pushed, ready to call out, 'Hey, it's me!' But the door didn't budge, and I didn't get any further than 'He—!'

Locked. She must have popped out for something. Or maybe she'd had to go to the school hall before I got here. I frowned. She'd been nagging at me to come to this thing, and now that I was here, she couldn't even be bothered to wait to see me?

Her spare door key hung from a tiny hook underneath her wooden bird-table in the front garden. I didn't bother being furtive about going to get it; I had no doubt that every man, woman and child living in Stoneguard knew exactly where my sister kept her spare key. I unhooked it and opened the door.

I could smell Lee as soon as I walked inside. It was a little bit of shampoo, a little bit of clean clothes, a hint of vanilla, a warm tone of dust. All of those were external, though; there was something more basic underneath, something that came from Lee herself. If I'd been transported here without knowing it in the middle of the night, before I'd even opened my eyes I would know that I was in Lee's house just from breathing the same air she had been in.

She probably knew my scent as well, too, though I couldn't tell you what I'd smell like. Socks, right now. Maybe the beer I'd drunk last night. I needed a shower.

'Hello?' I called, because although the locked door told me

Lee wasn't home, her scent told me so strongly otherwise that it was difficult not to believe it. But she didn't answer. She must've left minutes ago.

Oh well, she was probably there already, which meant I could take my time. I kicked my trainers off and walked across her hallway in my socks. The carpet here was some sort of natural fibre, jute or whatever, woven into a tight herringbone. It was new since I'd been here last, but it suited Lee's décor, which was all pale woods and pastel walls and filmy white curtains at the windows to let every bit of natural light through.

I'd only been to this house a couple of times. She'd had a housewarming party when she'd bought the place – when was that? Six or seven years ago now, I guessed. I'd been living in London but I hadn't been able to make it. Usually we met up somewhere else, because I had no desire to be in Stoneguard. I hadn't even gone inside her house on the Horrid Christmas.

I looked into the living room, a big room taking up most of the downstairs of the house. She had two white couches, bright scatter cushions, yellow walls, watercolours of the local area. There were fresh lilies in the big glass vase on the polished side table. Something new hung on the wall above the fireplace where she used to have a mirror: a picture of butterflies in an ornate gilded frame. Lee loved butterflies and flowers, delicate and beautiful things. When we were children she used to like sitting out in the garden as still as she could, waiting and watching until a butterfly would sit on her, unfurl its curled-up tongue and taste her skin.

I went straight through to the kitchen and glanced around quickly, enough to make sure Lee wasn't in there or that the door wasn't open to the back garden. It was all deserted.

Lee could have had a bigger house if she wanted it, especially these days, as director of Ice Cream Heaven. But she must've

88

liked it well enough. The house we'd grown up in had rooms that we didn't even go into, though they were kept impeccably dust-free by our mother's cleaner. Here, every room was well-used, clean and loved.

I couldn't imagine living in the same house for more than one or two years, not as an adult, anyway. But settling in seemed to suit my sister. She accumulated little homey touches – for example, the blue-painted bowl on the windowsill in the hallway, holding round beach stones. I could see her collecting them on a day at the seaside, tucking them in her pockets, thinking of the bowl and the sunny spot she'd put them. It was the sort of impulse I never had.

She had photographs hanging on the staircase walls. A parade of the past, smiles and poses and memories that were evidently fond for her. As I carried my suitcase upstairs I glanced at a group of framed shots, prints of Ice Cream Heaven advertising campaigns from the eighties: adorable twin girls, posing with ice cream. As fine-haired infants, plait-haired toddlers, giggling children, holding cones and dripping spoons.

Me and Lee, the Ice Cream Twins, growing up in adverts. I averted my gaze.

The spare bedroom, which was also her office, was at the top of the stairs, and it was empty. I dumped my case on the bed and went into Lee's bedroom. Her bed was made and the room was neat.

I opened her wardrobe and flicked through the clothes on the hangers. The scent of her was stronger here. Lee liked to wear whites and pastels and neutrals, linens and cottons. She had lots and lots of pink, and some charcoal grey and soft dark blue jumpers and a little black dress. I pulled it out and examined it critically. It was all right, but very conservative in wool crepe, hanging long in the skirt and with little cap sleeves.

89

Boring. I put it back and kept on looking. Trousers, skirts, blouses, little floral numbers, all lovely in their own way, but nothing that would suit me in the slightest.

I sighed and pulled out the black dress again, but when I turned to put it on the bed I saw a glimpse of blue cloth, partly concealed by the open bedroom door. I dropped the LBD and went to the door. The dress was hanging up behind it, as if Lee had put it aside specially. It was a silk shift in electric blue, the blue of sunny autumn skies.

That, I could do something with. I laid it down on the bed next to the rejected black dress, stripped and went to the bathroom naked to get in the shower. I would've liked to have spent a long time under the hot water, but even though I was in no hurry to get to the disco, Lee would be expecting me, so I quickly used her vanilla-scented soap and floral shampoo to wash the journey off me. All her cosmetics and creams were neatly laid out beside the sink; I borrowed her toothbrush and her mascara, blow-dried my hair, and went back to her bedroom to borrow some of her underwear (lace, but beige).

I didn't look at myself in the mirror on the back of her wardrobe until the blue dress was on. It skimmed over my collarbones and exposed my arms, nipped in at my waist and ended just above my knees. It wasn't revealing in the slightest, but it was flattering, simple enough to let the shape of my body speak for itself. I imagined Lee would wear it with a string of our grandmother's pearls; I was still wearing the bangle she'd given me. For a minute I was a little worried that she'd only have low court shoes or something, but when I checked her wardrobe again I saw a pair of indigo crocodile heels with little silver buckles on the slender straps.

'Nice one, Lee,' I said, and put them on. In the mirror, it wasn't exactly the outfit I would've chosen for myself – far too conservatively cut, for one thing – but it wasn't bad for that. And blue.

As twin girls, our clothing was bought for us in pairs: a red T-shirt and a blue T-shirt, matching skirts, white trainers with different coloured laces. As if the only way we could express our different identity was to wear the same clothing in different colours. Lee got all the pink, I got all the red, but we both liked blue and used to bicker over who got it. Occasionally some well-meaning but unimaginative person would give us completely identical outfits. At first I treated these gifts with the scorn they deserved, but soon I, at least, realised their usefulness. For example, if someone saw Lee Haven walking down the High Street during school hours, they'd assume she had a good reason to be out of school. Whereas if they saw Liza Haven, they knew she was up to trouble. Merely wearing pink could get me a few extra minutes, or even hours, unchallenged.

I wondered what Lee was wearing tonight.

Well. Only one way to find out, even if it involved putting myself through the torture of seeing my former neighbours and classmates. I left my dirty clothes and wet towel on the bedroom floor to pick up later. A quick cup of coffee to wake up my brain first, and then I'd be off. I whistled as I went down the stairs. Now that I was dressed and looking half-decent, I felt better about everything. What was the worst that could happen at this thing, anyway? I'd left Stoneguard, I'd had a successful and exciting life, with a career that most people could only dream about. I had worked all over the world in exotic locations and with rich, famous and talented people.

Well. Until recently. And a lot of the exotic locations were, in fact, in Canada. But nobody in Stoneguard was going to know that, were they?

I picked up my phone on my way past where I'd dumped my bag and tried calling Lee. It rang and rang without her picking up and went to answerphone. 'And you got annoyed with me for not answering,' I said. 'I'm at your house, waiting for you.' I hung up and went into the kitchen to put on the kettle. The indigo shoes clicked on the stone floor. I had to look a bit before I found the coffee, and when I glanced at the clock it was nearly seven.

Just then, the phone rang on the kitchen wall. It was loud in the silent house. I reached for it, expecting to hear Lee's voice telling me to get myself down to the school. 'I'm on my way,' I said into the receiver without bothering with a greeting.

'Lee!' cried a female voice that was definitely not my sister. 'Where are you?'

It sounded familiar, though I hadn't heard it for years – as if the owner were about to burst into tears. 'Mouse?' I said.

'What? Oh. Of course you're at your house.' She laughed, a little hysterically. 'Oh my God, I need you down here! It's a complete nightmare!'

'Where do you mean, "down here"?'

'The Headmaster's garden, of course! I thought you were going to be here an hour ago at least. I'm all alone here and the canapés are— well, there's a big problem.'

I frowned. 'You're all alone?' Maybe Lee was in the school building, putting up streamers or whatever.

'Yes! I looked all round the school for you – where are you?'

So much for that theory. 'Are you sure you're at the right place?'

'Of course I'm sure – there's only one school in Stoneguard! Why aren't you here? Where's everyone else? Oh God, do you think people have all forgotten? Did we put the wrong date on the invitations?'

'I'm sure that's not it,' I said, not even paying attention to what I was saying because I was trying to figure this out. If Lee wasn't at the school, where was she? Maybe she was picking up some stuff on her way. I hadn't seen her car out front, now that I thought about it. That must be it. But why hadn't she told the other people she'd be late?

'Oh thank God, I thought I'd made a horrible mistake,' Mouse was saying now. 'I tried your mobile like seven times but I couldn't get through. Why are you still at home, you told me you'd be—' In the background I heard a muffled crash. 'Oh no,' she wailed, 'that was the tray that hadn't fallen yet! Please, can you get down here now, I need you!'

Couldn't anyone around here organise anything without my sister stepping in? 'All right,' I said, 'I'll be there in a few minutes to help you, don't worry.'

'Oh, thank you, thank—'

I hung up. Wherever Lee was, she'd turn up soon enough. Right now, it was time to take this step backwards into the past.

Faking It

I walked to the school in my sister's indigo shoes. Despite the rain, tourists still trooped up and down the High Street, looking in windows at local guidebooks, crystals and essential oils and dowsing rods, handmade candles and, of course, locally-made ice cream. I clicked past them without making eye-contact. Across the street, someone came out of Ma Gamble's with a takeaway cup and raised their hand to me in greeting. I waved and moved on as quickly as I could, using my umbrella as a shield, before I'd have to stop and talk. I had enough of an ordeal ahead of me, thank you very much; I fully intended to have a large drink in my hand before I answered any questions about myself and why I was here. I passed the tiny stone library, and the tiny thatched cottage that now housed a building society, and the renovated medieval barn that was, according to the sign outside, now some sort of holistic therapy centre. The school was, unsurprisingly, down School Street. The original Victorian part of it, which was now the school hall, was a stone and red-brick building with long, thin windows. The 1960s-built wing huddled behind, as if ashamed to show its modern face.

When I was a child, it had seemed huge. Big enough to hold nearly everyone in my little world. Now it looked hardly bigger than the trailer they'd used for hair and make-up on my last film shoot in the desert, though much more sturdy and vastly more damp.

I folded up my umbrella and pushed open the door. It led to a coat-peg-lined corridor, smelling as I remembered it of dust and cabbage. A small table stood by the entrance, spread with leaflets about Alzheimer's disease, and there were balloons hanging from the doors to the hall. I couldn't tell you whether they were green or teal, and I didn't get a chance to look because as soon as I set foot in the building I was attacked by a whirlwind wearing a floral dress and an Alice band.

'Oh my God I'm so glad you're here!' cried the whirlwind, her hands clamped on my arms, walking backwards and dragging me into the hall. 'I have the most horrible thing to confess to! Alex and I had a glass of sherry before I went out because we couldn't get the babysitter, and it's gone straight to my head! I'm the clumsiest person in the world when I'm tipsy! And Phoebe spent the afternoon crying and holding on to my leg, then I was so busy giving all four of them their tea and not spilling baked beans on my dress I couldn't eat a mouthful, plus I hardly slept last night I was so nervous! What if it doesn't go well and everyone knows it was my fault!'

It had to be Mouse. I hadn't seen her since I was eighteen, but this was exactly the sort of adult I'd have expected her to grow up to be. The only appreciative difference twelve years had made in her was to add strands of grey to her off-brown bobbed hair, and to make her bosom more substantial. Her front teeth still protruded slightly, and her eyes were still frightened.

'Calm down,' I said. 'I'm sure it will all be fine.'

'You always say that, and you're right, but you haven't seen the food yet. Oh my God, those little sausages – I think they're burned.'

95

She steered me through the hall, which was festooned with green streamers and electrical cords, and straight out of the fire exit at the back. On the way I glimpsed a few people huddled around something near the stage. None of them looked like Lee.

'Who's here?' I asked as she pulled me across a corner of the concrete playground, rain pattering on our unprotected heads.

'Tania is doing the lights and Nigel and Jas are setting up the disco. They turned up five minutes ago.' She pushed open a metal gate with her flowered hip and we scurried across some grass to an open-sided marquee which covered nearly the whole of the so-called Headmaster's Garden. 'Where have you been anyway? You said you'd be here really early. I was sort of getting worried that something had happened to you because you're never late.'

Mouse still thought I was my sister. A fair enough assumption to make, I suppose, as I was wearing Lee's clothes and had answered her phone. And she'd had that sherry, which was obviously one sherry too many. 'Actually, prepare yourself for a shock. I'm Li—'

'Oh my God!' Mouse dropped my arms and scampered for the far side of the tent. My revelation upstaged, I followed her. At one end of the tent sat a beer keg emblazoned with *Druid's Ale*. Several tables stood beside it, covered with white paper tablecloths and spread with some sort of a buffet. Mouse halted at one of the tables, clutching her bob and looking as if she were about to cry.

'The tent!' she said, and pointed upward. I saw the problem right away; a branch of a leylandii was resting against one edge of the marquee roof, making the canvas dip down. Rainwater dripped in a steady stream from the canvas straight onto a platter of vol-au-vents filled with, it looked like, egg mayonnaise. By now very watery egg mayonnaise.

'Right.' I stepped around the stricken Mouse. It was a matter of seconds to climb onto the table and free the marquee edge from the leylandii branch, leaning back slightly to keep the dress from being spattered. 'Okay, what else?' I asked, hopping down, carefully so that my heels didn't sink into the earth.

'Oh, thank you! But it doesn't really matter at this point, does it? I reckon I've made a mess of everything.'

I surveyed the buffet. I could see what she was talking about. 'Wow, did you attack those sausages with a flame-thrower?'

'I know,' she said sadly, gazing at the tray of mini-sausages, all of them charred. 'The school ovens run really hot, I think. I left them in there for less time than Ma said, and they still got burned.'

'That explains a lot about the quality of the dinners we used to get when we were at school here,' I said. 'You know, for years I thought that lasagne was supposed to be char-grilled.'

'My lasagne usually turns out like that anyway. And look, this is what I was telling you about on the phone – the whole tray of little quiches slipped out of my hands and they're all broken now.'

'What's under this box of glasses?' I could see the edges of a platter underneath the crate. I picked it up and looked at the sticky lumpy brown mess.

'Oh no. Those were the bean croquettes.'

Mouse had gone all pale, except for a round patch of inexpertly-applied blusher on each cheek. She clutched my arm in despair.

'I've ruined it all,' she wailed. 'I knew I shouldn't have had that sherry. And – and what will Ma Gamble say when she sees what a mess I made of her food?'

Ah yes. Ma Gamble. That explained the wholemeal appearance of the quiche crusts and the presence of bean croquettes and large tubs of hummus. I squinted at the vol-au-vent boats, which I could now see weren't filled with egg mayonnaise but with some sort of tofu concoction. The leak had probably done us all a massive favour.

'She'll yell at me,' quavered Mouse.

Oh for God's sake, you're a grown woman, you're far too old to be afraid of the health-food freak who runs the local shop, I thought, but with admirable restraint, I didn't say it. Instead, I patted her on the back with the tips of my fingers.

'Ma Gamble isn't coming,' I said. 'She's in Bristol or somewhere. She'll never know. I certainly won't tell her.' In fact, I planned never to speak to Ma Gamble again in my lifetime, if I could help it.

'But what is everyone going to eat?'

'Well, the salad and the cheese tray looks fine still. And there's all that hummus.'

'We can't feed fifty people on salad and cheese! I've got lots of multi-packs of crisps at home, should I run and get them?'

There was a wildness in Mouse's eyes that told me she was about to break down and cry. I patted her again. 'Calm down. Don't worry. I'll sort all of this out. I think I can salvage most of it, actually.'

'Oh, thank you. What do you want me to do?' She reached for the quiche tray, but I interposed myself before she did any more damage.

'Tell you what, I'm dying of thirst. Could you run and get me a glass of wine? The largest you can find?'

'All the wine is still in the kitchen – Archie and Charlie said they'd carry it through when they came. I only brought in the one crate of glasses.' Her bottom lip wobbled.

'That's fine. You go to the kitchen and sort me out a glass, and I'll have this all in perfect order by the time you get back.'

She nodded and trotted obediently back to the school building, leaving me alone in the Headmaster's Garden with a leaky marquee and a ruined buffet.

Right. If I was going to get this done by the time she came back with my booze, I would have to work quickly. I suspected my ignorance of the culinary arts was of more benefit than inconvenience, as I had no rules to restrain me. It was like arranging a big-budget movie stunt with only a skateboard and a few smoke bombs.

The tofu vol-au-vents hadn't been worth saving even before the rainwater, so I tipped them straight into the bin at the end of one of the tables. The mini-sausages were the most obvious fix; I grabbed a knife from the cheese platter and cut the burned ends off each sausage, and then rearranged what was left on several recycled paper plates. A few lettuce leaves from one of the salad bowls scattered around, and there: mini-mini sausage bites.

The quiches were trickier. Fortunately, Ma Gamble's hummus was as thick and sticky as I remembered it. It made perfect cement to glue the bits of quiche back together, with the help of a butter-knife as a trowel. The resulting pastries were a little bit wonky, especially as I was working under time constraints, but I put half a cherry tomato on top of each one and they looked good as new. Nearly. Quiche sculptures completed, I turned my attention to the mashed bean croquettes. Using the hummus knife, I scraped the mess into a bowl and squished it up even more, into a lumpy paste. Crumble a bit of Cheddar on the top, scatter some more lettuce, and voilà! Bean dip. I pushed the bowl over near the crudités.

I stood back and surveyed my work. Not bad, really not bad. I was a one-woman buffet A-Team.

A small movement caught my eye from the bowl of salad I hadn't yet decimated for garnish. Perched on a ruffled leaf of lettuce, about to make the leap onto a slice of cucumber, was a delicate whorl-shelled, waving-antlered snail.

Organic produce. You had to love it. Hearing the hurried footsteps of Mouse returning, hopefully with a tankard of wine, I reached forward and flicked the snail off the lettuce. There was a small thud as it hit the grass on the other side of the buffet table.

'Here you go,' puffed Mouse, appearing at my elbow and giving me a glass full nearly to the brim with white wine. I took it and drank. The wine was chilled and delicious.

'This is great,' I said in surprise.

'Oh my God! What did you do? The food looks fantastic!' Her face beamed, childlike.

I shrugged, but I couldn't help a bit of a smile. 'I don't think it was as bad as it looked.'

'Lee, I've always thought you could do anything.'

I took another much-needed swallow of wine. 'Actually, that's what I was trying to tell you before. I'm not really—'

'Lee!'

We turned to see a woman hurrying towards us through the gate. She had artfully highlighted hair pushed back behind her ears to show off her diamond and pearl earrings. She looked vaguely familiar, but I wasn't sure if that was because I'd known her as a child, or because I'd seen very similar nose and Botox jobs all over LA. Her spray tan made her look a nice shade of tangerine. 'I'm having an issue with the projector,' she told us.

'Lee will fix it,' Mouse said confidently.

'I'll have a go, but actually the thing is I'm not—'

'Oh, will you, that's excellent. I swear it was working this morning when I had Rufus look at it and check it out, but I think I sort of dropped it a little bit when I was taking it out of the boot of the car, and now it won't light up.'

No wonder Ma Gamble found it so easy to intimidate everyone into doing as she liked; these people were crying out for a little bit of competence. I wasn't surprised that in Ma's absence, my sister was the one they looked to for sorting everything out. Lee might be far too nice and rather stuck in her ways, but she'd inherited the Haven can-do attitude. That was one thing we had in common.

The projector woman led me back into the school hall, to a table. I'd been expecting to see a clunky photographic slide projector; in fact, this was a sleek laptop projector, sat next to a sleeker laptop. Well. At least it was high-tech equipment these people were having trouble with.

'I really don't know what's wrong with it. I mean, a little knock shouldn't hurt it. This thing is supposed to be top of the range and if we can't get it working I'll have to call Rufus, and I hate to call him because he's at home with the police.'

'The police?' gasped Mouse. I raised an eyebrow myself. The Stoneguard police, as I remembered, somehow managed to be both inefficient and under-employed. Their principal activities were finding tourists' passports, listening to the local farmers' complaints about yet another crop circle, and turning blind eyes to locals who drove home drunk from the Druid's Arms.

'Yes. Can you believe it, his car was stolen this afternoon?'

'What?'

'Right in front of the house! Rufus came home for lunch

and then when he went back out again to get his briefcase from the boot, the car was gone. That's why he's at home now. We had to wait two hours for the police to show up.'

This didn't surprise me. My own run-ins with the local police had taught me they weren't the shiniest apples in the barrel, especially when it came to dealing with disappearing cars. 'It was probably some teenagers out for a joy ride,' I said. 'The car will turn up in a field somewhere.'

'I don't know, it seems like all the teenagers these days want to do is play their computer games. They've got *Grand Theft Auto*, they don't need to nick real cars. Not like your—'

Mouse elbowed Tangerine with more force than I would have thought her capable of.

'Kids these days, eh?' I said lightly, and turned my attention to the projector. I checked all the connections and the laptop. 'It must be a fault. Anybody got a screwdriver?' The women shrugged helplessly. Behind me, the first attendees were beginning to wander into the corridor from outside, shaking rain from their umbrellas, greeting each other in loud voices that echoed.

'I can ask one of the blokes,' suggested Tangerine. 'They might have a Swiss Army knife or something.'

'Never mind, I've got it sorted.' I opened Lee's clutch bag and took out her keys. They weren't the ideal tools, but I'd used a lot more awkward things on location. After unplugging the unit I unscrewed the back panel quickly and had a look inside. As I'd suspected, a connector had come loose from the circuit board. Ideally, it could use a smidge of solder but I twisted the prongs into position, switched the power back on, and waited for it to warm up again.

'And he said never mind, I should come anyway and enjoy myself, but the doctor says he must avoid stress and you remember how worried I was last summer when he had his surgery – oh!' Tangerine clapped her hand to her lip-sticked mouth in surprise and joy as a photograph of a rainforest scene appeared projected onto the stage curtains. 'You did it.'

'I told you, Lee's a wonder,' Mouse said, with as much satisfaction as if she'd fixed the projector herself.

'Oh, thank you,' said Tangerine, flinging her arms around me and giving me a Chanel-scented hug. 'Thank you so much. Rufus would have— I so hate to be the one to make him worry.'

'If you don't knock it around, it should be all right for the evening.' I patted her on the back as I'd patted Mouse's. I wasn't used to such effusive and warm thanks. I mean, people did normally thank me when I sorted something out, but it was usually with a slap on the back, or a thumbs-up if they were feeling really grateful. They didn't usually take me so literally to their bosoms.

But these were Lee's friends, and they thought I was Lee. Lee was the sort of person you hugged, whereas I valued my personal space. I remembered coming in from playing outside, sometimes, to find her sitting on the couch reading next to my mother, leaning against her side. In school she greeted her friends with hugs like these every morning, as if she'd missed them unbearably during the night.

It was interesting, seeing the world from Lee's eyes for these few minutes, if only to experience this casual affection. And how these people I hardly knew trusted me with their failures and worries, how they expected me to make things right for them.

Very strange. I took a swig of wine and realised that my glass was empty.

'You deserve another of those,' Mouse said, took it from my hand and trotted away.

Tangerine, looking much more relaxed, squeezed my hand and reached into her own clutch bag to reapply her lipstick. She looked more and more familiar to me, though I didn't remember anyone called Rufus living in Stoneguard, so maybe she'd imported herself a husband from somewhere else.

'So Liza couldn't make it, after all?' she said.

'Well, this might be a surprise, but—'

'It's not surprising,' she carried over me. 'To tell the truth, I never expected her here anyway. I know you were excited about it, Lee, but I think you're too optimistic sometimes when it comes to your sister. If you ask me, she never meant to come in the first place; she was just stringing you along to try to make you happy like she has before. What did she say this time? Was she still too busy with her precious career, jumping off buildings or blowing up cars or whatever she does for fun?'

I put my hands on my hips. 'That precious career is a very demanding one, and it takes up a lot of time and effort. You can't just go swanning off to a party if you feel like it.'

Tangerine smiled. 'There you are, I knew you'd stick up for her, even after all the times she's let you down and dodged her responsibilities.'

'There are different kinds of responsibilities. It takes a lot of work to make a movie into a blockbuster, you know. It's not just hurling yourself through a sugar window or two, there's lots of training and expertise involved. Only a few people in the world are good enough to do it safely and still have it look natural and dangerous.'

'I know, I know, you're proud of your sister. And so you should be, but—'

'Too right I'm proud of her, she's worked hard to get where she is today.'

'Right. Well, right.' My vehemence seemed to have taken the bitchy words out of Tangerine's mouth. 'I'm just saying you're a good person, Lee. Too good, sometimes.'

It was at that moment that Mouse reappeared with another half a pint of wine, so I just shrugged and took the drink. It was only after I'd had a sip and Tangerine had turned to Mouse and asked brightly, 'So how's it going potty-training Phoebe? Any accidents?' when I realised that, defending myself, I'd inadvertently talked about myself in the third person, as if I were indeed Lee.

Well. It made sense, when you thought about it. This woman was obviously prejudiced against me and my profession anyway. She thought my job was a joke and that I was some feckless waster hurling myself off buildings for fun. The only chance I had of opening her mind a little was to speak from the point of view of someone she respected. Which meant Lee.

'So four accidents in two days isn't too bad. All wee, and we've got laminate flooring, except in the lounge, but that carpet's been in the wars anyway from the other three, so we'll replace it when Pheeb's out of nappies. Do you think it's time to go into the Headmaster's Garden?'

It took me a moment to realise that Mouse was asking me the question. I glanced around the room; several more people had come in, all of them looking familiar, and were milling around looking at the streamers and tall windows. Nigel had begun to play some music, a bit of seventies soul. As I watched, I saw three men with varying sizes of beer bellies carrying crates of wine and glasses through the hall to the exit. 'Yeah, best go and make sure that lot don't neck all the booze,' I agreed.

So I went with my two new best friends, Mouse and Tangerine, through to the Headmaster's Garden. The rain misted my hair while we were crossing the short distance between the school and the marquee.

The early arrivals greeted the drink with a cheer that made me think several of them had stopped off at the Druid's Arms beforehand. They clustered round the drinks table while the three volunteer bartenders twisted caps, popped corks and filled glasses. Mouse and Tangerine went off to get themselves something and I was able to look around me for the first time, alone.

When Lee and I had attended this school, the Headmaster's Garden was the place where the teachers would slope off during break time for a fag, clutching mugs of disgusting instant coffee. Students were strictly forbidden within its wrought-iron gate and when we stole glances from the play-ground, standing on tiptoe to peer over the scraggly hedge, the garden looked like an Eden of wonders. We could see the end of a bench and a stone birdbath. It seemed green even in the depths of winter. In fact, most of the children at Stoneguard School in my time were convinced that the Headmaster's Garden had some sort of magical properties that made it exist in an endless, eerie spring. The flowers were different, the grass was a fairy carpet bed and a single bite of the apples from the tree we could see growing over the top of the wall would kill a child.

Of course I went in there. One Wednesday morning, first, when the teachers were all having their weekly meeting in the staff room. I opened the creaking gate with my heart in my mouth, anticipating wonders. But in actual fact, the garden was a scrappy piece of grass, well-trodden by teacher feet, and the bird-bath was full of fag ends. I picked up an apple from the ground, brought it back to the schoolyard, and ate it in front of a wondering crowd, who watched me like hawks the entire morning to see if I was going to drop dead during finger painting.

When I didn't, I grew bolder. I'd slip casually in through a gap in the hedge during break time, when the teachers were actually in the garden. The hole emerged behind the bench, and I could crouch there, breathing in second-hand smoke and listening to the teachers bitching about the kids and gossiping about each other. Then one of the boys, I think it was Martin Storey, got caught climbing through it. He told the teachers that I'd found the hole and dared him to go through it, and by then the teachers knew me well enough to believe him. Detention for three days for him, and a week for me. An early lesson in what happened when you let amateurs in on your tricks.

The garden was nicer these days. Someone had returfed it and planted some borders, and the bird-bath had water in it. The apple tree was gone, replaced by a second bench. With the marquee sheltering it from the rain, it looked more like the magical walled garden we'd always imagined it was, though of course the presence of various people clutching wine and beer spoiled the fairy-tale effect somewhat. I wandered over to the old bench and looked behind it, but my hideaway was clogged with nettles and a squishy lump of dog poop.

I knew you'd stick up for her, Tangerine had said. Even way back then, with the garden incident, Lee had told the teachers that I hadn't dared Martin to go through, that he'd decided to all by himself. It didn't do any good, of course, because the teachers shared Tangerine's attitude, that Lee would stick up for Liza. She was a good girl and she didn't want her sister to get into trouble.

But I wasn't a good girl. These people were all going to be sorely disappointed when they found out that I was here helping them instead of my sister. They probably expected me to be swinging from the light fixtures and challenging the blokes to fist fights.

Right now, though, they thought I was Lee, and when I came to think of it, I couldn't deny that the situation brought up some interesting possibilities.

All my life I'd wondered what it would like to be Lee. All I'd have to do was to play along for a little while, until Lee turned up, and I'd find out what life was like in her shoes. Then when Lee did arrive, which would probably be any minute now, we could have a good laugh about how I'd tricked everyone.

Could I do it, though? Many of these people saw Lee every day, and I'd seen her once in eighteen months. They'd probably notice the difference in our mannerisms. I didn't share any of the same daily knowledge, the things Lee was always so careful to know about others, like the names of Mouse's children, or indeed what Tangerine was really called.

Or Mouse, come to think of it.

I flicked one of the nettles with the toe of my shoe. If you brushed against nettles or touched them gingerly, they'd sting you. But if you grabbed them, they were harmless. You had to have the nerve.

'Lee?'

I adjusted my face and posture. Lee's smile was wider, her expression more open. She had a habit of gently twiddling a lock of her hair and she stood evenly balanced in her shoes, her posture straight yet relaxed. Then I turned around, spread my arms wide open, and gave the woman standing behind me a big, delighted hug. 'It's so good to see you!' I said, though I had no idea who she was.

What's-her-name smiled back without an iota of suspicion. 'Thank you so much for inviting me. It's fun to come back to Stoneguard for a visit. You look the same as you always did.'

My Lee-grin got a little wider. This was going to be easy. 'So do you.'

She laughed, though it was self-conscious. 'Well, I hope not. I've managed to lose about four stone since then.'

'Ah, of course, I meant you still look so young. So what are you up to these days?'

'Oh, you know, not much has changed since the newsletter I sent out with the Christmas card.'

'Of course. So you're still living in . . .' I tapped the side of my face, as if I'd momentarily forgotten.

'Luton. Still teaching at the secondary school there. Maths,' she added.

'Well, you always did love maths,' I ventured.

'Oh, me? No, don't you remember I completely failed my maths GCSE and had to take it again at Marlborough College? I was definitely a late bloomer when it came to maths. And other things.'

'Well, it looks like it was worth it. So is your other half here?'

She shifted her weight uncomfortably. 'No, I'm currently single,' she said in that sort of voice that tells you that 'currently' actually means 'have always been'.

'Lucky you. You'll have your pick of the single men tonight.'

'You know, that's exactly what I was thinking myself,' she said, looking around the room. I breathed a small sigh of relief. Who knew that this small-talk stuff would be so hard to get right? 'Who else is coming that's still single?'

'Um. Well, that's a good question. Let's see . . .' I made a face as if I was thinking, all the while scanning the room for someone, anyone I could remember the name of. 'Oh, Stephen Woodruff.'

'Stephen Woodruff is single? But isn't that his wife next to him?'

Sure enough, the weedy Stephen Woodruff had his arm

around a busty blonde, holding her waist as if he was afraid if he let go, she'd suddenly realise she was way out of his league.

'No, I meant that's Stephen Woodruff across the room there, and he was asking how you were doing. I'm sure he'd be delighted to see you again, why don't you go over and—'

'Stephen Woodruff was asking about *me*?'

'Of course, we often talk about you and wonder how you're doing. Now go ahead, don't mind me, I've got loads to do.' I patted her hand and nodded my head in the Woodruffs' direction.

'Well, if you're sure . . .'

'Definitely. We'll catch up a bit later. Say hi to Stephen for me!'

What's-her-name went off to the other side of the marquee and I watched as she greeted Stephen, who looked surprised and as if he had no more clue about her name than I did. Hopefully, he'd be as good as I was at faking it.

I smiled to myself. That had gone rather well, if I did say so. Of course what's-her-name hadn't seen Lee for ages. The real test would be if I could fool someone who saw Lee every day, someone who'd grown up with her. I'd fooled Mouse, but she was blinded by desperation.

I turned my attention to the table, where several new arrivals were beginning to pick at the repaired buffet. They all looked familiar. Everyone looked familiar here. I remembered what a relief it had been to escape to London when I was eighteen, if only to see a few strangers. There – the skinny bloke with the beard and the wild long black hair, loading his plate with marinated tofu skewers – it had to be Rock Hamlin. Rock was exactly our age, and he'd lived out on Rainbow Farm with his hippy family. For a couple of our teenage years, he'd had a crush on Lee, who'd always been agonising over how to let him down gently. He most likely had my sister memorised from spending hours gazing gloopily at her. He would be the perfect test of my Lee-skills.

I decided to give him a thrill. I went up beside him and slipped my arm flirtatiously around his waist. 'Hey Rock, how do you like the tofu?'

Rock's face went bright red. Wow, he really still likes Lee, I thought, until I realised that in fact he was choking on some tofu. I took my arm from around his waist and thumped hard on his back. He coughed violently, reached for a little napkin and spat something, hopefully tofu, into it. Then he wiped his eyes and turned to me. 'It's good,' he said. 'A little tough, maybe.'

'I think there was an accident with the oven.'

He nodded, dropped the napkin into a bin, and reached for some more tofu skewers. 'Did you sort out the balloon problem, Lee?'

Bingo! I hadn't even had to try, and he thought I was my sister. 'I think so, how do they look?' I asked.

'Good. Round.'

'What's going on with Rock Hamlin these days?'

He shrugged and pushed his long hair back with his free hand. 'Same as usual.'

Perhaps Rock wasn't the best person to choose to practise my small talk on. 'How's work?'

'Well, you know. The Heavenly Scoop is pretty chilled out.'

He worked in the ice-cream parlour, as one of Lee's employees? Whoops, wrong question to ask. Then again – he was thirty and still worked scooping ice cream. He probably wasn't the most astute of observers. I looked him over, under cover of pretending to be considering some tofu. He was wearing skinny black jeans and a skinny black T-shirt, and black hiking boots that had seen a lot of wear. He was more stylish than he'd been as a kid, wearing hand-me-downs all the time. But not much.

'And of course,' he continued, 'I'm up on the hill most evenings, looking for the aliens.'

I began to laugh, until I realised he wasn't joking.

'The aliens?' I managed.

He nodded. 'Yeah, I could really do with another ride in that spaceship, you know? I've told you about that, haven't I?'

'It's – well, I'm sure you have, but I'm not sure I recall all the details correctly.'

'It was a real trip being up there. It wasn't a flying saucer though, it was more like a cigar shape.' He popped another piece of tofu in his mouth, and has waited until he'd finished chewing to speak. 'It was the most incredible thing that has ever happened to me.'

'I can see how it would be.'

'So I'm sort of hanging around waiting for them to come back, you know. Doing the ice cream by day, meeting new people – same as usual. It's not too bad.'

He smiled at me; behind his beard he had straight white teeth. He wasn't the slightest bit my type – too skinny and hairy – but I wondered if my sister had ever gone there. Stuck in Stoneguard, Lee didn't have much of a selection of men to choose from. She'd avoided my question about her love life, come to think of it. I hoped Rock wouldn't get any ideas after a few more pints of Druid's Ale and want to dirty dance to the *Grease* Mega-Mix. My sister might do pity snogs, but I didn't.

'Can I get you another drink?' Rock asked, and I noticed my glass was nearly empty.

'Yes, please,' I said. He was weird, but he seemed harmless

enough. Maybe he wanted to get me drunk, but as I'd grappled with professional wrestlers, I didn't have much fear that he'd cop a feel without my permission. I held out my glass to him and he took it.

That's when everything went quiet.

I remember the first time I saw Jackie Chan in person. I was just starting out, doing a relatively low-budget martial arts flick in Hong Kong. I was both crass and new, but I was getting work through luck and persistence. Anyway, we'd wrapped for the day and a bunch of us went for a bite to eat in Lei Yue Mun. We were sitting at several plastic tables pushed together outside amongst the tanks of seafood, drinking beer from the bottle and eating spicy prawns and deep-fried oysters. The crew was mostly Chinese and were talking to each other in Cantonese. They'd switch to English if I asked them, but I was pleasantly tired, and happy to let the unintelligible conversation wash over me. To my left there was a box of small live crabs, with a little old man next to them on a stool, chain-smoking Marlboro Reds. Every few minutes, one of the crabs would climb, slow-motion, out of the box, and at the last possible minute, the little old man would reach out, catch the crab and put it back into the box.

I was watching this perfectly-timed ballet, when suddenly everyone went still. The market noise still buzzed around us, but the conversation dissolved, the beer bottles stopped clinking; it was as if a bubble had descended and trapped us inside it. I stopped watching the little old man and followed my colleagues' gazes. They were all fixed on a slight sturdy man wearing black sunglasses and a white linen shirt, and I felt the breath punch out of my body when I realised this was him, this was a legend walking amongst us. The man who had slid twenty-one storeys down the side of a glass building, and that was the least of it. He examined some squid and then he walked on, and we all exploded into conversation again.

The Headmaster's Garden wasn't as smelly as the Lei Yue Mun market and there was no little old man capturing crabs, but the feeling was exactly the same. For a brief moment, the babble of conversation paused. Its echo hung in the air, washed with the sound of the rain. Rock's fingers touched my glass, but he didn't take it, because he was looking off over my shoulder.

It was only for a split second, then the conversation began again, though its tone had changed; it was louder, higher, more excited. I turned and followed Rock's gaze.

A man had entered the marquee. He was tall and had that self-assured stance that makes men look even taller. He wore a blue suit, a white shirt and a pewter silk tie, and his thick brown hair was pushed back from his forehead. He had grey eyes, a wide mouth and well-defined brows. He was, quite simply, heart-stoppingly handsome.

Then I saw beneath the handsomeness to the person I recognised. He caught my eye, saw that I was watching him, and winked.

'I'll go and get your drink,' said Rock, and he disappeared.

On the other side of the marquee, Stephen Woodruff had practically run up to the new arrival, one arm still around his pneumatic blonde, the other extended to shake his hand. What's-her-name trailed behind them, looking a little lost, but still thrilled to see Stoneguard's resident aristocrat. In fact, several people began to cluster around him, as if he were emitting some sort of magnetic field. He smiled a big, white smile.

'Steve! Great to see you.' The two men shook hands vigorously.

114

In a dozen years, Will Naughton had not changed. Well, okay, he'd filled out into a man, and he no longer had that ridiculous hairdo he'd affected, deliberately cowlicked and tangled. And somewhere along the way he'd acquired the face of a god. But he still breathed money and privilege in that specifically English way that Hollywood stars could only aspire to.

I could still see the fantasy lists Lee would write in secret in the back of her exercise books:

Mrs Emily Naughton
Mrs E.M.H. Naughton
William and Emily Naughton
Will and Lee Naughton
Mrs William E. Naughton
The Honourable Mr and Mrs William Edward
Naughton
Lady Emily March Naughton
Lady Emily Haven-Naughton

Thank God nobody but me had ever seen those lists. If Will had got hold of them, he would've had a bigger head than he did already. I manoeuvred myself around to the side of the buffet table and pretended to be examining the placement of forks, all the time watching the fawn-o-rama going on.

'So how are things at Naughton Hall?' Stephen Woodruff was asking Will.

'Construction, construction, construction. We've basically had to gut the east wing and put it back up again. Still, we're nearly all the way there.'

'Not the Portman ceiling, I hope,' said someone very bent and bald. Could that be the vicar? Surely he wasn't still alive?

'Don't worry, Vicar, the Portman ceiling isn't going anywhere.'

'It's a national treasure, that ceiling. A national treasure.'

'I'm so glad you think that. We're doing everything we can to preserve it for posterity.'

Someone else asked, 'Have you got anybody famous coming? Any of your rock star friends?'

Will laughed. 'Oh, well, of course we try to be discreet.'

'This is my wife, Cheri. I've told her all about you, Will.' Stephen pushed her forward slightly and she simpered at Will, who took her hand in his and leaned forward to kiss her on the cheek.

'You look familiar to me somehow,' Will told her. She giggled, a movement that wobbled her breasts.

'You've probably seen her in the magazines. She's done some glamour work,' Stephen said proudly. 'I take all her pictures.'

'How fascinating. Lovely to meet you, Cheri.'

'Hi, Will,' said a quiet voice from the sidelines. What's-her-face smiled hopefully and lifted one hand in a bit of a wave. 'You probably don't remember me, I'm Marian Tarr.'

'Marian! You look great.' She beamed and blushed and looked like she'd died and gone to heaven when he kissed her cheek. I searched my memory for a Marian Tarr, but couldn't remember a thing. Not even a little twiddle of recall.

'Thanks, Will,' she was saying, her voice quite breathy. 'So do you. What have you been up to?'

He laughed and gave her hand an extra squeeze. 'What *haven't* I been up to. Getting by, running Naughton Hall, all the day-to-day things. What are you doing these days?'

She opened her mouth to reply, but someone called out first.

'Will!'

116

'Hey, it's Will Naughton!'

All at once it seemed that the marquee was full of people and all of them were rushing together at once, every one of them bearing drinks and smiles and competing for who could say hello to Will first.

'John! Great to see you! Mo! You're looking well, mate. Still selling those cars? Annabelle, how are the kids?'

I had absolutely zero desire to watch Will Naughton work a crowd. Abandoning the forks, I headed for the drinks table to get myself a glass of wine, since Rock hadn't reappeared.

'Lee Haven!'

The crowd parted for me and I found myself in a direct line to Will. He stepped forward quickly, took my hand in his, and kissed me on the cheek. His lips were warm. He smelled of a subtle woody cologne and he had quite a grip on him.

'Will Naughton,' I said.

'Look at this! You've done a brilliant job organising everything. The school has never looked so good.'

'It was no problem for me,' I said, which was probably the closest to the truth I'd spoken in forty-five minutes.

'Ah, darling, you're too modest.' Will squeezed my hand, which he was still holding. I extracted it.

'I'm surprised you know what the school looks like inside, seeing as you were swept off to prep school or something. And – Eton, was it?'

'I'd have rather gone to school here.'

I laughed. 'You're kidding me, right? I remember your school holidays started before ours and you used to ride your bicycle up and down School Street so we could all see you from the windows and be jealous.'

'You should have joined me.'

'Your twin sister did, didn't she?' Stephen asked. 'She was always bunking off school.'

117

'Not to join Will Naughton,' I told him. 'She had better things to do.'

'I wish she had. It got lonely cycling up and down School Street on my own all day.'

'You're certainly not alone any more,' I said.

'Not any more, since I've joined my beautiful date for the social event of the season.'

And Will put his arm around my waist, pulled me to him, and kissed me on the mouth.

Prince Charming

His lips were warm and his body firm against mine. It was only a quick kiss, but he'd obviously practised kissing quite a bit because it was textbook kissing-date-in-public procedure: grab woman, kiss her on mouth, release her, let your hand rest on her waist, smile.

I realised that my own hands were raised in surprise. I lowered them.

'Yes, of course you're my date.' It was my sister's dream come true. Which begged the question: why wasn't she here? And another: why hadn't she told me about her and Will Naughton?

'Wow,' What's-her-name, now Marian, said to me, her eyes wide. 'How long have you and Will been dating?'

'Good question,' I said, and turned to Will. 'How long have we been seeing each other, Will?'

'A few months,' he said, holding my gaze. I thought I saw a question in his eyes, but then he smiled and it was gone. 'Can I get you a drink, Lee?'

'The largest glass of wine you can manage, please.'

He went off to fetch it. Well, that was something, at least. As Lee, I could be served by The Honourable Will.

As soon as he was gone, Marian immediately grabbed my

hand. 'You're seeing Will Naughton! Why didn't you tell me?'

'Um. Well, as he said, it's early days. We're just, you know, seeing how it goes.'

'Oh my God, I had the biggest crush on him. I couldn't believe he remembered me! He is so charming,' she gushed.

'Yes, he is, isn't he?' I agreed, and we both turned to look at him, exchanging smiling greetings with Charlie and Archie who were manning the keg of beer. His clothes were better than anyone else's in the room, and he moved with confident ease. He looked exactly what he was: the son of the local viscount plonked down amongst the peasants.

And there was no way in a million years that Will Naughton deserved Lee. Even a complete twat should know his girlfriend from her sister. Even if it hadn't been that long that they'd been seeing each other, even if I was acting like her, there were plenty of ways that someone who really knew one of us could tell us apart. For example, surely he knew Lee's smell by now, and he'd certainly been close enough to me to be able to notice I didn't have it.

Then again, I'd used her shampoo, and her soap. And I was wearing her clothes. Maybe I did smell a bit like her. But underneath the fake chemicals and detergent, at that primal level, I was different. I was *me*, not her. Identical genes, different person.

I was probably doing Lee a favour by standing in for her; it showed up that Will wasn't a wonderful catch after all, if he couldn't even be bothered to know what his girlfriend smelled like.

Then again, maybe she didn't want to know he wasn't a catch.

'Here you are, darling,' he said, and gave me a glass of wine. He had a pint of Druid's Ale for himself, which was surely a departure from gin or single malt or heavenly ambrosia or whatever it was that the upper classes drank. 'Here's to you.'

'Thank you, darling.' I clinked my glass with his. Then I pictured my sister walking in right at that moment and seeing us. I stepped away from Will and pretended to be looking brightly around the room, in the efficient cheerful manner of Lee. 'So, is everyone here, do you think?'

'I'm not sure,' Mouse said. She started pointing at people and counting them.

'How many were there supposed to be coming, Lee?' asked Marian.

'Um . . .'

'It looks like we're nearly full up,' Will said. He wasn't wrong. The Headmaster's Garden had suddenly become quite crowded. You could barely hear the rain dripping over the buzz of conversation, and the throb of the music in the hall. 'Are you going to give your speech soon?'

'My speech?'

Will laughed. 'You haven't forgotten your index cards at home, have you?'

'Um.' That was Lee all over, preparing even a little speech and writing it all out on index cards, probably cute yellow ones. 'I might have done.'

'You'll have to wing it, then. Don't worry, you'll be fine.' He patted me on the back, a benevolent lord and master comforting a distressed little girl. 'Or I'll do it if you want me to. I've tried to forget everything I learned on the Oxford debating team, but I'm sure there are a few brain cells left that remember.'

With an heroic effort, I kept myself from rolling my eyes. Lee never rolled her eyes. 'I'm sure I can manage by myself, thank you.'

'I've got the spotlight set up for you, whenever you need it.' Tangerine had appeared next to Mouse. They made quite a double-act: Tangerine groomed to within an inch of her life, surgically modified and wearing clothes that had creases sharp enough to cut yourself on, and Mouse, who'd probably never heard of such a thing as eyebrow tweezers and looked like she only tackled the ironing mountain once every Leap Year.

No. Lee didn't think like this; Lee thought positive thoughts about everyone, which meant that everyone thought positive thoughts about her.

'Thanks,' I said, 'but it seems a little early to jump into the formalities. Why don't we let everyone chill out for a bit and enjoy. You've all been such a wonderful help to me.'

Mouse beamed at me. Tangerine beamed at me. There. It was quite an amazingly easy formula, actually: niceness given away equalled niceness back.

If you were Lee Haven, and everybody thought you were nice anyway. I wondered what Tangerine and Mouse would make of Liza Haven, the bad twin, swanning in and offering compliments left and right. They'd probably frown and think I was being sarcastic, or that I was after something. Which reminded me.

'In fact,' I said to Will, 'you should try some of the buffet, darling. I'll nip over and get you a plate.' I sent him a dazzling smile and squeezed through the assembled throng to the table.

'Oxford debating team,' I muttered, picking up a plate from the stack. I scooped out a big dollop of squashed bean-croquette dip and flung it on the plate, and put two of the most-crushed quiches beside it. 'Social event of the season,' I added, and added a few sausages, choosing the ones that looked the most like the fingertips of a charred hand. 'Would rather have gone to Stoneguard School,' I finished, picking up the leaf of lettuce that had had the snail on it, and laying it carefully beside my other offerings. Then I put my smile back on my face and gently excused myself all the way across the marquee back to Will's side.

'For you, my love,' I said sweetly, and handed him the plate. 'Excuse me for a minute, I'm going to powder my nose and practise my speech a bit.'

I noticed that when I left, everyone pressed closer to Will, hanging on his every word. Nothing new there, then. The whole town had always sucked up to Will, though you'd think with the passing years people would mature a little bit and see how sad it was to treat someone as a celebrity just because they were rich and good-looking. There were plenty of successful people in the room, after all. Like me, a Hollywood stunt woman. And Lee, if she were here: head of a thriving ice-cream business. Even teaching maths in Luton was more impressive than being born by chance into a wealthy family.

I walked around chattering people towards the marquee exit. Most of them greeted me, or rather my sister, but I just smiled at them and said, 'Got to run, be right back.' Across the garden I could see a group of people I knew were Ice Cream Heaven employees, Glenys and Dennis and several others; I waved at them quickly and hurried out from under the marquee, through the rain, and into the hall.

The disco was pumping out 'Boogie Wonderland', and Nigel Peach was nodding his head behind his decks, in imitation of a proper DJ. He waved at me as I walked through. Nobody was dancing yet, and the projector and laptop sat abandoned on their desk, waiting for an opportunistic thief to slip in through the open door from the street. Stoneguard people had too much faith in other people's honesty. Tangerine's husband had probably left the keys in his car and the engine running. It was hardly a shock that it had been stolen. Anyone with balls and a big enough swag bag could probably make off with half of the village's moveable property. It would be an interesting experiment to try, but I had other things on my mind at the moment.

I went into the corridor and peered out of the door. The rain was sheeting down, the air smelled of spread manure, and there was no sign of my sister. Ducking out underneath the small shelter above the door, I took my phone out of my bag and called Lee's number. 'Come on, sis,' I muttered as I pressed the buttons. 'Answer and get me out of this hellhole.'

It rang and rang, until the answering machine picked up. 'Hi, it's Lee Haven. I'm not home right now, but please leave a message and I'll get back to you right away. Thanks!'

She sounded sunny and fresh. I didn't sound like her at all, really. How come everyone thought I did? I hung up and dialled her mobile number. It cut to voicemail right away.

'Lee, it's me,' I said into the phone. 'I'm at the school, at your charity ball. Get here soon, all right?' *Oh, and by the way, your boyfriend is an arsehole*. But I didn't say that. It wasn't the best thing to leave on voicemail. Of course, when I saw her in person, I'd have no trouble saying that to her, and quite a bit more.

I hung up as a group of people came running up to the door, holding umbrellas and laughing with the effort of keeping dry. 'Lee,' one of them said. 'Hi.'

'Oh, hi.' I had no idea who any of these people were.

Fortunately, the woman in the lead held out her hand to me, as the others crowded under the shelter. 'Tina Wilson, of the dementia unit in Swindon? We've never met in person, only on the phone. It's so good of you to do this event. We're eager to spread awareness.'

'Of course.' I shook her hand as warmly as I could with it so damp. 'Thank you for coming.'

'How is your mother?'

Good question; I fell back on Lee's answer. 'About the same.'

She nodded. 'I hope you'll get in touch with me if I can help. A carer's job isn't an easy one.'

'Oh, well, I'm not a – a carer. Anyway, please come in, the dance floor is in the hall, and the food and drink are through there in the garden.' We went inside to the echoey corridor. The bass line of a disco song was thudding along it. The rest of the newcomers stood, folding up their umbrellas and looking at me, as if they expected me to say something else.

Lee would. I had no idea what to say. 'Excuse me, I was just on my way to the loo,' I said, and made my escape through the small door at the end of the corridor.

If walking into Stoneguard School had been like being tapped on the shoulder by the long finger of memory, walking into the girls' lavatories was like being assaulted with a brickbat.

They hadn't done anything to it since I was a teenager. In fact, they hadn't done anything to it since before World War II, as far as I could see. The black and white tiles on the walls and floor were Victorian; the child-size sinks were heavy porcelain rectangles with bevelled Art Deco corners. The pipes gurgled their endless complaint and the air reeked of bleach and mildew. I checked inside the furthest left of the three cubicles: the toilet was the same, squat with a black-painted wooden seat. The cistern was attached high on the wall, with a dangling flush chain, and there was a small gap between it and the tiles, a perfect place to hide cigarettes. If you stood on the seat, you could just reach the small window to blow smoke out of it. Dozens of children and a zillion or so rolls of toilet paper had come and gone, but nothing else had changed.

There was another, more modern lavatory in the main

125

wing, which got a lot more traffic. In my day, this one was only used by children taken short during assembly, or people like me, who wanted to be alone. Behind the cubicle door was the only private place in the entire school. Sometimes it felt like the only private place in Stoneguard. If you flushed the toilet, you could even cover up the sound of your own crying.

I pulled the chain and the toilet flushed with the same overabundance of water. This was one place eco-consciousness hadn't reached. The gush and swirl of water echoed off the tiles and I left the cubicle to wash my hands in the basin. In my high heels and adult body, I had to stoop over the sink to get my hands wet.

It was strange to see my own grown-up face in this mirror. I used to stare into it, my hands propped on the cold sink, trying to see what the other children saw, what the teachers saw. A reflection of my twin, a bad girl, a shadow of my mother at my age, maybe even an echo of my disappeared father? I'd practise my scowl and my pout and learn how to raise one eyebrow without moving the other. The faces of young people are so malleable. They haven't formed any lines or wrinkles yet, their eyes can be wide open and guileless.

In this mirror my familiar face looked different. It was shocking somehow. It felt as if I'd looked once in the mirror aged ten, and then glanced back again to see this adult person.

I closed my eyes and put on my Lee smile. Tossed my hair back over my shoulder, held up my chin at a jaunty angle, and then opened my eyes again.

For a moment, there was Lee. Then I caught my own eye, and it was me again. I stuck out my tongue at myself to confirm it.

Behind me, the door opened and Mouse came in. Her

cheeks were even more flushed than before, and her fringe had begun to stick to her forehead. I quickly put my tongue back in my mouth.

'Are you all right?' she asked. 'You've been gone for a while.'

'Just checking up on a few things. This place hasn't changed much, has it?'

She looked around. 'I never really liked this loo, I usually used the one in the new building. This one always smelled of smoke, and I—' She stopped, and shrugged. 'Anyway, I wondered if you were nervous about your speech.'

My speech. Or rather, Lee's speech. I'd almost forgotten.

'No. I mean – I'm really not sure what I'm going to say.'

'You'll be absolutely fine. I have faith in you.'

I met her eyes in the mirror. They were a sort of indecisive blue, but they were honest. She did believe in me. Or the version of me that she thought I was, anyway.

'That's really sweet of you.'

'What are you worried about, anyway?'

'I'm not worried. I'm not sure I'm the right person to do it.' Should I carry on pretending to be Lee? Or just stand in front of everyone and announce my true identity, like a character in a bad soap opera? I pictured myself ripping open the front of Lee's dress to reveal a sort of Superman costume underneath. Except instead of an 'S', there would be an 'L'. Though come to think of it, that wouldn't reveal all that much, as my sister and I had the same initial.

'Of course you're the right person,' said Mouse. 'You organised everything! Everyone's here because of you. So you can say any old thing. Nobody will care. I mean, they will care, but only because they care about you.'

'Yes.' True. Lee didn't have to prove herself. People naturally took her to their hearts. Lee could get up and smile and sit back down again, and everyone would applaud and say how wonderful she was. I was the one who'd always had to put on a show.

And I could put on a show. No problem with that.

'I think I'll have another glass of wine,' I said. 'Or five.'

Mouse giggled. 'I didn't think you were so much of a drinker.'

'Oh well, special occasions, you know. Care to join me?' I held out my arm, and she took it.

That's how the town bad girl and the town mouse walked back into the school hall arm-in-arm, like the best friends in the world.

It was strange. But it was sort of nice. In a very strange way. Though of course, Mouse didn't like me; she liked my sister.

And what was her name, anyway? She'd always been too much of a mouse for me to call her anything else. I thought back to morning roll-call in school, back to overheard conversations. Morrison . . . Anna. No, Annabelle. Annabelle Morrison. Though with four children, she might have a different last name now.

We'd gone through the hall, where two brave couples were starting to dance, and had ducked our heads on the threshold of the exit in preparation for avoiding the worst of the rain, when Mouse paused and said, just loud enough to be heard over the music, 'Can I tell you something and you won't get cross with me?'

I hated questions like that. How could you promise not to get cross? You couldn't shoosh away anger because someone wanted you to. Anger had a force of its own; it was stronger than just about anything else, even love. But Mouse was looking sheepish and I was being Lee, after all. And Lee didn't get angry.

'Whatever you want, Annabelle.'

She didn't seem surprised at the name, so I guessed I'd got it right.

'I always used to be scared of those toilets,' she said.

'Really? Well, I suppose they do have a bit of a scary flush.'

'No, I mean – I wasn't scared of the toilets, I was scared because of your—'

My phone rang in my bag. I pulled it out and checked the screen: Lee.

'Excuse me a minute, I need to take this.' I hurried to the side of the hall, away from the speakers, and pressed the answer button. 'Where the hell are you?' I said into the phone.

'Liza. You're at the school?'

Lee's voice was slightly breathless. In the background, I could hear something like a car engine.

'Yes. Are you driving here?'

'No, I'm—' She paused, and I heard a rushing sound, as if another car were going past her in the rain. I pictured her stopped in a lay-by, or maybe parked outside the school.

'I'm not coming,' she said, and she laughed.

'You what?'

'I can't, Liza. I need . . . to do something else. I want to take a break. I'm sorry.'

'You're not coming, after you went on and on at me about it?'

'No. I'm sorry. Something else came up that I thought would be more fun.'

'More fun? I thought this disco thing was right up your street.'

She laughed again. Obviously she was hugely amused by all of this, wherever she was. 'Well, things change sometimes.

You should know that. How's it going, is everything okay there?'

'Everything's fine. What do you mean, things change? Where are you? When will you be back?'

'I don't know. I'm all right, though. I'm having a great time. I need you to look after things for me while I'm gone. Will you do that for me? Please?'

'How long are we talking about?'

'Just – will you, Liza? Keep things going until I get back?' Her voice was urgent, a contrast to her previous nonchalance. I heard another swish as a car passed; it sounded like it was going too fast to be on School Street, or anywhere near Stoneguard. 'Please?'

'All right, but—'

'Thank you.' She sounded relieved, as if I'd taken a burden off her shoulders. 'Okay, have fun tonight. I'll talk to you soon. Love you.' Breezy again.

'But wait, what about—'

The line clicked, and went silent.

What the hell?

I dialled her number. It went straight to voicemail.

A gentle hand touched my shoulder, and I whirled around, as if Lee had suddenly appeared behind me. But it was Mouse.

'She's not coming after all?' she said sympathetically.

'No! I don't understand it – this was so important to her, and now suddenly she's not even here.'

'I don't think it was important to her. I think it's important to you, and you want it to be important to her, but it isn't.' She patted my shoulder again. 'I'm sorry Liza let you down, Lee.'

'No, it's—'

But I didn't finish. This would be the time to come clean about who I really was. But I didn't want to. Why should I?

130

Lee wasn't going to turn up; she had better things to do, apparently, than see her long-lost sister. And yet she was asking me to sort out her life for her.

I might as well enjoy being in her place for once. Spend an evening being everyone's friend and neighbour. See what it felt like.

'It's okay. She's busy doing other things. We'll just have to have a good time without her, won't we?'

'Yes!' She linked arms with me again. 'It's too bad your sister can't see how great you look, though. You were right, that blue dress is perfect for tonight.'

'Le— I told you about this blue dress?'

'You showed it to me, remember? When I was round your house to discuss the catering.'

'And I said I was going to wear it tonight?'

'You said it was driving you crazy having to save it. And I don't blame you, I'd have wanted to put it on for Will right away too!' She clapped her hand to her mouth. 'Whoops, did I say that?'

'You did,' I said, but my mind wasn't on what she was saying. I was wearing Lee's dress for tonight. Lee had bought it especially. But she hadn't put it on before she left to go wherever she was now. Which meant that she hadn't planned to come here in the first place.

'Anyway,' I said slowly, 'it's a good thing I decided to come tonight, instead of . . . doing that . . . other thing that I told you about.'

Mouse looked puzzled. 'What other thing?'

'You know, didn't I tell you?'

'No. You just said how much fun tonight would be and how excited you were to have Will as your date. Why would you decide not to come? You were the one who organised everything.'

'Exactly. That's what I mean.'

She tilted her head. 'I'm sorry, I think I might have missed something?'

'Never mind.' I smiled at her. 'We're here to enjoy ourselves, right? Let's enjoy ourselves. Come on, I need that glass of wine.'

We headed for the garden again, but people began spilling through the door into the hall, carrying glasses and plates and talking. And then there was Will. He smiled and ambled over. 'Nervous?' he asked me.

'About what?'

'Your speech. I think everyone's expecting it imminently.'

Oh. What with my sister asking me to take over her life for a little while, I'd forgotten all about that speech detail. 'No, I'm not nervous,' I said. 'Did you bring me some more wine, like a good little date?'

He looked surprised, but amused. 'No, but I'll go and get you some.'

'Never mind.' I took his half-full pint glass from his hand and downed the contents. The good people of Stoneguard were going to have to get used to the idea of Lee Haven drinking, that was all.

Then I went to the front of the hall and climbed the five creaky wooden steps to the creaky wooden stage. Up here, the smell from the musty curtains was stronger. I heard my heels clunking across the floorboards and the buzz of conversation in the room lessened, then stopped.

As crowds went, it was a small crowd, but the hall had been built for Victorian children and there was only just about room for everyone to stand with their drinks, with an empty space in front of the stage set aside for dancing. The last time I'd been up here, I'd set the stage on fire.

Not on purpose, exactly. But still.

From here I could see everyone individually. It was odd. In one sense, they were all strangers; I hadn't really spoken to any of them in twelve years, and had hardly spoken to them then, either. Years had made them taller or fatter or just older. If I'd bumped into most of them in LA, I would've walked straight by without recognising them. But in another sense, looking at their faces was like looking at the back of my own hand, so familiar that I didn't even have to process a recognition. Even though they had nothing to do with my life any more, they populated my memories and sometimes I saw them in dreams.

And of course, most of them didn't particularly like me.

That didn't matter, though. I didn't care about them either, but they liked Lee. And I was used to being the stunt double of someone much more popular. I stood straight in my sister's shoes and gave them my best Lee smile, in the centre of everyone's attention, and realised I didn't have the least idea of what I was going to say.

Nigel came up to the stage with a microphone. He gave it to me. Feedback screamed through the hall, and I winced and turned the volume down.

'Um. Hello everyone.'

'Hi, Lee,' called Archie Munt from the back.

'Hey, don't forget to leave some beer for the rest of us, Archie,' I said, and everyone laughed.

Right, this was easy! I could make the lamest jokes and nobody would care. Everybody thought Lee was wonderful anyway. The problem was, of course, that Lee wouldn't make lame jokes in this situation. Lee would say something sweet, warm and profound, something that would make you feel fit to burst with love and fellow-feeling and perhaps bring a little tear to your eye. I had never really been any good with speeches like that. And if I wanted to prove that I could handle Lee's life as well as she could, I was going to have to come up with something sweet and warm and profound in the next, oh, ten seconds.

Fuck.

And don't forget, she wouldn't swear.

'Okay, well, I'm not going to say much. Except to thank you all for coming. And –' inspiration hit me '– Tina from the Swindon dementia unit is here, so maybe she'd like to say something about what this evening is benefiting. Tina? Do you mind?' I saw her wave from the back, and she started forward through the crowd. 'Okay, great, please let Tina through, everyone. So I'll just say thanks for coming, and have a great time.'

Applause. I walked towards the stairs and then remembered something that Lee would never, ever forget, so I stopped and put my hands up for silence. 'Oh my God, I don't believe I forgot to say this! My only excuse is that I left my index cards at home.' I shrugged in the way that Lee did when she made a rare mistake, one of those 'whoops, sorry, but you'll forgive me because you love me' shrugs, and I heard affectionate laughter. 'I need to say thank you to everyone who made tonight happen. It wasn't just me, it was the drinks, and the food, and the venue, and the invitations, and the music, and the lighting, and . . .' I realised I was quickly heading into a minefield. Lee would thank each and every person who'd been involved individually. But although I could guess at a few people, I'd be sure to miss someone if I started to list them. Plus, I didn't even know Tangerine's name.

'. . . and everything. So please, a big round of applause for everyone who was involved with this, this thing here tonight, and everyone who wasn't – well, give yourself some applause anyway because that's the sort of place Stoneguard is. People are always looking out for you here. They know who you are.'

A lot of applause. Plus feet-stomping, whoops and whistles. I must have done something right.

Or more likely, that was the sort of place Stoneguard was.

For my sister.

Stairway To Heaven

Rather predictably, about an hour later I was considerably more intoxicated and was talking about yoga.

Candace Hopkins had seized upon me near the drinks table in the garden and was clutching my arm. She wore a sleeveless hand-knitted jumper made out of twiggy wool, a long, floaty dress embroidered with sequins, and more beads than seemed feasible.

'Lee, you look fantastic in that dress,' she said, wafting patchouli in my direction. She pinched my left bicep. 'You've been practising your *Chaturanga Dandasana*, haven't you?'

'You know it, Candace.' I remembered Lee had said she'd been doing yoga with Candace. All that peacefulness and serenity. Ew. When I couldn't get to the gym, my favourite work-out DVD was *Bar Brawl Basics* by Bruce 'Brute' Snyder. Brute was a legend. Still, I had to admit that Candace's arms were sculpted like Madonna's, so she was doing something right.

'I tried that DVD you lent me and could only last five minutes,' Mouse said beside me. She was halfway through her second glass of wine and her cheeks were violently flushed. 'After the kids are in bed all I want to do is collapse in front of the television.'

'Oh, try it again, Annabelle. It's so relaxing, so calming. You'll sleep better, too.'

'I do aquaaerobics every other day,' said the woman I now knew was Marian.

'You want to try yoga,' Candace told her, pushing a strand of ginger hair behind her ear. 'Of course it's not only for your body, it's for your spirit as well. It's my personal belief that doing yoga here in Stoneguard, so close to the ley lines and the circle, enhances the energy about a thousand times. I feel so energised when I've finished a session.' Her wide blue eyes went slightly vague.

'How's the love life?' the wine I'd ingested told me to ask her. I could see Will across the garden. He was taller than everyone else and his voice, both deep and posh, carried above the other conversation. Of course he was surrounded by adoring fans so he was being rather neglectful of me as his date, though I didn't mind that too much since I wasn't exactly sure what to do about him.

Lee wanted me to carry on for her and keep everything ticking along. But surely she didn't mean her love life, too. Aside from the fact that I didn't even like Will Naughton, I imagined she'd be pretty annoyed to find out that her sister had been hanging off him all night while she'd been gone doing God knows what. He'd kissed me once, which was once too many, but he'd taken me by surprise so I had an alibi for it.

On the other hand, I was Lee for the night. I'd committed to the charade, and I had to see it through. If I suddenly went all cold towards Will, he'd think Lee had gone off him, and that wouldn't do much for her burgeoning relationship. I had to play it carefully, not getting too close, nor seeming too distant. Since it was such a delicate balance, I'd pretty much decided to drink some more and ignore the situation for as long as I could.

'Oh, yoga helps with your sex life too!' Candace enthused. 'It makes you so calm and flexible, and so open to true feeling. Gil and I have never been happier. Though I think the crystals help too, and you remember how we redid our bedroom last autumn to take advantage of the energies flowing into our house from the stones.'

'That really worked out for you, then?'

'Oh, yes. It's blissful.'

'Maybe Alex and I should move the bed nearer the window,' Mouse said doubtfully.

'Do you think if I tried yoga I'd get a boyfriend?' asked Marian.

'Definitely. What you need to do though is get a crystal system going too, and maybe adjust your diet to get everything in alignment. Have you done any irrigation?'

I caught Mouse's eye. 'They're not talking about watering the garden, are they?' I murmured. She shook her head. Dear God.

'You know, I was thinking about trying that. Do you recommend it?' Marian asked.

'Absolutely. You can't benefit fully from yoga if your body is swimming in toxins. You need to flush it all out. Cayenne pepper and lemon juice, that's the trick.'

I suddenly had a bit more respect for these women. I thought I was brave for performing dangerous stunts, but they ingested pepper and acid and then stuck a tube up their bottoms.

This was fun. Actually, properly fun. It almost felt like I was hanging out with real mates. Everyone came over to chat, to congratulate me, to thank me, to stand in a circle and talk about yoga and irrigation. I seemed to be some sort of magnet of popularity, someone that people naturally gravitated towards and revolved around. In fact, I was attracting quite a circle of women, just as Will over there in the other side of the garden was attracting a circle of men – *and* Stephen Woodruff's wife, Cheri, who was hanging on Will's every word and arranging her body in such a way that her cleavage was visible to everyone in the garden, and most especially, Will.

'And you align the bed with the head pointing west, which is tricky in our case, because the ley line below our house actually goes from north to south, starting from the sunrise stone on the hill, of course. And we wouldn't want to sleep perpendicular to a ley line. So we debated and debated and finally we decided to buy a perfectly square bed, so that the head of the bed can point west, which preserves our passionate love, but we can sleep pointing from north to south, along the line, which keeps everything in balance, you know.'

I took another drink of wine, letting Candace's nonsense wash over me. To tell you the truth, Will Naughton wasn't such a hot date. Sure, he was beautiful, but if you were a dating kind of a person, which my sister was, you wanted your date to be attentive to you. You didn't want him to stay on the other side of the garden entertaining people with yah-yah anecdotes about restoring a massive family seat. You most especially didn't want him to be within ogling distance of a glamour model's assets.

But what was I going to do? I couldn't go over there and flirt with him, or remind him of his duties as a date. But if I stayed over here, he'd think that Lee didn't care. And she did. Or I thought she probably did, though she did seem to have done a disappearing act without telling her boyfriend.

'Excuse me a minute,' I said to Candace and Mouse and Marian and Tangerine and everyone else who'd clustered around. I crossed the garden, avoiding the more obvious soft patches in the lawn where my heels would sink deep down, and joined Will's circle. I didn't push my way between Will and Cheri; instead I stood on his other side, between him and Rock, smiling my sunny Lee smile and waiting for someone to pay me attention.

And they did; they always did for Lee. Will stepped back slightly to let me join the circle, and touched my waist as if to include me. He looked down at me and gave me his charming and polite smile. 'Hello, Lee, we were discussing who's likely to take over as thatcher now that Kester Burwood's retiring.'

This would probably be a subject of great and abiding interest to my sister, but I really didn't give a straw for thatchers. 'Great,' I said, 'you carry on.' I turned to Rock. 'Rock, don't you think it's about time you asked me to dance?'

Rock blinked, and then he blushed to the roots of his wild hair. I almost regretted what I'd said, until I saw Will's face. He was the picture of barely-hidden chagrin. *His* date had the temerity to dance with another, lesser man?

That would teach him to neglect my sister.

'Yeah, sure, that sounds like fun,' Rock said, recovering himself. He glanced briefly at Will.

'You don't mind, Will, do you?' I asked him sweetly. 'You're obviously pretty busy talking about the thatcher.'

He smiled again and shrugged, taking his hand off my waist. 'What the lady wants, the lady gets.'

'Excellent. I think Nigel might play the *Grease* Mega-Mix soon, and I wouldn't want to miss that.' I threaded my arm through Rock's and we left the garden and went off to the hall.

The PA was pumping out 'Wannabe' by the Spice Girls, and several people were having a go, stepping to the beat and flapping their arms around. It was quite frighteningly close to my expectations of what the entire evening would be like, but I swallowed my forebodings and went out on the dance floor with Rock. This was probably a dream come true for him, anyway, dancing with his schoolboy crush; I shouldn't ruin his moment.

I closed my eyes, channelled my inner Scary Spice, and let the beat take me. When I opened them again, Rock had a look of fierce concentration on his face and was sort of jerking himself around to his own private rhythm. He looked like a man who didn't often get the chance to dance, but he was determined to go with the flow. I grinned at him and his concentration melted into a grin back at me. I did a little turn as the song ended and the next one began. It was 'Relight My Fire' by Take That.

Lee was a Take That fan. She had every album in the 1990s and played them continuously. She had a crush on Jason Orange and she Blu-Tacked posters of him to the wall on her side of the bedroom. I, of course, countered by putting on Nine Inch Nails' *Pretty Hate Machine* whenever I got my hands on the CD player. I would never, ever admit in a million years that actually I quite fancied Robbie. And that I maybe once in a while hummed one of their songs, when I was alone and no one could hear me.

But tonight, I was Lee. I could like Take That all I wanted to.

I laughed out loud. I shimmied back and forth and wiggled my hips and tossed my head. I felt the other people on the dance floor laughing too, and I kept on dancing, feeling the rhythm in my chest. I was thirteen again, only better. When Lulu came on to sing about walking on through the night, I sang along, and when the chorus came, I raised my hands up in the air and waved them around.

Several more people joined us on the dance floor and DJ Nigel, encouraged, put on Blur and then Kylie Minogue for a bit of a nineties dance fest. By this time, everyone was singing along and the room was packed. Even Rock, who was a Hawkwind fan if ever I saw one, pointed at the ceiling and hopped on one foot, his hair bouncing around to the beat. He was enjoying himself hugely, so I went with it, through that song, through another.

Take That was on again when I looked to the side of the dance floor and saw Will. He was standing near the DJ table, but he wasn't talking to Nigel. He'd taken off his suit jacket and loosened his tie, but he wasn't dancing either. He was standing perfectly still and watching me.

What happened next was probably the alcohol's fault – the organic sulphite-free white wine – and possibly the fact that I was trying so hard to act and think like Lee.

But I'd learned from many, many years of experience that if I have a few drinks, I get horny. I start feeling itchy in my skin and I begin to look around the room for a likely-looking lad to help me scratch. So that was possibly another explanation: his personality aside, The Honourable William Edward Naughton was quite simply the most objectively attractive man in the room.

All of this sounds quite logical. But there was nothing logical about the way his grey eyes followed my every move. Or the bolt of lust that sizzled through me, wobbled my legs and clutched at my chest and made me lose all the air in my lungs.

I met his gaze and we looked at each other. Robbie Williams sang 'Everything Changes' and I felt my lips parting and my mind whirling, telling my body to close the distance between us.

Then someone bumped into me and said, 'Whoops, sorry, Lee.'

'Uh. Oh. No problem,' I said to Marian, who it was, and the music changed to the Beatles singing 'Twist and Shout', and when I glanced back in Will's direction he'd leaned over to speak with the DJ.

Right. Right, no big deal. I fancied my sister's boyfriend for like a split second. I didn't really fancy him. I didn't even like him. It was taking all my acting skills merely to spend time in the same room with him without rolling my eyes or threatening to kick him. That one, momentary lapse of judgement was probably a good thing because it would help me act my part more convincingly.

Still, the uncontrollable lust thing was a bit worrying. I remembered what I'd said to Lee when she'd first invited me here, and I danced up closer to Rock. He was nodding his head and playing air guitar in the manner of George Harrison.

'Is Pete the caretaker here tonight, do you know?' I asked him. 'You remember, the old bloke with the glass eye?'

'He retired and moved to Bognor Regis.'

'Well. That's one temptation gone, anyway.'

'Pardon?'

'Nothing. Don't worry about it. I think I need another drink.'

The song was ending. I turned to leave the dance floor and collided straight into someone. Crisp white shirt, pewter silk tie, a woody scent, two hands that rested on my bare upper arms to steady me.

Will.

'It's my turn for a dance,' he said. The music stopped, then it changed to slow guitar picking, atmospheric recorders over the top. 'Stairway to Heaven', the longest song in the universe.

'I really need a dri—'

'Dance first. Just one.' He put one of his hands on my waist, wrapped the fingers of his other hand around mine, and brought them both to rest on his chest. Then he pulled me subtly closer and began to move.

I didn't have a choice. Well, I did – I could think of at least sixteen ways of breaking his hold on me and tossing him to the floor, every last one of them hugely satisfying – but Lee wouldn't do it. Therefore, I couldn't either.

So I put my hand on his shoulder, and I danced with him.

Stupid wine. Stupid, stupid wine. It made my hands tingle where I touched him. It made me notice he had broad, well-muscled shoulders and that I liked dancing with a man so much taller than me.

Damn. I looked around the dance floor. Maybe I could find another man, who was attractive, and also discreet, who would kindly agree to get off with me tonight after everything was finished, and not tell anyone about it. I didn't have much to choose from. I wasn't going there with Rock; I'd bruise myself on his hip bones and choke on his hair. Archie was drunk enough to be willing but most likely not able, and besides, I doubted he could keep his mouth shut. One-Eyed Pete was in Bognor Regis. I briefly considered proposing a partner-swap to Stephen and Cheri Woodruff, but the thought made me feel sick. And that story would be all over Stoneguard within about thirty seconds.

I was stuck with my sister's boyfriend.

'So, have you been having fun?' I asked brightly. If we talked, I was bound to be reminded what a wanker he was, and that would be like a drenching with cold water.

'Yes, I have. Thanks for inviting me.'

'Don't mention it.'

'Your dress is lovely.'

'Thank you.' This was probably my cue to give him a compliment in turn, but I couldn't bring myself to do it. Besides, surely he'd had enough toadying from the other

Stoneguard peasants. I tried to think of something else to say. There were several problems with this, though. I didn't want to mess up and ask him a question that Lee would know the answer to already. I didn't want to let it slip that I didn't like him. And I definitely didn't want to let him know that I fancied him like mad, especially now, with my ear close to his chin, close enough to hear his soft breathing over Robert Plant.

So much for the idea about using talking as a distraction.

'Nice night for it,' I said at last.

'Yes.'

'Pity about the rain, though.'

'Yes.' He cleared his throat. 'How's your mother?'

'About the same.'

'Oh. That's . . .' I could practically hear him trying to decide what to say. That's good that she's not yet completely demented? That's too bad that she's still going crazy? 'She must have been disappointed that your sister couldn't make it.'

I welcomed the flash of irritation. 'I seriously doubt it. Liza and my mother never really got on. They can barely stand to be in the same room as each other.'

'Really? You never told me that before.'

'I thought it was self-evident. Besides, you know me; I don't like to dwell on the negative.'

'No.'

We lapsed into silence. I tried to look over Will's shoulder so I could drift away and think about something else, other than the fact that Will was a good dancer, smooth and easy and holding me close, not close enough to be plastered all over him but close enough so that it was difficult to pay attention to anything other than his warmth and his body and the little places where I brushed against him as we moved, at the elbows and the hip. I focused on his hand where it held mine against his chest. He had neat nails, long fingers, those veins that on the back of a male hand signify strength and competence. I looked away, but because I didn't want to look into his face, I ended up staring at the side of his neck, at the space underneath his ear, where his hair had grown a bit out of its haircut and was beginning to curl under.

I wanted another drink. I wanted to run out into the rain. If he said something, I'd be able to follow his lead in conversation as I was in the dance. Why wasn't he talking? I thought that the whole point of posh prep schools and public schools was to give the upper classes the ability to make mindless small talk on any occasion. He *had* been making mindless small talk, for hours now. It was only now, with me, that he'd gone mute. This silence was driving me crazy. It let me imagine things. Like leaning forward a little and pressing my lips to the hollow behind his ear where his hair was curling.

I cleared my own throat. 'Penny for your thoughts,' I said.

He paused for a beat before he said, 'You're different tonight.'

That was it. I'd been sussed. My heart thumped, though I shouldn't have been surprised. 'How am I different?' The walk, the talk, the general cynical outlook to life?

'I've been trying to figure that out. The dancing, maybe.'

'You mean, this dancing with you?' Right. Maybe Lee had been taking ballroom dancing lessons and I'd missed a cue for a twirl or a dip or something.

'Partly. It's—'

I made a mistake and looked up into his face to see why he'd cut himself short. He was looking down into mine. My heart thumped again, but in a different way.

'No,' I said quickly, 'I always dance like this to Led Zeppelin.' I focused on his hand again, and the shoulder of his shirt.

146

'Then maybe it's something else.'

The coloured lights played off his white shirt, first red, then green, then blue. They were making me quite dizzy.

'This difference,' I heard myself saying, 'do you like it?'

'I'm trying to figure that out, too.'

The tempo picked up for the rock-y bit at the end of the song. I took my hands away and stepped back. 'Want a drink?'

'How about another dance?'

I shook my head. 'I'm really thirsty, Will. You go on, though. I'll just nip next door and get myself a drink. Cheerio!'

I didn't look back to see what he was doing with himself, but instead hotfooted it out of the hall. Unbelievably, it had finished raining outside so I didn't get the dousing with clammy water that I needed. Mouse and Tangerine were lingering by the gate. They each had an ice cream cone in their hand and they waved me over before I could pass them.

'It's going really well, isn't it?' Tangerine said.

'Yes, brilliantly.'

'Is Will having a good time?'

'He's trying to figure that out.'

They both laughed, evidently taking it as a joke. Maybe it was. I wasn't sufficiently acquainted with Will Naughton's sense of humour to know.

Tangerine took a lick of her ice cream. Her tongue was pink and wet and left a trail across the buttery yellow. Not for the first time, I wondered how a so-called civilised society could endorse a food that required you to show your tongue to all and sundry as you ate it.

'I hope you don't mind,' Tangerine said after she finished licking, 'but we got the ice cream out already. You looked like you were having so much fun dancing and since we have to

147

vacate the hall by midnight we haven't got much time left.'

'Can you believe, the ice cream totally slipped my mind? Thank you both for thinking of it for me.'

'It's really good.' Mouse took a lick of her own cone.

'What flavour is it?' Tangerine asked.

'Um . . .'

'Goody Two Chews,' Mouse said. 'Caramel ice cream with toffee and marshmallow.'

Ugh. The mere thought of so much sweetness made me want to shudder. 'I'm glad you like it.'

'We put the tubs and cones on the table with the scoops so everyone could help themselves. Is that okay? I did think maybe you'd planned on serving it yourself.' Mouse's worried look crept back.

I remembered scooping ice cream. Your fingers froze, your wrist and shoulder ached, you got chilblains on your palm. And you ended up reeking of sugar and cream. I wasn't averse to physical discomfort, but in the case of scooping ice cream, it was adding injury to insult.

'No, no, no, that is absolutely fine.'

'Are you going to get a cone?'

'I – don't think I'm in the mood for ice cream right now.' No. I didn't want sickly cold. I wanted something cool and sharp, like another glass of wine. Or even better, something warm and spicy. Like Will's skin.

Really no. Not my sister's man.

I shook my head and realised that I was more drunk than Lee probably ever got. I grinned, and lurched forward and threw my arms around both of these women. 'You are absolutely the best, did you know that?'

They both put their arms around me with no hesitation at all, and we had a group hug.

A group hug. Yesterday, the mere idea of a group hug

would have sent me screaming for the hills. Stoneguard really was rubbing off on me. I straightened up and took my arms back.

'Right,' I said, 'who wants another drink?'

'Thank you for coming! Yes, thank you for coming too! Oh, it was a pleasure to organise it. Walk home safely, now. Yes, you're right, we should definitely get together for coffee soon – you have my number, right? Oh, I'm so glad you enjoyed it. Yes, the ice cream rounded off the evening nicely, didn't it? Take care! See you soon!'

Shaking hands, kissing cheeks. I now knew what politicians felt like, canvassing for votes and spreading bullshit. I stood by the door, my back to the jamb, wishing goodbye to all the other happy Stoneguardians in various states of inebriation. The door was helping me to stay upright, and also relieving some of the pressure on my back. My months of physical therapy hadn't quite prepared me for hours of dancing in high heels. The ache was beginning to shoulder through the cushion of wine and ibuprofen, and it was taking all my willpower to stay nice and not tell these people to piss off home so I could go back to Lee's house and lie down.

I hadn't seen Will for some time. He never turned up to get his ice cream, and he stayed well away from the dance floor when Nigel finally, at last and at my drunken request, played the *Grease* Mega-Mix to finish off the evening. He'd probably left without bothering to say goodbye. Apparently he'd decided that he didn't like the 'different' Lee after all. Some date. Some charmer. I was personally going to corner Lee when she got back and tell her that she needed to kick her posh totty to the kerb.

People staggered out into the cool wet night, their footsteps and conversation echoing loudly in the rural silence. Mouse

149

appeared from the hall. Her cheeks were violently flushed, her headband askew. She held a bunch of keys in one wobbly hand. 'Are you shure you don't mind lockin' up?' she slurred.

'No problem, you go home.'

'I am going to be *shooooo* hungover tomorrow.'

'Get that husband and those kids of yours to let you sleep in.'

She grabbed my hand. 'Can I tell you shomething? I haven't schlept past shix ay-emm in nine yearsh. Nine yearsh. Can you believe it? I love my kidsh but hellooooo!' She clapped her hand to her mouth. 'Whoopsh, that was loud.'

'Are you okay to walk home?' I asked her.

'Umm, shure. Lived here all my life, know it like the back of my hand.' She tried to focus on the back of her hand to illustrate her knowledge, but I saw her eyes cross.

'Rock!' I called. With the rain stopping, the moon had come out, casting silvery light everywhere, and I could see Rock's slim figure a few metres away, on the pavement. He was gazing up at the stars. 'Can you walk Annabelle home, please?'

'No worries.' He came back to the door.

'I'm all right, really I am, I can find my way home. Let me jusht – hey, where are my shoesh?'

'In your other hand,' Rock said. 'Come on, Belle, let's get you home and get a cup of cocoa down you.'

'Cocoa, I love cocoa. I mean, I really really *love* . . .'

'Good night, Lee,' said Rock over his shoulder to me.

'Lee!' Mouse ran back to me, and nearly floored me with another big-bosomed, wine-scented hug. 'I love you! You are *shooooo* . . .'

'Yes, thank you,' I said. 'Go with Rock now, and I'll see you soon. Thanks for all your help.'

'Okay, right, okay, okay. Rock? Where are you?'

I thought of something. 'Rock?'

'Yeah?'

'Don't let her get abducted by aliens, okay? I don't think she's up to it.'

'They're not coming tonight. Come on, Belle, lean on my shoulder.' The two of them walked off unsteadily. Rock was taller, but Mouse was wider, and she was evidently a little difficult to keep on a straight path.

And then I was alone. No more former neighbours, no more cheesy disco. No panicking about food or offering of drinks. The voices of people going home floated over the still air to me. A sheep bleated. Then it was quiet.

Well. What an interesting evening. I looked down at the keys in my hand. Who would've ever thought that Liza Haven would be entrusted with the keys of the school? I smiled, and stepped out of the building, and closed and locked the door behind me.

All things considered, I hadn't done too badly. Nobody had sussed that I wasn't Lee. Her reputation as an organiser was entirely intact, and her reputation as a drinker was considerably enhanced. I hadn't argued with a single person, even when they'd been slagging the real me off. I hadn't sworn, I hadn't shocked anyone, and I especially hadn't taken my sister's boyfriend round the alley behind the school for a quick, breathless, amazing shag.

My feet throbbed and my back ached. I bent down and took off the indigo shoes. Under my bare feet, the stone steps were cool and wet and felt wonderful. I started down School Street, whistling the chorus to 'Summer Lovin''.

'I never knew you were such a *Grease* fan.'

The voice came from the shadows cast by the school. I jumped, twisted in mid-air, my hands up in a defensive

151

position. There were footsteps and Will Naughton stepped into the moonlight.

'Jesus Christ!' I yelped, putting my hands back down quickly. 'What are you doing lurking out here?'

He smiled. His eyes and teeth gleamed in the moonlight, and his shirt showed dull silver. 'I'd said my goodbyes already and you seemed to be pretty busy sending people off. I thought I'd get a breath of fresh air before walking you home.'

'You don't need to walk me home.'

'Of course I do.' He held out his hand for me to take, but I kept mine resolutely by my side. Not seeming to notice the snub, he started walking in the direction of Lee's house, and unless I wanted to stand alone on the pavement and watch him go, or follow him like a lovelorn puppy, I didn't have much choice but to walk along with him.

What was he on about, presuming he'd walk me home like some sort of olde worlde pre-feminist knight in shining armour? Did he expect me to swoon at his feet or something in gratitude for his manly protection?

'You honestly don't have to walk me home,' I said. 'I mean, that's very . . .' I made myself say it '. . . *chivalrous* of you, but it's not like I'm going to get mugged here in the middle of Stoneguard. The worst thing that's going to happen is stepping in some sheep sh— manure in my bare feet.'

'I noticed that you made sure Annabelle had someone to walk her home.'

'Yes, but Annabelle is utterly smashed. She'd end up in a field cuddling up to a cow and thinking it's her husband.'

Will chuckled. It was a deep rich sound, like espresso coffee. And I wished I hadn't noticed that. I concentrated on the cold pavement under my feet.

'I think it's incumbent on me to make sure you don't do the same,' he said.

'I would never cuddle up to Annabelle's husband.'

'That's a considerable relief to hear.'

'Why do you talk like someone out of a book?'

'What should I talk like?'

'I don't know. It's— surely you can drop the whole Oxford-educated lord of the manor accent every once in a while, can't you? Loosen up? Say "innit" or something?'

'Innit.' It sounded wholly alien in his mouth, like Prince Charles talking about getting down with his homeys in the hood.

'Never mind.'

Stoneguard had one streetlight, and it was planted right in the middle of the High Street, between Ma Gamble's Wholefood Emporium and the Mysteries of the Stones bookshop. The other partygoers had dispersed already, and the light made the town look even more deserted. The thatch on the buildings hung over the road and cast furry shadows. When I wasn't wearing shoes, Will seemed taller. This small nakedness on my part felt strangely intimate.

'You're doomed to be posh,' I said.

'And don't you feel sorry for me?'

'Terribly. It must be so dreadful to have more money than God.'

At that, he laughed right out loud. The sound echoed off the shops and buildings.

'Shhh, you'll wake up the whole town,' I said. Not that I cared about the whole town and their sleep. No, it was because I liked his damn laugh and I wanted to laugh too. This alcohol really had a lot to answer for. Thankfully, tomorrow I'd wake up sober and in my right mind, and have absolutely no desire to get into Will's pants.

'Of course. Sorry.' He lowered his voice significantly to ask, 'When does the clear-up begin tomorrow?'

'Archie and Charlie have volunteered to do it all themselves. I'll believe it when it happens.' We'd reached the corner of Church Street, and I stopped. 'Well, good night then.'

Will had carried on walking half a step before he twigged I wasn't coming too. 'What do you mean, good night?'

I pointed ahead, down High Street towards the dark horizon. 'Naughton Hall is that direction, don't you remember? It's very nice of you to walk me to my street corner, but I can take it from here, thanks.'

He grasped my arm. 'I'm not leaving you on the street corner. I'm your date and I'm walking you right up to your door.'

'I know it's protocol, but you can really make an exception this time. What's going to mug me, an owl?'

'No, Lee. I'm going to make sure that this date has a proper ending.' He began walking us down Church Street. All the lights in the houses were off, the curtains drawn. I'd forgotten to put on Lee's outside light, too, so her house was also in shadow. The darkness reminded me of all the people curled up in bed inside, warm and snug. It made me feel even more alone with Will, especially as he was silent again, which was giving me space to think.

What did he mean, a proper ending? Did he mean a handshake-and-a-peck-good night ending? An all-right-just-one-more-drink-for-the-road ending? A grab-each-other-open-the-door-and-fall-onto-the-hall-carpet-and-have-wild-explosive-sex ending?

I racked my drunken brain for excuses. I wasn't used to resisting temptation and my willpower could only hold out for so long. If Will even came in for an innocent coffee, I wouldn't last long enough for the kettle to boil. Maybe I could tell him I was having my period.

We paused, and I realised we were at Lee's garden gate.

Will opened it and walked me down the short pathway. Something was blooming in the darkness; I could see the flowers like faint stars, and smell their scent. We reached the front door and we stopped. Right, what was my best ploy here? Could I pretend to be really drunk and throw up on his shoes? No, with my luck, his so-called chivalry would extend to carrying me into the house and putting me in a hot shower. Stripping me naked, and putting me in a hot shower.

I fidgeted. Will stood there. I glanced up at him and saw he was gazing down at me.

What was it with this man and his intense scrutiny? Was I an interesting specimen or something? I cleared my throat.

'Will—'

'Lee—'

We spoke at the same time, and both immediately shut up. He was still touching my arm but he didn't have a hold of it, which was good as it gave me the additional option of bolting if he made a move. The warmth of his fingertips on my bare upper arm was almost unbearable.

'Go on,' I said.

'No, the lady goes first.'

'I wouldn't dream of interrupting you because of outdated sexism.'

'Please, humour me. Say what you were going to.'

'I was going to say thank you for a lovely evening, and I'm absolutely knackered, so if you don't mind I'm going to go straight to bed – I mean, straight to sleep. So good night.'

He kept on gazing at me. It was as if he hadn't heard what I said, or was expecting something else. His eyes were very dark and the air smelled of jasmine and rain.

'Anyway, good night,' I said again.

A faint frownline appeared between his eyebrows. I didn't suppose he was used to being turned down at the end of an evening, but it would probably do him good. His ego would undoubtedly bounce back anyway, like a posh gorgeous rubber ball.

He didn't move other than the frown, and it suddenly occurred to me that he might be about to swoop down and try to take me by surprise with a kiss again, so I pulled away from him and busied myself finding the keys in my handbag. I slotted the correct one in the door, fortunately on the first go, and turned it in the lock. Then, and only then, with my escape route open behind me, did I stretch up and give him the briefest of brief kisses on his cheek. 'So thanks, Will, be careful of those owls on the way back to Naughton Hall, won't you?' I said cheerily, and then hurried into the house and closed the door behind me.

I could smell his aftershave on my lips, right under my nose. I stood with my back to the door, listening, waiting for him to step up to it and knock. But I didn't hear anything. Was he standing there among the flowers like a tall, dark and handsome garden gnome? Without turning on the lights I crept into the front room and twitched the sheer curtains aside the tiniest amount so I could peep out.

He was gone. The garden was empty. I breathed a sigh, half of relief and half of guilt, because for a split second, down deep in my gut, I had wanted my sister's boyfriend to be outside waiting for me. And that was all kinds of wrong.

I went into the kitchen and snapped on the lights. The tiles were bright, hand-fired in orange and lime and yellow; the cabinets were pretty country-style pine, with a plate rack mounted on one wall. I searched the cabinets until I found a bottle of whisky right at the back. I doubted Lee drank it much; she probably had it for entertaining or for baking. Pouring myself a large measure, I sat down at her rustic kitchen table and kicked off my shoes. Then I took a long drink, long enough to fill my head with whisky instead of Will Naughton's sandalwood aftershave.

Well. I'd survived the disco. Even more than that, I'd done a smashing good job. And I'd had a taste of what it was like to be Lee Haven: to have everyone as a friend, to be the centre of love and approval, to be endlessly included and made to feel at home. It would have been different if I'd come as myself. I would have met suspicion and awkwardness, stilted conversations and silence. I wouldn't have had Will Naughton looking at me that way, that intense way, in a quiet jasmine-scented night.

I took another gulp of whisky, then noticed with surprise that the glass was empty, and refilled it. I had a fun life. I had an adventurous life, and an independent life, and a lonely life.

My sister had a wonderful life.

A Wonderful Life ✤

She's walking between her house and the school for the sixth time today when she sees Rufus Fanshawe getting out of his car. It's a glossy black machine with slanted headlights and a bonnet curled like a sneer. She raises a hand to greet Rufus, but he goes straight into his house without glancing in her direction.

It's warm today, threatening to rain, as if the world is waiting on the brink of something. The kind of day that makes you uncomfortable in your clothes, that makes you look towards the hills for something different and new, when your mind should be full of leaflets and paper plates and who's going to collect the tickets at the door. As she walks by she glances through the window of the car.

The keys are dangling from the ignition.

Her heart thumps once and she doesn't think. She opens the door, sits in Rufus's seat, and turns the keys. The engine purrs into life.

She holds her breath and touches the accelerator. The purr turns into a growl, but the car doesn't move. For a moment she's sure she's been caught and she looks around frantically. The street is empty. One raindrop spatters on the windscreen.

What would she say if she were caught? 'I got in by mistake'? 'Tania asked me to run an errand for her and use her car'? She hasn't got any talent for lying; she would probably tell the truth. 'I wanted to see what it felt like. I wanted to do something different.'

Then she realises that she's not moving because the handbrake is still on and she laughs, relief and adrenaline zooming through her veins. It feels good enough so that she releases the handbrake and presses the accelerator again.

She can hardly believe she's doing this. She can hardly believe how great it feels. I'll just drive to the end of the street, she thinks, and then I can bring it back and park it in the same place and Rufus will never know. But when she gets to the end of the street, she turns right and keeps going. Then she turns right again, down Hill Farm Lane.

Someone will see her. She knows everyone in town, everyone knows Rufus's car, they'll see her and though they won't stop her, they'll think about it later when they hear that his car has gone missing, and they'll say, 'Oh yes, I saw Lee Haven driving it this afternoon. I thought she'd borrowed it?'

But nobody passes her on the narrow lane. She drives to the end, carefully so as not to nick the paintwork on the loose stones. Then she's at a T junction at the A road. Right is back to Stoneguard. Left is Devizes.

She turns left. The rain spills and patters.

They call it 'joy riding' for a reason. Her foot is on the accelerator and one hand is on the wheel. She likes driving with one hand, negligent, controlling the big car with merely her wrist and fingers. It's nothing like the way she normally drives.

The car is sleek power under leather seats and a gleaming bonnet. She's approaching Devizes, thinking for the thousandth time that she can never see the signs without thinking of that dirty rhyme of her sister's, when she remembers that she might be recognised there. She takes the first sharp right, back north. The road winds past farms and cottages, the windscreen wipers swishing, and she turns on the radio, something loud enough to block out the reality of the world outside.

A curve comes up too fast and she twists the wheel. For a split second she's out of control and she hears branches scraping against the polished paintwork, then the tyres have a grip on the road again and she's speeding forward, faster than she would have thought possible, faster than is wise. The memories are spinning along behind her, lost in the slipstream. It feels so, so good to let them go, if only for right now.

A white roundabout sign looms up in front of her. There's a blue label pointing towards the M4. She barely slows down for the roundabout, takes it in fifth gear, makes a split-second decision, and shoots off to the left. She doesn't even care where the motorway goes; she wants a long, straight run in the car. She's been stuck in one place, going round in circles, for too long.

When Bristol comes she sees the familiar signs and says, out loud, 'I need to go back now before Rufus notices the car is gone.' And then it hits her: he's already noticed. She's been gone long enough now. In fact, not only will he have noticed by now, but so will a good proportion of Stoneguard.

So when she sees signs for the M5, she follows them. North, because she can go further that way. Her running has become, all at once, running away – and to cover up the thought of that she turns up the radio even louder and drives, through the rain, as the sky darkens and her life goes on without her. This is a big car, a car that's meant to shield you from everything and create its own little bubble of comfort: leather seats, climate control, suspension that cushions every bump on the road and makes it disappear.

After a while, she doesn't know how long, she glances at the clock and thinks, with an odd detachment, The ball must be going on by now. Then she realises what that means and sits up straight in her comfy driver's seat.

The ball depends on her. All these people depend on her.

She pulls off into a service area and stops the car near the back of the car park, as far as she can from the sterile lights of the services. She doesn't quite dare shut off the engine; it will be too quiet. When she looks at her phone, it has eight messages on it, and ten missed calls. She hasn't even heard it ringing once. The last number on there is her sister's, so she dials it.

Liza answers after four rings. 'Where the hell are you?'

This is such a typical Liza way to answer the phone. In the background, she can hear thumping music, something from the eighties – Duran Duran maybe. That's the real world, there, going on without her.

'Liza. You're at the school?'

'Yes. Are you driving here?'

'No, I'm—' She twists a lock of hair around her finger and looks at the yellowish lights all around her. She doesn't know where she is. She doesn't have a map. She's been driving for nearly three hours – how did that even happen? If she turned around right now, she wouldn't be back till the ball was over.

She did all that work for it. Lee sits in her leather seat and waits for the disappointment, the guilt to hit her. Oddly, it doesn't.

'I'm not coming,' she says, and laughs because it's so strange.

'You what?'

'I can't, Liza. I need . . .' She needs to know why she doesn't feel bad. She should feel bad. She's stolen a car and she doesn't

161

even regret it. She's ignored all her responsibilities. There must be something wrong with her. '. . . to do something else,' she finishes. 'I want to take a break. I'm sorry.'

'You're not coming, after you went on and on at me about it?'

'No. I'm sorry.' And yet she isn't. She has this odd calm, and a sense of euphoria floating over everything. To cover up for it, she says quickly, 'Something else came up that I thought would be more fun.'

'More fun? I thought this disco thing was right up your street.'

She laughs, again. It sounds wrong in the confines of the car, but she knows it's the kind of reasoning that her sister will accept. 'Well, things change sometimes. You should know that. How's it going, is everything okay there?'

'Everything's fine. What do you mean, things change? Where are you? When will you be back?'

'I don't know. I'm all right, though. I'm having a great time. I need you to look after things for me while I'm gone. Will you do that for me? Please?'

'How long are we talking about?'

'Just – will you, Liza? Keep things going until I get back? Please?' She holds her breath and bites her lip. If Liza says no, that's it. She'll have to go back to Stoneguard. And it isn't like Liza to say yes.

'All right, but—'

'Thank you.' She takes a deep breath and puts her hand on the wheel, ready to drive some more. To drive and drive until she's forgotten everything and everyone. 'Okay, have fun tonight. I'll talk to you soon. Love you.' She turns off the phone, properly off so it won't even ring, puts the car into gear, turns the radio up again, and drives back onto the motorway.

But it's no good now. The phone call to her sister has broken the spell; it's reminded her there's something beyond the present moment. She puts her foot on the accelerator and remembers the rush of elation she got earlier, speeding down country roads, and wonders, is that how Liza feels? And then that leads to wondering about what Liza's doing at the school hall. Is she antagonising people? Why did she come, anyway? Was it to make up, or was it one of her impulses, something not thought through, something she'll get angry about when it doesn't turn out the way she'd hoped?

And what about the ball? That was probably what most of the messages were about. From Annabelle, or Tania, or Will.

She shakes her head and keeps on driving.

Maybe there was something about Mum. They wouldn't know to get in touch with Liza, they wouldn't know she was in town. Maybe something's happened.

She needs to go back.

She's just passed a junction; she'll get off at the next one and turn around. Or she could check her messages, make sure there's nothing to do with Mum. She can't do that while she's driving, though; she's read that using a phone whilst driving is as impairing as being legally drunk. Yet another reason to get off at the next junction.

The next junction comes, heralded with blue signs. Lee keeps on driving. And through the next, and the next. And the next. She's chewing her lip now, gripping the wheel hard, as if the car's making the decision, not her, and she's along for the ride.

She can't go back. She's *stolen a car*. This isn't something small, not something slipped into her bag that she can say fell in there by mistake, or she forgot to pay for it. It's not something she can just apologise for and everyone can forget.

163

She's taken something big and expensive, something important. Rufus loves this car.

Oh my God, what was she thinking?

The radio is suddenly too much of a distraction. As she shuts it off, the headlights dim, and she's thinking she must have touched something wrong by mistake when the engine sputters out.

'What?' she says, and glances at the dashboard only to see that the petrol gauge is on zero. 'Oh no.'

Fortunately, she's in the left-hand lane. She puts the car in neutral and coasts off onto the shoulder. The car stops, and she puts the handbrake on and finds the hazard light button. An eighteen-wheel lorry shakes the road and buffets the leather-lined shell of the car with its wind as it passes.

What you're meant to do, as a wise motorist, is to get out of the car and ring the rescue services. She carries a membership card in her purse for occasions such as this. Then you're meant to wait for the yellow rescue vehicle on the embankment near the car, behind the guard rail, so that you're safe from any other vehicle which happens to plough at full speed into your stationary car.

But she can't do that. Her membership covers her for cars other than her own, but not, she's pretty sure, for cars stolen from your neighbours and driven several hundred miles at random in the middle of the night.

She gets out of the car. From outside, it's sleek and black. She can understand now why Rufus is out there polishing it every Sunday morning, making the bonnet shine like the carapace of a precious beetle.

But he won't be polishing it this Sunday morning. Because it's Sunday morning already, or close to it, and the car is here with her. Wherever here is.

And she remembers Rufus's bypass operation last August,

and how worried Tania was, and how this is going to cause him even more stress.

Another lorry thunders past.

She looks back the way she's come, and then ahead of her. She hasn't a clue whether the nearest junction is before her or behind. Whichever way she goes, she'll be abandoning the car, someone else's car. There are no rules for that procedure. Should she leave the keys in the ignition? But then someone else might steal it, someone who doesn't know Rufus.

She's not thinking like a car thief. A car thief would hope that someone else would steal it, because it would make it harder to trace it back to her. But another thief wouldn't get very far without petrol, anyway. She puts the keys behind the sun visor, closes the door, and takes two steps away on the hard shoulder.

She's not a car thief. She opens the door again, finds the keys and locks the BMW's door before she puts the keys in her handbag. She'll post them back to Rufus.

But she can't do that, then everyone will know for sure that she took it. Because she is a car thief.

Vehicles whiz by her, shaking the hard shoulder beneath her feet. None of them slow down. She'll post the keys back. She owes it to Rufus.

The flashing of the BMW's hazard lights fades behind her as she walks, until it's less than a blink. The motorway isn't lit except by the headlights of the cars going past in her direction and against her, but now that the rain has passed, the moon is full. It lights up raggy scraps of clouds in the sky. It looks like a painted sky in a black-and-white horror movie. It's too clichéd to make her frightened, and anyway, she's been out a lot at night recently. As she walks she looks back down at the tarmac of the hard shoulder, which is gleaming with wet. Fortunately, she's wearing sensible shoes.

Fortunately? What's she on about, *fortunately*? What's she doing out here anyway? What difference does it make what shoes she's got on?

The road lights up from behind her, casting her shadow. A long, dark Lee, walking God knows where. The shadow shrinks rapidly and the car zooms past, leaving her with no shadow and its retreating red eyes. She pictures what she must look like – slender and vulnerable, completely incongruous at this time, in this place. You'd think someone would stop and offer me a lift, she thinks, and then rejects the idea. At speed, motorists will barely have enough time to register her presence before they're too far past her to bother to stop. Besides, it's illegal.

She laughs. The noise, between cars, is loud.

Her breath goes in and out and her heart beats faster than normal. Her senses are sharp, her head clear. The night air is scented with motor oil, tarmac and wet grass. To her right, the painted white line glows in the moonlight and leads her forward. On the verge ahead of her, something small moves and she sees the bright reflection of an eye. An animal of some sort, probably a rabbit. It's used to cars but spooked by the presence of a human. It rustles back to safety and is quiet. She likes rabbits. There are lots of them on the hill in Stoneguard, grazing along with the sheep. They've grown up with tourists, so they don't mind humans. Sometimes, on a sunny day, she takes a picnic to the other quieter side of the hill and lies on the grass there watching the rabbits and the sheep. They live their lives in small circles of eating and sleeping and mating, sticking together for security.

When she was younger and there was more time in the day, she was a voracious reader, and she remembers *Watership Down*. That was a story about rabbits forced out of their homes, who had to keep moving forward and face all kinds of

166

perils. They had to act against their nature, riding on boats or tempting foxes.

A car speeds past her saying *grrrrrRRRRR*, an angry predator rushing in for the kill. It blows oil-scented wind at her.

She remembers reading the book late into the night, long after her mother had gone to bed and Liza had sneaked back into the house. She held a torch under her duvet, escaping into the world of the rabbits and how they overcame their timidity, their instincts, everything inside them that told them to keep safe.

Lee is out here in the dark on the side of the motorway, right now, because she wants to escape. The impulse has been growing day by day, and today for some reason, it's built up in her like a kettle shivering with unreleased bubbles and then it burst out into steam. The simple fact is that right now, not knowing what the next few minutes hold, she feels alive. Terrified, but alive. She could call the AA to come and get her, she could confess to stealing the car, and maybe, probably Rufus would tell the police she borrowed it, or Tania would convince him to say that, and the gossip would die down eventually or she could get Ma Gamble on her side to minimise the damage. She could be back to her old life in time for Sunday lunch with Mum.

But that fills her with more dread than the darkness ahead, the strangers in cars, the road stretching for she doesn't know how long till the next junction. So she starts jogging in her flat shoes.

She told her sister that she wanted a break. And that, at the heart of it, is the pure truth. She wants a break. She wants to break. Put on the brakes. Break a habit of a lifetime.

The words thud with her feet on the tarmac, and in the headlights of an approaching car, she sees a blue sign up ahead. She's at the junction already.

She should be at the school, at the ball she's organised, having fun. No, that's not true. It started out as a fun idea, but mostly, it was responsibility for other people's fun. If she'd been there tonight, she would have been thinking about the food or the music or Will or, especially, Liza. It wouldn't have been fun at all.

Maybe that was why she took the car – for a moment of fun. But what was fun about taking something that belonged to someone else?

Behind her eyelids, she has a quick flash of stolen turquoise nail varnish, and then she blanks it out as she starts up the slip road. She's got more pressing problems right now – like where to go in the middle of the night. It's got to be past midnight.

In the distance, she sees lights, services. A roundabout and a petrol station, a motorway hotel.

She's made enough decisions for today, all of them the wrong ones. She'll be fresher tomorrow.

She'll be able to figure out how to take this all back.

Dancing In The Moonlight ✸

BRRING! BRRING!

The phone rang with all the good cheer of a jackhammer pounding into my skull. I groaned into the darkness and pulled the duvet over my head.

BRRING!

Who the hell was calling in the depths of night? Instinctively reaching my hand out towards the phone on my bedside table, I encountered empty air. Then I remembered that my phone wasn't there because I wasn't in my apartment in LA, and I wasn't in a hotel either. I was in Lee's house.

I sat up and pushed my hair back from my eyes. The curtains weren't drawn, and the moon still cast enough light so I could see where I was. For some reason, I'd gone to sleep in Lee's room, on her bed. I was naked. I couldn't remember stripping off or lying down here, but that could have something to do with the several medicinal whiskies I'd consumed after shutting the door on Will.

BRRING!

The upstairs phone was across the room, on Lee's dresser. She must've had the ringer turned way up because I could hear the downstairs phone going off, too, in a shrill echo.

Right. Well, it was Lee's phone, so it wasn't going to be for me. I could lie back down and relax, and—

What if it was Lee, calling me?

I jumped out of bed and grabbed the phone off the cradle. 'Hello?'

'Ms Haven?'

Not Lee, a stranger. I considered saying, 'No,' and hanging up, but then it struck me with a chill that this could be someone calling to tell me about Lee, to say she'd had an accident, was hurt somewhere. Was never coming back.

'Who's this?' I said quickly.

'It's Brianna Milton, I'm on night duty up at the house. I'm sorry to disturb you at this hour, especially with your party tonight, but your mum's gone missing again.'

'Gone missing? It's . . .' I looked over at the digital clock. 'Three in the morning.'

'Yes, she was quite active earlier this evening and I thought she'd sleep, but apparently she wanted a little wander. Should I—'

'A *little wander*? What are you on about? The woman's sick, she shouldn't be out of bed at this hour! You're her nurse, are you?'

There was a pause. Then the woman asked, 'Are you all right, Lee?'

'I'm fine, it's my mother I'm worried about. Where has she gone? Why aren't you trying to find her?'

Another pause. 'Well, usually I stay here in case she wanders back, and you go after her, but if you'd like to do it differently . . .'

Usually? How often was this nurse letting my demented mother out of the house in the middle of the night?

But she thought I was Lee. It was easier if I was Lee. There were fewer questions to deal with, and I could find my mother

170

and get her back to safety and then go back to bed to sleep off this whisky and wine. I swallowed down my rage and said, 'Yes, that's probably best. How long has she been gone, do you know?'

'I went to get a cup of tea and a sandwich, and when I came back to check on her she'd unlocked the French doors and they were open. She can't have been out for more than fifteen minutes.'

Fifteen minutes. Christ. And she was probably dressed in a thin nightgown, completely off her trolley, hitchhiking to Spain or something. 'Right. Right. I'll get dressed and go out looking for her right away. Keep a look-out, will you?'

I hung up. 'Fucking hell.' I flipped on all the lights, then tore open Lee's chest of drawers, found a pair of jeans and a T-shirt and pulled them on without bothering with underwear. Then I ran downstairs and shoved my bare feet into a pair of hiking boots that stood near the door. I was halfway out of the house before I remembered to bring the keys with me. Then I went outside into the dark, still night.

Where would she go? I stood on the front path for a moment before I realised it was pointless to try to figure out the thought patterns of a demented woman. The best thing to do was to head for her house, and then make a sweep in circles trying to find some trace of her. She couldn't have got that far, and even with my lopsided running, I was bound to be quicker than she was. Especially if I used Dog Shit Path.

Instead of turning left down Church Street toward the High Street again, I ran right, towards where the road bent right at the church. The moonlight picked out details of the lych gate, with the spiky yews either side of it. I opened the gate and cut through the churchyard, a shortcut to the lane running behind it.

The church loomed to my left, with its squat square tower

171

showing darker than the hill behind it. Graves poked up, each with their own shape and shadow. Running, I wove between them, not bothering to follow the gravel path, using my memories instead. The ground dipped and rose with the coffins underneath, and Lee's boots were loose on my sockless feet. It had been only a few hours since my last drink but at the moment I felt stone cold sober.

An obelisk rose into the starry sky like an upside-down ice-cream cone: my grandparents' grave, bigger than any of the others in the churchyard. I touched the stone briefly as I passed and ran to the corner of the churchyard. Someone had tacked a sign next to the stile. I couldn't read it, but I could guess what it said because some things never changed. I launched myself up over the stile and nettles stung my bare arms. Then I was on the lane beyond, running through a pitch-black tunnel between the wall and a hedge. The gravel crunched and rattled under my feet.

This part of the lane was used mostly by locals walking their dogs. Tourists didn't like it because even during daylight you couldn't see anything on it aside from fences and hedges, and of course, dog shit. From the churchyard it followed backs of houses along the bottom contour of Stoneguard Hill. I ran down it as fast as I could, until suddenly it opened out into moonlight. Here it met the tourist car park and continued as a narrower chalk path that wended its way, carrying hundreds of visitors a year, up the hill to the stone circle. The path was empty now, and I followed it up the slope.

The gap in the hedge was somewhere on my left. Once upon a time I could have found it with my eyes closed; it was my escape, my road to adventure. But now I scanned the darkness of the hedge for the place where I used to push through out of my mother's garden into the freedom of the hill and the fields. I tried to remember the exact placement of

172

the bushes and trees and rocks, but I couldn't quite make a picture in my mind. I'd always found it by instinct, not by knowledge – the skin-memory of a thousand scrapes from winter holly and summer bramble. I recalled how the hedge would try to grow itself together in the days between my passage, as if it wanted to block me and trap me inside.

I stopped. What an idiot. Of course the gap wouldn't be there now, twelve years later. It would have overgrown the first summer I was gone.

'Shit!' My voice should have been loud in the silence, but the grassy hill and the hedge muffled it. I was going to have to go back down to the car park and around via the High Street to my mother's house. Which meant I'd lost several minutes of time.

I turned around ready to run even faster, when something caught my eye further up the slope of the hill. A glimmer of white on the chalk path, the same colour as the night-blooming flowers in my sister's garden. It could have been a scrap of rag, a paper from a tourist's sandwich, but then I saw it move and realised it wasn't something small nearby but something bigger far away. A ghostly figure walking up the hill.

'Mum!' I yelled and ran up that way instead. The path wound around the hill in a gradual ascent for visitors not used to steep climbs. I left it and scrambled up the grassy slope, pulling myself up with my hands and feet through long grass and over rabbit holes, my breath loud in my ears now, closer and closer to that figure. It was bone-thin and walked with a single-minded determination, back straight, hands barely swinging. Even in the middle of the night, incongruously in her nightgown under the stars, my mother's walk was so distinctive I could hardly believe I'd mistaken her even briefly for a bit of litter.

I hauled myself over a tussock and reached the path behind

her. 'Mum!' I said again, but she kept on walking as if she hadn't heard me. Up the hill, following the path, narrow in her flannelette gown. Her feet were bare.

My mother's feet were never bare. She wore shoes outside, slippers inside, sandals on rare trips to the beach. But now she walked on, mindless of the rocks on the path or the white chalk that coated the bottoms of her bare feet.

I'd been alarmed before, pissed off, urgent. She took another step and I heard the tiny sound of her footfall and for the first time I was afraid.

'Mum?'

I didn't quite dare touch her. I hurried past her on the grass bordering the path, and stood in front of her. I'd had a crazy idea her eyes would be closed and she'd be sleepwalking like you see in cartoons, but her eyes were open. In the moonlight they were aglitter. Her cheeks were hollows and her dark hair was streaked with silver. All the colour was leached from her skin and if she hadn't been walking, still walking, straight past me as if I weren't there, I would have thought she was dead.

I wanted to bolt down the hill quicker than I'd come up it. Instead I turned and walked the two steps to catch up with my mother. 'Mum,' I said again, and I touched her elbow.

I hadn't touched my mother in years. She was thinner.

She stopped and turned her head to look at me. 'Oh, it's you,' she said, in quite a normal voice. Matter-of-fact, calm and authoritative, as if she were talking to one of her suppliers for her ice-cream business, or the gardener who came to prune her roses.

Yeah, don't bother to be glad to see me or anything, your daughter you haven't seen in a year and a half. 'What the hell are you doing out here in the middle of the night, Mum?'

'Walking, of course.'

'Walking where?'

'To the stone circle.'

'Why on earth would you want to do that at three o'clock in the morning?'

'Because—'

She stopped and I saw that blank look come back, the expression she'd had when she walked straight past me. As if my mother had suddenly stepped out of her own mind and left her body there empty. Nobody home.

'Mum? Why were you walking to the stone circle?'

She blinked. And then in the moonlight I saw something that was more scary than the blank zombie-mother, because it was something I could never in my life have imagined.

My mother looked afraid.

She shrank back from my hand on her elbow and drew her hands up to her chest, as if to protect herself. Her eyes darted back and forth, looking at her surroundings in a random way that seemed to make no sense of the patterns she saw. 'Where am I?' she asked, and all her matter-of-fact authority was gone.

'You're on the hill, leading up to the stone circle. You escaped the house while the nurse wasn't looking.'

Eyes still darting, as if she could only take in bits of information at a time, she whispered, 'It's dark.'

'Yes, it's the middle of the night.' I heard my voice being unexpectedly gentle. As if she were the child, and I was the parent, though maybe more like the parents I'd seen on television or in other people's houses.

'Where am I?' she asked again.

'I said already. You're on the hill.'

'Where?'

'In Stoneguard. Behind your house.'

'Where's that?'

'In Wiltshire. In England.'

'But where am I?'

'You're *on the hill*, Mum.'

'Oh. Oh.'

'Anyway, I think we should get you back to bed.'

'Oh. Yes.' She nodded slightly, and then shook her head. 'Why is it dark if it's morning?'

'This is going to go on all night, isn't it?' I said, mostly to myself, with a lot more exasperation than gentleness now. 'Come on then, Mum. Let's get back down the hill.'

I put my hand on her upper arm again to turn her around and guide her down the path. She moved slowly, shuffling her feet. Something seemed to surprise her and she looked down. 'I'm not wearing my shoes.'

'No, you bolted out barefoot apparently. Are you okay? Do your feet hurt?'

'Of course not, I'm perfectly healthy.' She began to walk, quite briskly, down the path. I went along beside her.

Okay. This was totally surreal. I seemed to have my pick of two or three different people who flitted at will through my real mother's body. I walked alongside her, watching the path in front of her for obstacles. Her feet seemed so bony and pale, nearly the same colour as the chalk path. Her toenails were unpainted. She looked as if she'd snap a toe or two if she hit a rock, like that one, there, that sat in the middle of the path. 'Watch out for that rock, Mu—'

She stepped over it and kept going.

'Why were you going up to the stone circle?' I asked, figuring I might as well take advantage of her apparently lucid moment.

'How did I get out here? Was Harvey sleeping?'

'Dad's—' Then I remembered what Lee had said, that sometimes my mother forgot that my father had left and when Lee reminded her, she got upset. I left the sentence unfinished.

'And the girls?'

'We're sleeping. Or should be,' I added under my breath.

'Oh. I must get to work then.'

She stopped and made as if to turn around and walk back up the hill. I gripped her more firmly on the arm and put my other arm around her. 'No, Mum, it's time to get back to the house now. Come on.'

She gave up her ascent and began walking downward again. 'Did you tell Doris that we are making Darkly Divine tomorrow?'

'Yes.'

'Did you double-check the sales figures?'

'Yes. Down here, Mum.' She was veering off the path, over the grass.

'No, this way.'

'No, we have to go through the car park and up the High Street. This way.' I pointed forward. She tugged at my arm, her feet resolutely pointed off the path toward the hedge.

We were the same height, but she was no match for me in weight or physical strength, not these days. Still, she was bloody persistent, like one of Derek Hunter's terriers on a lead, so after a moment's resistance I said, 'Oh what the hell, ten more minutes won't hurt,' and went along with her to see whatever it was she wanted to see. She walked straight for the hedge and then, stooping, went through it.

It was my passageway. I recognised its position, its angle, the flattened grass at its entrance that hadn't been flattened by my feet. I ducked and followed my mother through. The path emerged between two flower beds and half behind a stone sun dial in the back garden of the house I grew up in.

The windows were ablaze with light. My mother was

already walking across the lawn towards the conservatory door. She tried the handle and seemed puzzled to find it locked.

'Do you use that gap in the hedge all the time?' I asked her.

'What gap in the hedge? There's no gap in the hedge. It's quite safe. Do you have the key for this door?'

'Let's try the front door, they'll be looking out for us,' I said, and guided her around the brick Victorian building. This time she walked docilely by my side. The front door was unlocked and we walked straight in.

The hallway was the same as it had always been, with patterned tiles on the floor and dark engravings on the walls. The coat tree held my mother's jackets, Barbour and tweed, a navy cardigan and a purple anorak I'd never seen before. Her boots and wellies were lined up neatly below, next to an umbrella-stand with curved handles protruding. There was a different smell to the air, something I didn't have time to identify because as soon as we set foot in the place a large woman with a mass of frizzy ginger hair came scurrying in. She wore trainers and an horrendous smock-type top covered with pictures of blue and pink teddy bears.

'Mrs Haven! There you are! You've had us worried!'

My mother stopped stock-still and gave the woman a steely glare. 'What have you been doing? Where did you go?'

'I haven't gone anywhere, Mrs Haven. It's you who has gone for another wander. But your daughter found you, isn't that nice? Why don't you come back to bed and I'll make you a lovely cup of tea?'

She had a saccharine voice to match her top that made me instantly grit my teeth. My mother's face didn't change. 'I should not be able to get out of this house at night,' she said. 'You should be locking the doors and securing the windows and you should have me under constant supervision. That is what I pay you for, not the condescension nor the lovely cups of tea. You are not my nursery maid. You are, at least during the night-time hours, my jailer. Am I making myself clear?'

This was my mother, back with a vengeance. The nurse's eyes went wide. 'Perfectly clear, Mrs Haven.' The saccharine had been knocked out of her.

'Good.' She turned to me.

In the full light, I could see that she had lost weight, but she'd lost none of her upright posture, nor the flash in her dark eyes. In her nightgown and bare feet streaked with chalk she looked as formidable as she ever had in her best business suit. Somehow, she seemed taller now than she had outside.

For the first time since the Horrid Christmas, I was faced with my mother. My real mother, not the ghostly confused creature out on the hill. She looked at me and I looked back at her. I'd thought about this meeting. What she would say, whether she'd reproach me or thank me for abandoning her.

I was too old to care what my mother thought. But I found myself holding my breath, poised to fight or to fly.

She studied me slowly, looking from my hair to my feet, much the same way she used to study our uniforms before we went off to school every morning. I had to restrain myself not to adopt the old position with my shoulders slumped, my hips cocked, my chin thrown back to show her I didn't care. And then I remembered that I was wearing Lee's clothes, and I could breathe again. Of course there weren't going to be any recriminations or arguments; I was dressed up as the dutiful sister. Her favourite. And I'd just rescued her.

But surely, if anyone could tell me and Lee apart, our mother could – when she was in her right mind, like now. Surely she loved Lee at least well enough to know when someone else was standing in front of her.

179

'Do you know who I am, Mum?' I asked her. My voice was much smaller than I wanted it to be, nearly the voice of a little girl.

'Yes,' she said, and my heart leaped or sank, I wasn't sure which. Her nose wrinkled. 'You're covered with dog droppings.'

She turned on her bare heel and walked through the door into the living room, leaving the saccharine nurse gawping at me. I looked down at myself, sniffed, and then picked up my feet to look at their bottoms. Lee's boots were, in fact, smeared with dog shit. From the looks of it, it had originated with several different canines.

'I went through that alley where everyone walks their dogs,' I said to Bianca or whatever her name was. 'You know the one?'

She shrugged. 'I live in Swindon,' she said. 'But you'd better take your shoes off if you're going to stay here. Your mother's got a tongue on her, hasn't she?'

'You should have known her twenty years ago. Don't worry, I'm going.'

I walked back along the High Street. The sky was just beginning to get light, fading from black to dark blue. I stomped my feet on the pavement to dislodge some of the dog shit and I thought about how my mother had changed in nineteen months. And the ways she hadn't changed. Trust her to be the only one to notice, in a crisis, that I'd stepped in filth.

I wondered if she really knew who I was.

Unknown Territory

I used to date a guy who was in a rock band. He said that Sundays were God's gift to help you recover from Saturday's drinking so that you could start Monday's drinking with a clear head. I dumped him when he started greeting Sunday mornings with a bottle of Michelob, too.

But in this case, he was at least partly right. I lolled in Lee's bed until late in the morning, glad that in my drunkenness the night before I'd chosen to sleep in her bed instead of the guest bed. I'd only slept in that bed a couple of times, but I remembered it as lumpy and creaky. Then I got up to get myself a cup of tea and sat in the sunny kitchen, wearing my sister's dressing-gown. I found some bread and made myself some toast, and spread it thick with peanut butter and jam.

I had to admit that I'd done a great job with the disco. It had gone without a hitch and nobody guessed that Lee wasn't really there. And I'd found my mother in record time, even if I did tread dog mess all over her hall tiles.

But there was unease gnawing at my stomach, and a growing feeling that something was wrong. Because my sister was still missing.

I'd been expecting Lee to walk into her bedroom and wake me up. I thought back to the phone conversation we'd had.

She'd been in a car, and she'd said she was fine but that she had to get away for a while and she wanted me to keep things going for her until she got back.

When would that be? What was this sudden going off for a break anyway? If she was supposed to be going away, why would she let me, and everyone else, believe she was going to be home? My sister wasn't manipulative, or calculating. I couldn't picture her intentionally deceiving anybody, and especially not me.

So maybe it was a spontaneous decision, to go away. There was fresh milk in her fridge, eggs and bacon and vegetables and some salmon with an expiry date of – I got up to check – tomorrow. You didn't stock up on supplies if you were planning to take off on holiday. Unless, of course, you thought there would be someone, such as your sister, at your house to eat them. The house was tidy, but Lee was always tidy. It had smelled of her when I came in yesterday; did that mean she'd recently been in the house, as I'd thought, or did the house always smell that way? I sniffed the air, but all I could smell was toast.

It didn't feel right. But she'd been so breezy on the phone. She wouldn't act that way if she were in trouble. Would she?

I put my dirty plates in the sink and went back upstairs. I looked in her bathroom; her toothbrush was by the sink. Surely my sister would never go anywhere without her toothbrush. But then again, maybe she had two toothbrushes, one for home and one for travel. I had half a dozen of them, depending on which bag I ended up grabbing on my way to the airport. I touched her towel, hung up carefully on the rail, but of course it was dry. I thought back to yesterday, when I'd taken a shower: had the tub been wet, as if she'd just used it?

I couldn't remember. I thought it probably was, but I could

be wrong. Her make-up was arranged in a neat basket next to the sink. I counted mascara, eyeliner, eye-shadow, blusher, lipstick – but again, she could have spares of everything. She was that sort of person, organised and forward-thinking.

I went to the bedroom and looked in her cupboard. There was a suitcase on the bottom and an overnight bag on top of that. I opened her drawers, but it was impossible to tell how many clothes were gone, if any. I sat on the unmade bed. I should have visited my sister more often. Then I'd know what suitcase she used, what her favourite clothes were, which shoes she wore every day and wouldn't dream of going away without.

I tried to think of the one thing that my sister would never, ever go away without – and found that I didn't know. As familiar as I thought Lee's life was, it was, in fact, strange and unknown territory.

Mouse might know. Will might, too. They didn't know Lee had gone away, but they would know what her most necessary possessions were. Wouldn't they? Were they the people who were closest to Lee in Stoneguard? I didn't know that either, though they seemed logical enough places to start. Maybe I could figure out a way of asking them, without giving away the fact that Lee was gone.

But what would I do with that information? If she'd taken her favourite shoes and bag, it meant she'd intended to go away, but it didn't tell me how long she'd be staying. If she had left them, it either meant that she'd gone away spontaneously, or that she didn't mean to be gone for long. Or maybe that she had a new pair of shoes that she liked better.

I could try to amass the raw data, but I didn't know how to assemble it. I couldn't read my sister's mind. All I could do was wait for her to come back, not knowing where she was, what she was doing, whether she was in trouble.

Because as much as I didn't believe in twin psychic connections, I was really beginning to feel that Lee was in trouble.

Someone knocked at the door.

I jumped up from the bed and ran downstairs. I'd left the spare key on the hallway table. It could be Lee, if she'd lost her bag. I flung open the door.

It was Charlie and Archie Munt. For cousins, they didn't look much alike, but the surprise on their faces was identical. Maybe they weren't expecting to have the door answered by someone wearing a dressing-gown and bed hair, with no slippers and disappointment written on her features.

'All right, Lee,' Charlie said. 'Just got up?'

Interesting. So I still looked like Lee when I was more dishevelled than she'd ever been in her life. Then again, context was everything; I was wearing her clothes and standing at the door of her house.

'I'm a little worse for wear today,' I said.

'Too much wine, eh? Good for you. There's nothing wrong with letting loose once in a while. Anyway, never you fear, we've come for the keys to the school so we can do the tidying up. You can leave it all to Archie and me, and go back to bed.'

'Okay.'

They looked even more surprised. Evidently they were expecting Lee to be more insistent about helping. But it seemed to me that Lee had probably done enough already, and it was time someone else took some responsibility, preferably someone who hadn't been up at three in the morning rescuing their mother. They trooped into the house after me while I went to get the school keys out of my handbag. I noticed that Archie was peering down the corridor towards the kitchen.

'Who are you looking for?' I asked him.

'Oh! Oh, me? I was going to say hello to Will Naughton if he was here.'

'He's not.'

'Oh, well, that's fine, just wanted to say hi. Wanted to tell him to make sure to keep his car doors locked. We stopped by the Fanshawes' on the way over here. Rufus still hasn't got his Beemer back.'

'Probably find it in some field somewhere,' said Archie.

'That's what I was saying to Rufus,' said Charlie. 'Joy-riders.'

'Unless it's one of those professional thieves. They take them and respray them and put new number-plates on. Whole thing takes about ten minutes, then they sell them on. Saw it on telly.'

I got the keys out of my handbag and held them out. Neither cousin seemed to notice.

'Rufus said he couldn't get hold of the insurance company since it's a weekend so he's driving the missus's Focus. Mad enough to spit, he is. Haven't seen a face that red in a long time.'

'Still, he'll be all right, his insurance will cover it.'

'Not if he left his keys in the car.'

'Well, they don't have to know that.'

'Going to be pretty obvious if the car's found burned-out somewhere with the keys still in the ignition.'

'Well, here are the keys to the school,' I said. Neither of them made a move to take them, so I shoved them into Charlie's hand.

'Good party last night,' he said.

'Yes, very good,' I agreed.

'We carried on afterwards at the Druid's Arms. Viv did a lock-in for us. Didn't get home till, what, Archie, two in the morning?'

'Two-fifteen. I checked the clock when I got in.'

'That Stephen Woodruff's wife is something, isn't she? You know she used to be a model?'

'Yes, I do,' I said. I shifted from foot to foot and wondered if I was going to have to throw them both bodily out of the house. The movement made the dressing-gown gape open slightly at my chest, and I saw both of the cousins glancing at the revealed cleavage and then looking away to resolutely focus their gaze on the cream-coloured walls.

'Glamour model,' said Archie. 'She had a few last night. Nice girl.'

'Not the sharpest tack in the barrel.'

'But her heart's in the right place.'

'Looked like we had most everyone there last night. The only one of the usual suspects I could think of who was missing was Ma Gamble. And your twin sister, of course.'

'Haven't seen her in ages.'

'Might have seen her in a film, come to think of it, but I wouldn't have known it was her. What's she look like these days?'

'Quite a bit like me,' I said.

'Yes, that would make sense.'

'So, we'd better get going and do that clearing up,' Archie said. Neither one of them made a move to leave.

'We've got the boot filled with bin liners,' Charlie said. 'Archie even brought a mop. Don't think that thing's ever been used.'

'I mop my floors once every six months whether they need it or not.'

'You wanna come round and do mine some time?'

'Do I look like your wife?'

Dear Lord, I could see why it took forever to get anything done in this town. It was going to take dynamite to move these two out of the house. God knew how long they'd stay if I actually went so far as to offer them a cup of tea.

I decided if I was going to be standing here half-naked listening to the cousins' interminable duologue, I might as well get some useful information while I was at it.

'Do you remember that holiday I was talking about taking?' I said suddenly. They looked surprised again, but I couldn't quite tell if that was because of the content of my question or because I was actually participating in the conversation.

'Holiday?' said Charlie.

'Yes, you know I was saying I needed a break and I was going away for a little while?'

They thought about it, which was the longest they'd been silent since I'd opened the door. Finally Archie shook his head. 'Can't say I recall.'

'There was that jolly to Paris that my Cathy wanted to take on the Eurostar with the girls, but she said you said no to that,' Charlie put in. 'Didn't want to leave your mother or the business for too long.'

'Right. I must have been talking to someone else,' I said.

'A holiday sounds good, though,' Archie said brightly. 'Now, somebody was saying that they went to Butlins – who was that?'

'You haven't got kids, though, so maybe save that for later, eh? Cathy is mad keen to go to Ibiza. I tell her, "What are we going to do surrounded by all those E'd up ravers?" "Lie by the pool," she says. Mind you, I saw it on one of those holiday programmes and they said—'

I faked a yawn, stretching my arms up above my head so that the dressing-gown rode up and then gaped even more in front. Charlie stopped talking and quickly averted his eyes; Archie followed suit, a split second later.

'Well, thank you so much for volunteering to do the

cleaning up,' I said, going to the door and holding it open. 'I really appreciate it.'

'Um. No worries at all. Best get going then. See you Monday, Lee.' Miracle of miracles, Archie stepped out of the door.

'Later, Lee.' Charlie followed suit and I waved and smiled and closed the door behind them.

At last. I went back upstairs and got straight into the shower. I intended to stand under the spray for a good long time, but the smell of Lee's shampoo and shower gel made me wonder even more where she had gone. So I washed quickly, dried off with Lee's towel, and pulled on a fresh pair of her jeans and a T-shirt. I'd throw my own clothes in the laundry in a minute. I was still rubbing my hair while I dialled her mobile number on the upstairs extension.

'You have reached the messaging service for oh-seven-seven-four . . .'

I hung up. Then I redialled. 'Turn on your phone,' I said to the pause after the recording. 'And ring me to tell me where you are. I had to rescue Mum from the side of the hill last night, and I've had the Chuckle Cousins blathering on at me today. Call me right now, all right?'

I put the phone down and waited. Last night she'd called not long after I'd left the message, which meant she was monitoring her voicemail, anyway. After five minutes I went downstairs to make a cup of tea. I pinched a few biscuits from the crockery jar and ate them with it; I seemed to be starving, which wasn't too surprising as I hadn't eaten last night. No way was I going to touch that buffet.

The phone still didn't ring. I wandered into the living room with another cup of tea and some more biscuits and turned on the television. I watched the rugby for a while, but even violence and manly thighs couldn't distract me from the fact that my sister wasn't calling me back.

Right. I was obviously going to have to do my own investigation if I wanted to find out where she'd gone. The living room was spotless; the only clue there were the fresh flowers on the table. They hadn't even begun to wilt. But even if she was planning to go away, Lee would find it impossible to believe that her guest could get along without flowers, even if that guest were me, who could kill anything green by standing within two feet of it. All they told me was that Lee had gone some time yesterday or late the day before.

I went to the hallway and nosed around for some post. I hadn't seen any before, but I thought maybe I'd been missing something. But there wasn't any, even though she had a sweet little basket on the table for keeping things in like outgoing letters or her keys. The most likely place for real clues was her spare room upstairs.

The door was open, and my suitcase full of dirty clothes sat on the bed. The room was neat, like the rest of the house, and decorated in pastels, like the rest of the house: blush-pink walls, matching curtains and duvet cover on the single bed in a pretty fabric with a small flower pattern. The bedstead and chest of drawers looked old-fashioned, though I couldn't tell whether that was because it was old or because it was new and had been sanded down or whatever to look old. Lee liked all that antiquey stuff, so it probably was actually old. The desk had an in tray with some papers stacked in it, a chunky mug full of pens and pencils, a folder holding what looked like promotional materials for Ice Cream Heaven, a desk lamp and Lee's laptop, which was open. Firework patterns snaked across its sleeping screen.

Bingo. I pulled out the chair, sat down and pressed a key to wake up the computer. There was a spreadsheet open, something about invoicing, but that wasn't what I was looking for. The computer beeped to tell me there were new email messages. I hovered the mouse over her email icon, and then I saw a calendar icon on her desktop and clicked that instead.

It came up as a week's view, and the grid was filled in with a chequerboard of colours and abbreviated appointments. It seemed that my sister had a colour code for different things. Blue, for example, for *M's Dr. Appt* and *Visit M*. The red stuff seemed to be about work: *Mtg w Geoff H, Pick up @ printers*. Yellow for *Yoga*. My name, *LIZA*, was typed in capitals in bright orange on yesterday's entry. Below that, in green, was *WILL*. And below that, in magenta, *CHARITY BALL!!!*

Did you buy a new dress and use three exclamation points for something you were planning to miss?

As it was Sunday now, the week in front of me was the one that had just passed. I didn't see the word *Holiday* anywhere. I clicked ahead to next week. It looked as though she had a solid work schedule ahead of her on Monday, with several appointments all typed in red. Blue visits with Mum Monday, Wednesday and Friday. Yellow yoga Thursday. Assorted purple appointments every evening. There was hardly an empty hour between nine in the morning and nine at night. Same for next week. And the next. I had a thought and clicked backwards to last week, but there was nothing obvious there either, no appointments with travel agents or days booked off. Unsurprisingly, there were quite a few magenta things, presumably having to do with the dance. Green *Coffee w W* on Wednesday afternoon. Orange *London w Liza – Jett 7.45* last Sunday.

I clicked back, and back, and then got the bright idea of viewing the calendar a month at a time. Every day was bands of colour. Red, blue, yellow, green. May, April, I saw green first date with Will writ large in March. February, January, then into last year. I didn't see a single blank stretch of holiday. She was a busy woman, my sister, though probably most of it was second nature to her and she only looked busy because there were so many colours jostling for space in her schedule.

These are my lists, my mother's voice said in my head.

They were similar. But different. They didn't mention turning off the gas, or how to get to the train station. They were the lists of someone who was busy, not someone who was sick.

But I blinked and saw the image of my mother in her nightgown on the side of the hill. Surely my sister hadn't wandered away like that? Forgotten where she was? Was Alzheimer's even hereditary?

I shook my head. No. Not possible. If my sister were going crazy, I'd be going crazy too. And I wasn't going crazy.

Except I couldn't drive.

'Stop it,' I said aloud in the small room. 'This is your hangover talking.'

Right. Keep looking for clues. I hovered the mouse above the email icon again.

On the one hand, it was wrong to read someone else's email, more wrong than looking at their calendar. On the other hand, it might help me find out something that I really should know. On the third hand, Lee would be almighty pissed off with me if she discovered I'd been snooping through her inbox. I sighed, got up and went into the bedroom, where I dialled her number again and got her voicemail again.

On the fourth hand, since when had I been bothered by moral dilemmas anyway? I went back to the laptop, promising myself I'd only look at the subject lines of her emails to see if there was anything about a trip or a holiday or a break. Then I could deny actually reading her emails, since I'd only read the subject lines. Though if I found anything, I'd read it.

Her email was also all compartmentalised, with separate

folders for separate topics. The Ice Cream Heaven folder had several sub-folders, too. I went straight to Personal, where there were two new messages on the top. One said something about a Rolex watch, and one was from Will Naughton. It had been sent this morning, and the subject line was *Good morning*.

I scrolled down. Most of the past few weeks' emails had been about the dance in some form or other. I recognised most of the names. There were more from Will, sometimes several in a row, as if they'd had a bit of online banter. Some invitations from people in the village, quite a few that looked like gossip, more that had the subject line *Hello* or similar. It was strange to read emails like this, a list of subjects; almost like a poem that made no sense, with random repetitions that made no rhythm. My own email was on there, with my flight details on it to London.

There wasn't a single email subject about going away. Then again, the ones with the vague subject lines could be about anything.

The computer beeped a new message again, and I scrolled up to the top to see it. It was from Will, again. This one said *Good afternoon*.

I looked away, at the mug full of pencils and pens and the flowered curtains and the lumpy bed. Then I looked back.

He probably wanted to chat about last night. Maybe even why I'd sent him packing instead of inviting him inside. Which meant, in a strange way, that these emails were actually for me. I remembered how he'd looked last night in the garden and how the scent of him had clung to my lips. I reached my finger to the mouse pad to open the emails.

The phone rang – not Lee's landline but my mobile. I jumped up and went to the bedroom to answer it. 'Hello?'

'Toast and yogurt and tea. What about you?'

It was Lee's voice. I didn't care what she'd had for breakfast. 'Where the hell are you? Why aren't you back yet?'

'I'm – in a hotel room.' I heard her sigh, an unknown number of miles away. 'How are you?'

'A bit puzzled, to tell you the truth. And worried. What are you doing? I came to visit you, I thought you were all hot on it.'

'I am – I was – I mean, it's difficult to explain. How did it go last night?'

'Fine. It was the party of the century.'

'Were people asking for me?'

I hesitated. 'They certainly expected you to be there.'

'What did you tell them?'

'Not much. I don't know much. What's going on, Lee? It's not like you to up and leave. You haven't taken anything with you.'

'It was a bit sudden. I'm okay, though.'

'Why aren't you answering your phone? Or is it only me you're not talking to?'

'I'm not talking to anyone. I – need a break, like I said.'

'When will you be back? Later today?'

She hesitated. 'Do you need to work on Monday? Or is it just a fact-finding thing, like you said?'

I sat down on the unmade bed. I wasn't sure where this was going. 'I don't need to work on Monday,' I said cautiously.

'Do you think you could hang around in Stoneguard for a little while longer? Just, you know, take care of things for me?'

'Like what things?' I pictured her full, coloured schedule.

'Oh, you know, like pop into Ice Cream Heaven and see how they're getting on, check in with Mum, take messages on my phone, things like that.' She was nonchalant, but it didn't sound as natural as usual. 'I've got my diary on my laptop, it's in the spare room. You can have a look if you don't mind.'

'Why can't you do all of this yourself?' Silence on the other end. I thought maybe she'd hung up. 'Lee? Is something wrong? You can tell me.'

'I just can't come home for a little while. I can't explain it, not to you, not to anyone else in Stoneguard. It's not a big deal, really, it's only . . . I really do need that break. I'd really appreciate it if you helped me, Liza.'

'I don't know the first thing about the ice-cream business, and you know what it's like with me and Mum. I think you should come home. And what about Will Naughton?'

'Will can take care of himself. Liza, I really need you to do this for me. Please.'

I heard her on the street with snow falling around her, asking me not to go. I heard her in London asking me not to argue. *Please*.

'Right,' I said.

It wasn't quite an agreement, but that's how Lee took it, because she immediately gushed, 'Oh thank you, Liza, thank you. I really appreciate it, so so much, you don't even know. Okay, listen, I have to go, but I'll call you soon. Love you, bye.'

She rang off. 'What the hell?' I said to the phone in my hand.

I began to dial her number again, to demand some more answers, like for example what was really the matter and how long she wanted to me to look after things for her, but the doorbell rang downstairs.

'They haven't heard of having Sunday to yourself in this bloody village.' But I abandoned the phone and went downstairs to answer the door.

She stood on the doorstep. She wore a tie-dyed Grateful Dead T-shirt, trousers that looked as though they were hand-woven out of hemp, and Jesus sandals. Aside from slightly more silver in her hair, she looked exactly the same as she had when I'd last seen her up close, more than twelve years before. Former British Army Major Doreen Gamble, locally known as 'Ma'.

'Good morning, what's this I hear about bean dip?' she said.

Ma Gamble knew everybody. She knew everything. She was the chair or vice-chair or secretary of every committee, club and association in Stoneguard, and there were a lot of committees, clubs and associations in Stoneguard. Her Wholefood Emporium was a hub of gossip which spread its spokes out into the community. Every time you went into her shop for carob or mung beans or a cup of Fair Trade tea, you learned some titbit of information which stuck to you, like a virus, and which you then released into the wider world to spread pandemic-like to everyone you met.

Aside from my mother, Ma Gamble had been my childhood nemesis. When she had caught me nicking from her shop, she had taken me by the ear – *by the ear!* – this was in the nineties, not the Middle Ages – and marched me to my mother's office to suggest I was sent to military school. My mother didn't send me to military school, but she made me put on every item of clothing I owned and work every Saturday afternoon for a month stacking pallets in the freezer.

I had great pleasure in anything I managed to steal from under Ma Gamble's nose after that. I didn't care what it was – organic sweets, beer, a packet of lentils, a Fair Trade cotton dishcloth. When I bought coffee there I'd grab a handful of sugar packets instead of one, smirking at her openly as if to say, 'Go on, ask me if I really need all of these.' In return, she wrote my mother a note asking if she had considered getting me therapy.

That got me another month's worth of Saturdays in the freezer.

So with Ma Gamble standing in front of me asking me about bean dip, my first impulse was to flip her a v-sign and slam the door in her face.

Then I actually looked at her. She was standing with her feet apart, her hands on her hips, a classic combative stance, but she was smiling. Not with her mouth, which was pulled up on one side waiting for my answer, but with her eyes, which were sparkling and crinkled in that way that means *I like you. I might be yanking your chain, but I like you.*

I was Lee to her.

And in a real way, how I behaved in the next two minutes would determine whether I continued pretending to be Lee. Because if I revealed myself as Liza to Ma Gamble, the entire town of Stoneguard would know it as soon as I slammed the door.

'Good morning, Ma,' I said. 'Won't you come in for a cup of tea?'

Why was I being nice? Why didn't I slam the door? Was it because I *wanted* to keep on being Lee?

'Haven't got the time, I've got kale soup on. I saw Fenella Dearborn at the station when I arrived from Bristol and she said that Jasbir had told her this morning on his walk that he had really enjoyed the bean dip. I didn't make bean dip. Where did it come from?'

'Bean dip?' I said, stalling for time. Mouse had been terrified of Ma; I couldn't drop her in it though she'd been the one doing the dropping. And smushing the bean croquettes. 'Oh, I whipped that up myself yesterday afternoon. I had some kidney beans I had to use, so I thought I might as well bring it to the party.'

Her brow furrowed. 'That's funny, I could have sworn Fenella said it was a azuki bean dip.'

'No, definitely kidney.' I didn't know one bean from another. If you asked me, azuki sounded like a Korean scooter. 'You know how things get distorted with gossip.'

'She also mentioned cherry tomatoes on the quiches. She said it was cute.'

'That was me as well. I was getting a little whimsical, I'm afraid.'

She was silent for a moment – which would probably have made Mouse wet her pants. Then her frown loosened and she gave me an indulgent smile. 'Oh well, I suppose it was your party. You were probably thinking about ice-cream sundaes with a cherry on top.'

'Probably. It's a hazard of the profession.'

'Your sister didn't turn up then.'

'No, something came up.'

She tapped her teeth with her finger. 'I'd be curious to see how that one turned out in real life.'

I bet you would. I fought an impulse to say, 'Well, look at this then,' and turn around and drop my jeans to show her my arse.

I got round it by clutching the doorframe until my fingers went white and saying lightly, 'She's very happy in her life and in her job.' If Ma Gamble got hold of the fact that I was currently unemployable, that too would be all over the village in seconds. 'She's very in demand,' I added.

Why? Why did I care what she thought, what the village thought? I pushed the question back into the recesses of my mind.

'As long as she's not dead or in jail, I imagine your mother's satisfied. How's she doing today?'

'My mother or my sister?'

197

'Your mother,' said Ma Gamble in a tone that showed she had had her final word on Liza Haven.

'Mum's about the same.'

'You haven't gone for Sunday lunch? You always go for Sunday lunch, before the Ley Line Preservation Society meeting.'

I did? The calendar flashed before my eyes; yes, I seemed to recall a blue appointment for today, which I hadn't paid much attention to as I'd thought it was a reminder to ring Mum. 'I'm a little worse for wear, to tell you the truth. I'm not used to drinking so much wine.'

'Ah, I see.' Now my hangover was going to be talked about for the rest of the day. 'Well, send her my regards when you see her. Tell her she's always welcome for coffee at the Emporium, like the old days. You'll have to come in later so you can tell me all about the dance.'

'I wouldn't dream of depriving you of a single detail.'

That might have been a little bit too sarcastic for Lee, because Ma Gamble shot me a sharp look, then mellowed again. 'Oh well, I've heard a great deal already from Archie and Charlie and Will Naughton, and of course I've seen Stephen Woodruff parading his new wife around in church. Pretty one, isn't she?'

'You've seen Will?'

'Yes, jolly as ever. He would have done well in the Army, like the Princes, you know.'

'What did he say when you told him that?' I knew she'd told him. Ma Gamble wasn't one for keeping her opinions or knowledge to herself.

'He thanked me kindly for the compliment. Charming manners, Will Naughton. Oh, by the way, while I'm thinking of it, we've had a run on Praline Paradise. Can you send some more over tomorrow morning?'

'Of course.'

'And Toffee Euphoria. And Strawberry Fields. And you might as well send over some Triple Chocolate Bliss while you're at it. Barbara Raymond's having problems dealing with her husband's wandering eyes. She's all right during the week, it's the weekends that are the killer.'

'Maybe I should make a special batch of Quadruple Chocolate Angelic Choirs Singing Hallelujah and get it sent to her house on Friday night.'

'Goodness no, don't encourage her. I'm hoping to get her to try a macrobiotic diet soon. She'll be done with the indulging and ready for a little purging. Is that a new flavour? What was it, Quadruple Chocolate Hallelujah?'

'No, I just made it up off the top of my head in response to Barbara's emergency.'

'I see. Well, must get back to the kale soup,' Ma Gamble said. 'Goodbye. Don't forget the ice cream.' She turned around and walked down the garden path.

'Don't forget the ice cream,' I mocked in a sing-song and totally childish voice once she couldn't hear me, and shut the door. What was it about this place that made me act like a kid, when I wasn't acting like my sister?

I wandered into the kitchen. Last night I'd been Lee because she'd asked me to take care of things for her, and it was easier that way. I'd been Lee with Archie and Charlie because I'd been taken by surprise.

So why had I been Lee with Ma Gamble? It had been the perfect time to reveal my true identity. I'd get the satisfaction of telling her to get her podgy nose out of everyone's business and she'd get the satisfaction of badmouthing me to everyone in Wiltshire. A win-win solution all round.

But I'd put one over on Ma Gamble. It was even better than the times I'd swiped things from her shop, because then, she'd known I was at it and was waiting to catch me. This time, she was totally deceived. Ma Gamble, who thought that she knew everyone in Stoneguard better than anyone else, tricked by a pleasant voice and a clothes swap. Liza Haven one, Ma Gamble zero.

My stomach grumbled. Clearly peanut butter and biscuits weren't enough and my body had decided it was time for lunch. I was about to open the fridge to poke around again when I remembered what Ma had said about Lee always going to our mother's house for lunch on Sunday.

No. No way. I'd seen her this morning on the hill. That was more than enough for me.

She'll be worried you didn't come, Lee's voice said in my head, like a conscience.

'Bull crap, she probably can't even remember what day it is,' I said out loud, but there must have been something in the air that made me more susceptible to moral acts because I went to the phone and picked it up and dialled the number I remembered from my childhood, wondering what on earth I was going to say to my mother.

The phone rang a few times and then it was picked up. 'Haven residence,' said a calm, competent female voice. 'Serena speaking.'

'Hi there, Serena, it's Lee.'

'Hello, Lee,' said the voice, warmth in it now as well. 'I've just arrived to see how your mum's getting on. I hear you were out on rescue duty last night.'

'Yes, well . . .' I couldn't think of any pleasantries that applied to finding your mother nearly naked walking up a hill in the middle of the night. 'Anyway, I was just ringing to ask if my mother was expecting me for lunch?'

'I think she's very tired today – from last night, you know. She seemed happy with a quiet bowl of soup in her room.

She's a bit out of it today, a little confused, but she's all right, quite placid.'

I pictured her in the moonlight, standing with a blank face. *Where am I?* A shiver went across my skin.

'You take today off, Lee, you take a rest, you deserve it. We're all fine over here.'

It was the kindness, the warmth that got me. Here I was, offering excuses not to see my ailing mother, and this woman was happy to have me do it.

'No, no, I should come over,' I said, because Lee would say it. She'd mean it, though.

'Really, there's no need. She's resting quietly. You have an afternoon to yourself, or do something nice with Will.' Was there no one who didn't know Lee's love life? Except for me, of course.

'Well, if you're sure.'

'I am. We'll see you later in the week.'

'All right then. Bye.' I tried to add her name but realised I'd forgotten it between the beginning of the conversation and now. 'Bye,' I repeated instead.

'Bye, Lee.'

Well. That had gone better than I'd thought. In fact, everything had gone better than I'd thought since I got here to Stoneguard, and it was all down to my name change. It was actually easier being Lee. People got on with you, they didn't argue with you. They assumed you were kind and honest. You were the apple of everyone's eye and after all this time as a bad seed I deserved to be an apple, especially if I was going to have to stay here for a little while longer.

But I wished I knew what was happening with my sister.

Ice Cream ✿

Lee's and my grandfather was a dairy farmer called David Haven. His own great-grandfather, John Haven, began the herd with a single cow, fulfilling the needs of his own small family, and slowly acquired more cattle. John's son, my great-great-grandfather, also called David Haven, built the walls around the pastures following one of the Enclosure Acts or another. According to modern archaeologists, the Haven dairy farm stone walls incorporate pieces of several megaliths which were probably lifted from an avenue which once spanned the distance between the River Kennet and the large Neolithic stone circle overlooking Stoneguard, which gives the village its name.

(I'm quoting almost verbatim from the family business brochure, by the way. I'm assuming it's more or less accurate; even if it isn't, it was the catechism of my childhood, so it might as well be, as far as I'm concerned. There's a nice picture of my ancestors for you: exclusively male, enclosers, cow-collectors and looters of ancient monuments for building materials.)

Anyway, I've never understood politics or the wording of family business brochures, but the enclosure somehow meant that my family were able to grow their herd in leaps and bounds or however cows grow, acquiring a reputation for fine breeding stock and for fresh, sweet milk and cream, supplying the families in the local area. By the time my grandfather David Haven inherited Haven Dairy in 1935, it was one of the biggest in south Wiltshire.

Whenever I think back to that time in my family history, back before my mother was born, I picture a vast field of cows, packed tight as sardines, mooing and jostling and banging their fat dangling udders against each others' legs, leaking milk and shitting. I see my grandfather as a protruding human head and shoulders over the bovine surge, as if he is drowning in his own cattle. This isn't the official image; the photograph in the brochure, which is also on the wall of my mother's former office – now Lee's – shows him dressed in a rather stiff suit and dusty-looking hat, with his hand on the horned head of a single black-and-white cow. In the background, you can see the part of the wall that was nicked off the prehistoric site, and next to it is the charmingly old-fashioned truck which used to bring the milk in urns to the station in Swindon and thence all the way to the milk-starved masses in London.

There were no cows any more at Haven Dairy. The barn had been transformed into the ice-cream factory, and a new archeologically-correct stone wall, containing no ancient artefacts, had been built between the factory and the farmhouse where my mother had grown up. The fields had been sold off long ago.

The farmhouse was whitewashed and thatched, with roses around the door. When we were children, Lee and I used to visit our grandparents here and our grandmother would give us milky tea and hard ginger biscuits. My grandmother was always in her kitchen, and my grandfather was always outside. Even though all the cows were gone and my grandfather was retired, he would walk the fields as if he were visiting ghosts.

They died when Lee and I were seven, first my grandfather in the summer and then my grandmother in the autumn, as if she couldn't bear to be without him. I'd asked my mother if we could move in and live there, in the low-ceilinged rooms that were always warm, but she sold it to a company which rented it out as a holiday cottage.

As a teenager, I'd sometimes hang out with the sons of the families who rented it, from London or Manchester or America. They never invited me in and I never told them I knew every room as well as my own face. This morning there was a big car parked outside, one of those clunky ones beloved by families with several children, and a row of wellies lined up outside the door.

Ice Cream Heaven's administrative offices were in a purpose-built brick building off to one side of the factory barn. It was late Monday morning by the time I opened the metal swing gate and walked down the tarmacked path to the offices. There were several cars parked outside.

Lee still wasn't back. I'd tried to go to bed early last night, mostly because there wasn't anything else to do around here, but my back had started throbbing from inactivity and damp, and it had kept me up until nearly two in the morning, stretching and watching rubbish on TV. The phone, which I'd put beside my pillow, had woken me up at half nine, bolting me upright in the bed with immediate visions of my mother wandering around like a zombie.

It was Mouse, sounding rushed and flustered. 'Oh! Good morning! Are you okay?'

'Yes,' I answered, reaching back and spreading my hand out over my lower spine. It was better this morning, but I didn't think Mouse wanted to know that.

'Oh good. I was wondering since you're not here yet, and Ma Gamble said you were looking a little pale yesterday, I thought you might have a cold or something. Is your mobile switched off?'

'I think it's broken.' Where was the 'here' I was supposed to be? A safe guess, given the day and time, would be Ice Cream Heaven. But why would Mouse be calling about that? 'Are you there already?' I risked.

'Yes. I couldn't believe I got here on time this morning, Pheebs was an absolute terror and refused to put on her sandals, finally I had to take her to the childminder in her slippers. Upsy Daisy ones, she takes them to bed with her. Anyway I was so excited to show you I could actually do it, nine o'clock on the dot, and then you weren't here.'

'Sorry,' I said. Lee must have hired Mouse, I could only imagine out of pity. Typical. So was Lee always so punctual that being half an hour late on Monday morning was worthy of a check-up phone call?

Scratch that thought. Of course she was.

'Oh well, can't be helped, I'm sure I'll manage it again one day. Did you oversleep? I didn't wake you up, did I?'

'No, no, just running a little bit late this morning.'

'I know all about that! Well, it's a relief to hear you're not dead in a ditch somewhere. You'll be in soon then?'

'Sure.'

'Great. I'll hold the fort here. See you soon!' Mouse rang off, and I swung my legs out from beneath the duvet. I was standing up when the phone rang again.

'Hi,' said Mouse again as soon as I answered it. 'Sorry, forgot to ask, the whole reason I called you before was because Dennis was asking for the invoices for D.F. and Co. Do you know if you've printed them already and where they are?'

'You've – checked the usual places?'

'Yes, they're not there, and I checked three times because you know I often overlook things.'

'Okay, well, can you print them yourself?' I bent over double, the hand that wasn't holding the phone pressed flat to the floor. Yeah, that felt good. Marv would be pleased with my flexibility.

There was a pause. 'Um, well . . . don't you have your laptop at home?'

'Oh. Yeah, I do.' Crap. 'Are you sure you don't have the invoices anywhere else?'

Another pause. 'No, I wouldn't have them, no. Are you okay, Lee?'

'Of course,' I said, upside down with my hair brushing the carpet. 'Why?'

'You sound a little funny, that's all.'

I straightened up. 'Everything's fine. So you need me to come in with the laptop, then.'

'Yes, please.'

'Right. I'll be twenty minutes.'

'Okay,' she said, instantly bright. 'See you then. I'll hold the fort – oh dear, I already said that, didn't I? Well, see you in a tick anyway. Bye!'

To tell the truth, it was more like sixty minutes before I'd taken a shower, had a good stretch out, got dressed in Lee's clothes and walked through the churchyard and down Dog Shit Path (carefully avoiding the lumps this time), up the hill, through the stone circle, down the other side, over the stile, and down the lane to what used to be Haven Farm and now was Ice Cream Heaven. The stone circle was whirring and clicking with Japanese tourists and I walked through it without really looking at anything, which was quite a feat while passing twelve-foot monoliths. But the grass was wet and cool, the sky was blue, the air was green-scented and fresh, and by the time I got to the cottage door I felt okay, or as okay as I could reasonably expect to be when walking through a door I'd never expected to darken again.

I stepped inside. Somewhere in the back of my mind I expected an alarm to go off, shouting, 'Wrong twin! Wrong twin! This twin does not belong!' as if my mother's intentions for her business were wired into the building's electricity. But all that greeted me was a small squall of chaos.

The office itself had hardly changed since I was a child. It was open-plan, occupying nearly the entire building except for what I knew were a small kitchen and two store rooms at the back. The walls were stark white, the large desk in the centre of the room was gunmetal grey, the carpet was brown. Framed photographs lined the walls, though they failed to lend any cheer or personality. The sole bit of beauty in the room came from a vase of yellow freesias on the grey desk. Their petals drooped and their scent, as it reached me, was rather bruised.

Mouse, in another shapeless patterned dress, was busy at a photocopier in the corner of the room. Her back was to me, but as soon as I walked in she turned around and began to hurry in my direction. A pile of papers fell off the shelf behind her and scattered diagonally to the floor.

'You're here!' she cried, and I felt as if I'd stepped in a time machine back to Saturday night.

'I am. Good morning. Sorry, the battery on my alarm clock must have gone.'

'Oh, the same thing happened to Dr Percy last week. Is that a new handbag?'

It wasn't, but it wasn't Lee's, either. It was mine; I'd grabbed it without thinking about this charade I seemed to be playing. 'Yes, it is. How are you doing?'

She threw up her hands. 'Well, I'm photocopying those purchasing orders. It's three copies of each, isn't it?'

'Yes.'

'Jonny's in the back getting some flags and wobble boards ready.'

So Jonny Whitehair was still around. The silver Vauxhall outside must be his; the dusty estate car screamed 'Mouse!' all over. The others must belong to the factory workers and the ice-cream van drivers.

I sniffed the air. 'Any chance of a coffee?'

'Of course.' Mouse scurried off to the kitchen. I wondered what her official job title was. Receptionist? Secretary? Dogsbody? She couldn't be up to much if she wasn't sure how many copies to make or how to print out an invoice.

Oh well, not my problem. I was just filling in. I went to my mother's desk, now my sister's, and sat down in the leather chair. I'd never sat here before. Rebellious as I might have been, I'd never dared.

It felt like a leather chair in the middle of a bland office.

I unzipped Lee's laptop bag and powered the thing up. That was a difference in the office; there was an up-to-date PC on Jonny's desk, and another on what I assumed was Mouse's. The photocopier was a new one, and there was a laser printer next to it. At least Ice Cream Heaven moved slightly with the times.

Lee was supremely organised, of course. Once the laptop was going, it was easy enough to find the folder marked *Invoices* and to select the most recent one for D.F. & Co. I sent it to the printer, three times to be safe. It seemed a pretty simple thing to come all this way to do, so I flicked through the papers in Lee's in-tray. Purchasing orders, promotional material, press clippings, a big violet folder marked *Production Schedule*, a Post-It note dated this morning and saying *Edmund*

Jett rang, pls return the call. There was nothing with big red flags on it saying *Must Do Now!* so it could probably all wait till Lee got back. Whenever that was.

The laptop chimed with new emails, so I checked them. There were seven in the ICH file, two more in the ASG file, one in the Mum file. In the Personal file, there were a dozen unread messages – six that had come in this morning, four last night, and still those two emails from Will from yesterday. *Good morning* and *Good afternoon*.

My fingers tapped on the keys, lightly enough not to depress them. If I didn't reply to messages from Will, he might think Lee had gone off him. There was no danger, really; I'd only been attracted to him because of the alcohol. In the cold light of day, he'd probably appeal to me as much as a wet fish. Or a bowl full of ice cream. Wet-fish-flavoured ice cream. That was it.

'Here you go, coffee.' Mouse put a mug down near my elbow, on a little handmade ceramic coaster. 'Where are your flowers today?'

I glanced at the wilting freesias. Of course Lee brought in fresh ones once a week. 'I was going to bring some from the garden, but I thought I'd get here as soon as I could.'

'Oh. Well, these are probably good for another day?'

'Probably. I've printed out the invoices for you.'

'Thank you! I'll give them to Dennis. But I hope you don't mind . . .' Annabelle bit her lip, her brow furrowing with worry.

'Don't mind what?' From the way she was looking, I wouldn't have been surprised if she said she'd set the factory alight by mistake.

'I told him I'd just email the invoices straight to D. F. and Co.'s head office. Is that okay? I know I should have checked, but you said you were going to be here in a few minutes and

209

he waited, but then the driver had to go and I hated to ring you if you were getting ready to come in.' She spat it all out in a breathless stream, twisting her hands together as if she really were admitting arson.

'You're going to send the invoices electronically?'

'Yes. I'm sorry if it's not okay. I should have checked, I really should have. I'm sorry. But you know, I rang them first to make sure it was okay if they got it a little bit late and by email, and they said it was fine.'

'Well then, that's good.'

She frowned even more. 'It is?'

'Of course it is. It sounds like you did the right thing. It's more efficient for them to have their invoices on the computer, I'd think. But anyway, you cleared it with them first. So it's fine.' She didn't look like she believed me, so I said, 'Well done.'

She broke into wreaths of smiles. 'Oh, that's fantastic. I thought as soon as I said it to Dennis that maybe I was making a mistake, but he seemed to agree with me so we went ahead. I'm glad it's okay. I'll ring you first next time.'

I took a drink of my coffee. She'd made it how Lee liked it, with milk and one sugar, but I needed the caffeine badly enough not to care. 'There's no need, M— Annabelle. You seem to have good instincts for this sort of thing.'

'Oh.' She blushed. 'Anyway, I'll let everyone know you're in, and they should be in here in a few minutes.' She scurried out of the room.

That confirmed it. Lee must have hired Mouse out of friend-ship or charity. The woman couldn't make the simplest of decisions by herself, and this wasn't the sort of thing you bothered the head of the company about. How many children did she have, anyway? You'd think that would inspire some sort of decision-making ability, being responsible for young lives. But maybe it just cauterised the adult part of your brain.

I went back to Lee's computer. Probably I should read the Ice Cream Heaven emails, try to do some work, or at least fake it. I opened the ASG folder instead, thinking maybe that could be the clue I'd been looking for yesterday. Maybe it stood for Absconding Sister . . . Gossip? Getaway?

Alzheimer's Support Group. The return addresses were all the same; it was an email loop. Right. Well, fair enough. Lee probably wanted support, or more likely, she wanted to offer support to people in the same situation she was in, people who had relatives with Alzheimer's.

And obviously it was easier to exchange support with total strangers over the internet, than with her own sister.

I gritted my teeth and clicked straight over to the Personal file. The ten messages on top were all from people who had been at the dance, and from their subject lines they were obviously thank-yous. I opened the bottom message, the first one from Will.

To: Lee <emilyhaven@icecreamheaven.co.uk>
From: Will <will@naughtonhall.com>
Date: 23 August 09:54:06
Subject: Good morning

. . . Though I have to confess that I nearly didn't make it home last night. A bloodthirsty gang of owls ambushed me as I passed the pub, stole my wallet and my shoes and left me for dead. Those birds can pack a punch.
W x

That was it? A lame joke about getting mugged by owls, which had been my idea in the first place? I'd been expecting some smarmy compliments, at least.

211

And what was with the email address? *Naughtonhall.com*, as if he had to advertise the fact that he lived in this big old aristocratic house? Lee totally had to drop this guy.

I felt no compunction about opening the later email, now.

To: Lee <emilyhaven@icecreamheaven.co.uk>
From: Will <will@naughtonhall.com>
Date: 23 August 14:35:50
Subject: Good afternoon

Alarmingly, in my last email I seem to have forgotten to mention how ravishing you looked last night. 'So shows a snowy dove trooping with crows', etc etc. I must have been hungover to neglect it, please do forgive me.
Your legs looked great, too, Juliet.
Fancy lunch tomorrow? I'll pick you up at one.
Romeo x

Ah. That was more like it. Well-worn compliments, a pretentious quotation, a fatuous apology and the invitation that couldn't conceivably be refused. But it would be refused. I was sure not to fancy Will today, and I had no desire to have a cosy little lunch with him in a country pub somewhere. I hit *Reply* and rubbed my hands together, thinking of what to say to turn him down flat. Charmingly, of course, as Lee would, if she ever had the guts to say no to Will.

'Afternoon,' called a jovial voice, and I reluctantly looked up to see Jonny Whitehair emerging from the back room. In twelve years, his stomach had grown and his hair had gone white enough to match his name, though it was so perfectly snow-white that I suspected some chemicals had been involved. Jonny must have been in his mid-sixties by now, but his hair was still abundant, combed back from his forehead in a glossy white wave. He wore a short-sleeved shirt with several index cards and a ballpoint pen stuck into the chest pocket, and a flowered tie.

Jonny Whitehair would never change. He'd be laid out in his grave wearing a short-sleeved shirt with index cards in the pocket and a flowered tie. Still, I didn't have to force the smile I gave him. 'Hi, Jonny.'

'My favourite girl,' he said, and kissed me on the top of my head. He smelled like the spearmint gum he'd started chewing when he quit smoking, and for a minute I missed all the years of kisses on the top of my head from Jonny Whitehair. Though in those days, it had been his favourite girls, plural, and pieces of gum sneaked to us when my mother wasn't looking.

'How are you doing?' I asked him, though I knew what he'd say, the exact words. *Oh, can't complain.*

'Oh, can't complain.' He went to his chair and sat down, leaning back and putting his feet on the desk. This used to drive my mother crazy, which was one reason I liked it so much.

'How's Hazel?'

'Oh well, the arthritis is getting to her something awful, but you know Hazel. She won't say a word. We got those sponge things to help her with the cutlery on Saturday; she has trouble holding it, her hands.' He curled his hands up into two stiff Cs, the shape of arthritis.

'She must miss doing her needlework.' I had no idea how I remembered this; I hadn't thought about Hazel Whitehair in ten years at least. But being in the same room as Jonny made me recall their tiny cottage, stuffed full of cross-stitch. Cushions, tablecloths, framed samplers. You could barely move in there.

The adults in my childhood world were old, now. They used to be powerful, tall and knowing, vital and eternal.

Somewhere in the past years they'd shrunk. They'd become mortal. They were curled with arthritis or night-wandering the hills.

'She'll never stop doing the bloody needlework,' Jonny said in a mock-growl, and I laughed.

The outside door opened and Mouse bustled back in, followed by Glenys, Brenda and Doris. Glenys was Charlie's mother and Archie's aunt, Brenda was Archie's mother-in-law, and Doris – well, Doris was related in some way to the entire town, it seemed. Her ancestors had bred like flies, and so had Doris. Like Jonny, these three women had all been working at Ice Cream Heaven for forever. It didn't look like Lee had changed the staff much, except for hiring Mouse.

They'd taken off the protective clothing they wore in the factory while they were making the ice cream, but Brenda still wore her white mesh hat. They all smelled strongly of raspberries. 'Morning,' said Doris to me. 'I heard your alarm clock's broken, eh?'

'I wish I needed an alarm clock,' Mouse said wistfully. 'Jo and Mimi jump on the bed every morning at six sharp.'

'I know, can you believe it?' I said cheerfully. 'I think it needs a new battery.'

'That's what I said when I heard you weren't in yet. I said, her alarm clock needs a new battery.' Glenys shook her head sadly, in the manner of a Cassandra who has predicted catastrophe to an unbelieving public. 'Same thing happened to Dr Percy last week.'

'Archie says the dance was good fun, eh?' said Doris.

'It was great,' said Mouse. 'I haven't had so much fun in ages.'

'It turned out really well,' I said.

'Your sister didn't make it, though?'

'No, she was too busy at the last minute.'

'Is that a new handbag?' Brenda asked.

'Yes, I got it in Swindon, do you like it?'

'Ooh, yes. Quite sporty.'

'And how's *your mother*?' Doris's voice hushed for the last two words, as if she were speaking of the dead.

'About the same.'

'Ah.' They all nodded. I wondered how many times I was doomed to repeat this same conversation, exchanging the same information with people who were slightly different versions of each other. It was as if any topic was a piece of gum that had to be chewed and chewed repetitively until all the flavour had been sucked out of it. And then chewed a few more times, for good measure.

'Where's Dennis?' asked Jonny, rubbing his hands together as if he was waiting for Christmas dinner.

'On his way. He's picking up the spoons, eh?'

The three women were also showing signs of age. Doris was beginning to show the rounded shoulders of osteoporosis, ironic in someone who had worked with milk and cream for nearly forty years. Brenda's hair was grey and cropped short in an old lady cut. Glenys's hair was dyed a shade of mahogany that never occurred in nature, but she had deep grooves of wrinkles lining her cheeks and forehead and joining the corners of her nose and mouth. Aside from the whole going out of her mind thing, my mother was actually better preserved than her employees.

I wondered why they were all standing in the office, instead of making ice cream. They didn't have a daily inspection, or anything? Surely after more than half a lifetime, they could get on with it and make the ice cream by themselves. They were Ice Cream Heaven's dream team, hand-picked by my mother when she started up the company in the 1960s, and supplemented by other workers according to season and demand. Maybe this was a little ritual, everyone coming in to trade gossip on a Monday morning. Was I supposed to say something, or make tea for everyone?

They weren't looking at me expectantly, though. They seemed to be looking at the door. Presumably waiting for Dennis, who was Doris's nephew, and his—

His spoons.

The truth hit me with a cold splatter at the same time that the door opened and Dennis walked in. He had his hands in cold-proof gloves, because he was holding a plastic freezer tray full of 500 ml cartons of ice cream, and spoons.

Shit. It was a shelf-life tasting day.

'I've got Vanilla Valhalla, Pistachio Paradiso and Toffee Euphoria that are six months gone, and Holy Moly Melt, Bee's Knees, Nutty Nirvana and Banana From Heaven that are twelve,' Dennis announced. Everyone said, 'Mmm,' excitedly. Jonny smacked his lips. They all reached for spoons.

I eyed the cartons. They were all so . . . cold. And sweet. I recalled the way the fat from the cream coated your tongue, how the frozen stuff shocked your mouth, ached on your dentalwork, sent a shiver down your spine. Melting and leaving nothing. A hundred thousand dinnertimes when I'd sat and watched the hill of ice cream in my dessert bowl transform itself into milky soup while my mother watched me. Long hot afternoons freezing in the back of the van, waiting for a customer, and days in the glass-fronted goldfish bowl of the ice-cream parlour with my wrists aching and chilblains on my hands while the weather called me to be outside. Photo shoots with cones and sundaes and chocolate drips on your ice-pink dress, bought especially, which you were supposed to keep clean.

The melting was the worst. It melted so easily, as if to

remind you of impermanence. Solid into liquid, with that slimy state in between, slick and cold, meaning nothing. And then to recapture it, you had more. Always more. An endless circle of ice cream, never filling you up, empty as loveless hands.

I swallowed the spit in my mouth. Doris and Glenys were already prising the lids off, exposing flat frozen surfaces, white and cream and brown and yellow.

'Oh, and Rum Raisin Rapture,' added Dennis. He popped open another lid.

Raisins, plump with juices. They studded the ice cream like fat brown flies. The squish between your teeth and the burst of soft innards.

The employees of Ice Cream Heaven hung over the tubs, licking their lips. I stepped backwards, sending the executive chair spinning backwards on its wheels across the carpeted floor.

'Are you all right, Lee?' Mouse asked. Her spoon was touching the virgin vanilla.

'You look a little green, eh?' Doris added.

'I'm not feeling that great, suddenly,' I said. Everyone's face instantly registered concern.

'You probably really are coming down with something,' Mouse said. 'Ma Gamble did say you didn't look well yesterday.'

'And you never sleep late, even without an alarm clock,' Glenys added. 'You must be sick, I was saying so earlier.'

'Something going around,' said Dennis.

'Yes,' I said. I was never sick, hated fussing, and viruses bounced off me as if I were wearing plate mail. But I'd been defeated by a few tubs of ice cream. I couldn't eat it. Not without blowing my Lee cover. 'I think I'd better go home and lie down. I don't want to spread any germs.'

217

'Do you want me to drive you home?' Jonny's spoon already had a scoop of Pistachio in it, but he put it down on the tray.

'No, no, I think fresh air will do me good. Honestly, Jonny,' I added, because he was about to protest.

'We'll do the testing tomorrow,' Doris said, beginning to replace the lids on the tubs.

'No!' They had all begun to put down their spoons, but they stopped and looked at me. 'I mean, there's no sense in changing the schedule. You're all experts, you can do the tasting.'

They all continued to look at me. They appeared to be shocked. I guess it was unheard of for Lee Haven to turn down ice cream.

'It's fine. Really, you do it. I trust you.'

Silence. At last, Jonny said, 'Well, if you're sure.'

'Of course I'm sure. I'll just go home, and I'll be back tomorrow.' I reached for my handbag with one hand and for the laptop with the other.

Mouse made a small alarmed noise, diverting my attention. She was biting her lip in the way I'd come to recognise. 'Is there something wrong?' I asked her.

'I – well, it's basically only the invoices, really. I sort of need—'

'Oh. No problem. I'll leave the laptop here for you then. They're right in the "invoices" file, you can't miss them.'

Everyone was still staring at me. It was beginning to get a little bit weird, as if my own home town had turned into the setting for *The Wicker Man*.

'You do know how to use the laptop, don't you?'

'Of – of course I do, that's fine, yes.' She swallowed visibly.

'Great.' Quickly, I closed the windows with Will's emails,

and was about to shut down the email programme, but looking at the folders reminded me. 'Actually, would you mind having a look through the ICH file on my email, to see if there's anything that needs dealing with today?'

Mouse looked as if she were a deer in headlights. 'Um. Yes. Okay. If you're positive you don't mind.'

'I'm positive.'

'You're sure you won't stay for some ice cream?' Jonny had recovered enough from whatever it was to pick up his spoonful of Pistachio. It had begun to go soft around the edges.

'No, no, thank you, best get to bed.' I made quickly for the door and had it halfway open when I remembered something else. 'And could you please ring Ma Gamble, Mou— Annabelle, and ask her what her order was she wanted sending around this morning? She told me yesterday but it's slipped my mind.'

'Um . . .'

'Thanks. Thank you, everybody! I'll see you tomorrow.'

The scent of grass and animal dung on the air outside had never been so welcome. I walked quickly, aware that they would be watching me from the window. I rubbed the back of my hand against my forehead, as if to feel for a fever. It wasn't until I'd reached the gate and closed it behind me that I felt I'd escaped.

And not only the shelf-life tasting, either. I'd be long gone by the time Will turned up to take me to lunch. And if he came to the house, I'd have the perfect excuse not to answer the door.

Secrets

Of course the one thing I'd forgotten about living in a small town is that people don't leave you alone if you're ill. The house phone started ringing as soon as I got in. I answered it the first few times, hoping it was Lee, but when I'd had the third neighbour asking if I was okay and could they bring me anything, and by the way wanting to have a nice cosy gossip about Saturday night, and by the way had I heard that Rufus Fanshawe's BMW had been found on the M6 outside of Preston, I decided enough was enough and I turned off the ringer. Lee could ring my mobile.

Nobody else had rung my mobile, to offer work, for example. Huh. Big surprise.

I drew the curtains in the front room, moved the coffee table out of the way and treated myself to a good long session of Tai Chi to loosen up my body. I'd decided I needed more of a workout and was poking through Lee's CDs to see if she had absolutely anything kick-ass amongst the acoustic singer-songwriters, when the doorbell rang. I ran upstairs and peeped out of the guest bedroom window, keeping myself to one side so I wouldn't be visible.

I spotted the car first. Who wouldn't? An Aston Martin DBS V12 in British Racing Green, such a thing of beauty and speed and elegance that I had to catch my breath. It was parked on the street and I was one storey up but I could practically feel the vibrations of its 6-litre V12 engine, taste the chunky responsiveness of the steering.

I lusted after it. God knows if I'd be able to drive it, even if I were to get behind the wheel. It was like heaven dangling just out of reach.

Then I saw a movement on the path below, and I realised who the car belonged to. Will, of course, here to pick me up for lunch, or to check on me if he'd found out I was supposedly ill.

He was wearing casual cotton trousers and a short-sleeved blue polo shirt, and he had committed that aristocratic fashion crime of draping a light jumper over his shoulders, which in my opinion instantly made any man resemble a little old lady.

That was a relief, anyway. I could never in a million years fancy someone who draped a jumper over his shoulders. He was looking around, clocking the drawn curtains in the living room. He appeared to be giving the bird-table more than a casual glance, and for a moment I wondered if he was looking for the spare key to let himself in, and then it occurred to me that he might have a spare key of his own, and then he stepped out of sight near the door and rang the bell again.

We waited, both invisible, for longer than I would have expected. Then he reappeared walking back down the path. My perspective meant that he was foreshortened closer to the house, but as he walked toward his car he became taller. He opened the door without having to unlock it – *watch out, Honourable Will, someone's nicking pricey cars and driving them to Preston* – and climbed in. I had to admit, the jumper didn't quite distract from the purely aesthetic effect of a high-spec

221

man climbing into a high-spec car. I heard the gorgeous roar as he started the engine and then he pulled off, slower than I would have.

But not much slower.

I retreated from the window and went back to my workout. First, though, I had a sneaky peek at the front door, in case Will had left anything behind. A note, flowers, a footprint. Nothing. Good thing I didn't actually like him, or else I'd feel a bit miffed.

Someone else came to the door while I was doing some cool-down stretches, knocking rather than ringing the bell, but I didn't bother checking this time. When I went to the kitchen to get a glass of water and maybe poke around with thoughts of lunch, I noticed that someone had pushed a note through the letter box. It was written in a crabbed hand on the back of half a gas bill. *Dear Lee, J said you were ill, left something on your doorstep for you, pop it in for 30 mins at 180°. Love, Hazel.*

In LA, nobody ever left anything unsolicited outside your door except for graffiti and junk mail or, if you were unpopular, flaming paper bags full of dog shit. I opened the door and found a white covered casserole dish. When I picked it up it was still warm. I brought it to the kitchen and opened it: tuna pasta casserole, the kind made with tinned cream of mushroom soup and frozen peas, and crumpled-up crisps sprinkled on top. Hazel Whitehair had never really fitted in with the organic wholefood school of cooking.

I scooped up a plateful and stuck it in the microwave, and then ate it at the kitchen table with a glass of milk. It was salty, but comforting, a bit like Jonny's kiss on the top of my head. I could picture Hazel holding a rolling-pin in her curled-up hands to smash up the crisps.

In the shower, I tried to plan ahead. It had been nearly

three days since Lee had left, and she'd refused to tell me when she'd be back. There was a real chance that I was here for the foreseeable future. For today, at least, I could stall, and maybe tomorrow too, but soon I was either going to have to come clean with everyone, or renew my efforts to be Lee. With my belly full of neighbourly casserole, and my muscles relaxing comfortably in her shower, I was inclined to keep on with the latter, for the time being anyway.

Meanwhile, it was time for me to work on finding out where my sister had gone. Somewhere, deep down inside, I knew she was in trouble. The world felt out of step. Even if she wasn't admitting it, something was wrong with Lee.

And if she wasn't going to tell me why she'd disappeared, I'd have to find out for myself.

Two and a half hours later, I had found very little dust and only three items of interest. The downstairs didn't hold any secrets, except for some high-quality chocolate she'd stashed behind the mustard in the kitchen. She had a lot of photographs in the living room, whole shelves full of albums arranged by date. I didn't bother looking into the older ones, but I glanced at one or two of the more recent. They were full of get-togethers and parties, picnics and barbecues, company dos, country walks with friends, tubby children blowing out candles. Always groups of people, always my sister smiling. Lovely. Nothing I didn't know already. I put them back on the shelf.

The papers in her home office didn't reveal much either, though I put all the ones that had to do with recent Ice Cream Heaven business to one side to look at later. If I were to carry on as Lee, I'd have to have some idea of what was going on with the company. I could have a crash course tonight, with a glass of wine or two. My mother had thought I was too incompetent to have anything to do with the business; it would be supremely satisfying to prove her wrong.

I found Lee's bank statements. There weren't any records of her withdrawing any large amounts of cash for a holiday, or anything else out of the ordinary. Her bedside books were a historical romance, and a thick book about Alzheimer's. There was a crossword puzzle book and a packet of condoms in her bedside table drawer. Maybe she and Will had sex and then did word puzzles together. Wahoo.

But I didn't want to think about my sister's sex life with Will, so I shut the drawer quickly.

I found the most interesting things underneath her bed. This was totally predictable, but for some reason I looked there last, because as long as I'd known Lee, she'd never hidden anything. She did everything in pure sunlight, and why shouldn't she? But there was a basket underneath her bed, made out of soft woven jute, next to a single, solitary dust bunny.

I pulled out the basket, which had a yellow ribbon woven through it, proving that Lee even made sure the hidden things suited her décor. There were two rather scratchy woollen jumpers on top, homemade by the same person by the looks of them, and hideous. I smiled. Evidently someone had given Lee rather horrible Christmas presents and she didn't dare to throw them away. If this was the calibre of her deepest secrets, I wasn't going to come up with much. I tossed them aside and looked underneath. There were only three things there: a plastic bag, a paper folder and a heavy cream envelope.

The plastic bag clinked as I took it out. I dumped the contents on the hardwood floor: half a dozen bottles of nail varnish, two lipsticks and a container of cotton buds. Two of the nail varnish bottles rolled away from me, back under the bed.

I retrieved them and lined them all up on the floor. The lipsticks were still sealed in plastic, and the nail varnishes didn't look used, either. They were all different colours, one deep purple and another blood-red. There was even a turquoise one. Not really colours I could see my sister wearing.

Fashion mistakes? Bad impulse buys? But why, then, was she hiding them?

I stuck them back in the bag and turned to the folder, but I was disappointed again. It was full of documentation about the antique restoration and reselling business where Lee used to work part-time. I remembered her chattering on about it on the phone; she was always finding some lost treasure and getting all excited about researching its origins. I hadn't paid a whole lot of attention, as it was all Greek to me. The folder held some sales receipts for individual pieces, a few photographs of furniture, several auction catalogues. There was a flier for the business – Clifton's Furniture it was called, and two business cards: one for Timothy Clifton, owner, and one for Emily Haven, associate.

So what was secret about this? An old job, so what? There certainly wasn't anything incriminating in the folder, no evidence of stolen furniture or ripping off clients.

Maybe I was mistaken, and this wasn't a hidden box, after all. Maybe it was someplace she stashed stuff prior to throwing it away, so she could see if she really wanted it or not before she actually got rid of it. But I could never picture her throwing out jumpers that someone had knitted for her. She'd keep them out of sight and get them out every now and then when she was going to see the person, to make them feel better.

The last thing was the envelope. There was something ominous about a closed envelope. It could contain anything; maybe even something I didn't really want to see. I opened it.

It was a Christmas card, on heavy paper with a picture of a branch of mistletoe. Someone had written in the card with a fountain pen: *Next year in Bath? Love, T.*

It could all mean nothing. She could have picked up the cosmetics in a car-boot sale as a job lot because she liked one of the shades, and was keeping the other ones to give away. She could have filed the folder under her bed because she didn't have anywhere else to put it. The card could have been sent any time, it could mean anything. She'd been spending quite a bit of time in Bath a few years ago, with the antique stuff. With Timothy Clifton. Was that the *T* who'd signed the card?

I tried to remember if I'd had any conversations with Lee about Timothy Clifton. I remembered his name, and I recalled that Lee had always been very enthusiastic and talkative about her antiquing. I didn't remember anything about a relationship, and I didn't think I'd heard anything about it for a long time. But was that because there was nothing to discuss, or because Lee was keeping something from me? Or was it because I hadn't really been listening?

I turned over the card, and turned it over again. I sorted through the file. So much knowledge was public in Stoneguard, and my sister's life seemed so straightforward. Living in the same town she'd grown up in, with nothing ever changing. Genetically, we were identical. For half of our lives, we'd shared the same memories. I'd assumed I knew everything about her.

But it looked like I didn't.

Betrayal

At lunchtime on Tuesday I was contemplating another plateful of tuna pasta casserole when I heard my sister's voice.

'Hello,' she said, and I jumped in my chair and looked around wildly to see how she'd appeared without my hearing her come in. 'I'm not home right now,' she continued, and I realised it was the answering machine picking up a call I hadn't heard because I'd turned off the ringer the day before. I let out a sharp breath and sat back in my chair, heart banging in my chest.

'So please leave a message after the beep.' Beeeeep.

'Lee, it's Naomi here, over at your mother's. Mrs Haven is having a good day today, bright as a button she is, and she keeps asking to see you. Annabelle said you weren't well when I rang the office just now, but I thought maybe if you didn't think you're catching and you felt a bit more chipper later on this afternoon you'd like to pop round. All right then, cheerio!' Dial tone.

I swung my feet. On the one hand, I had no desire to see my mother. On the other hand, if I stayed away for too long, it would begin to look suspicious.

On the third, if she were lucid, it would be interesting to see how my mother treated Lee. It could help me fit in another piece to her puzzle. Maybe she'd know something about Timothy Clifton, if I could drop him into casual conversation. Since yesterday, I'd found nothing more about him in the house. He wasn't even in my sister's address book in her desk drawer.

I went upstairs to put on some make-up, then checked that the coast was clear of well-meaning Stoneguardians before I left the house. When I opened the door, I found another casserole, a basket of butter biscuits, and a pie.

I knocked on my mother's door. Since I'd left home, I'd always knocked when I visited; the big Victorian place had never felt like my home, and it certainly wasn't any more. Lee, as my mother's favourite daughter and caretaker, probably walked right in using her key, but I didn't have it and the door was locked, for obvious reasons. Yet another nurse answered, this one a comfortably middle-aged lady with a moustache on her lip and a ruddy dot of good humour on each of her cheeks. I wondered if it was usual to have so many different nurses, or if my mother just drove people so crazy that they couldn't stand it for long.

'Hi, Naomi,' I said. 'How are you?'

'Oh, wonderful, bless you for coming out when you're poorly.' Naomi enveloped me in a talcum-powder-scented hug, squeezed, and let go. 'What is it, something you ate?'

'No, just the time of the month, I think.'

'Oh, you poor dear. I used to suffer horribly before they yanked all my plumbing out. Well, you spend tonight curled up with a hot water bottle, and in the morning you'll feel right as rain. Mum's watching a bit of telly.'

I masked my astonishment at this woman calling my mother 'Mum', and the idea of my mother watching a bit of telly in the afternoon. My mother did not watch a bit of telly in the afternoon. She turned on the BBC news at ten o'clock in the evening, before going to bed. Otherwise it remained blank-screened and lifeless.

Naomi led me through the entranceway to the parlour, where again, I had to work hard to hide my surprise. I hadn't seen this room when I was here the other night. It wasn't the parlour any more. Not everything had changed; there was the same green striped wallpaper that made the ceiling seem more remote, the same green velvet curtains at the bay window. All the former furniture was there, heavy and glossy mahogany that seemed to weigh down the very air. But it had been shunted sideways to make way for a modern hospital-style bed that sat in the middle of the room. It had snow-white sheets, perfectly wrinkle-free pillowcases and a green flowered coverlet. Our mother's dressing-table had been carried down from her bedroom, and it sat against the far wall. The room smelled of air freshener. Beside the bed, not two steps from it, was a sturdy white metal chair. There was a green cushion on the seat and a knitted throw on the back, but it couldn't disguise the pot underneath the seat, nor the function of the chair.

That bed and the smell and the commode said so much. It said 'illness' and 'decline' and 'old age'. It was a more tangible sign than my mother's night wandering or her confusion on the side of the hill. It said nothing was the same, that my mother's strict house rules were gone forever. The room where she'd held court with clients and workers, where she'd been the most powerful person in her world and in mine, was now her bedroom and her bathroom and her prison.

It told me, though I hadn't precisely known this before, that my mother never had visitors other than my sister and now me. Or I hoped that she didn't. Because a person who accepted visitors here in this room where she slept and used the toilet could not be, could never be, my mother Abigail Haven.

I didn't know why I wanted her to be the same in this way, not to have lost her dignity that had cost me so much of my own happiness and freedom as a child. But the clenching in my chest told me that I did.

And I couldn't show this, not only because I was being Lee but because it was so contrary to everything I'd ever felt about my mother when I wished she'd unbend a little, be a little bit more human. A little bit softer.

So I said, 'Hi Mum!' cheerfully in the direction of the television. I could see the top of her head over the back of her leather armchair. The same one she'd sat in to tell me and Lee the news about her diagnosis during the Horrid Christmas. Beyond the chair, *Countdown* was on the TV. I walked around so that my mother could see me without getting up, Naomi following.

Mum raised her eyes from *Countdown* and glanced at me. 'Oh, it's you,' she said, in exactly the same words and tone that she'd used on the side of the hill early Sunday morning.

'Yes, I've come to visit. Naomi said you were asking for me.'

'I wasn't asking for you, I was asking for Emily. Why would I want to see you?'

A surge of – relief? Adrenaline? Anger? My mother knew who I really was. At this moment, anyway.

'No, Mrs Haven, this is Emily right here,' said Naomi, touching her gently on the arm. 'She was feeling poorly, but she wanted to see how you were today.'

'This is not Emily, it's Elizabeth. Be quiet, she's about to choose the letters.'

Naomi shot a look to me, a look of apology and sympathy.

I shrugged, in a way that might signify that I was used to such misidentification.

'Would you like a cup of tea, Emily?' the nurse asked me.

'I'd love one, thank you, Naomi.'

'Mrs Haven? Tea?'

Mum nodded curtly, not taking her eyes off the screen where the slender woman was pulling letter cards out and lining them up on a shelf. I walked with Naomi to the doorway, out of earshot of my mother.

'I'm so sorry,' Naomi whispered. 'I thought she was more herself today. She's never made that mistake before.'

'That's absolutely fine,' I said. 'It's quite understandable. After all, Liza and I do look alike. Thanks so much for the tea.' I touched her arm in a gesture of reassurance, and she went off to the kitchen, leaving me alone with my mother, whom I'd just betrayed.

It was a small betrayal. Nothing, really, next to the years of her making me feel like the second-class twin, the bad twin. And how could it hurt her, since she was already knee-deep or further in dementia? She most likely mistook people for each other all the time.

Except she'd never done it with me and Lee. I knew it, and would have known it even if Naomi hadn't told me. As soon as our eyes had met I could tell. Even in my mother's most addled mind, she knew the difference in worth between her two daughters.

I went back to her and sat down in another chair. It might have been the one I sat in at the Horrid Christmas, or it might have been Lee's. They were identical in every way. 'It's good to see you again, Mum,' I said.

Her eyes flickered to me. 'Do not lie, Elizabeth. You have no desire to see me.'

'I'm Emily, Mum.'

'I just told you not to lie, young lady.'

I sighed. 'All right, you've caught me. I'm Liza.'

'That's better. Why are you here?'

'Do you want the easy answer, or the complicated answer?'

'I see you haven't lost your smart mouth.'

I sat back in my chair and crossed my arms over my chest. 'Lee's asked me to look after some things for her.'

'Where is your sister? Why isn't she here?'

'No, it's my turn to ask some questions, Mum. Do you remember seeing me Saturday night, or rather Sunday morning? Do you remember why I was there? How I found you?'

She set her mouth into a firm line and focused on the television.

'You're still not taking any medication, are you?'

'Forgive me if I think it is the height of insolence for you to ignore my existence and then suddenly return to ask me the most personal of questions.'

'You're not taking anything, then.'

The smallest twitch of her eyebrow confirmed it.

'Mum, there are drugs you can try. I've seen advertisements for them – they're on American television, for Christ's sake. You can't just let this happen.' I gestured to the room, the bed, the commode.

'Elizabeth, it has already happened. My choices do not affect you. You do not belong here.'

'Here we are, a lovely cup of tea,' chirped Naomi. She had a tray in both hands and put it down on the mahogany table between our two chairs. The cups were my mother's best, normally saved for occasions of high state, for example when a business acquaintance came to tea. I personally had never drunk from one. My mother took hers without protest. Her standards had slipped.

'Emily?' It took me a second to realise that Naomi was

speaking to me, holding out my cup of tea. I took it.

'This is my daughter Elizabeth,' my mother said. 'I don't know where Emily is. Elizabeth refuses to tell me.'

'Mrs Haven, this is Emily right here.'

'Naomi, would you mind getting us some biscuits if you have any?' I asked. 'And maybe a glass of iced water for Mum, as it's quite stuffy in here. There's no hurry, though.'

The nurse nodded, understanding my tacit request for privacy, and bustled out.

'That woman is deluded,' my mother said. 'She can't even see that moustache on her face.'

'These are your best porcelain cups,' I said.

She looked at the cup in her hand. Her eyes appeared to go out of focus slightly, as if she were studying something in the air behind the cup. 'Oh,' she said.

'I don't know where Lee is,' I told her. 'I haven't seen her. When I got to Stoneguard, she was gone.'

'Gone?' my mother said, but she didn't look away from the air.

'She rang me to tell me she was all right, but that she had to go away for a little while. Did you know anything about this? Did she tell you she was going somewhere?'

'No.'

'Really? You don't remember her mentioning anything about it?'

'My memory is not what it was, for obvious reasons.' But despite her diction, her words were emptier than they had been before, as if a bit of her had suddenly gone away. On the telly, one of the contestants had come up with the anagram INAUDIBLE.

'I was wondering if you could help me to figure out where she's gone.'

'Why would I know? I never leave this house.'

I could contradict her on that, but an argument about her night wandering wouldn't help me find out about Lee. 'I thought you might know something about what she's been doing. Maybe you talked about her going on a holiday.'

'No, I don't think so.'

'She hasn't called you since Saturday?'

'No.'

'Are you sure?'

'Of course I am not sure.'

Some of the testiness was back, which was probably a good sign. 'Do you remember a man called Timothy Clifton? Lee used to trade antiques with him.'

Mum appeared to be thinking, though she could be watching television. I waited until the contestants had started doing maths to prompt her. 'Mum? Do you remember Timothy Clifton?'

'I don't know.'

'I think she worked pretty closely with him. You don't think he ever came to the house, or to the office?'

She shook her head. 'I don't know.' The cup on her lap listed to the left. I reached out and took it and put it back on the tray. Was this the way it was all the time, moments of clarity so sharp they were painful, and then these lapses downward?

'Nobody seems to know she's gone on holiday. Not at work, not her boyfriend. I just think it's weird.'

'A holiday,' she said. 'Maybe at the seaside. It's the best place for ice cream, you know.'

I knew. It was the only holiday we ever had, as children – days visiting Ice Cream Heaven parlours on the coast. Looking out of the windows at the other children playing on the sand. 'So you do know where she's gone?'

My mother frowned. 'No, I do not. What about the business?'

'I'm taking care of it.'

'*You* are?'

'Mum, I know you think I'm a waste of space, but I'm not. I can fill in for a few days without causing a disaster.' And I damn well would, now, to prove her wrong. I was going to study those Ice Cream Heaven documents tonight until I had them memorised.

'It's not for you.'

'We'll see about that. *You* could always come and take over again. If you cared about getting better instead of rotting away here in this parlour.'

'I will not get better.'

'You certainly won't if you—'

She turned to me, suddenly and fiercely. 'Where is your hairbrush? Where is your jumper? You cannot go to school in that state.'

'Biscuits and ice water!' announced Naomi, coming in with another tray.

'Where is your satchel? Where is Harvey? Why is it so quiet?' She seized my wrist.

'Oh dear,' said Naomi cheerfully, 'perhaps it's time for a rest.'

'I do not want a rest, we have the hygiene inspectors coming.'

'Maybe it is time for me to go,' I said, getting up, but she held fast to my wrist. Her fingers were as strong as they'd been Sunday morning. I stared at them. My mother had touched me so rarely. Probably more in the past two days than in the past twenty years. I could not prise her fingers one by one from my arm.

'Emily's a good girl,' she said to me.

'Yes, I know. Mum, I think I'd better go now.'

'It's *Deal or No Deal*,' Naomi told her.

'Oh, yes,' said my mother. She turned her attention to the television, and I pulled my arm away.

My phone beeped with a text as I was walking home, weaving between the strolling groups of tourists on the High Street. I checked it.

I'm fine so don't worry. Have u been telling people I'm ill? L xx

I rang her immediately, but it rang and rang and I swore aloud, knowing she had her phone right there in her hand, her thumb probably still on the *Send* button, and she wasn't answering. A fat tourist wearing a Milwaukee Brewers T-shirt gave me a dirty look for swearing in front of his wife, but I kept on walking. When it got to Lee's voicemail I hung up.

What the hell was she playing at with her cryptic little messages, making me turn into some sort of Nancy Drew to work out where she'd gone? She knew I hated it in Stoneguard; she knew I didn't like pussyfooting around. A short, hard kick to the midsection, or a high-speed escape – those were my preferred methods of solving problems, not this snooping and pretending and asking questions, not this sitting helplessly by and feeling guilty while my mother slid into death. It would serve Lee right if I took off and went llama trekking after all and left everything here to rot.

I stabbed her number again as I rounded the corner into Church Street. I'd leave a message telling her about how confused Mum was and how she'd been asking for her. That would bring her back.

I wasn't even listening to the phone ring, thinking about what I'd say, so I was taken by surprise when she actually answered.

Freedom

She's in a pub full of strangers. It flashes with fruit machines and a wide-screen television showing Sky Sports. The lights glint off her glass, which is full of red wine. It's been so long since she's had an alcoholic drink in the afternoon. She's always had to get back to work, or go to see Mum, or do something urgently. But now she's got nowhere to go, nothing to do except for being herself.

She turns her phone over in her hand. Well, she does have quite a bit to do. She could return some of those messages. Ring Liza.

She's actually been in this pub before. It's across from the hospital where she took her mother once, about this time last year. While Mum was going through the battery of tests, Lee slipped out to have a coffee. She could've had one in the hospital, but she had had enough of sickness and clinical spaces and she wanted something more normal. She wanted a few minutes free of worry.

It didn't work; worry followed her across the street and through the pub doors and sat with her while she drank her coffee and didn't read the magazine she'd bought. Guilt followed her too. Why had she really convinced her mother to come to the hospital for more tests? She wanted hope for

Mum, but she wanted hope for herself, too. She pictured a doctor coming in with a print-out of a brain scan, handing it to her, and saying, 'Good news. You're free.'

Lee looks across the pub at the table where she sat last year, and sees herself there, twisting her hands, biting her lip. She remembers how she finished the coffee quickly, scalding her mouth, to get back to the hospital. Not that there was anything to do there; she ended up sitting in a chair not reading her magazine again. But the uncomfortable chairs and the clinical smell felt like a slight penance for wanting freedom for herself more than health for her mother.

Now here she is again. Why? It's not as if she liked this place the first time. It's ugly and corporate-feeling, a chain pub like hundreds of others all over the country. Everything the Stoneguard Residents' Association loathes. She's ended up here because she doesn't know where else to go.

She left Preston this morning on the train. She couldn't wander the town any longer, and two and a half nights in that bland hotel were enough. So she took a chunk of cash out of her bank account and went to the station, where she lingered in front of the ticket counter for ages, trying to gather up the courage to buy a ticket to Stoneguard, or even Swindon. She couldn't do it. In the end she got a single to London, which was at least in the right direction. She could have gone to Edinburgh or something. So her conscience isn't totally dead yet.

London is more baffling than she's ever found it before. There are so many choices. The Underground map looks like a wall of doodles made by an exceptionally tidy child, and every name on it is a world of its own. Olympia, where the gods sit. Swiss Cottage, Elephant and Castle, Temple, Bank. Normally, she's confident on the Underground and can navigate to wherever she has to go. But today, she has no schedule. She could go to any of these places. In the end, she got on the yellow line, the Circle. The simplest one, going round and round in a soothing loop. She sat on the train until she recognised a station and then she got off. And came into this pub, ordered a large glass of red wine then turned her phone on, which was probably a mistake.

It beeped and rang as the messages and missed calls mounted up. It's not as if anyone else would be bothered, with the noise of the Sky Sports and the fruit machines and the drunks talking over their lagers in the corner, but each new noise sounded, to Lee, like the voice of another person in Stoneguard. Someone else she's left behind and let down. Then the beeping and ringing stopped, as if the phone were sulking.

Now she sips her wine and turns her phone over in her hand. Over and over, a small thing in metallic pink like a raspberry frozen in ice. If she threw this away, she could be disconnected from everyone. Nobody knows where she is. Nobody could find her, not for a few days anyway, and by then she could be gone again.

And then she thinks of what's going on while she's gone. It's been – she looks at the clock on the front of the phone – nearly seventy hours now. The charity ball is finished and everyone's talking about it, whether it went really well, or was a complete disaster. Did they miss her? Have they sent the police out after her? Have her flowers been watered in the garden, the house plants on the windowsills? Has Liza separated the recycling from the normal rubbish? How's Mum? What about Ice Cream Heaven? What does Will think?

No. If she starts worrying about everything, she'll get on another train back to Stoneguard, and she can't do that. She's not ready to explain why she took off in Rufus's car. Not ready to face the failure and the shame.

She chucks her phone back in her handbag, and takes a gulp of wine. From the corner, there's raucous laughter and when she glances over, the group of men are all looking at her. 'Awright, love?' calls over one of them. She looks away quickly.

In situations like this, a phone is a lifeline. It's a barrier to hold up, to say, 'I'm busy and don't want to be disturbed.' She takes the phone out again and begins to check who her missed calls are from. Annabelle, work, Will. Liza, over and over again. None from the police, so that's a good sign. Maybe. There aren't any from Tania or Rufus either, and thank goodness, none from Mum's phone. She doesn't feel brave enough to listen to her messages, but she does check the most recent texts.

HOPE U FEL BETTER SOON. From Archie.

Get well! Try lotus position and echinacea! Candace xxoo

She frowns. Echinacea isn't something you suggest to car thieves to make them better. Maybe nobody knows yet. The thought isn't particularly comforting, as it only reminds her how unlikely it is for her to be doing the things she's done.

'C'mon, gizzus a smile!'

She pretends not to hear the drunken order and to be wholly absorbed in writing a text message.

I'm fine so don't worry. Have u been telling people I'm ill? L xx

She sends it to Liza. It would be a relief if Liza was telling people she was unwell, that she was cooped up in the house. Liza would be able to lie like that quite convincingly. And it would make a change, Liza being the one to keep her out of trouble.

The phone begins ringing within minutes of her sending the text. She reaches for it to turn the ringer off, but someone speaks to her first.

'Drinkin' alone, love?'

One of the lager drunks from the corner has come over and is standing next to her table. It's impossible to tell how old he is; his face is mottled from alcoholism and his irises are pale blue in his bloodshot eyes. His trousers hang off his too-skinny hips.

'Yes, thank you.' She smiles – it's impossible not to smile, even to him – but only a little and she glances away quickly. Maybe if she's polite and distant, he'll realise she's not interested and go away.

'Well, that's no good. All right if I join you?'

'Oh, I'm, er, waiting for someone.'

'We can wait together.'

'Oh, thank you, that's very kind, but I think I'm all right here by myself, really.' She takes the phone in her hand, as an excuse for some privacy, but as soon as she picks it up it stops ringing. Bother.

'No no no, sweet'eart, I'd love to keep you company – know what I mean?'

She scrambles for a way to put him off, but he puts his half-empty pint down on the table next to her glass and slides onto the bench beside her. She can smell beer and cigarettes and unwashed clothes.

'I'm really quite happy by myself,' she says, but she knows it's futile. Her stomach sinks.

'Pretty little thing like you shouldn't be alone, yeah? So, do you live round here, love?'

'No.'

'That so? Where you come from?'

'Wiltshire.' She doesn't want to answer him, but she's trapped in this politeness, this knowledge that this is how you behave. But he's ignored politeness, he's got his own rules and he's using hers against her. He's mocking her. Surely he knows she doesn't want to talk with him. She clenches her hand.

'What's your name then?'

'It's—' Tell him anything, something untrue. But she can't think of anything. 'Emily.'

'Hi, Emily, I'm Puggy.' He holds out his hand for her to shake. There are black scabs on the back of his knuckles. He knows she doesn't want to touch him and he's waiting for it. A better person wouldn't care that he's smelly and drunk and scabby. They'd see the humanity inside this man and connect with that.

Her phone rings again. 'Sorry,' she says to the man and she grabs the phone and answers it. 'Hello?'

'Oh thank God for that, you *do* actually exist. Listen, when the hell are you getting back here, because I'm sick of taking care of your life?'

It's Liza, of course. And Lee doesn't hesitate in order to choose the best and kindest response, doesn't think about Liza or her feelings at all, actually. She feels the river of anger she's been holding back for so long burst its banks. It spurts out, through her clenched hands, though her gritted teeth, and she says back, 'It's about time you took care of something.'

'What's that supposed to mean?'

'I mean how many responsibilities have *you* got? How many have *you* ever had? It's your turn to find out how normal people live.'

'I never wanted to live like normal people.'

'Well, sometimes you have to. You have to put yourself in someone else's place and think about how they might feel. Not just swan off always thinking about yourself.'

'Like how you're swanning off now, for example? Where are you?'

She looks around the pub, her gaze settling on the table across the room where she sat a year ago. 'It doesn't matter.'

'Lee, I don't know if you noticed wherever you are, but it's a business day today. You've got a lot of people at Ice Cream Heaven who need you to be there. I've already run your party for you, and I didn't even want to be there. Then there's Mum—'

'My business. My party. *Our* Mum.'

'As far as I'm concerned, it's all yours. Mum has made it pretty clear she doesn't want me around anyway. And Jesus, she's really lost it, have you noticed?'

Lee stands up so fast that she bangs her hip on the table, but she doesn't care. Her heart is hammering and she feels sick. She doesn't even see the drunk next to her gazing at her in blurry astonishment. She can't see anything but the chair where she sat the last time she was here, alone, because her mother took her help for granted and her sister didn't want to know.

'Yes, I've noticed,' she says, 'because I see her every day. I talk with her, I deal with her, and maybe now you can see what it's like.'

'She's a prisoner in that house and half the time she doesn't understand what's going on. She watches *game shows*, Lee. How have you let her get like that?'

'I haven't let her get any way. She's got Alzheimer's, remember?'

'Never leaving the house isn't Alzheimer's, it's pure stubbornness. Have you even tried to talk her into getting some treatment?'

'Don't you dare judge me!'

She screams it. Around her, the voices cease. There's only the beeps of the fruit machine. Even the sport on the telly has gone quiet for a moment, as if terrified by her outburst.

But Lee's not terrified. She's riding a wave of anger and adrenaline, so fast she can't control it. There's a power in

243

letting go. Almost like how she felt when she was driving the stolen car through the dark without direction.

'I've been looking after you since the day we were born,' she continues. 'Every time I had something I loved, you spoiled it. Every time you got into trouble, I had to get you out.'

'I never asked you to—'

'And now that Mum's ill, you're the one who washed your hands of everything and left me to deal with it all. You think because she rejected you that you've got an excuse. Poor Liza, the black sheep, nobody loves you. You get to be tough and free and act like you don't care while I get to make every decision. You don't even know you're being selfish, it's so normal for you.'

'Right, *I* see what you want. I'm supposed to stick around where I'm not wanted, am I? Stay in this shitty little town and take the kicks and keep on smiling.'

'That's what I do, isn't it? It's your turn now. Let's see if you can do a better job.'

Liza starts to say something back, but Lee hangs up. Then she turns off the phone with a jab of her finger.

'Blimey. Got a mouth on yer, don't ya?'

She whirls around, bumping her hip again. The drunk is still sitting there, watching her.

'You can fuck off and all,' she says. She snatches her glass of wine, tosses what's left of it down her throat, then grabs her handbag and leaves the pub before he can even get a word in.

Outside, a cab is passing and she flags it down. 'Where to, love?' asks the cabbie.

She's breathing hard, as if she's been running or fighting. She glances back at the door of the pub, half-expecting the drunk man to come after her, maybe with his friends. Maybe she's just been very stupid, but right now she feels great. Her

244

hands tingle, her feet are dancing, her spirit is tripping on air. She gets into the cab and slams the door. 'Just drive for a minute,' she says.

They're not even two streets away when the guilt kicks in. What is *wrong* with her? Stealing a car, yelling at her sister in public, telling a complete stranger to eff off?

This is not what she does. It's completely out of character. It's more like how Liza behaves: selfish, reckless, angry. And liking it is even worse.

'I need to stop it,' she whispers to the window, to the shops and pubs and traffic. 'I need to get myself better.'

If she could cleanse herself, somehow, wash away all these negative wrong emotions, bring herself back to where she's supposed to be. But how? Can you even do that? She pictures sunlight, flowers, the smell of incense and forgiveness.

'Decided where you're going to yet, love?'

They pass a grey church, and she's tempted. But the answer isn't there. It's in herself, somewhere. She needs to look inside at her own shadows, at the anger that's been eating at her like a dark hidden spider. She needs calm and distance. Somewhere to think.

'Can you please take me to a travel agent?' she asks.

Showing Them All

I turned off the phone and flung it into a bush.

'Fine,' I said. 'You just watch. I *will* do a better job.'

I stomped up to Lee's gate. Church Street, fortunately, was deserted, so nobody had witnessed my argument over the phone, though I wouldn't be surprised if curtains were twitching like crazy all over the place.

How dare she have a go at me? She was the one who'd disappeared before her own party, who'd left her own confused mother without letting her know first. I was expected to come in and pick up the pieces – and on her terms, too, not mine. It reminded me of a time when I'd been called in late for a commercial shoot for a shampoo ad, of all things, filmed on a trapeze. The woman they'd hired originally was inexperienced, had fudged her CV, and was therefore absolutely rubbish and amateur, so her stunts looked like they were done by a clumsy twelve year old. But the director, who had no idea what he was doing either, straight out of some god-awful film school and a nephew of the CEO of the company, wanted me to replicate what she'd done, only 'fancier, you know, with a few more kicks and spins and stuff' so they could edit my footage onto hers. Of course the problem was that her holds and positions were all wrong to begin with, so I had to do all of my moves beginning with her bad positions. Nearly broke my wrist.

'Forget it,' I said out loud. I wasn't going to do things Lee's way. I'd do them my way, and I'd do them better, and I'd prove to Lee *and* my mother that they were wrong. The thing was, I'd have to still pretend to be Lee – otherwise, nobody at Ice Cream Heaven would take me seriously.

Then, when Lee came back, I'd reveal myself as the bad twin, and watch people's chins hit the floor in astonishment.

There was a large bunch of flowers on Lee's doorstep: yellow and pink roses wrapped in a froth of tissue paper. I picked them up and read the card. *Get better soon, and by the way answer your bloody phone. Will.*

There. That was better boyfriend behaviour. Treat 'em mean, keep 'em keen. It looked like Will Naughton was responding to my own way of doing things, too. For a split second, I thought it would serve Lee right if I stole her boyfriend, but then I rejected that right away. Selfish, she'd called me. Thoughtless. I wouldn't give her the satisfaction of being right.

Very well. I might have to fake running an ice-cream business, but I did know how to handle high-performance motors, high-grade explosives – and men. I'd work a bit of my magic on Will so that when Lee came back, she'd have the most attentive, eager, ultra-posh boyfriend in the world. And it would all be down to me. Was that the behaviour of a thoughtless person?

I'd show them all.

Of course, ten minutes later, I was crawling through the bush looking for my phone.

I was up with the sun the next morning and jogged a long and circuitous route to Ice Cream Heaven, along lanes and bridleways. The sky was clear blue for once and a breeze

247

tripped along the top of the hedges. Fluffy seeds and insects danced in the air, birds twittered, sheep baaed. Dew clung to grass blades and spider webs. It was like running through a postcard. I didn't see a single human being, though in one direction I could see the stone circle on the top of the hill, and through the trees in the other direction I could glimpse the ancient chimneys of Naughton Hall. I ran through a field of rustling wheat, vaulted the stile, trespassed across a pasture, skirted some cows flitting flies away with their tails, and came to the factory the back way, over fields that used to belong to my grandfather.

Running cleared my head and the air cleared my lungs. My stiffness wore away with every step I took. I was light on my feet as I jumped the gate and my trainers crunched the gravel around the old barn and the two empty Ice Cream Heaven vans, painted with clouds and flowers. Nobody was here yet, of course; it wasn't even half past six.

I walked round to the front of the office block, stretching my arms and spine as I went, and let myself in with the key I'd found neatly labelled in a box in Lee's house. All the blinds were drawn; I left them that way and went in the half-gloom to the lavatory, where I had a quick wash and changed into Lee's skirt and blouse. I poured myself a large glass of water in the kitchen and then sat down at Lee's desk and fired up her laptop. Assuming everyone else was on time and not early, I had about two and a half hours to go through Lee's computer and desk to learn everything I could about running Ice Cream Heaven. I'd been up till past midnight last night studying the files in her house, and comparing them to my memories of what my mother had done when we were kids. This morning, I wanted to learn Lee's schedule and anticipate everything she needed to do today, so I'd be prepared. I read production schedules, recent invoices, ordering schedules, meeting minutes, sales directives, memos, everything there was.

It was absolutely clear that I was never going to be able to take over the business and do as good a job as Lee from a standing start. I didn't have the experience, or the expertise, or the interest. I might be able to fake it for a few hours or even a few days, but sooner or later I was going to trip up and betray myself or make a major mistake that could damage the company. Not – let's be clear about this – that I gave a rat's arse about Ice Cream Heaven. But I'd sworn to prove Lee wrong, so I couldn't ruin the business, or lose any customers, or make a costly mistake.

No, I had two things going for me. One was that every person at Ice Cream Heaven, except for Mouse and myself, had been working there for donkey's years and could probably do their jobs in their sleep. The other was that I had no compunction about lying through my teeth.

The water was still undrunk when I heard a car drive up outside. It was ten to nine. I got up and began drawing the blinds, as if I'd just arrived myself. Glenys, Doris and Brenda all got out of the car and I waved cheerily at them through the window. They'd want to go through my supposed illness, and I wanted an excuse to go into the factory, so I joined them outside as Dennis pulled up on a beat-up Yamaha. The engine coughed when he stopped and it was splattered all over with mud and God knows what else, but it was a nice little machine and I allowed myself half a second of an appreciative glance before I greeted everyone.

'Feeling better?' asked Glenys as we walked together to the factory entrance.

'Much, thank you. It's amazing what a couple of days in bed can do. And thank you for the biscuits, they were lovely.'

'Ah, we were baking anyway.' She ducked her head. I stood and watched as Doris, Glenys and Brenda pulled on their protective coveralls and boots, and Dennis began to dress himself up in the full-winter outfit that would keep him warm for his spells in the freezer.

'You coming in for a look-see?' asked Doris, handing me a hairnet. I nodded and put it on before we went through the glass door into the factory proper.

It was relatively quiet; the machines hadn't started yet, though there was the constant hum and blast of the freezers. Doris and the others set immediately to work, checking the mixtures, flipping switches, going to the pallets of packaging and to the walk-in, and I wandered the concrete floor reacquainting myself with the nuts and bolts of my family business. The big flavour tanks stood in a regimented row, waiting to be connected to the pumps so that their liquid contents of milk, cream, sugar and flavouring could be mechanically whipped with air and frozen into a semi-solid, ready to be squirted into tubs. I sniffed the air: strawberry. Brenda confirmed my inference by reappearing with a plastic bucket filled with frozen strawberries, which she began tipping into the fruit feeder where they would be mixed into the ice cream.

The blast freezer looked as if it had been updated, though that was hardly surprising; freezing technology must have moved on a bit since I was a kid. I only glanced into the big storage freezer because I had more than enough memories to last. It looked the same, with shelves stretching up to the ceiling, all of them loaded with pallets of ice cream and ingredients.

Enough. It wasn't as if I was going to be making the actual ice cream myself. I waved at the production team and threw my hairnet into the bin by the door as I left.

When I came back into the office, I heard whistling from the direction of the kitchen, and Jonny Whitehair appeared in the door, a teaspoon in his hand. 'Cuppa?'

'Love one,' I said. 'No sugar though, I'm trying to cut down. Got to keep my girlish figure, you know.'

'You don't look a day over twenty,' said Jonny.

'Ah, Jonny, still the flatterer.'

'I'm sorry to tell you this, Emily, but when you're as old as I am, every woman under fifty doesn't look a day over twenty.' He went back into the kitchen.

The front door opened and Mouse rushed in. She was wearing a brown blouse with a toothpaste stain on the front of it, a denim skirt with a crooked hem, and the omnipresent Alice band. 'Sorry I'm late,' she gasped. 'I couldn't find Mimi's pants.'

'Jonny, tea for Annabelle too,' I called. She flashed me a grateful smile and dumped her huge canvas handbag on her desk.

'How are you feeling?' she asked.

'Well-fed. I've had more casseroles than I can get through in a week.'

'Ma Gamble said that Will sent you roses.'

'Yes.' I'd put them on my grandparents' grave. I figured they wouldn't mind where they came from.

'He was very disappointed yesterday when he couldn't take you out to lunch. He said he'd booked a table at Madigan's.' She sighed. 'I wish I could go to Madigan's. That said, sometimes I'd be grateful for a McDonald's so I didn't have to cook every night.'

'Don't tell Ma Gamble you yearn for McDonald's,' I said.

'I think she knows. I can see it in her eyes when she looks at me.'

'Tea, tea, and tea,' said Jonny, coming in and putting a mug

251

on each of our desks. I glanced around the room. Open-plan offices were fine for ease of communication and making cups of tea for each other, but they weren't ideal for more confidential conversations.

'Thanks, Jonny,' I said. 'Annabelle, do you want to bring yours outside with me? It's a beautiful day.'

Mouse looked around in a panic, as if my asking her outside was tantamount to saying I was going to sack her. Jonny sat at his desk, his feet up, and began to whistle. 'Uh, don't you want to check the orders and invoices?' she said.

'Already have. Come on, we're wasting precious sunshine.'

We went outside and across the gravel and tarmac to one of the old stone walls. Across at the loading bay, Archie and Charlie were stocking the ice-cream vans; they waved at us in tandem. I sat down and Mouse perched beside me, if you could use such a delicate word for Mouse. She held her mug in one hand and with the other she was pleating her skirt.

'Lee, I'm so sorry if I messed up the purchasing orders for today. You weren't there, and I knew we needed them, and so I just went ahead and did them. I couldn't think of what else to do.'

'Annabelle, do you think you messed up the orders?'

I could see her thinking about it. Personally, I had no idea if she'd messed them up or not.

'I didn't think so when I was doing them,' she said slowly.

'Well then, don't worry about it.'

'Really?'

'Really.'

She seemed to relax, and she took a drink of her tea. 'Thanks, Lee. That's a relief. I'm glad I did it right.'

If she didn't, we'd be finding out about it soon enough. Meanwhile, I had to keep the company ticking over without the least idea how to do it. 'Annabelle, how long would you say you've been working at Ice Cream Heaven?'

'About a year? No, more than a year, because when I started Pheebs was cutting her molars and I remember I was changing the worst nappy of my life when you rang and asked if I wanted to meet up and talk about a job.'

I chuckled outwardly, though inwardly I was wondering at how a person could measure her life by horrible nappies. 'Wow, has it been that long already?'

'I know. It seems like yesterday.'

'Do you think you're happy here?'

'Of course I am,' she said very quickly.

'What would you see your position as in the company?'

Evidently I was better at business-speak than I'd anticipated because she looked worried again. 'Is this some sort of yearly review or something?'

'Something like that. Really it's touching base, making sure we're making the best use of you, et cetera.'

She fidgeted. 'Well, you know, I see myself as a very small wheel in, you know, a bigger machine. And that machine being Ice Cream Heaven, basically. Or should it be a cog? A small cog. You know, the things that make other things go more smoothly. Or is that grease?'

'Right. That's – very good. I was thinking on a more basic level though, Annabelle, about what exactly you do here.'

'You mean, what do I do on a daily basis?'

'That's it.'

'Oh, okay. I make the tea, of course, except in the mornings sometimes when Jonny gets in first. And I do the photocopying. And filing, too, when something needs to be filed. I help with the tasting, though really I'm not much good at that, because it all tastes great to me. I leave you messages if you happen to be out to lunch, or ill, though that doesn't happen too often, obviously. And – um . . .'

I waited.

'Sometimes I make coffee, too,' she added after a while.

'Okay, that's great. So Monday and yesterday you had to do quite a bit more than usual, in terms of responsibility.'

'Oh, yes.'

'Did you enjoy it?'

'Um – well, I was a little bit worried, in case I messed up, but otherwise – yes, it wasn't bad.'

'Excellent. Because I was thinking, it's time I made more use of your skills, and yesterday happened to be a great trial period.'

'You – you want me to do more?'

'Exactly.'

'But I don't really know how—'

'And you'll never learn unless you start doing it, will you? Did you think you could do the orders for tomorrow, before you did them?'

'Well, I wasn't sure.'

'But I was. I knew they'd be fine. So starting today, I'd like you to pick up a few extra duties for me. You can do all the orders from now on; pop round and see Doris during the afternoon, and sort it out between you. Then you can type them up. Are you all right with that?'

'Um – I suppose so.'

'And I think it's time you had more of a hand on the coal face, as it were. So I'd like you to take over handling the bulk of the email and phone queries. To start out with, I'll forward the emails I think you're okay to handle, but in a day or two, I'd be expecting you to go through my inbox and funnel off the tasks you can do yourself. Basically, it's upshifting your job description to be something more like a PA. If it all goes well, we'll review your pay scale, too.'

Mouse's eyes were wide. 'I – Lee, I'm not sure about this. I mean, I will absolutely do my best, but I can barely get here on time, so I don't think—'

'I trust you,' I said firmly. 'I know you can do this.'

'Do you really?'

Of course I didn't. I doubted that Mouse could find her elbow most days. But all I needed was for her to hold it together moderately well on the less important stuff, so I could concentrate on figuring out what was going on. *Plus*, a little voice whispered in my head, *if she screws it up it will be her fault, not yours.*

'Of course I trust you, Annabelle,' I said.

She bit her lip. In fact, she looked as if she were about to begin to cry. Instead, she flung her arms around me. 'Oh, thank you, thank you, Lee. You don't know how much it means to me, to hear you say that.'

I patted her back. Now, here was a definite advantage of being Lee Haven. Lee could push off responsibility onto other people, and they saw it as a compliment.

Whereas if Liza Haven pushed off responsibility, she was accused of being selfish and uncaring. Where was the sense in that?

Mouse was still hugging me, so she couldn't see that I was frowning.

'Annabelle,' I said over her shoulder, 'can I ask you a question? Something totally unrelated to your job?'

'Certainly.' She stopped hugging me, wiped her eyes, straightened her blouse, and smiled a little sheepishly.

'What do you think about my sister Liza?'

In the distance, a cow mooed. Mouse looked as though she were weighing her words, apparently not something she did very often.

'I was always a little scared of her,' she said at last. 'She used to call me Mouse.'

'You did used to be pretty timid.'

'Yeah. I suppose so.'

'Do you think she's selfish for having her own career and not helping me run the business?'

'Um . . .'

'But surely you have an opinion. People in Stoneguard always have opinions.' Especially about things that have nothing to do with them.

'I think – well, obviously it's really amazing what she does for a job. And you do a really amazing job here. So it's all fine.'

'But do you think she's being selfish for not helping out?'

'Not with the business so much, no.'

'With other things? My mother, for example?'

Mouse sighed. She shook her head, but it was the kind of headshake that didn't really mean no. She drank some of her tea, and looked out at the landscape around us. The hill topped by stones, the thatched cottage with the strangers' car in front, the green and yellow fields rolling away.

'My mother and my sister never got on,' I told her. 'They could barely stand to be in the same room together. It's not as if our mother even wanted Liza around to help.'

'Right.'

'It would probably cause lots more stress for everybody.'

'Probably.'

'It's not being selfish if you get on with your own life because nobody else needs you. That's just being realistic.'

'I suppose not. I mean, I suppose so. I don't really know anything about it, obviously.'

'No. And my mother doesn't want help, anyway. She's determined to do everything her own way. So what is Liza supposed to do?'

'I don't know,' said Mouse. 'I suppose – well. I don't know.'

'No,' I said. 'I don't either.'

We sat there for another minute. A bird flew from the hedge into a tree, and then another one followed. In the distance, a single-engine aeroplane circled and dipped. A Cessna, but I couldn't tell from here what model. I could just about hear it above the breeze in the leaves.

'Anyway,' Mouse said, 'you're sure about the email?'

'Definitely.' I stood up and stretched. 'Let's go inside and get started.'

Old Flames

For the next two days I observed the staff of Ice Cream Heaven, under guise of having friendly chats. It really wasn't difficult to talk to people in Stoneguard, even if you were hiding your identity; all you had to do was to ask questions, listen carefully and pass the same information around. By five o'clock on Thursday, I'd learned a great deal about how the business and factory worked on a daily basis. And by passing routine enquiries on to Mouse, production matters to Doris, distribution queries to Dennis, sales information to Jonny, I'd had to do very little actual work. Everyone else, of course, was running around like a blue-arsed fly. Jonny didn't even have the chance to put his feet up on his desk.

I was congratulating myself on a job well done and planning where I could take an evening run without being spotted by too many people when I heard a car drive up outside and beep its horn. A minute or so later, a man in a dirty T-shirt, dirty jeans and dirty boots came in the door. He had dirty blond hair tied back in a ponytail.

'Afternoon, Stone,' said Jonny, putting down his phone.

'Hi there, Stone,' said Mouse.

'Peace,' said Stone. I recognised him now: Rock's brother.

He held up a set of keys in his dirty hand, and tossed them to me. I caught them in mid-air.

'Here are your wheels back,' he told me. 'I had to wait an extra day for the converter to come in. But it's all sound now.'

I twirled the key ring around my finger. The fob was a sparkly enamel flower. Stone had evidently betrayed his hippy credentials enough to become a mechanic for foul carbon-producing automobiles. Though he was still nice and grubby, which was something of a relief.

'Thanks,' I said. 'It's good to have it back.'

'I got some funny looks driving it.' His white teeth showed up bright in his dirty face. 'Not my usual colour.'

'Good thing everybody knows you, or you'd probably be reported as the car thief,' Jonny said.

Stone shook his head. 'If it don't run on bio-fuel, I don't drive it.'

Ah. There it was. Stoneguard all over. 'Thanks, Stone, I appreciate it. It's nice of you to deliver it here, too.'

'No problem.'

I got up and looked out the window. Even though I'd never seen it before, I knew which car was Lee's. It was the ice-lolly-pink Mini parked next to Jonny's Vauxhall. White roof, round fog lights and, apparently, a bio-diesel engine.

I thought about driving it and my hands went slick.

It's not a particularly fast car, I told myself. *It's not even a Cooper. This thing has a 1.5 litre engine at most. It will pootle around the country roads like a little safe insect. It is a dinky pink car running on chip fat.*

'Actually, Stone,' I said, 'would you mind dropping it off at my house for me?'

'Nope, not at all.' He held his hand out for the keys. 'I'll put them through the letter box.'

'Thank you so much.'

'Peace, everyone.' Stone waved and left.

I closed my eyes for a moment. This was not a good state of affairs. Not good at all.

'Are you getting a lift home from someone?' Jonny asked me.

I swallowed. 'No, just fancied a walk,' I said lightly. The phone on my desk rang and Mouse looked at me questioningly, as she had all week. I nodded.

She pushed the button to transfer the call to her phone and picked it up. 'Ice Cream Heaven, Annabelle speaking, how can I help you?' I had to give her credit, she didn't stumble at all over it this time, as she had earlier. I began to gather together some files I wanted to study.

'Oh, Will, hello!' she said. Her voice did the excited, breathy thing that I kept hearing when people spoke with Will. 'Yes, fine, thanks. Yes, they're fine too. Well, except that blueberry jam doesn't wash out, and Jo still absolutely refuses to have anything to do with maths. Yes, she's here, would you like to speak with her?'

I shook my head violently, waving my arm and mouthing, 'No! No!'

'Um – wait a minute, she might not be here. Just a sec.' She put her hand over the mouthpiece. 'It's Will Naughton. Don't you want to talk with him?'

As Will was likely to know exactly what was going on, I gave up all pretence of being quiet and said, 'No, I'm on my way out of the door, I'll talk with him later.' I shut up the laptop without turning it off and swept it and the files into my arms.

Clearly incredulous, Mouse said into the phone, 'Sorry, Will, she's on her way out of the door. She'll talk to you later. Um, well, no, she says she's going – well, I can try, but I don't think— okay.' She held the receiver out to me. 'He said to give you the phone whether you liked it or not.'

I hugged the laptop and files to my chest and skipped backwards, dodging the receiver. 'No, no, gotta go. Bye, everyone!' I hurried out and onto the footpath through the fields. Behind me, everyone was probably speculating about why I hadn't taken Will's phone call or driven the Mini. Bloody Stoneguard.

I had other things to think about, though, as I walked over the hill to my sister's house. Lee's car being with Stone brought up some questions. I'd assumed she'd driven to wherever she was going, but evidently not. Train, taxi, tourist coach, bus? Had she gone off with someone else – someone other than her boyfriend? I remembered the Christmas card from the mysterious T. Was that it – was my sister was having an affair?

I shook my head. Emily Haven was not the type to have an affair.

Then again, last week I would've said that my sister wasn't the type to disappear into thin air leaving all her responsibilities behind.

The Mini was parked in front of Lee's place. I regarded it as I would an adversary. It sat there, looking pink.

When I opened the door to the house, the phone was ringing. Something about the timing gave me an inkling of who it was, so I let it ring.

'I'm beginning to think I've lost some of my considerable charm,' said Will Naughton's voice to the answering machine. 'Put me out of my misery and give me a ring. I've got something I'd like to show you.'

I bet you have, I thought. I erased the message.

I'd had the excuse of supposed illness to get out of Lee's evening arrangements up till now, but Friday I bit the bullet and went to a Stoneguard Residents' Association meeting. It was in the back of Ma Gamble's Wholefood Emporium, in the space she kept specifically for gatherings such as this, among sacks of lentils and loose tea. I drank Fair Trade coffee and tried to keep my mouth shut as much as possible. It was as boring as I'd expected it to be. At about nine thirty the meeting broke up so everyone could heatedly discuss the latest heart-stopping news to hit the town, which was that some do-gooder had posted the keys of Rufus Fanshawe's BMW back to him. I'd heard the speculation about this particular bit of gossip about fifteen million times already. I finished my coffee, yawned widely and excused myself to go home.

The folder and the Christmas card from under Lee's bed were on the kitchen counter; I retrieved the business card, sat down with Lee's phone, and dialled Timothy Clifton's number.

'Lee?'

Well, someone had her number programmed into his phone, anyway, though they didn't work together any more. Interesting. 'No, it's her sister, Liza. Is this Timothy?'

'Yes, it is. You're Lee's twin? The one who lives in America?' It was a deep voice, pleasant, with the slightest West Country accent. He sounded a little guarded.

'Yeah, except I'm in Wiltshire now, at Lee's house.'

'Why are you calling?'

'Well, I'm trying to track Lee down, and I thought you might have some idea where she is.'

He paused. 'Why are you trying to track her down? Isn't she in Stoneguard?'

'No. She seems to have taken a holiday without telling anybody.'

'She what? That doesn't sound like her. I can't imagine Lee keeping any secrets.'

'Apparently she has. I came to Stoneguard to visit her, and she was gone.'

'You don't think she's in any danger, do you?'

'She's rung me to tell me she's all right.' I decided not to mention my nagging feeling that she wasn't. 'But she won't tell me where she is. I thought maybe you'd know where she was and why she went there, but I guess I was wrong.'

'I haven't spoken with Lee in over a year now.'

And yet you still have her number in your phone. 'Did you and she have a relationship?'

'You'd better ask Lee that yourself.'

'Well, I would, if I could get hold of her. You don't know anywhere she might have gone? Her favourite holiday spot? Any long-lost friends to visit?'

He paused for a moment, evidently thinking. 'No. I don't recall her ever going on holiday, except to visit you around her birthday. And she's never lost any friends. Except, maybe, me.'

'It wasn't a good break-up?'

He laughed, though there wasn't any humour in it. 'She doesn't tell you much, does she? I thought twins were supposed to be close.'

'That's the common perception.'

'What made you think of ringing me?'

'I found your business card in her house, in a place that I thought might be significant. And a Christmas card from you.'

'Did you? She kept that?' He paused again. 'Listen, Liza, I'm very sorry I can't help you. But will you tell me when you've found her? Call me and let me know she's all right. Please?'

'It sounds like you still care about her.'

'It's impossible not to care about Lee. Goodbye, Liza.'

I put down the phone. So that had told me exactly nothing, except that I didn't know anything, and that Lee wasn't as open a book as I'd thought she was.

I put down the phone. And went to get myself another glass of Lee's emergency whisky.

Sundowning

I woke up a split second before the phone rang. I opened my eyes, realised I was lying on the couch with all the lights on and an open folder on my chest, glanced at the darkness beyond the undrawn curtain at the window, looked at the empty bottle on the floor and the clock on the mantelpiece and saw it was three minutes past three, and then the phone rang.

It could be Lee. Or Timothy. Or even Will. But none of them was likely. I answered the phone with the words, 'Is she wandering again?'

'Oh hi, Ms Haven, yes, she managed to unlock the conservatory door this time, I can't think how.'

'I'm on it.'

This time, I wasn't drunk (not much, anyway) and I knew more what to expect. I was still dressed so I pulled on Lee's trainers and let myself out. For the first time I noticed that Lee kept a torch next to the front door, probably for events such as this. It cast a circle of yellow light on the road ahead of me. As I went through the lych gate to the church, a swift shadow bolted through the graves; I caught a glimpse of orange tail.

My grandparents' gravestone pointed up to the dark sky. I touched it as I went past, murmuring a greeting to Nan and

Grandad. I then climbed into the alley, shining the torch on the ground to light a clear path. I didn't run, but I did walk quickly, to the end of the alley and across the car park and onto the chalk path up the hill. Although it had been a sunny day, clouds had crept in with darkness and there was no moon or stars. The torch made it seem darker, too, by making a contrast and casting shadows. Still, I spotted the white nightgown against the dark hill without any problems.

She'd got a bit farther up towards the stones this time. I used the path instead of cutting across, though she was moving more quickly than I'd expected and she was about three-quarters of the way up the hill before I caught up with her. She was looking straight ahead into the darkness, walking with the same determination as last time.

'Mum,' I said, and touched her on the shoulder.

'I'm not your mother,' she said, without looking at me or stopping.

'I'm sorry to say that you are. Come on, let's go home.'

'I have to go up here.'

'No, Mum, it's the middle of the night. You need to go home and go to bed.'

She didn't answer, just kept on walking.

'Mum!' I took her arm this time and tried to gently hold her back. She jerked out of my grasp.

'Stop,' she said and kept going forward. The path here was steeper than lower down, and had steps cut into it, each held together with a plank of wood.

'No, *you* stop,' I told her. 'You can't go up there, and I really don't want to carry you down. Come on, let's go.'

She kept walking. I had to climb a couple of steps behind her.

'Mum, it's quarter past three in the morning.' She took no notice. 'Quarter past three, Mum. Listen, if you want to come up here during the day, we can do that. I'll come over tomorrow. How about that?'

'No.' Another step, and another. Her feet were bare again. I'd have to mention to the nurse to at least put her to bed in slippers, if this was going to be a regular occurrence, which apparently it was.

Jesus. Why couldn't they keep the doors properly locked? Surely it couldn't be that hard to keep an elderly lady in a solid Victorian house. The thing had been practically a fortress when I was living there. I'd had to perfect my lock picking and climbing-out-of-window skills by the time I was eleven.

'Mum, that's enough of this, now. It's time to go home. Come on.' I took her arms, both of them this time, and more firmly so she couldn't shake me off. She tried to move forward, but I planted my feet, so she leaned forward and tugged. 'Stop it, Mum, you'll hurt yourself.'

'Let me go. I need to see.'

'No, Mum, you can't see anything, it's the middle of the night. Come on, now. Back to bed with you.'

'No.' Tug. Tug. She was putting her whole body into it. My fingers dug into her arms, maybe hard enough to cause bruises. I let her go, as gently as I could, but she still staggered forward a bit and then carried on walking.

I moved round so I stood directly in front of her, blocking her way. I could get her to do what I wanted, quite easily in fact, but I'd rather persuade her.

'Mother,' I said, as authoritatively as I could. I shone the torch in her face, which made her blink. 'You can't go up the hill. It's the middle of the night. You must go home and go to bed.'

She stepped to the side. I blocked her. She tried the other side, and I blocked her that way, too. Right, left, right, left, all the time with her looking over my shoulder, never in my face, and never shielding her eyes from the torch light even when it shone directly in them and made her pupils contract into tiny holes. Finally, she charged forward and ploughed straight into me.

I'd fought bigger and stronger and more skilled opponents and kept my ground, but none of them were my mother. She didn't have the weight or strength to knock me over, but she kept pushing and pushing, using her hands and her shoulders. Barefoot, she was slightly shorter than me and I could smell the old-fashioned cold cream she rubbed into her face every night. Her breath came in pants and small grunts, like that of a trapped animal. She pushed. And pushed again. Her toes scrabbled against the chalk.

'Mum,' I said in despair. 'Don't.'

She didn't alter her position or gather her strength for a harder push. She kept on applying pressure, steady and horrible. Her nails curled into my chest, through Lee's thin T-shirt. Around us, it began to rain.

'Please stop, Mum. Please. Or I'll have to force you. Please don't make me.'

Was she even in there? Could she hear me? Or was she a single desire, not even a person any more, just an impulse?

I'd been fighting with my mother for as long as I could remember. My earliest lesson in life, learned probably before I could even walk, was that my mother never lost. Even when I grew up and I had physical strength and skill, she was more powerful. She was the adult, and I was the problem. The only way I could win was to move away. To leave her. Joy rides, night escapes, rebellions in my mind and in my actions, always tugging against the cords she wove to bind me where she thought I should be, who she wanted me to be, until finally I broke free and only the other side of the world was far enough.

And here we were. Another battle. Except this time she was the problem, and I was younger and stronger and sane.

She let out a long, keening moan of frustration, wordless and inhuman, and that was enough. No more. 'Right,' I gritted and stuffed the torch down the waistband of my jeans. I took hold of her where I knew I could and within half a second had whirled her around in my arms to pin her back against me, helpless.

'We are going back home, Mum,' I said.

She couldn't struggle in this position, couldn't do anything except what I wanted her to. I had years of martial arts experience behind me. Her feet were free to walk, so I propelled her back down the hill, supporting her on the steps. It was painless, I knew. I'd been in this position myself. I wasn't hurting her. And what dignity was there to remove when she was barefoot and wearing a nightgown outside in the dead of night, with no one to see her but me?

We slipped through the gap in the hedge, with me going first backwards, dragging her after me so she wouldn't be scratched by the holly and bramble. Once we were on the lawn, she went limp. In the light cast from the house's windows, I could see her eyes were half-closed and her mouth was half-open, as if she were lapsing back into sleep. I adjusted my grip, draped her arm over my shoulder, and held her up by the waist to support her back to the house. The nurse met us at the door.

'Oh, there you are, Mrs Haven,' she said cheerily to my mother. 'I'm so sorry about this,' she said to me.

'Why is she doing it?'

'It's normal. Sundowning, we call it. People with dementia seem to naturally become more confused in the dark.'

'It's natural?'

She nodded. 'Twice in a week is unusual, though, so perhaps

she's unsettled about something. Come along, Mrs Haven, let's get you tucked up again.'

Mum went willingly with her, head drooping, hands limp, back to her bed.

In my own bed, or rather Lee's, I lay with the window open to the night noises and tried to relax enough to go back to sleep. I could still feel my mother's hands on my chest, pushing.

On the hill I'd thought she sounded like a small trapped animal, but lying here I couldn't stop thinking about a bird trying to get through a glass door. Battering and battering, pecking and pushing, destroying feathers and beak and hollow bones.

One time when I was very young, a bird, a starling, had smashed into one of the windows in the conservatory. I'd found it lying on the grass, fluttering one wing. I picked it up and brought it inside. My mother, I knew, would order it back outside immediately so without permission I took it over the fields to my grandparents' farmhouse. My grandfather was standing outside the door, squinting at the distant fields. I held the bird up to him. Its heartbeat was so fast it felt like a trembling.

He examined the bird, touching it carefully with his fingertips.

'Can you save it?' I asked him.

'It's got a broken wing, I think,' he said in his soft voice, barely louder than the whisper of starling's feathers. 'Leg as well.'

'But you can fix it, right?'

He touched the iridescent green feathers on its breast, the small pale specks that looked like stars. 'It's a wild animal. It can't survive injuries like this. Without a wing, it can't fly or find food. Even if it healed, it would be crippled and in pain for the rest of its life.'

'But it–it was just flying. It didn't mean to run into the glass.'

'These things happen, Elizabeth.'

'So one accident, and it's no good any more?'

He stopped touching it and put his hands back into his pockets. 'It's best to put it out of its misery.'

'You want me to kill it?'

I had just turned seven. And I was small – my sister and I were small as children, a legacy of the cramped space inside our shared womb. My grandfather assessed me. He couldn't want me to kill the bird, could he? Not me? I squirmed and rubbed one of my feet against the back of my other leg.

'I'll do it,' he said, but I clutched it against my chest.

'Put it out in the back of the garden,' he said at last. 'A fox will find it. Or a cat. That's the way nature works.'

He looked away again, at the fields surrounding his house. There was an odd expression on his face, odd enough so that I looked out to where he was staring, but there wasn't anything there.

In my sister's bed, now, I kept my eyes closed and listened to the rain pattering on leaves outside. The way nature works. One thing eats another, the old and injured fade and die. Disease blocks my mother's brain and strangles out her memories. A circle, decline and fall and regrowth, natural and just and so horrible that we fight it. We build vast edifices, fences and barriers of stones, to keep something eternal. To keep death away.

The pattering rain sounded like the starling's heartbeat and breath, quicker than thought. Long ago, when I was seven and my father had left us not long before, I'd put the damaged bird in a box and tried to splint its wing with Sellotape and cotton wool, and while I was winding more cotton around its rough-skinned leg, it stopped moving and its eyes went dull and it was dead. I tried to revive it by putting my mouth over its beak and breathing air into its tiny lungs. But nothing happened and I sat for a long time looking at its tortured body and the pain I had forced it through. I'd buried it by the hedge, deep so no fox or cat could find it.

My grandfather died soon after that and I thought, for a very long time, that it was because of me, because I couldn't do what he wanted me to do.

Sleep rubbed away at the edges of my mind. I thought of paths and circles, white stars in darkness. Fast, fast cars, speed and freedom, the moment of dead numbness before the pain begins.

In my dream, I held the starling, alive and broken, in my hands. I was big, it was small. I hated its weakness. It pounded its wings against my breast, making a high keening sound of frustration through its fragile beak. This was all its own fault. Why did it want to fly into a door anyway?

I clenched my fists. I felt its bones cracking and its feathers breaking. It sounded like the crunch of a pine cone underfoot. Something sharp pricked my palm. I dropped the bird's twisted body near the hedge and looked at my hands. There was a single dot of blood, and a black feather touched with beautiful, oily green.

When I woke up it was morning and my fists were still closed tight, my jaw aching from grinding my teeth.

Joyriding

The knock was so gentle that I didn't even know, until I opened the door, that it was a cop.

'Morning, Lee,' said Mikey Mercer, or rather PC Michael Mercer, standing, as always, like an apology for himself. The shoulders of his uniform were too wide for his stick-thin frame. 'Sorry to bother you on a Saturday morning. How are you?'

'I'm all right, Mikey, you?' I didn't make a move to let him in. Neither Mikey nor any of his colleagues had ever caught me at anything while I was growing up, which had made him beneath my notice. And it had been a long time since I'd done anything much more illegal than speeding. But in my world, policemen did not make social calls.

Maybe this wasn't a social call.

'Has anything happened to my sister or Mum?' I gasped out. *I knew it*, a little voice said inside me. *I knew she was in trouble and now it's too late.*

'No, it's nothing like that, your family are all fine as far as I know.' He looked even more sheepish than before. 'Do you mind if I come in for a few minutes?'

'Oh. Of course.' I stepped back to let him in, because that was what Lee would do. 'Cup of tea?'

'That would be very kind of you, Lee. No biscuits though, I'm heading home for lunch after this.' He followed me into the kitchen and stood, shifting from one foot to the other, while I switched the kettle back on. Mikey was the sort of policeman that tourists liked. He was always ready to give directions or a little history lesson about Stoneguard, he enjoyed standing out in a prominent place and wandering round the tourist car park, and if anything went wrong, he could issue an apology like nobody's business. Whether he had ever actually solved any crimes was doubtful.

I tried to remember the name of his wife, but the blast of panic had obliterated most of my recall. 'How's your family?' I asked instead.

'Fine, we're all fine. Posey's enjoying school. We got the poor dog fixed last week and she's hating her cone.'

This could go on all day. Fortunately I'd just boiled the kettle so I hurried his cup of tea. When I turned to put it in front of him, I saw that he was kneading his hands.

'Looks like it's shaping up to be a hot weekend,' he said. 'That must be good news for an ice-cream business.'

'Is this an official visit, Mikey, or is it just for chit-chat?' I asked. It wasn't how Lee would have asked it, but he didn't seem to notice; his hands pulled at each other.

He took a deep breath. 'Well, you've probably heard about Rufus Fanshawe's vehicle being stolen. Terrible thing, especially in a place like this where everyone looks out for each other.'

'It's certainly been the talk of the town.'

'Have you heard the news that it was found abandoned on the side of the M6 near Preston?'

'Yes.'

'Well. It was right near a CCTV camera, as it happens.

They have them on the overpasses up there. They monitor traffic, mostly.'

'So what does this have to do with me?'

He shifted. He kneaded. He rolled his shoulders around in his too-big uniform and bit the inside of his lip. I waited.

'Yes, well, I am sorry about this, but you were filmed getting out of it.'

I'd been standing up. At this, I sat down.

'What?'

'It's pretty unmistakable, I'm afraid. The chaps up North sent it down and we made the ID right away. You were wearing your pink raincoat with daisies. I don't want to put you out, but do you have that here, by the way?'

'I – don't know.'

Jesus Christ, what was Lee doing getting out of a stolen car?

'It's only that it would help with the, um, enquiry. Sorry.'

'I just remembered, I took it to the cleaners in Marlborough. Mikey, there's got to be some mistake. When was this?'

'Last Saturday night. Or sorry, rather Sunday morning, about one o'clock.'

My mind raced forward. She'd actually stolen a car. My sister, Lee Haven, the good twin, was Stoneguard's infamous BMW thief.

No wonder she'd been so cagey about where she was. She must be shitting bricks.

'Well, you've definitely made a mistake, Mikey,' I said. 'I was here in Stoneguard at the charity ball until past eleven on Saturday night. Half of Stoneguard was with me, so there are a good few witnesses. There's no way I could have driven Rufus Fanshawe's car to Preston by one. And wasn't it stolen earlier in the evening, anyway? Everyone was talking about it that night.'

'Well, yes. We did think of that, you being here in the town and all. Who was the last person to see you, by the way?'

'Will Naughton walked me home.' At the name, Mikey's face screwed up even more with anxiety. At least there was one good thing – I had an aristocratic alibi.

'Ah, yes, of course – well, that's fine, thank you. But, you know, and forgive me for mentioning it, there is someone else who looks exactly like you.'

'My sister?' I did my best to look shocked. 'I'm sure she'd never do such a thing.'

'Of course, of course I'm not jumping to any conclusions, we're speaking hypothetically here. No offence intended. But there is some understanding that your sister is actually in this country currently?'

I got back up and fetched my cup of tea. 'She's working in London, yes.'

'And there was some expectation that she might have been coming to your charity ball?'

'She couldn't make it at the last minute. Work.'

'Yes. Yes, of course, that does make sense, but the thing is, have you talked with her recently?'

'Yes, I have, a couple of days ago. She didn't mention anything about stealing Rufus's car.'

'Do you think maybe, and I'm sorry to have to ask this, I realise it's an intrusion, but do you think maybe I could have your sister's contact details?' He took a little pad of paper and a pencil stub from his pocket.

I gave him my own mobile number. 'I'm sure there's some mistake, Mikey. Liza and I don't even really look like each other any more.'

'Yes, well of course the thing is that the camera's resolution is quite good, but it was dark and everything. Still, the resemblance is quite striking. If we hadn't known it was impossible, we would have been willing to swear up and down it was you. And then there's the raincoat, of course.'

'Liza wouldn't be seen dead in a pink flowered raincoat, believe me.'

'Ah, well you see there, that's a good point in her favour.' He put the pad and pencil back in his pocket and recommenced kneading his hands. 'So, Lee, I thank you very much for your time, and you know we're duty-bound to follow up every lead we get, as unpleasant as the possibility might be. It's a serious crime, car theft.'

He avoided my eyes as he said it, and drank his tea quickly, in three or four gulps that must have been in danger of scorching his throat. It was probably the biggest risk he'd taken recently. Unlike, apparently, my sister.

What if Lee had left fingerprints or something behind? No – her fingerprints wouldn't be on file. But she could have left something else in the car that could identify her. Or other footage could turn up. Or there was the writing on the envelope that had held the car keys. It would have to be pretty overwhelming evidence to lead this lot to a conviction; but it could happen.

'Let me walk you to the door,' I said, keeping my face calm while my mind was racing.

'Oh yes, of course.' Mikey put down his cup, and went with me to the front door. 'Well, it has been good to see you, Lee, sorry about the circumstances.'

'No problem, Mikey. Whatever I can do to help, though I think you're barking up the wrong tree with my sister. Give everyone my regards at home. Did you say you were headed there for lunch?'

'Yes, Kim likes me back when I can make it. Can't always, though – you know how duty calls.'

'I do.' I ushered him out of the door. 'Take care.'

As soon as I'd closed the door, I was rushing to the window in the front room to watch him go. To my relief, he took a left and went towards the High Street. Mikey lived at the other end of Stoneguard, down Milk Lane. Once he'd rounded the corner, I had a clear hour at least to do what I needed to.

The first thing I did was to call Lee. No answer; phone turned off. What a surprise.

So, Plan B. Whatever that would turn out to be.

I had no idea where the Fanshawes lived, so I raced upstairs and found Lee's address book. Fortunately, she was as meticulous about keeping her address book as she was about everything else. I found the address in seconds and, pausing only long enough to put on some shoes was away, out of the house and down the street.

The Fanshawes' house was a thatched flint and brick cottage on School Street; I remembered it as always being a bit dilapidated, but now it was impeccable. The hedges were trimmed to within an inch of their life. The incessant gossip had taught me that Tania Fanshawe, who'd grown up in Stoneguard as Tania Blunt, had moved to London, married, and brought her husband back with her for a better life in the country.

A black BMW 535i saloon was parked at the kerb. It was cleaned and polished inside and out, but I had no doubt that this was the car in question, back from its adventure to Preston in one piece. I was surprised they were still leaving it on the street, but then again, seventeenth-century cottages didn't really come with garages. And this was Stoneguard, after all.

Any idiot could drive a BMW saloon, they did the driving for you, practically, but this was a powerful car, especially after Lee's chip-fat Mini. What on earth would have possessed her to steal it?

And how? I tried to imagine Lee, in her daisy-print pink mac and our grandmother's pearl earrings, bent over the ignition of a BMW, trying to hotwire it. I couldn't. Maybe it was the pearl earrings; maybe it was because I couldn't imagine her taking the time to learn how to do such a thing. Unless she'd really listened carefully to my teenage tales about joy riding. But even if she had, a modern BMW's ignition system was far more complicated than anything I'd hotwired in my youth. She'd never do it.

No, she hadn't had to; I suddenly remembered that the keys been left in the ignition. She'd just have to get into the driver's seat and go. And then she'd posted them back, which was an utterly Lee thing to do. That fact alone confirmed that the CCTV cameras hadn't lied.

Which only left two questions. Why did she do it? And how could I get her out of it?

I hurried up the gravel path and knocked on the door. Tangerine, aka Tania Fanshawe, answered, and I put on my best sunny smile and held my breath, because the next half a second would tell me if Mikey had been here yet, to tell them Lee had been spotted abandoning their car.

'Lee! How lovely to see you. How are you? Please, come in.'

The Botox disguised her true expression somewhat, but her voice didn't lie. She was genuinely pleased to see Lee, and gave her a kiss on either cheek to prove it.

'Rufus and I were having a glass of wine before lunch, would you like one?'

'I'd love one, thanks. Actually I wondered if I could talk with you and Rufus about something.'

'Of course, anything.' She ushered me into a sitting room straight out of the pages of an interiors magazine feature about country cottages. A balding man wearing ironed jeans and slippers stood up from his armchair when I entered. There was an open bottle of red on the table next to him.

'Lee,' he said, shaking my hand warmly and kissing my cheek as well. I had become somewhat used to the sort of greetings my sister got as a matter of course, but for the first time, the friendliness made me feel a little guilty. My sister had done something against these people, and I was deceiving them, too.

I brushed it aside. 'How are you doing, Rufus?'

'Oh, all right. We got the car back yesterday, as you can see. It was a mess from the fingerprinting powder or whatever, but I've polished it up good as new now.'

'I'll get another glass.' Tania disappeared, and Rufus gestured me into a chair.

'To tell you the truth,' he said in a low voice, 'Tania's been more worried than I have. I think she thought I was about to keel over about the whole thing. I keep telling her I'm good as new after my bypass, but she worries.'

'I'm glad you're better,' I said truthfully. If Lee had killed old Rufus by mistake, she would really freak out. Tania returned with a glass and began fussing over pouring some wine. I accepted it and took a sip, wondering how much I'd be allowed to drink before they kicked me out.

'I don't have a whole lot of time,' I said, 'so I'll cut right to the chase. Has Mikey Mercer been to speak with you?'

'No, not today.'

'Okay. Well, he's been to see me, and the news is that he thinks he's identified who stole your car. My sister, Liza.'

The shock on their faces was quite comical. Even Tania managed it. It would have been worse if they'd known Lee had stolen the car. 'What – how – why?'

'I'm not sure. The only thing I can think of is that she came back for the ball after all to surprise me, and saw your keys in the ignition, and couldn't help herself. She's got a – a bit of an obsession with fast cars.'

'But why would she steal ours?'

'I don't think it had anything to do with you. I think it was just the car. It's a very nice car. I'd want to drive it myself.'

Tania nibbled on a manicured nail. 'I mean, I know there were all those rumours way back when, about Liza liking to do a bit of joy riding, but I wouldn't have thought—'

'No, I wouldn't have thought so either. All I can think is . . . well, she must have had a moment of madness. Liza hasn't been very happy lately. I think there are . . . problems at work.' I swallowed; this was the first time I'd said this out loud, even in the third person.

'Problems at work don't make you steal someone else's car,' fumed Rufus. 'What is she playing at?'

'Rufus,' Tania warned him quickly.

'I know, I know. Lee's your friend and you've known her for a long time, and presumably her sister too, but there is just no excuse for that sort of behaviour.'

'True,' I said. 'None at all. And I know she feels awful about what she's done. And . . .' I took a breath and crossed my fingers by the side of my leg, where they weren't visible '. . . I've come here to ask you if you'd consider not pressing charges.'

'Not pressing charges!'

'Shhh, Rufus. Lee, I know you're always defending your sister, but she's gone beyond the pale this time.'

'But think about it,' I said. 'You've got the car back, safe and sound. No damage at all, it looks like. You don't even have to use your spare set of keys; she sent them back. If that doesn't show she feels sorry for what she's done, I don't know what will. I'll recompense you for the petrol and the mileage and whatever else needs doing. You don't have to make a claim on your insurance. And it would make things so, so much better for Liza. And for me.'

Tania was shaking her head. 'Lee, you're too good.'

'Believe me, I'm not. I'm just – really worried about my sister. I didn't think she'd do something like this. There's something wrong.' My throat closed up.

Rufus and Tania exchanged a look. 'We'll need to think about it,' Tania said.

I tried to recall whether I'd ever done anything against Tania when I was living here. Anything to make her dislike me so much. I couldn't remember any specific event – but I'd never exactly gone out of my way to make anyone in Stoneguard think well of me. I was reaping that harvest now.

And because of it, Lee could end up in jail.

'Mikey Mercer's on his way over here after he has had his lunch,' I said. 'There isn't much time to make up your minds.'

They exchanged another look. 'Lee,' said Rufus slowly, 'I trust you. If you truly think this is the best thing for your sister, I won't press charges.'

'Oh, thank you, thank you so much.' Relief flooded through me and I jumped to my feet to give both of them a hug and a kiss. 'You won't regret it, I promise you.'

'If Liza is as messed up as you say, though, you need to do something to help her get better.'

'Don't worry, that's exactly what I'm going to do, starting right now. Oh, thank you both so much! I really appreciate it.'

'Well, as you say, there's no harm done really.' Rufus stood to see me out. Tania stayed in her chair; her eyebrows couldn't move much, but I got the distinct impression she was frowning underneath. Still, I didn't think she'd go back on their decision. They both really did trust Lee.

'Except for the stress and worry,' I said. 'If there's anything I can do to make up for that, please let me know.'

'Just help your sister,' he said, and closed the door behind me.

I waited till I was past the BMW and back around the corner before I leaned against a wall and exhaled loudly. That had been a close escape. And not a fun one. I'd almost cried in there, from anxiety and desperation, and mostly because nearly everything I'd said in the Fanshawes' house, about both me and my sister, had been true.

'Dammit!' I threw my phone down on the kitchen table. Why didn't Lee turn her mobile on? Of course, now it had a more sinister meaning: she was on the run from the law, and possibly something else. I thought of the first phone call she'd made to me, while I'd been at the dance. She'd been in the stolen car then. She must have been terrified.

What would make my sister do such a thing?

I made myself a cup of coffee, barely paying attention to what I was doing. All of her friends, including Will, didn't even know she'd gone; they wouldn't know what was wrong, and I couldn't tell them why I was asking without giving away Lee's secret. I couldn't ask Mum, for obvious reasons.

The thought I'd had before struck me again, and I nearly dropped my spoon. Our mother was losing her mind. Had madness put Lee behind the wheel of that car, the same impulse that drove our mother to climb the hill at night?

I'd dismissed that idea before, but I hadn't known then quite how weird things had become.

I gave up on coffee and wandered into the living room. Her lilies were drooping and dropping pollen on the polished table. I went over to pick up the vase, to take them out to the back garden and dump them on the compost heap.

As I was reaching out for them, my eyes went to the new picture hung over my sister's fireplace, the one in the heavy Victorian frame: the butterflies, the ones I had thought suited my sister so well. From the angle I was standing right now, I could see that it wasn't a painting, after all. Each butterfly had a small but definite shadow to it. They were real.

I put the vase down and went over to the fireplace. Up close, it was clearer that the butterflies were real. They had been dead a long time. Their wings were spread, each one a jewel of colour made up of millions of glistening dustlike scales, spots and eyes and stripes and blotches, a carefully segmented body, six perfect needle-legs, and two antennae in graceful curves. Underneath each butterfly there was a note of its name, Latin and English, in copperplate pencil writing.

And through each body, holding them upright, trapping their wings into stillness, was a silver pin.

Inner Peace

It's hot. A dry heat, so different from Wiltshire summers, and the air is perfumed with salt and warm herbs. Lee climbs up the narrow dusty path to the summit of the hill. The view from up here is astounding: the brown and green island stretches out around her, olive trees, white buildings, a blue-domed church. And further away, the luminous turquoise sea.

A goat bleats. Lee takes her mobile phone from her pocket and holds it up high, as if showing it the view. There's a rumour that there's mobile reception here, though on the welcoming pamphlet it says very clearly *We discourage use of mobile phones and other media devices, as distractions from finding inner peace.*

But there's something she has to say, something that's been burning inside her since before she stepped off the ferry. No meditation or *asanas* or relaxation is going to help her find inner peace until she gets this off her chest.

Her phone beeps into life in her hand. The sound is incongruous here, in a place that looks as if it hasn't changed in thousands of years, not since the days of Poseidon and Aphrodite. She watches as the messages pile up; there are fewer now, only two texts and two voicemails. The only missed calls listed are from her sister.

Don't they miss me? she thinks with a pang, and then tells herself this kind of thinking is not the way to inner peace. She dials her sister's number.

Liza answers within a ring. 'Thank God,' she says, 'I've been trying to get in touch with you since this morning. Are you all right?'

She's been expecting anger that she could soothe with apologies and serenity. Not this concern, which sounds almost like panic.

'I'm fine. Are you okay? Is everything all right there?'

'Well, yes and no.'

'Mum? The business?'

'They're all fine. Where are you?'

She breathes in the herb-flavoured air. Oregano, or thyme. 'I'm in Greece. On an island.'

'Bloody hell, you really have swanned off on holiday.'

'I'm on a yoga retreat. I . . . felt like I needed to be cleansed.'

She's expecting a retort to this, too, but there's only a pause, then: 'Lee – are you really all right?'

'Yes.' No. She's not sure. 'Liza, I'm calling because I wanted to apologise. I shouldn't have got so angry at you on the phone the last time we spoke.'

'Why not?'

Again, the response is a surprise to her. 'Because – because it's wrong to take out your anger on people you love. I might not always agree with your choices, but that doesn't mean I should be screaming and shouting at you. Especially when you're taking care of everything for me at home.'

'It seems to me that it's better to let your anger out than to let it fester inside you.'

'Yes, well, maybe it's better for you. But I don't work that

286

way. I never have. I can't remember the last time I really argued with someone, except—'

'Except that Christmas, in the street, with me. I'm sensing a pattern here.'

It sounds like Liza is smiling. 'You're not taking me seriously.'

'No, I'm taking you really seriously. If you're angry with me, I'd rather know it. You can't be perfect every minute of every day, Lee. You can make mistakes.'

She gazes at the sea, pure and glittering with gold. 'I can't.'

'Everyone does.'

'Not me.'

'Lee, I know about the car.'

'What?'

'I know you took it.'

It's not hot any more; it's freezing. 'Who else knows?'

'It's okay, nobody else does. Only me. And Rufus got it back all right, everyone's fine.'

Breathe. She tries to remember the techniques she's been practising. They don't work.

'Why did you take it?'

Tears well out of her eyes. 'I didn't mean to. I was – it was – too much. There was too much going on, and nothing had changed, but it was all feeling so heavy on me – Mum, and the business, and Will, and the ball, and Stoneguard, and you were coming and I was afraid we'd argue again. I wanted to escape. And I saw the car, and I just – got in it.'

'You felt like speeding away.'

'Yes.'

'And it felt good, didn't it? Like you'd left everything behind and you were free.'

'Yes,' she says again, but quietly. Then, louder, 'But it was wrong, I shouldn't have done it. It's like arguing with you – I should know better. I should *be* better.'

'It's a one-off, Lee. It's over. Stop torturing yourself about it, you'll only make it worse.'

'But it's not a one-off.' It bursts out of her.

'You've stolen *another* car?'

'No, just little things, but—'

'Those nail varnishes and lipsticks under your bed?'

'Oh, God.' Guilt twists her guts. 'I don't know what's the matter with me. There's something really wrong, there must be.'

There's another pause. Then Liza says, hundreds of miles away, 'You know what? Personally, I like you a lot better with a few flaws in you.'

Lee wipes her wet face. 'I wanted to be more like you for a little while. I wanted not to care about anybody except for myself. I'm sorry for saying it, but it's true.'

'It's not true. I care about you. You might think it looks like I don't, but I do. I've been worrying here.'

Lee sniffs.

'Don't cry.'

'I want to cry.'

'All right, cry then.' Liza's got laughter in her voice. 'Wimp.'

'Witch.' But she giggles through her tears, a small bit of sweetness.

'Well, listen, I'm not very good at putting myself in someone else's shoes, but I'm going to take a guess and see how I do. Basically, you've been too busy being a good girl for the past two years to have any fun yourself. You don't do anything but look after Mum and the business, and I'm betting you've hardly allowed yourself any time to spend with Will, either.'

She swallows. 'You know about Will?'

'You and Will are the talk of the town. Perfect couple, right? Except when you took off you didn't tell him.'

'I couldn't tell anybody, Liza. I *stole a car*.'

'Yeah, in broad daylight, in a place where everyone knows you by sight. Damn, Lee, you've got a lot more guts than I thought you did.'

Liza sounds admiring. This is totally messed up.

'This is totally messed up! You're not supposed to be proud of me for this! It's wrong!'

'It's the first time you've rebelled in thirty years. It makes sense it would be a big one.'

'So you're saying this is some sort of – midlife crisis?'

'I'm saying you never have any fun. You've colour-coded every hour of your life. You need to cut loose.'

'And go on a crime spree?'

'Just relax. You've been away for days now and things haven't fallen apart. Rufus has got his car back, nobody knows it was you. Mum isn't going anywhere, the business hasn't gone under yet. Enjoy your Greek island. Sunbathe, drink some retsina. Throw some dishes.'

'It's a strict vegan diet here. No alcohol.'

'Sounds like a blast.'

'But you can't stay in Stoneguard, you've got your work to get back to.'

'I can take some time off.'

Love for her sister fills Lee, brighter than the sunshine all around her. She never would have believed Liza would put her own life aside to help her. Maybe because she never asked before. Maybe there's always been this connection, deep down, despite their differences.

'So how long are you in Greece for? Not that I care, I just want to know when to start warning the department stores to lock up their nail varnish.'

'Liza, don't.'

Liza laughs, that big throaty laugh that Lee could never quite accomplish herself. It's too dirty, too unfettered and gorgeous.

'Come back when you can,' she says. 'And stay in touch, okay? So I know you're safe.'

'All right. And . . .' She knows she should discuss Ice Cream Heaven, and Mum, and everything she's left behind and which has probably ground to a halt. But she needs a bit more inner peace before she wrestles with those repercussions, so she settles for, 'And thanks for looking after everything for me.'

'No problem. I sort of like being the good twin for a little while. Take care of yourself, and don't worry.'

As Lee thumbs off the phone, she knows that the latter is impossible. She's going to worry, phone or not, outside world or not.

But maybe, for a change, she really can take care of herself.

Kidnapped

What on earth was the point of a Ley Line Preservation Society? As far as I knew, ley lines, if they existed at all, were more or less indestructible, created by magnetism or polarity or whatever the hell it was supposed to be. They certainly didn't require the great and good of Stoneguard to assemble every second Sunday afternoon in Marj Parker's cat-filled living room and discuss how the lines could be 'protected' from the 'hazards of modern life'. If people didn't want a mobile phone mast near Stoneguard, surely they could think up a better protest than this.

But I did not say a word. I kept my jaws clamped shut and thanked Marj at the end of the meeting and kept myself from brushing the cat hair off my clothing until I could get out of sight.

Candace stood on the front path fanning herself. 'It's so muggy, Lee, do you want a lift home?'

'No, thanks, I can do with the exercise.' *And also, if I have to smile any bloody more, my lips will fall off.* I'd already spent a completely miserable hour eating dry lamb and dry roast potatoes with my mother, during which neither of us spoke more than necessary. The small-talk options had seemed rather limited, since I couldn't really say, 'Well, turns out your perfect other daughter has stolen a car.' Or 'How did you like that jujitsu hold I put you in the other night? Inescapable, isn't it?'

Or maybe it was because if we spoke, I'd have to confront, again, the extent of her decline. It seemed easier to sit across from her at the table while she glared at her lunch.

I lingered near Marj's sunflowers, pretending to admire them, so that I wouldn't be caught up by any other ley-line preservers on their way home and have to refuse all their offers of lifts too. Then I set off. Marj lived a couple of miles outside of Stoneguard proper, just off the A road heading to Swindon. There was a nice swathe of grass between the hedges and the road which was fine for walking, though the cars whooshed past at speed. They made a hot breeze which did nothing to cool off my skin.

I'd dreamed about crashing the Ferrari last night. The brief moment of freedom from gravity, and then the crunch of everything breaking. Fire and pulling. I'd woken up at four in the morning gasping and covered in sweat, and hadn't been able to get back to sleep. And I hadn't quite been able to get behind the wheel of the Mini today to drive to Marj's house. It was safer to walk.

When had I become the type of person who played it safe?

I wiped sweat off my forehead, and pushed back my hair. I was wearing a floaty white dress of Lee's which should have been lovely and cool. The Mini had air conditioning, I was sure of it.

Behind me, I heard a car approaching, then slowing. One of the meeting attendees, offering me a lift. I lifted my hand to wave them on, but then I heard the lovely throaty purr of the engine, and turned to look.

It was British Racing Green. The Aston Martin DBS. The front window was rolled down and inside was Will Naughton.

'Are you stalking me now as well as wooing me?' I asked.

'Get in,' he said. 'It's too hot to walk.'

'It's England, not the desert.'

'I've got air conditioning.'

I hesitated. On the one hand – Will. On the other hand – an air-conditioned DBS. It was only a couple of miles, and I wouldn't be driving.

On the other hand – maybe not. I did not want to have a panic attack in front of Will Naughton.

'I'll walk.'

The car kept pace with me. The clouds were low in the hot sky, and I felt a warm raindrop on my bare arm.

'I'll pick you up and put you in the car if you prefer,' he said.

'I'd like to see you try.'

He stopped the car, unfastened his seatbelt and began to open his door. So much for that bluff. I opened the passenger door and got in. Café-au-lait-coloured leather interior, classic round dials on the dash, Will's long-fingered, strong hands on the wheel. The air smelled of leather and sandalwood. I buckled the seatbelt and he pulled away from the kerb.

My heart stuttered. I sat on my hands and breathed deeply. The engine was a lovely low growl, a subtle vibration through the seat leather, and cool air feathered over my heated skin. Rain pattered on the roof and windscreen. I sat back. I was breathing, I was still in control. It was all right, for now at least. We were hardly going over thirty-five.

'What were you doing, walking down the A road on the hottest afternoon of the year?' Will asked.

'What are you doing, driving down the A road on the hottest afternoon of the year?'

He indicated the back seat with a jerk of his head. 'I had to pick up an AKG D12.'

I looked. There was a silver case on the seat, about the size of a small shoe box. 'Well, I'm none the wiser now.'

'It's a microphone.'

'Okay.'

'How about you?'

'I'm on my way to a rendezvous with my MI5 contact to pass on top-secret insider info about Ma Gamble's tofu burgers.'

'That's a lie, because I personally told MI5 all they could possibly want to know about Ma Gamble's tofu burgers last week, on the side of the A34.'

'You cad. Give a man a James Bond car and he thinks he's can outspy the professionals.'

'You're a horrible liar.'

'If only you knew the truth about that. You'd be shocked, you really would.'

'So why are you walking? Hasn't Stone finished with your bio-diesel conversion?'

'He has. I just felt like walking.'

'How's it run?'

'Not bad. You're not thinking of letting Stone at this car, are you?'

We'd stopped to wait at a roundabout. He ran his hands over the wheel, almost protectively. 'It's a moral dilemma. On the one hand, we should all be reducing our carbon footprint. On the other, I've been away from Stoneguard long enough to think that a precision V12 engine is a thing of beauty that shouldn't be messed with.'

'So you're not letting him touch it.'

'Not on your life.'

He smiled at me, just a flash. He was gorgeous, damn him. My body went all hot.

Damn me.

'Wait a second,' I said, as he continued around the roundabout. 'This isn't the way to my house.'

'No, it isn't.'

'Where do you think you're going?'

'For a drive.'

'I don't have time for a drive.'

'What do you have to do instead?'

I tried to think about what colour Lee had put in this afternoon's schedule, and I must have hesitated too long, because Will said, 'I thought so.'

'Will, take me home.'

'No. You haven't spoken to me in days. I'm not letting you out of this car until I've got you where I want you.'

Jesus. This man spoke like a romance novel hero. And even worse, I seemed to like it.

I thought it had been the booze obscuring my judgement on the night of the dance. I couldn't really be attracted to this man. Maybe I hadn't had sex in too long. Maybe it was the car.

Maybe it was the way his sleeves were rolled up to show his wrists and forearms. Maybe it was the way he filled the car with his voice and scent and presence. Maybe it was how he drove, not showily like many men with powerful cars, but with calm competence.

I pushed my sweat-dampened hair back behind my ears. 'Kidnapping is quite an interesting way to show a lady you're interested in her.'

'Did you like the flowers I sent?'

'Were those flowers? I thought they were another of the

neighbours' casseroles. I wondered why they tasted so odd.'

'You were in the other day when I came round. I saw the curtains twitch. Why didn't you answer the door?'

'I thought I was probably contagious.'

He raised an eyebrow. Why was I looking at him instead of the car, or the road?

'All right, I'll admit it,' I said. 'It's because you were wearing a jumper draped around your shoulders.'

'Ah. You were hiding from me because you didn't like my fashion choices.' He navigated another roundabout, accelerating into the turn.

'I'm sorry, but sometimes it's necessary.'

'Do I pass muster today?'

Jeans faded at the knees. A white cotton shirt. Hair casually rumpled. A bit of dark stubble on the chin. I looked out of the window again.

'Did I ever tell you about Timothy Clifton?' I asked. It was a risk, but less of a risk than continuing this banter that was dangerously close to flirtation.

'I don't remember you mentioning him. Why?'

'Oh, no reason. He was someone I used to work with, that's all. He sent me a text.'

'I thought your mobile was broken.'

Whoops. 'Um—'

'I understand. It's that particular kind of broken where you only take calls from people you want to speak with.'

'If only you knew how true that was.'

'I'm sorry that one of those people is me.'

He sounded sincere, and a little bit sad, too. For the first time I wondered if playing hard to get was a bad idea, whether it might break Lee and Will up, instead of making him keener. But what was my alternative?

He drove in silence. I watched the hedges and thought

about the route I'd take, if I were free to choose where to take this car. If I could drive it without fear. The M4 – too crowded and straight. A346 – eh, boring. We weren't headed that way anyway. A4361 – could be, there was that nice stretch between Winterbourne Monkton and Broad Hinton where you might get a bit of speed up, that is if a tractor didn't pull out in front of you, and with the hills rolling around you, you could feel almost as if you were flying.

'Are you going on the M4, or the—'

'A4361. Then the back way through Ogbourne. The motorway's too predictable.'

I settled back. I wasn't going to be able to get out, so I might as well enjoy it as much as I could. He seemed a careful driver, anyway.

I'd been listening enough to everyone at Ice Cream Heaven that I could make small talk about the good people of Stone-guard in my sleep, but Will didn't seem inclined for conversation right now. I looked out of the window. I tried not to notice the long muscles of his thighs whenever he pressed the clutch or the brake. Instead I listened to the roar of the throttle, muted and contained, like a wild animal in a cage.

'Are you up for a bit of speed?' Will asked me.

Was I?

'Why not,' I said. Keeping my muscles relaxed. Keeping my breathing calm.

Will opened it up a little and the DBS leaped forward like a sleek cat. Rain beaded and blew off its windows, and I felt that for the first time in days of standing still, I was moving again. We drove, faster and faster down the clear road, hedges and fields no more than green and yellow blurs. He hardly slowed to turn left down a minor road but the DBS could handle it; it held the road and sped ahead on the narrow ribbon of asphalt.

This was it. The hedges were high and the road turned and climbed. A pheasant exploded from the left and I jumped despite myself, but it missed the car by inches and hurtled back into the field.

I wasn't frightened at all.

'Faster,' I said. It wasn't what Lee would have said but I couldn't help it. The corner of Will's mouth curled up, his hands gripped the wheel, and he pressed the accelerator.

An English car, in the English countryside. It shouldn't make a difference in the way the car handled and felt, but it did. As if we were a very fast part of the scenery. And why wasn't I frightened? Was it because I wasn't supposed to be the one in control? We cut through the rain, glimpsing a white horse cut into the chalk hill face below us, and then followed the ridge of the hill with nothing above us but the vast grey sky.

The road bent and then dipped downhill. A village lay nestled below us, thatched roofs in a padding of green trees, the steel-grey of a twisting stream. If Will put his foot down a little bit more we could probably fly over it. I opened my mouth to tell him so, and that's when we turned a blind corner, hidden by hawthorn, and I saw the tractor.

It was an old one, battered, red and smeared with mud, hauling a trailer stacked with empty cages. It had pulled out of a gap in the hedge on the right, and was lumbering its slow way down the hill towards the village. A thin cloud of blue exhaust trailed behind it, and clumps of mud from its wheels littered the road. Straw drooped from the cages, dripping rainwater.

It never ceases to amaze me how many details your mind can register about an object when you're hurtling towards it at upwards of seventy miles per hour.

'Shit!' I yelled and my hand reached for the wheel,

instinctively to take charge while my feet pressed uselessly on the car floor where there was no accelerator or brake for me. Will only breathed in sharply. I hardly heard it above the engine and the sound of the tractor and my own heart.

He braked and turned the wheel and the DBS nudged to one side as if it had been brushed by a giant's finger. For a sick second, the tyres slid on the wet, muddy tarmac. And then they gripped, and the car went forward instead of sideways, and tried to throw itself past the tractor on the left of the narrow road. I judged the distance with my eyes, between the trailer at its widest point and the high thorny hedge on the left.

I could make it, or could have once, with not a lot of room to spare. But Will?

I glanced at him. His brows were drawn down, his hands gripping the wheel, his head forward in fierce concentration. I anticipated the crunch, the crash, the jerk as the seatbelt pulled us backwards against a G-force of seventy miles per hour. The heat and the pain.

I screamed and the sound was every nightmare I'd ever had.

I saw the ridged tractor wheels, somehow obscene in their wetness, then the red of the body and a smeared glimpse of the farmer's pale and yelling face above the dull green of his raingear. There was a scraping and a snapping of twigs from the other side of the car as it grazed the hedge.

Then we were past, shooting forward again, clear and free. My breath had been punched out with my scream and I couldn't haul it back in, couldn't move, couldn't blink. Grey crept around the edges of my vision.

'Crazy motherfucker city drivers,' said Will.

My breath came back, all at once, and I burst out laughing.

I turned to Will and he was laughing too, a big laugh that opened his mouth wide and he caught my eye and we were laughing together.

'I think we gave that farmer a heart attack,' I said.

'I think we gave me a heart attack. Christ, it was fun.'

His right hand on the wheel, his left reached out and took mine. I gave it to him gratefully. I put my finger on his wrist and felt his pulse thumping hard and fast. For a moment, our hearts were beating exactly in time.

Then the road turned sharply again and he took his hand back to steer, and I rubbed mine against my leg because I could feel the heat of his skin on my fingers.

'I hope you didn't scratch the paintwork,' I said.

He shrugged, his eyes on the road. 'It happens. Better than having a flattened tractor on my bonnet.'

'True. That was good driving, Will. I didn't think you'd make it.'

There was a passing place on the left before the village began, and he pulled into it and stopped. He grinned at me. The car was purring as if proud of itself.

'You know what?' he said. 'I knew I would make it. I'm not quite sure how, to be truthful. I'm a good driver, but not that good. Things seemed to slow down, and I could see everything so clearly. I saw the car going through that gap before it did. I knew exactly how it would fit, even the wing mirrors.'

'It's the danger,' I told him. 'It focuses the mind. You have time to memorise every detail.'

'It was incredibly stupid. I'd do it again, though.'

'Let's.'

The tractor drove by at that point, and the driver gave us the finger as he passed. Since he was going so slowly, the gesture lasted a good long time. He made wanking movements with his other hand, too.

'Then again, he might have a shotgun in there,' I said.

Will waited until the tractor was out of sight and then he put the car in gear again. 'We'll cut through the back of the village and onto the main road. I don't think I want to cross his path again, now that I think of it.'

'Scaredy-cat.'

'Let's call it the better part of valour.' We turned right at the tiny village pub and zig-zagged for about a quarter of a mile before we were on the A road back to Stoneguard. The DBS pulled smoothly out and was soon doing a steady, calm fifty. The rain stopped and the sky turned a freshly-washed blue. My body buzzed pleasantly with the after-effects of adrenaline, and I relaxed in my seat.

Most idiots who can buy high-performance motors don't have the first idea of how to use them. The car owns them, not the other way round – like the Pipe King. Whatever his other faults, in less than thirty seconds, Will had shown his mastery over his machine. A mastery I might never have again.

But I'd seen the possibility of it, in our near-miss.

'Ever taken this thing out on a track?' I asked him.

'Once or twice.' He smiled. 'Since when have you been interested in cars?'

'Oh. Well, I'm a little more interested because I've spent so much time talking with Stone about mine, you know. And I think I saw a *Top Gear* about this model, or something like that.'

'Lee Haven, you're a woman of many surprises. The minute I think I know you, you pull something new out of the hat.'

'Full of tricks and secrets, that's me.'

We were approaching Stoneguard; even if you couldn't see the stone circle looming in the distance, you could tell by the preponderance of brown attraction signs. I began to wonder if I was going to invite Will into the house for a drink. My fingertips could feel the ghost of his grip on them; as soon as I thought about it, it was a struggle not to raise them to my mouth to see if I could taste his skin. It was very much a bad idea to invite him into the house. But the afternoon was beginning to have its own momentum. I wasn't sure if I could stop it.

But before we got to the town, Will slowed down and indicated. 'Where are we going?' I asked.

'I'd have thought that was obvious.' We turned right and passed through a set of vast open stone and iron gates. Frozen statues of griffins holding shields perched on the top of either side of them. Their beaks were curled in fierce grins, and the shields held the crest of the ancient Naughton family.

'I don't recall asking you to take me to Naughton Hall.'

'You've been avoiding me for over a week. I'm not going to let you out of my sight for a little while. That's going to be easier to do on my territory. Besides, you haven't been in the house since we started construction.'

The gravel drive curved with leisurely elegance between stately chestnuts, through grounds studded every now and then with wild flowers and sheep. With all the loose rock, it would be a perfect place for really gunning the accelerator, pulling the hand brake and leaving a lovely fishtail trail. But Will drove steadily and slowly. Probably the blue blood running in his veins compelled him to behave properly within the boundaries of his ancestral home.

'I've got a lot of work to do at home, actually.'

'I'm sorry about that. But I'm sure you can spare me an hour or two, in return for all the messages I've left on your phone.'

The Hall lay in front of us, growing bigger by the moment.

It was made of red brick and grey stone and black beam, millions of windows with their tiny panes glinting in the sun. A whopping great symbol of privilege and wealth, and the man beside me was taking me to it as if he still exercised the right of an aristocrat over his subjects.

'Will, you can't force me to come to Naughton Hall if I don't want to.'

'On the contrary, I'm afraid that I can.'

All that brief alliance that I'd felt with Will while he was driving melted away, and I saw him again as he was: stubborn, arrogant and spoiled, someone I hated to concede any-thing to. I could open the door and jump out of the car, and walk – or run – to Stoneguard. But what was the point? Stoneguard wasn't my territory either. As long as I was pretending to be Lee, I was going to have to deal with this man, and try to walk the fine line between stepping closer and pulling away.

I hadn't been to Naughton Hall since I was a young child. I remembered it as cavernous, ancient and cold except for a small semi-circle of vicious heat around each fireplace. You were not allowed to run there, or yell, or play with any of the things, even though there were swords and pikes on the wall of the gallery, and a real suit of armour. The armour had been far too much of a temptation on my final visit; after I was caught trying on the helmet, I was never allowed to darken the Hall's Elizabethan doors again. On the rare occasions when our family was invited, my mother left me at home with a brave babysitter and brought Lee with her as the Haven twin who could be trusted to behave appro-priately.

I crossed my arms, and when Will stopped the car at the impressive front door and got out, I stayed exactly where I was until he came round and opened my door for me. My feet crunched on the wet gravel, which gleamed like tiny jewels. Will held out his hand to me, but I didn't take it. It might be Lee's dream to be lady of the manor, to sweep into her fairy castle on the arm of her Prince (well, Son-of-a-Viscount) Charming, but it wasn't mine. I'd walk into Naughton Hall under my own steam. I wondered if I'd still be banned, if Will knew who I really was.

Walking beside him, I could see how perfectly he suited the place. Even in his casual clothes, clothes that anybody could be wearing, there was something about him that exuded poshness. His upright posture, maybe; the strength of his nose and jaw which probably went all the way back to some Norman's nose and jaw. He walked with the ease of a person who belonged here amongst these stones and treasures, who knew that dozens and hundreds of his relatives had walked these same paths and corridors before him, and that more would walk here after he was gone. A long permanent line of Naughtons stretching both ways in time, all with that same nose and jaw and posture, so far you couldn't see the end in either direction.

I wondered if he expected my sister to provide his share in that line of heirs for him. I wondered if he thought about that line of heirs every time he had sex, and then I wondered again if he and Lee had slept together, and then wondered why on earth I should care about their sex life or why it should make any difference to me. I was wondering so hard that I got to the bottom of the worn steps leading to the pitted oak front door before I realised that Will wasn't walking beside me any more. He was standing a metre or so down the path, next to a monstrous and beautiful clump of lavender, watching me with amusement.

'Aren't we going in?' I said, annoyed at his smile.

'Yes, but my father would never forgive me for my breach

of manners if I had a guest at Naughton Hall and didn't take her to greet him.'

'Oh. Okay.' I thought that's what we had been doing, but maybe Lord Naughton was round the back having Pimm's on the lawn between rain showers or some such. I came away from the front door and walked alongside Will. The lavender breathed its old-fashioned scent into the air, and bees hummed lazily in the dropping sunshine. Although the grounds through which we'd driven up had been left for pasture, the lawns around the house were precisely trimmed. Not a single daisy or dandelion marred the velvet surface. The troops of faithful gardeners probably used nail scissors around the flower beds. We passed mullioned windows and walked through a yew arch into a topiary.

Only the rich could have enough time, money and greenery on their hands that they thought carving animal shapes out of hedges was a worthwhile pastime. We walked by a peacock, a dove, a bear, a lion and a griffin like the pair on the gates, all clipped out of perfectly serviceable bushes. Will had to duck underneath the griffin's outstretched paw, which loomed over the path to bat any unwary walkers who happened to be over six feet tall. 'My father's idea of a little joke,' he said to me, which only confirmed my beliefs.

The topiary ended with another yew arch, and we followed a winding path past several greenhouses and through an extensive herb and vegetable garden. It stretched in all directions, full of various plants and poles and shiny things tied to string, all the way up to a big wooden barn and, it appeared, beyond. The Naughtons certainly believed in keeping their gardeners busy. If the peasants revolted, the family would probably be able to shut the gates and live under siege conditions for months without ever having to venture out for food.

I expected Will to take me to another lawn, maybe a tennis court or a swimming pool. Instead he led me up to the front of the barn, which had a huge door with a human-sized door cut into it on one side. It had been painted a glossy dark green, not unlike the colour of the Aston Martin, and the cobbles in front of it were swept clean, with pots of bright geraniums clustering around. Apparently even the farm animals had to be tidy here at Naughton Hall.

'Aren't we going to see your father?' I asked. 'Or are we stopping off for a roll in the hay?'

He only laughed, and knocked on the barn door before he opened it and gestured for me to enter. I shrugged and went in.

My first thought was that the horses and sheep had opened up an antiques shop. Then I realised that the air smelled of pipe tobacco and furniture polish, not livestock, and that there wasn't a single wisp of hay to be seen. The barn, in fact, had been converted into a human living space, with the indoor walls covered with white plaster between the black beams, and polished oak floorboards underfoot. Not that you could see much of the walls or the floorboards, because the whole living area that I could see was crammed full of furniture and rugs and paintings.

'Father, we've got a guest for tea,' Will called into the jumble of priceless antiques. 'Come through,' he said to me, and led me through the barn – no easy feat, as in some places there were only narrow walkways between pieces of furniture. In a small clearing surrounded by sideboards crammed with porcelain, sat a chintz sofa and chairs, and a wooden rocker with a scarred table beside it.

'He must be out in the garden, still. He'll be in in a minute, he's a creature of habit. Please have a seat. I'll get the tea.' He went through a door which I presumed led to the kitchen.

Will was getting the tea? Where were the servants? The adoring flunkies and the pomp and circumstance? For that matter, why was most of the furniture from Naughton Hall in the barn, even one that had been rather nicely converted?

Of course, there was all the building work going on. Will had been talking about it at the dance. They must have moved themselves and all their belongings in here for the duration.

'Hello!' Lord Naughton appeared from somewhere and strode through the antiques. He was a lean man, with hair greying at the temples, wearing a checked shirt rolled up over his forearms, corduroy trousers with very dirty knees, and wellies. 'Wonderful to see you, Lee, no don't get up, I'll kiss you from here.' He bent over me and kissed my cheek. There was an air around him of freshness and soil, and he went to the wooden chair and sat in it.

'Aphids,' he said, taking a wooden pipe from one shirt pocket and a pouch of tobacco from the other. 'Evil little buggers. The ladybirds can't keep up with 'em, they're stuffed to the gills. I've spent most of today picking 'em off by hand and drowning 'em.'

'That – sounds interesting.'

'Wish it were; they come back overnight and I do it all over again. How's your garden by the way, girl? That Rhodochiton doing all right?'

'Yes, it's wonderful,' I hazarded. It was pretty unlikely that Lord Naughton was going to make a special trip into Stoneguard to nose around Lee's garden.

'You must take some runner beans with you. I think I could feed the five thousand on runner beans. Oh, here is my son with the tea. Did you get what you needed in Swindon, William?'

'Yes, I did.' Will was carrying a large silver tea-tray, piled high with porcelain and an enormous and rather magnificent

Chinese tea-pot. He put it on a highly-polished table and gave me a glass of water from it. I drank it, surprised he'd noticed I was thirsty.

After pouring three cups of tea and handing one to his father and one to me to replace my drained water glass, he sat down beside me on the sofa. It wasn't a big sofa, more like a love seat, and his weight made the cushions go down. He should have looked wrong sitting on a chintz love seat. He looked entirely damned comfortable. He leaned forward and snagged two biscuits from a plate on the tray and handed me one. It was a Bourbon. I took it.

'I wanted to show Lee around the work in the Hall,' he told his father.

'Good, good.' Lord Naughton took a long draught of tea. 'Ah, that washes the aphids away. How's that twin of yours?'

'She's fine, thank you, Lord Naughton. She's very busy with her film career.'

'Spirited girl, your sister, though rather hard on the furniture. I don't think Cousin Malcolm has been the same since she took his head off.' He nodded to the corner, where I saw a familiar suit of armour. It had a distinctly rakish tilt to the helmet. 'Can't say I blame her, I did the same thing myself a few dozen times when I was a boy. Glad to hear she's doing well. How's your mother?'

'Mum's about the same,' I said. I should really get this phrase tattooed on my forehead.

'Hm, yes, but what's that when it's at home? Is she lucid, still? Is she recognising you?'

'She definitely recognises me.'

'Terrible disease. My Aunt Iphigenia had it – you remember her, William. We could see her in flashes, and then the next minute –' he snapped his fingers – 'gone. Then the flashes disappeared, too. Waste of a good woman.'

'Mum's got excellent care, I think.'

'She would. That woman's always been proud, demanded the best. Quite right, too. She won't see anyone, I hear.'

I wondered if posh people dunked their biscuits in their tea, decided I didn't care and did it anyway. 'She's a very stubborn woman.'

'Well, stubborn is good. It'll help her hold on a bit longer. You look tired – does she wander at night?'

'She picks the locks.'

Lord Naughton threw back his head and laughed. His laugh was very much like his son's. 'Once my Uncle George found Auntie Gin a mile and a half away from the home, sitting at a bus stop at midnight. She told him she was waiting for the stagecoach to Newmarket.'

I didn't quite feel like laughing, but I did smile. Lord Naughton helped himself to a handful of biscuits.

'The most difficult part for George was the anger.'

'Your aunt was angry?'

'No, no, Gin was always quite placid, bless her, right up until the end. No, George was angry. We all were, to some extent.'

I sat up. All by themselves, my arms remembered putting my own mother in a lock-hold and forcing her down the hill, into her bed. Defeated.

This was not where I'd expected this small talk to go.

'Why – why were you angry?' I asked.

'Sounds monstrous, doesn't it? But it's maddening, an adult acting like a child. And it isn't like normal illness, because they won't get better, and my aunt was healthy as a horse for years. Only her mind was gone. Terribly unfair. It's easy to be angry.'

'But I've been—'

But I've been angry at her all my life, I was going to say. But

Lord Naughton was looking at me with grey eyes that were like Will's, and Will was looking at me, too. And it wasn't something that Lee would say.

'It feels wrong to be angry at someone who's helpless,' I said instead. That was something Lee would say, but it was also true, and I was surprised I was saying it. It was the understanding in Lord Naughton's face that brought it out. And the relief I felt saying it. 'It's like bullying a sick old woman. It's a horrible way to feel. If she were whole, herself, I could argue with her. But she's not. The whole thing makes me feel nauseated.'

'Yes, yes, that's right.'

'I want her to be herself again so I can be angry with her properly. It doesn't even make any sense. I should be . . . kind.'

'You are kind,' Will said. He touched my hand, and I pulled it away.

'Let's talk about something else,' I said.

'How's her garden?' Lord Naughton said immediately.

'Awful. I don't think anyone's looked at it all summer. You should come round and have a look.'

He tamped down the tobacco he'd put in his pipe. 'Might do, might do. If you think it might help her out. Hate to see a garden like that go to waste.' He stood. 'Now come and give me your opinion about these marrows.'

Will stood as well. It seemed to me that his father was precisely the amount shorter than Will to be able to walk under the topiary lion without ducking. 'She'll have to take a look at them some other time, Father. I'm taking her around the Hall now.'

'Of course, well, stop by the marrows if you get a moment.' He sat back down and struck a match.

We went out into the enormous garden. Alone with Will,

and the feel of his hand still on mine, I felt embarrassed about revealing my feelings about my mother. I cast about for a new topic. 'Does your father really do all of this?' I asked.

'Oh yes. It's his main occupation these days. I'm sorry, he's desperate to talk about it. He doesn't get much chance.'

'Do the gardeners mind him hanging over them all the time?'

'We haven't had a gardener since Thewkson died ten years ago.'

I stopped and looked around me. Veg in all directions, as far as the eye could see. And the hulking fantastic shapes of the topiary in the background. 'All by himself?'

'Except for the dark days when he forces me out here with him to pull weeds. I don't think my father could bear to have a gardener any more. He likes his control. It's a Naughton trait.' We skirted a herb garden which breathed green scent into the evening air. 'I wish he'd get out more, but he's reluctant to leave the comforts of home and garden.'

'He really should go and see my mother one Sunday,' I said. 'She says she doesn't want visitors, but I think that's ridiculous.'

'I'll try to persuade him to do that. I think it would be good for him. Thank you.'

I snorted. 'Don't say that too quickly, we don't know if she'd kick him out.' We passed the giant lavender bush again. 'He spoke almost fondly of my sister,' I said. 'That's a first around here.'

'Is it? Give her my regards when you speak to her next, will you?'

'She didn't like you very much. Too posh by half.'

He laughed. 'And you?'

'I'm not too posh at all.'

'That wasn't what I was asking.'

'I know.' The Hall loomed in front of us, all pointed gables and flashing mullions in the lowering sunshine. We approached the front entrance, where I'd mistakenly tried to go in earlier. 'Why do you want to show it to me?'

'We couldn't get in here last time you visited. But it's a lot further along now.' He took a big bunch of keys from his pocket.

'Oh, that's what that was,' I said. 'I thought you were just happy to see me.'

'So you were looking.' We walked up the steps to the front entrance, our feet fitting neatly in the dips worn by thousands of other feet, and he unlocked the door. Directly inside the door was a rack holding rows of orange hard hats. He took two and handed me one.

I was actually beginning to be curious about Naughton Hall now, if it was dangerous enough to need hard hats. Will strapped his own on and picked up a torch from the rack, too. 'The power's out?' I asked.

'In this part. We've had to set up a generator for the workmen so they can see what they're doing. It's fine in the rest of the building, where we've finished working, but this part is the problem.' He held the door open for me, and I walked into the cavern that was Naughton Hall.

Trespassing

It wasn't quite dark in here. The windows let in slanting light at ground-floor level and at first-floor level, too. Still, it took a moment or two for my eyes to adjust to the difference in illumination, and at first all I could see were shadows and more shadows. Some were deep and solid, like the corrugated shadow where I thought I remembered the big oak staircase. Others were spindly, criss-crossing like a thick vertical spider's web. The floor was dull grey and seemed to be undulating. Will shone the torch over my shoulder and between that and my eyes getting used to the darkness I began to be able to make out the room.

Dust sheets covered the floor, which accounted for the illusion of movement. The dark wooden panelling walls were largely obscured by a network of metal scaffolding poles, stretching two storeys up to the ceiling.

Yes, the ceiling . . . Will pointed the torch upwards when he saw me tilt my head. The first thing the circle of light illuminated was a big belly in pink flesh tones, girdled with rings of rolling fat and punctuated by a deep navel. I wrinkled my nose and he panned the light over so I could see more of the painting. It was of a particularly obese cherub, with legs like doughy tree trunks, cheeks like burgeoning apples, and a pair of delicate angel wings protruding from its massive upper back.

'Surely those wings could never hold that thing up,' I said. 'It's against physics.'

'Portman had a very ripe imagination,' Will said, and played the light over more of the ceiling, revealing more fat cherubim and a gaggle of voluptuous nymphs dancing their scantily-clad way over a field of flowers.

'So this is the Portman ceiling everyone was going on about.'

'The very one.'

'I don't remember it as being quite so . . .' I searched for a word that Lee might use, something tactful. *Fantastic*, maybe. No, that implied admiration. My gaze got caught on the shepherd who was partnering the nymphs in their dance. He had, from the looks of it, a rather large set of keys underneath his tunic.

'Fleshy?' Will suggested.

'That'll do. Your family's into this sort of thing, are they?'

'Another William Naughton commissioned it in 1752. It's the only Portman ceiling in existence; he was primarily a sculptor, but apparently that William loved his work so much he wanted it painted onto his home where everyone could see it as soon as they walked in. The rest of the Naughtons have been regretting it ever since. Though probably none as much as I do.'

'So you're taking it down?'

Will laughed. 'English Heritage would have my balls for garters. No, we're repairing it. It's the most valuable part of the house – a work of major art-historical import. You wouldn't believe how much money and how many hours of meetings it's required.'

'But it's hideous.'

'You're telling me. I used to spend many a Sunday afternoon shooting wads of paper up at it through a pea shooter. There's one still over here, look.' He shone the light on one of the nymph's bare breasts; I could just about make out a small lump of whitish something near her pink nipple. 'It's an eighteenth-century mural painted on sixteenth-century plaster. It's a wonder it's lasted as long as it has.'

'If you let it fall down, you wouldn't have to look after it any more. You could say that time took its natural toll.'

Will shook his head. 'My father wouldn't hear of it. We have to preserve it for posterity, and for the occasional Portman scholar who comes round and has spontaneous orgasms about it.' He played the torchlight over the scaffolding and sighed. 'At least living in the barn we don't have to look at it any more.'

'It's rather odd, seeing Lord Naughton in the barn surrounded by all his worldly possessions,' I said. 'A little bit as if Queen Elizabeth and Prince Philip decided to pack up all the furniture in Windsor Castle and move it to a three-bed semi in Reading.'

He laughed. 'We're not that posh. And my father's at an age to appreciate the central heating in the winter.'

He opened the door and switched on a light. I blinked, dazzled after the half-light of the hall. 'Games room,' he said.

I took off my hard hat and stared. It was like stepping from the past into the present. If not for the dark wood panelling on the walls, I wouldn't have thought I was in the same house. The first impression was of televisions; two enormous flat screens hung on opposite walls, in front of semi-circles of leather armchairs and couches. One was hooked up to snakes of video game controls. A big green-felted billiards table dominated the centre of the room, and a fully-stocked bar

315

stretched along another wall. There was a pinball table, an audio system made to look like an old-fashioned jukebox, and six mounted heads of stags high up on the walls.

I was glad Will had brought me to this room now. Because over the past hour or so, I'd almost begun to like him. He drove a good car well, he had a sense of humour, he made tea and he didn't like hideous art even if it was priceless. But the games room took that liking and quite rightly smashed it to pieces under my heels.

This room was a playboy's paradise. A place where he and his similarly rich mates could kick back, watch sports, have gentlemen's bets over the billiards and drink themselves silly. It must have cost thousands of pounds just in televisions.

He'd turned his father out of his home and made him live in a barn, for this?

'Very impressive,' I said coldly. 'I'm sure you can't wait to use it.'

'Oh, it's been used already. It's the most popular room in the house.' He touched the billiards table with affection.

How could my sister stand him? And she'd called *me* selfish, for going off and leading my own life. I clenched my teeth.

'Of course,' he continued, 'you can't tempt rock stars out into the middle of Wiltshire without offering them some compensations.'

'Rock stars, models, actresses,' I pretended to agree. 'And the super-rich, of course. You all have such tiresomely low boredom thresholds. And of course you can't be expected to go to the pub in town.'

'Well, some people do prefer the pub,' Will said. 'It's offering the choice.'

'How thoughtful of you.' I tossed my hard hat onto the billiard table and marched across the room and through another door. I could hear Will following me. It led to a short corridor, lit by modern recessed lighting, and into a vast dining room. I remembered this room, with its long gleaming table and dozens of chairs, where footmen or whatever they were called would stand at attention, ready to cater for the Naughton family's every whim. Will had renovated this, too. Gone was the long table, replaced by several glass tables of varying sizes and modern chairs. It looked more like a hotel dining room than an ancestral home.

Did he really expect Lee to be impressed by this? 'Lovely,' I tossed over my shoulder, and went through into the next room. The library, with another television and several desktop computers.

Will, annoyingly, was having no trouble keeping up. 'The main wing of the house is mostly the social area. The real business is all in the east wing. Shall we?' He held out his arm for me. He really should know better by now. Seeming not to notice my snub, he opened yet another door and took me down yet another corridor. 'This wing is more modern,' he told me, 'early nineteenth century. It's not of any historical importance, fortunately, so it's been easy to get at the wiring, and the walls are nice and thick. Which makes it better for the noise.'

The noise? What was he putting in the east wing, anyway? I fleetingly pictured S&M dungeons, whipping posts and iron maidens – hell, why not a full-fledged menagerie with elephants and lions?

Then he opened the door and we walked into a recording studio.

I'd never been in a recording studio before, my job requiring me to produce spectacles rather than noises, but I knew what it was, because what other kind of room had waffle-look walls, microphone stands and a full drum kit in the corner?

I remembered the microphone with the spy name, on the back seat of his car. Apparently Will Naughton fancied himself as a bit of a pop star. I looked around the room, trying to figure out what on earth I could possibly say that wouldn't show my utter incredulity and contempt.

'This is the smaller one,' he told me. 'I've got two more, one quite a bit larger, and two mixing studios as well.'

Three recording studios. Even the richest, most spoiled would-be musician didn't need three recording studios and two mixing studios.

'Once we get the ceiling sorted out we should be able to take some bookings, maybe one artist or group at a time until we work out the glitches. But I'm hoping within six months we could be running to our full potential, with several bands living and working here at once.'

I touched the acoustic walls, then tapped my finger on a cymbal. The metallic ringing was much louder than I'd have expected. Apparently Will Naughton had renovated Naughton Hall into a high-spec rehearsal and recording studio. Turfing his father out into the barn as he did.

'Forgive me if I'm being stupid, Will,' I said slowly. 'And forgive me if we've talked about this already. But can you just run me through your reasons for turning Naughton Hall into a recording studio?'

He sat down behind the drum kit and banged the bass drum twice before he spoke.

'I trust you, Lee,' he said.

'Okay,' I said, not sure where he was going with this.

'And I appreciated your honesty about your mother's condition. I know it's not easy to talk about it. I know my father appreciated it too. And I think the idea of getting my father to visit your mother is a stroke of genius. He'll do it because he'll think he's helping a neighbour, but really it will take him out of himself for a little while. He spends too much time with the garden and his memories.'

'I'm glad you think it's a good idea. Why have you changed the subject?'

'I haven't, really. You asked why I was turning Naughton Hall into a residential recording studio, and I'm assuming that you don't want the answer that I've told everyone else, that it's about wanting to bring the family fortunes up to date in the twenty-first century. I think you want the real answer, and that's about my father. And how he's broke.'

'Broke.'

'The tactful term, I believe, is "cash-poor, land-rich". Only we're not land-rich any more, either; we had to sell off most of the property aside from the Hall and the garden years ago. My father is very good at growing marrows, but less good at finance. After my mother died, he made some poor decisions. A lot of them had to do with preserving the Portman ceiling. It was as if he'd lost my mother and couldn't bear to see that collapsing too. He threw money at it, and most of it didn't do a bit of good.'

'Aren't there grants and things to preserve stuff like that?'

'Yes. And my father was too proud to apply for any of them. And, of course, there was all the capital needed just to keep the rest of the Hall in decent repair.' He picked up a pair of drumsticks and used them to beat a light rhythm to accompany the words he was saying. 'I had a decent salary as an A and R man for Tornado Records, but compared with what the Hall needs to keep it at a liveable standard, it's a drop in the bucket. Never mind the damn ceiling, which sucks money like a limpet. Of course, I didn't know any of this until about two years ago when my father sat me down for a heart-to-heart. He should have told me years before, when I could have done more, but by the time it got bad enough to tell me, it was too late. Even once we'd applied for the grants and got them, it was a huge shortfall. As it was, we had three options – sell the house, open it fully up to the public, or try to make it into a going business concern. Either of the first two options would kill my father. This way, he gets to live in the grounds, and if we make a success of it, at least we've got something to pass down to the later generations.'

'You really do think that way, don't you? About later generations?'

He shrugged and thumped the bass drum again. 'It's been bred into me, I suppose.' Then a drum roll and a cymbal smash, as if he'd told the punchline of a joke.

'It must be costing millions, though, to do up this place. And convert the barn, too. Why don't you use that money to keep the place as it is?'

'Banks, oddly enough, are more willing to lend money for a project they might see a return on, than sinking their cash into a big old house. You might as well toss it into the fire. Come on.'

He got up and went through another doorway set into the wall, into a control booth full of equipment: switches, gauges, monitors, like the bridge of some science-fiction spaceship. Then back into the hallway, which had been fitted with fire doors.

This was difficult to comprehend. Will Naughton wasn't rich at all. He was probably poorer than my sister was, seeing as she had a controlling interest in Ice Cream Heaven.

'What about the Aston Martin?' I asked.

'I got a deal on it from a teenage singer I signed to Tornado. It was the first thing he bought when he had a number one single, and then of course he couldn't drive it, so he sold it to me cheap. I should probably give it up, but I can't seem to bring myself to. Besides, it's useful to project a solvent image when you're presenting business plans to the bank.'

The weirdest thing about all this was that nobody in Stoneguard was talking about it. A cat had kittens and it was gossiped about for months. But the lord of the manor was utterly broke, and nobody squeaked a word. 'Why aren't you telling people this?'

'My father prefers it if I keep quiet about the dire financial straits situation. Personally, I think it's better to be honest and open. It's not as if Stoneguard is going to turn against us for not being rich. I think it's more likely they'd turn on us for deceiving them. But he's a proud man, and I can't fault that. The investors like it, too; it's better PR for the business if it doesn't look as if we're as desperate as we are.'

'But you told me.'

He met my gaze, his grey eyes serious. 'I know it's a strange time to choose to tell you all this, but I did.'

'Why?'

'Mostly, because you asked. Nobody else has.'

'And do you want me to keep quiet about it, too?'

He paused. 'You can make your own decision about that, Lee. I know you don't like deception. I don't either. If it were out in the open, my father would probably find it easier to cope with than he fears. But I don't think he's quite ready yet. Maybe after the studio is up and running, and we don't have so much to worry about any more.'

'Right. I'll – think it over.'

'One thing I've learned from all of this is how much my father trusts me. I'd never known how much, until I came back home and started this project. He's left everything in my hands – and I mean everything. His whole future and his whole past. It's an honour, but it's a huge responsibility, too. I suppose you must have felt the same way when your mother signed Ice Cream Heaven over to you.'

I thought of my sister, who'd dreamed of being mistress of this place. Who was loved by everyone, who shouldered responsibility, who kept secrets and who had disappeared.

Whose man I was talking to right now. And he'd told me a secret he should be telling to Lee.

We left the studio and Will showed me some other things, but I was only paying cursory attention. The feeling was growing on me, ever stronger, that I shouldn't be here. I was trespassing too much on my sister's life.

So when Will opened another door that took us outside, to a part of the garden I hadn't seen yet, I said quickly and cheerfully, 'Well, Will, that was very nice but I've got to get home now.'

He'd registered my total change in mood; he raised his eyebrows. 'So soon?'

'It's getting late, and remember it wasn't my idea to come here anyway. Will you take me in your flash car, or should I hop over the fence and walk?'

'Lee,' he said, half on a sigh.

'Hop over the fence, then. Okay, see you later, thanks for the tour.' I began to turn away, and he put his hand on my arm.

'Don't go yet. I think we need to discuss something, don't you?'

'Oh, I think we've done enough discussing for one day. And I do in fact have lots of things to do, so maybe we can talk about all of this later. Much later. I'll call you, okay?'

'No. We need to talk about this now.'

The authority in his voice set my teeth on edge. 'Will, you will *not* tell me what to do.'

'And you won't continue to drive me crazy without us at least trying to sort this out.'

'I told you: later.' I began to walk away. And then something happened that I never could have expected. If I had expected

322

it, I would have prevented it with a single movement of my arm, or a feint to the side.

Or maybe, to tell the truth, I wouldn't have.

Will grabbed me from behind. Then he flipped me in his arms so that he was holding me cradled in the crooks of his elbows, in much the same manner as a swamp monster holding a helpless damsel in a B-movie.

Then he started walking, carrying me with him.

I could have broken his hold in any one of dozens of ways. But Lee wouldn't have. And I, God help me, didn't want to. I liked the way his chest felt against mine, the way his arms felt around me. The warmth of his breath on my neck.

This wasn't drunkenness. It wasn't even the fact that I hadn't had sex for months and months. It was attraction, pure and simple, for a man who could talk smart and drive a fast car and had the face of a god and yes, for one who was responsible and took care of his father. A man who was perfect for my sister.

'Very mature,' I said. 'Using force.'

'I've already kidnapped you, I might as well go all the way.'

'Where are you taking me? The dungeon?' Or to his bedroom, I thought, and I couldn't suppress a shiver. He carried me through the fragrant bushes, into the centre of the topiary. The animals cavorted around us, their shadows long in the late sun.

'Feeding me to the hedge animals? Is that what your ancestors did to insubordinate peasants?'

'Generally we chopped them up first. Are you going to run away? Or do I have to put a lead on you?'

The idea of being tied up by Will Naughton should not make my body turn to warm liquid moosh. It did. I was screwed.

'I won't run away,' I said.

He brought me to a cast-iron bench and set me down on its cold seat. Then he sat down beside me. You'd think that the lack of bodily contact would get rid of the attraction I felt for him, but being close to him yet not touching made it worse, because I had such a recent memory of what it was like to be in his arms.

'Okay,' I said, 'I'm listening. What do you want to say?'

Considering he'd gone to such lengths to get me to listen, it was faintly surprising that Will didn't speak right away. Instead he stared at the lion that was directly in front of us, and I watched his profile.

'You've changed,' he said, at last. 'Since the dance. You're different.'

Well, hallelujah, give the man a medal. But despite my sarcastic inward thought, my real response was relief. 'Is that so?'

'Yes. You're not returning my phone calls, for a start.'

'Have I always returned your phone calls before?'

'Within about two minutes.'

'I suppose I've been busy.'

'I don't like it.'

'Gosh, I am sorry. Next time you ring, I'll make sure to drop everything and—'

'Why are you so angry with me, Lee?'

'I don't get angry.'

'You're certainly acting it. For a minute or two today I thought you weren't any more, but now here we are again. We both agreed to break up, remember? We both thought this wasn't going anywhere.'

My mouth was open from talking, and it stayed open.

Lee and Will had split up?

'I . . .' I started, but I had no idea where to go from there, so I stopped again. 'You did a very good job of pretending to be my boyfriend at the dance,' I managed.

'Well, that's what we agreed. You wanted a date, I wanted to go, we were friends. Was it something I did that night that's made you so angry? I've been trying to work out what I could have done wrong, but I can't think of anything. And I've been trying to work out whether it's you that's changed, or if it's me.'

My head was whirling with this. Will wasn't Lee's boyfriend. They'd agreed to split up, and Will had only been her date out of – what? Friendship?

'I'm not really sure why I'm angry,' I said slowly. 'It's probably because I didn't feel like getting dumped right before the big party I'd planned.'

'But I didn't dump you. Or if I did, you dumped me right back. Maybe I was reading it all wrong. I really thought you were fine with us breaking up. I thought you seemed relieved when I mentioned it. You're the one who said we're perfect on paper, but in person there was just nothing there. And then I thought you were going to be the one to tell everyone we weren't dating any more, but I haven't heard a word from anyone else. Every time I talk with Annabelle, she seems to think you and I are most definitely together.'

'That's because she does think that.'

'Why? Are you regretting what we decided? Do you want us to still be together?'

'It's not that, it's – I haven't got around to telling her.'

'Because I'm regretting it,' he said.

He put his hand on my leg. Big and warm and so not supposed to be there. I should run.

'What do you mean, you're regretting it?' I said.

'I've never been attracted to women who didn't want me, and I've never ended a relationship where I wanted it to continue. But you haven't been returning my calls, you're refusing to see me, you won't touch me, you won't even meet my eyes when we're talking, I have to kidnap you off the side of the road, for God's sake. You're this good girl full of snappy put-downs and sexy comebacks and this really shaking honesty, and it's made me want you more than anybody else I've ever wanted before.'

Oh.

Damn.

'I – don't want you any more,' I said, but my traitor voice was shaking and my traitor body didn't get up off the bench. Not even when he put his other hand on my chin, and tilted it up towards him.

'I think you're lying,' he said, getting closer, close enough for his breath to caress my lips, close enough for me to put my hand on his chest though I knew I shouldn't, and feel his heart beating hard and fast. 'And I think you're a terrible liar.'

'No, a very good one,' I whispered, and then I couldn't whisper anything else because he was kissing me.

The Bad Twin

And it was, I am not joking, the best kiss I had ever had in my entire life. In the ancient garden, surrounded by animals made out of plants, Will Naughton fitted against me like the missing piece of a puzzle. His hands tightened on me and his mouth moved against mine, and despite all of this I might have been able to resist him, might have been able to summon up the crumbling remains of my decency and push him away if at that precise moment his tongue hadn't touched mine and he hadn't made that low sound of male desire in his throat. My body melted, my scruples melted, everything disappeared except for his mouth and mine, and he pulled me onto his lap and took my head in his hands and kissed me deeper.

And I kissed him back.

At times like this, all your blood tends to desert your brain to rush to your erogenous zones, and kisses like the ones Will was giving me are like a drug. You have one, you want more. And more. The most primitive part of your brain takes over all your rational thought, and then you want more than kisses, you want to get naked as quickly as you can, because that primitive part is yelling, 'Come ON, let's ensure the survival of the species, right NOW. I don't CARE if it's not a good idea!'

It wasn't a good idea. But for the life of me, my blood-starved, yelled-at, rational part of my brain couldn't figure out a reason why. Lee and Will had broken up, right? He was free and single, and so was I, and we were obviously compatible, and dear Lord he shifted me on his lap and that was a definite erection rubbing against my thigh, and his teeth felt straight and strong against my tongue and his lips had just the right amount of warmth and pressure and what would he feel like inside me?

I groaned. He dipped his head and kissed my neck. I leaned my head back and let him. In fact, my fingers pushed between the buttons of his shirt and touched the hot skin of his chest. He nipped my throat and kissed up to my ear, where his breath sent shivers all the way up my back.

We were both free agents, my primitive mind told me, male and female perfectly suited and randy as hell, and we really, really should be getting it on right here on the grass in front of the hedge peacock. I unfastened the top button of his shirt, and slipped my hand inside.

'Lee,' he muttered roughly into my ear. And my rational mind suddenly woke up.

You're a good girl, he'd said. *We're perfect on paper*. I was kissing Will Naughton, but Will Naughton was kissing my sister.

I pulled my hand out of his shirt as if I'd been stung, and then scrambled off his lap to stand on the path. 'Will,' I gasped, 'we shouldn't do this.'

I'd moved so fast that Will hadn't had a chance to react yet; he still sat with his hands just about where I'd be if I were still on his lap. In the lengthening shadows he appeared half in focus, his hair mussed and his shirt in disarray.

'What?' he said. He reached for me, but I stepped back, and he put his hands on the bench. He began to look less confused than angry.

'I think – I think it's best if we stay broken up,' I said.

'But that's ridiculous. We broke up because we agreed that there wasn't any spark between us. And now . . .' I saw that he was looking at my boobs, where my nipples were standing out through my shirt. 'There is most definitely a spark.'

I could still feel the memory of his erection against my thigh, the heat of his skin. 'There isn't a spark,' I lied.

'There's such a bloody big spark it might as well be a forest fire, and you know it. Nobody kisses like that unless they mean it, and you've never kissed me like that before.'

Damn, damn and blast and damn again.

My primitive brain was wrong. Will Naughton wasn't a single man. He was my sister's man. They'd been meant to be together from the beginning. I could step into my sister's shoes, I could run her business and live in her house and sleep in her bed, but I could not sleep with a man who had ever been hers.

I might be a bad twin. But I couldn't be as bad as that.

'Listen, Will,' I said as calmly as I could, trying to channel Lee and logic. 'Okay, we had a good kiss. But that's not going to make a relationship, is it? Not a lasting one.'

'We could make it last all night, for a start,' he said, and he stood up. I could see that he was still aroused. This did not help my resolve or my argument, so I dragged my gaze away up to his chest, but that only reminded me of touching him, so I looked at his nose instead. That aristocratic Naughton nose, passed down intact through generations.

'I need more than that,' I said to his nose. 'There's more to a relationship than sex, sex, sex. I think we got it right the first time. We should definitely break up.'

'You're not making any sense. First you say we should split up because we're not attracted enough to each other. And now you're saying we should split up because we are attracted to each other.'

'You're right, I'm totally crazy, which is another reason we can't be together. Who wants to date a woman who keeps on changing her mind? We'd better stay well away from each other.'

'Give me five more minutes,' Will said, reaching for me again, 'and I think I can change your mind for good.'

I backed away quickly. 'Don't, Will. I can't.'

'But why not?'

'I just – can't.'

His arms crossed on his chest. 'What the hell is going on with you? This doesn't make any sense at all. One minute we're friends and I'm doing you a favour by not telling people we've broken up, the next you're mad at me, then you're flirting and playing hard to get. Five minutes ago you were practically tearing my clothes off and now you don't want me to touch you. Are you playing some twisted game with me?'

Attack is the best form of defence. 'And you're so conceited that you can't get it through your thick head that I don't want to go out with you? You should snap your fingers and open your car door and I should hop right in? All right, oh high and mighty Naughton male, let's have sex because you feel like it now? I don't think so.'

'And you're so holier-than-thou that you can't take any responsibility for this at all. Well, let me tell you, Miss Perfect Haven isn't all that perfect after all. It's like you're two people, you're so different. In fact—'

I literally saw the truth hit him. It changed his expression, his stance, everything. From an exasperated man arguing with his girlfriend he became someone different, someone taller, incredulous, and very, very angry.

'Fucking bloody hell,' he said. 'You're Liza, aren't you?'

There was only one thing for it. I couldn't run, I couldn't

deny it. I stood up to my full height and I faced this man, finally, as myself.

'Yes,' I said. 'I'm Liza.'

He'd been talking about a spark? I could practically see them lighting up the topiary, shooting back and forth between us like our words. Adrenaline, and honesty, do funny things to your perceptions.

'Since when?'

'The night of the dance.'

'Where's Lee?'

'Greece. She left without telling anyone. She says she needs a break.'

'And you've stepped into her place and lied to everyone.'

'That's right.'

'Why?'

'She asked me to take care of things for her. And I thought it would be fun.'

'You've been telling barefaced lies for days now because it's fun?'

'No.'

'No, you haven't been lying?'

'No, it hasn't been fun. Lee's life is a stone drag. But she wanted me to take care of things, and I knew nobody at Ice Cream Heaven would take me seriously if I walked in there. So I've been acting like her.'

'That doesn't explain why you lied to me.'

'You want to know why I lied to you?'

'That would be nice.' Will Naughton angry and righteous was actually quite an impressive sight. I could see how his ancestors would have looked, high on horses, wearing plate mail and carrying enormous sharp swords. I could also see why the feudal system went out of fashion, because righteous anger got really old, really quickly.

'To tell you the truth,' I said, 'I thought that if you couldn't even tell the difference between your girlfriend and her sister, you probably deserved to be played with a little bit.'

'Hold on a minute. You're saying that *you* lied to me, and it's *my* fault? That's the most twisted thing I've ever heard.'

'That's funny, because it seems to me that about ten seconds ago you had your tongue down my throat and you couldn't tell that I wasn't my sister. If that's not twisted, I don't know what is. Women are obviously interchangeable for you, which in my mind, makes you a completely shitty boyfriend. I'm relieved to find out that you and Lee have broken up.'

'You *didn't know we'd broken up?*'

Immediately I knew I'd made a mistake because if he'd really had a broadsword in his hand, it would have been pointed at my throat. I took a step back.

'What the hell have you been playing at, Liza? Have you been trying to manipulate my relationship with your sister?'

'No more than you have, by suddenly changing your mind about being with Lee when something about me attracted your dick.'

'It's you that attracted me, and you knew it from the beginning. Flirting outrageously, playing hard to get. Does Lee even know you've been doing this?'

Here I was on shiftier moral ground. 'Not exactly, no. But she did ask me to take care of things for her.'

'And that kiss just now was taking care of things for her, was it? I don't know what kind of chip you've got on your shoulder, Liza, but obviously it's your plan to humiliate me in any way you can, and by the way, I don't appreciate it when you drag my father into the mix.'

'Your father . . .' But I couldn't defend that. Lord Naughton was so blatantly harmless, so obviously genuine. And he didn't even hate me for ruining his Cousin Malcolm. 'This doesn't have anything to do with your father.'

'Of course not. You're deceiving the entire village for your own amusement, without any thought of how it might affect everyone else.'

'I don't owe Stoneguard anything. Everyone here has always hated me.'

'If they don't hate you already, they will after they hear about what you've been up to.'

'And I bet you can't wait to blow the lid off my deception, lord and protector of the town that you are.'

Will was shaking his head. 'Oh no. I'm not blowing the lid off anything. It's your job to come clean with everyone. Especially everyone who trusts you.'

'That's where you've got it wrong. Nobody here trusts me. They trust Lee.'

'If you're there, they trust you. Though God help them, because you couldn't be more different from your sister.'

He hurled it at me like an insult, and I raised my chin.

'That's right, I couldn't be more different from Lee. For example, it's me that you want to fuck.'

I heard him draw in a breath, either in shock or because he wanted to argue. But I didn't wait to find out.

'Good night, Will, and thanks for the righteous indignation. I appreciate it.'

And I turned on my heel and left the garden, and him.

Holding The Fort

After I left Naughton Hall, I spent much of the evening doing the most ferocious jujitsu possible when my only opponents were air and an imaginary aristocrat. Early Monday morning, I spread the contents of my suitcase out on the bed, all the clothes I hadn't yet bothered to wash: jeans, T-shirts, lots of lycra.

They should have looked familiar. They looked like a stranger's clothes.

Unsurprisingly, none of them were remotely suitable for running an ice-cream company. I had no need for business clothes in my normal life. I never wore a suit unless I was dressed as a stunt double.

But I had nothing soft, either. Nothing pretty. No patterns or colours, no scarves or jewellery, nothing beautiful to look at in itself.

This had never bothered me before. In fact, I'd never really noticed it before. It didn't make sense to buy lovely or delicate clothes anyway; with my lifestyle, I'd probably ruin them before I had the chance to wear them twice. Lee had time for nice things, as well as having the eye for them. She liked to be surrounded by beauty. And there was nothing wrong with that.

In fact, I was beginning to like it a little bit.

I stood there, on Monday morning with half an hour before I was expected at Ice Cream Heaven, and debated with myself whether I was going to put on my clothes or Lee's. Whether it was time to end this charade and own up to my identity.

I reached for a pair of my jeans. And then I thought about what Will had said. *If they don't hate you already, they will after they hear about what you've been up to.*

I shouldn't care if people in Stoneguard hated me. It wasn't as if it was anything new. I'd left Stoneguard behind for bigger, better things.

Bigger and better things like the life in this suitcase? a little voice in my head niggled. *Possessions you don't like, an apartment you don't live in, a job you're not able to do any more?*

I shook my head. I didn't need my own nagging voices to add to Will's. He'd been condemning enough.

But the truth was this. For some reason, I did seem to care if the people in Stoneguard hated me. Will Naughton and his holier-than-thou act deserved to be taken down a peg or two. But I'd felt a genuine pang of guilt when Will had mentioned that I'd been deceiving his father. Lord Naughton seemed so harmless. And kind. And in debt up to his eyeballs.

And then look at Mouse. She was scatty as hell, but she was trusting. Despite being a mother herself, she looked up to me – to Lee, rather – like a little girl needing guidance to find her own way. Jonny Whitehair, with his cheery kisses. Rock and Stone and their wacked-out ideas. All the casserole-givers, all the well-wishers and cheery wavers.

The minute I showed up as Liza Haven, all of that trust and cheer and camaraderie would be gone. That shouldn't bother me. But it did.

To say nothing of my stint as leader of Ice Cream Heaven.

Who would take directions from me as myself? The minute I walked into the office dressed in my own clothes, everyone would go into panic mode. Look at what had happened the one day I'd shown up late. The only reason Mouse had been able to cope was because she'd believed I had faith in her. The same went for the rest of the factory: they expected to get orders from Lee, and they thought I was delegating responsibility out of trust and faith. If they knew it was because I honestly didn't have a clue about running the business, the good effects of all that supposed trust and faith would be gone.

I would mess up the business. Exactly as my sister and my mother expected me to. I'd confirm everything Will thought about me.

I stuffed my clothes back in my suitcase and put on a pink skirt.

The Guardian Business Profile, 20 February 1998.

We All Scream for Ice Cream

The trend for small, locally-owned food producers is nothing new to Abigail Haven. From a family of dairy farmers, Haven has single-handedly built an ice-cream empire in the south-west of England over the past thirty years. Starting with a fleet of ice-cream vans and a rash of ice-cream parlours, she soon expanded into restaurants and supermarkets and captured the nostalgia market for English holiday ice cream. Her advertising campaigns featuring her own twin daughters emphasised the family-centred appeal of her product.

The imported brands of Häagen-Dazs and Ben & Jerry's made ice cream into luxury premium products in the eighties, when Ice Cream Heaven was already a mid-range family brand. Refusing to stay still in a competitive business, Haven jumped into the high end of the market, introducing new branding, new packaging, and a tradition of launching innovative flavours twice a year: a wholly new limited-edition ice cream or sorbet invention each summer, and a new twist of a traditional favourite at Christmas-time. Last summer saw the sharp, creamy Cloud Lime and Christmas brought Eggnog Elysium (winner of a Gold Medal in the Best of British Foods Contest). With this dual-pronged approach, Haven appeals to affluent consumers looking for something new, and established markets wanting a variation of a familiar Christmas or summer treat.

I put the article down on my desk, among the other clippings in the archive. I didn't really need to read this stuff. It wasn't as if I didn't remember all of it myself. Two new flavours a year, every year, the bane of my existence. Lee and I would be expected to hand-deliver single-serving samples to everyone in the neighbourhood in the summer, and serve scoops at our mother's annual Christmas afternoon drinks party. We'd have to watch, over and over again, as people lifted their spoons to their mouths and smacked their lips and rolled their eyes in an ecstasy of tasting. I remembered the Cloud Lime of the article; it looked vaguely like radioactive snot. But as a limited-edition flavour, it sold shedloads. People would queue up for it on the first day.

My mobile rang, and when I saw who was calling, I took it outside, out of listening range of the rest of the office.

'Liza? It's the first of the month and I'm calling to check on the payroll. It should be sent through today so that—'

'It's taken care of,' I told Lee.

'Oh.' It clearly wasn't the answer she'd been expecting and despite myself, I felt a little charge of triumph. *See, you thought I'd fuck it up too. And I haven't.*

Then I thought about kissing Will Naughton.

'How's Greece?'

'Relaxing,' she said, though half on a sigh. 'The people are nice here, they really know their yoga. Have you gone through Mum's care schedules with the agency?'

That, I hadn't done, though I'd been planning to; it was marked on Lee's schedule, like everything else. 'I will.'

'It really needs doing because they keep on putting new people in, and they get a little intimidated with Mum unless you're there to show them the ropes. How is she?'

'Generally pissed off with life.'

'Well, that's a change then.'

The sarcasm was unexpected and unlike Lee, and it made me laugh. 'Are you still freaking out?' I asked her.

'Yes. No. Maybe. I've had time to think. The problem is, I'm not sure what I'm supposed to be thinking about.'

'What did you have for breakfast?'

'A fruit smoothie.'

'Me too.'

'Really?'

'No.'

It was her turn to laugh. I tucked the phone between my shoulder and my ear and sat on the sun-warmed stone wall.

'Is everything really going well there?' she asked. 'Because I can be back anytime, if you need me. I really can. If you want me to.'

It didn't take a genius to hear the reluctance in her voice. Or to remember the pinned butterflies on her wall. 'No, everything's pootling along fine. Just holding on, waiting for you to get back. This place practically runs itself. I could

338

probably join you in Greece and nobody would even notice.'

'I'm glad you think it's such an easy job.'

'It's not that,' I said quickly, 'it's just that you've got a really comprehensive schedule all sorted out, so all I have to do is follow along and everything gets done.'

'Oh,' she said. 'Do . . . you remember Mum's lists?'

'I don't think I'll ever forget them.'

'They were weird, and they frightened me, but I've been thinking, they're actually pretty admirable. She had a problem and she worked out how to cope with it.'

'Well, that's Mum.'

'She doesn't make them any more. She doesn't need to, now she's got people looking after her.'

'She should make a big one and put it on her door: *Don't escape at night.*'

'Oh no, has she been doing that again?'

'It's fine. I can cope with it. I . . . I can see how your life hasn't been as easy as I thought it was.'

She didn't reply to this. I wished we weren't so far apart, so I could see her face; and I was also glad of it, so she couldn't see mine.

'Do you really think I ruined everything for you when we were kids?' I asked.

'Why do you ask that?'

'You mentioned it when we were talking before.' I shifted on the wall.

'Oh. Well. Yes, sometimes. Like remember that Christmas pageant where I was Mary?'

'The one where I had to be a sheep and I thought it would be funny to come out smoking a cigarette and I set the stage on fire by mistake.'

'Yes, that one. I . . . really wanted to be Mary.'

'Oh.' I hadn't thought of that; I'd been too busy being

punished at the time. 'That's the one where Will Naughton was Joseph. You liked him even then, didn't you?'

She exhaled sharply. 'Liza, why are we always bringing up the past? It doesn't matter any more.'

'The thing is, I'm starting to think that every time we talk about the past, we're really talking about the present.'

'That's a very insightful thing for you to say, Liza.'

'Maybe. Still, you and Will got it together anyway, right? It just took a few years.'

'Oh.' She laughed, high and forced. 'Yes. A few years.'

'Yeah.' I waited for her to say more. A beat, two beats. *It's your job to come clean with everyone*, Will said in my memory. *Especially everyone who trusts you.*

I didn't say anything, either. I wished I hadn't brought it up.

'Well, I'm glad the payroll is all done,' she said at last. 'And if Dilwar sends you an invoice for the website, don't pay it. I'll do that when I get back and I can check his work. And then I'm not sure I wrote this down, but could you chase up Yann at MWP's about reprinting those one-twenty-five-mil covers, because it's completely holding up the schedule for Goody Two Chews. We were supposed to have that all sorted weeks ago.'

'Jesus Christ, Lee, it's only ice cream.'

'Ice cream is *important* to this family, Liza.'

'To you.'

'To you too. You needed something to hate as much as I needed something to love.'

I blinked. 'Now who's being insightful?'

'Like I said, I can be on the ferry this afternoon and a plane tonight, if you need me.'

'I don't need you,' I said firmly. 'We are all fine here. Absolutely fine.'

Jonny Whitehair looked up when I came back in. 'How's my favourite girl?'

'Great, as usual,' I told him.

'What do you want me to do today, boss?'

Mouse had sorted out the payroll. Jonny had decided not to pay Dilwar until he coughed up the goods. Doris had rung Yann. I hadn't even known that these things were normally Lee's job until she told me. The business was, in fact, running itself, though Lee hadn't liked to hear it.

Because the people working in the business trusted who they believed I was, and they believed I trusted them in turn.

'Jonny, I have total faith in you as director of sales,' I said. 'What do you think you could be doing today to make the business grow?'

'Me, myself?' He pointed at his chest in a comedy gesture.

'You, yourself. I want to hear your ideas.'

He cocked his head to one side. 'I've always had a bit of a fancy for cruise ships and trains.'

'Cruise ships and trains?'

'Sure. We cater for people on holiday all summer long, and then in the winter the holiday trade tails off, right? Well, people on cruise ships are on holiday whatever the weather. People on trains, too – the long-distance routes. I suggested it to your mother a few years ago, said I'd pop down to Portsmouth for a few days and talk to the ferry companies for a start, but she didn't seem that interested.'

I could understand my mother's reaction. The market sounded plausible enough, but Abigail Haven was only interested in ideas which had come straight from Abigail Haven. 'Well, I think it's a great idea,' I said. 'Get on the blower and make some appointments. Ask Annabelle to book you a hotel. Take Hazel along, if you like.'

'Lovely jubbly.' It could have been my imagination, but Jonny seemed to go back to his desk with an even jauntier step than usual. Would he have reacted that way to the know-nothing no-good twin telling him to go off and follow his instincts?

Definitely not.

Then I checked through the papers Mouse had prepared for me, as a formality more than anything, and told her I was going to spend the rest of the day doing a bit of a business review. I made myself some coffee and got stuck into Lee's records again.

Because now, I didn't only have to keep Ice Cream Heaven ticking over. I had to use my time here, even if it was only a few more days, to make it even more successful, even better, because I didn't only have to prove myself to Lee and my mother. I had to prove myself to Will Naughton, too.

Somewhere through my third cup of coffee, I noticed something in the sales figures. Ice Cream Heaven had not cornered a new market for nearly two years. There were new outlets, some shops and restaurants, mostly in the south of England, taking existing products. But nothing big, nothing like the cruise-ship coup Jonny was thinking about. No really new venues.

Of course, my sister had been learning the business. It was understandable that she wouldn't be willing to take any big risks in the first few years she was in charge. And she was following in the footsteps of the Ice Cream Queen, our mother. Compared to the booming business I remembered when we were growing up in the eighties, growth was bound to be conservative now.

Some instinct made me turn to her marketing records, where I saw something not so much conservative as unbelievable. So unbelievable was it, in fact, that I had to look through her files on paper and on her laptop three times before I could believe that the relevant material hadn't been misplaced somewhere.

Where was this summer's special edition flavour?

I went back to the marketing materials. Usually I'd expect to find press releases, fliers, designs for posters and signage. But there weren't any, not for this year's summer. Not for Christmas, either. In fact, the most recent launch material was for Rum Punch Perfection, and the date on that was one year before the Horrid Christmas.

'Annabelle,' I called over to where my assistant was busily filling in a spreadsheet, 'where's my new marketing folder?'

She looked up, confused. 'Your new one?'

'Yes, the one with all the stuff from the past financial year?'

'Haven't you got it in your hands right now?'

'Isn't there a newer one?'

She shook her head. 'There might be, maybe I missed seeing it. But I only remember that one, there. That's got this year's summer adverts in it, hasn't it?' She came over and hovered as I checked. It did.

'So you've got another folder?' she said, looking anxious. 'I'm sorry. What colour is it?'

'Oh, you know what – I was just thinking of these ads and I must have overlooked them. My mistake, sorry.'

'That's all right,' said Mouse, going back to her desk. 'Actually it's a relief to know that even a good record-keeper like you can make mistakes.'

She was right – Lee *was* a good record-keeper. Yet Ice Cream Heaven hadn't developed a single new flavour since our mother had retired. Nor it had gained any new clients of note, or effectively changed in any way with the change of management. In fact, the only way it *had* changed was to become more conservative, more stagnant. For all her preoccupation with the company, my sister had been treading water since she'd taken over.

The Talk of the Town

'Ouch,' I muttered under my breath. 'Ouch, ouch, ouch ouch ouch.'

'Sixty more seconds, ladies. Feel the energy running through your chakras.'

I'd jumped out of burning buildings. I'd beaten up Samuel L. Jackson's stunt double. I'd survived a car accident that should have crippled me for life. But holding my body in the ridiculous contortion known as the Eagle Pose was one of the most painful experiences I'd ever had outside a hospital bed.

And I seemed to be the only person who was finding it painful. Five women of assorted shapes and sizes posed motionless around me, their faces suffused with tranquillity. I gritted my teeth until Candace finally, blessedly, said, 'Now relax.'

Lee had yoga every Thursday night, and this week I didn't have the excuse of a feigned illness, so I went along. How hard could it be? I thought. Even after nearly three weeks without a gym at my disposal, I was still in good shape. Probably better shape than most of the ladies meeting in Candace's spacious conservatory/yoga studio, who ranged in age between sixteen and eighty and mostly didn't look like world-class gymnasts. I figured I'd be at least as good at it as anybody else.

I was wrong.

I collapsed onto the mat, breathing hard. My exercise routines had always been kinaesthetic, preferably involving the fastest movement I could do. Who knew that holding still could be so difficult? I was red-faced and sweaty, and stayed that way all through the final stretching-out routine, done to the strains of some haunting, new-age music involving pan pipes.

'You haven't been practising at home, have you?' Candace asked sympathetically when the song was done, handing me a towel. Like her yoga outfit, it was aqua and covered with embroidered stars.

'Obviously not as much as I should have,' I said. 'Thanks.'

She tsked at me. 'Here, take this and put it in your bath tonight. I got it from the new aromatherapist who's in town – you know, the girl from Reading who set up in the holistic health centre. She's absolutely amazing. This one should help relax muscles and will prevent you being sore tomorrow.' She plucked a dark blue bottle from a shelf next to a towering aloe plant, and gave it to me. 'Oh, and do you have a labradorite?' She pointed at some walnut-sized crystals arranged on her windowsill.

'I . . . don't think so.'

She picked up a silvery grey one. 'Take one of those, too, and keep it by your bed. It will enhance healing and help psychic connection.'

'Thanks.'

'Tomorrow you'll feel better than ever.'

I doubt it, I thought. I could only hope that Lee got back before next Thursday so I'd never have to go through this yoga hell again.

On my way home from Candace's, I bit the bullet and dropped into Ma Gamble's Wholefood Emporium. Lee's fridge was nearly bare. The bell jingled over the door when I walked in, and I saw there was a meeting. The centre of the shop had been cleared to make way for a circle of chairs, all containing various members of the Stoneguard community holding clipboards. There was a table in the middle which held, as far as I could tell, a heap of dirt. A circle of chairs shouldn't naturally have a head, but when Ma Gamble sprang to her feet I could tell that she was at it.

'Lee!' she cried. 'Come in, come in! Have you come to join our Friends of the Earthworm meeting?'

'Thanks, but actually I was just looking for some bread.'

'Of course. Please, Friends, carry on without me.' She bustled over to the wooden display shelves that held various loaves of bread, all, according to the signs around them, *Handmade* and *Local* and *Organic*. 'We're monitoring *Lumbricus terrestris* this week,' she said to me in an undertone, 'but between you and me, Maureen is getting a little uppity about the water table. You know Maureen and her relationship with the rain. She was out shaking her fist at the sky on Tuesday, Joe Bilton saw her. Here you go, this loaf has flax seed in it, that will keep you regular. How's your mother?'

Bath oil for relaxing, crystals for healing, bread for shitting – it seemed that people in Stoneguard had a remedy for everything that ailed you and weren't afraid to talk about it in public. 'Mum's about the same, thank you,' I said. 'If you have a bread that's good for Alzheimer's, I'd appreciate it.'

I'd been joking, but Ma Gamble brightened. 'Not bread, but look at this here.' She grabbed my arm and brought me down the herbal supplements aisle. 'There have been some studies about milk thistle.' She gave me a plastic bottle.

'I'm not sure she'll take this,' I said, turning it over in my hand. 'She's not so keen on alternative therapies. Or any therapies at all, to tell you the truth.'

'Powder it up and slip it into her tea,' Ma Gamble advised me, walking with me to the till. 'Or try it in Coca-Cola, you can barely taste it. Much as I hate to advise anyone to consume such a horrible thing, corporate giant pigs.'

In the centre of the room, the Friends of the Earthworm had clustered round the central dirt heap. 'Asphaltisation,' hissed Maureen Lilly.

'Ass-what?' said Jasbir innocently. Nigel Peach produced a pair of what I could only assume were tiny callipers and began poking at the dirt.

'As you can see, the group has got very large,' Ma Gamble said to me. 'And it's such important work we do. Without the humble earthworm, our ecosystem would be nothing but dust. We've got the fundraiser for the *Driloleirus americanus* planned a week Saturday. The giant Palouse earthworm, it's horribly rare, you know. What can we put you down for?'

'A donation? Of course, that's no problem. I'll get Jonny to send round some catering tubs. Maybe the flavours that look most like dirt – like Divine Chocolate Chip and Holy Moly Melt? You could rename them with sort of wormy names, like Compost Surprise.' Ma Gamble frowned. 'And some cones,' I added, but she didn't look any happier.

'Actually we've put you down to be in charge of the publicity,' she said. 'And the scavenger hunt. We've got the green by the car park, and we're putting up a marquee.'

I thought about Lee's full calender. She was busy enough, and I didn't even know when she'd be back. 'I'm sorry, but I don't think I'll be able to do that.'

Ma Gamble looked shocked. 'I'd have thought you'd want to help save the earthworm.'

'I do. That's why I said I'd donate some ice cream. You can sell it and keep all the proceeds. Tell me what you want, and I'll sort it out for you.'

She stared at me, as if someone refusing to take on a load of work for a group they didn't even belong to, was the most astonishing thing in the universe.

'I can do the scavenger hunt,' said Jasbir behind me.

'I'll do the publicity,' said someone else.

'No, I will.'

'I can help.'

'You don't even know who to call.'

'I do! I think.'

Their argument was interrupted by the bell jingling again over the door.

'I forgot the eggs,' said a too-familiar voice, a voice that made my heart leap and my stomach sink and, annoyingly, made my skin shiver all over into recognition and longing.

I turned from the till to face the door. There stood Will, wearing jeans, a paint-spattered T-shirt and a polite expression that hardened into stone the minute he saw my face.

'Hello, Will,' I said, sweeter than evil Coca-Cola. 'Fancy seeing you here.'

I could see him trying to decide how to reply. Meanwhile, the argument behind us had stilled. 'Miss Haven,' he finally said. The words fell like ice into the silence.

Out of the corner of my eye, I could see Ma Gamble pause on her way to pick up a box of eggs. On the one hand, she had a customer to serve. On the other, there was some juicy gossip unwinding itself right there in her Emporium in front of all the Earthworm Friends, and she couldn't bear to miss a millisecond of it.

This didn't concern me so much, however. I was more interested in how Will Naughton's grey eyes narrowed, how his handsome mouth compressed. How very far we were at this moment from when we had kissed, only a few days ago.

'There's quite a gathering here,' Will said to me. 'Have you come to make an announcement?'

This would be the place for it. Ma Gamble could spread information more quickly than any other mortal, and a good chunk of the town was gathered here already. Maureen was holding a worm up, dangling it from her fingers. Its squirming was just about the only movement in the room.

'No,' I said. 'I came in for bread. But don't let me stop you from making an announcement, if you want to.' I raised my chin, and dared him with my eyes.

'I meant what I said. I'm leaving it up to you.'

'Always the gentleman. You really did learn some wonderful manners at Eton and Oxford, didn't you?'

'Yes, and I've learned some other very interesting things, especially lately.'

He held my gaze with his and we both stared, neither willing to drop it. It felt as if we were each pushing against the other, our feet planted firm, our bodies struggling.

God, his strength. I felt his thighs underneath me and his body pressing against me. It felt as if every breath was full of him. As if he was inside me all the way to my fingertips. I could taste him on my tongue.

I couldn't, wouldn't back down. But if he didn't turn away, if I didn't say something, I'd fall into his arms, and that would be the worst defeat I could imagine.

'Is your father coming round to see my mother's garden on Sunday afternoon?' I asked, in a tone of voice that made it clear I was changing the subject on purpose. But without dropping my gaze.

I was surprised to see his face flush suddenly, as if his cold anger had turned to heat. His eyes, so calm and righteous before, snapped fire and I realised that he thought I was bringing up his father to remind him of the secret he was keeping himself, about the family's fortune. I opened my mouth to correct him, to say I hadn't meant that at all, but how could I say anything without giving away the secret?

'That's my father's decision,' he said, fury barely restrained in his voice. And then he turned away from me, to Ma Gamble. 'It turns out I don't need eggs after all. Thanks anyway.' Without catching my eye again, he went out through the door. As soon as it closed behind him it felt as if someone had turned off a giant electricity switch. I bit my lip and nearly sagged back against the counter.

Then I remembered the audience. So I smiled instead.

'What a magnificent worm,' I said to Maureen.

'Er,' said Maureen. 'Um, thanks.'

Ma Gamble couldn't bustle up to me fast enough. 'Lee, what's up between you and Will? Have the two of you fallen out?'

All of my dismay at having inadvertently insulted Lord Naughton, my tension and frustration at confronting Will again, the strain of having to be Lee, even the throbbing from my over-extended muscles, channelled itself into anger against the busybody standing in front of me, and a fierce sympathy for my twin. For God's sake, did Lee have to watch every single word she said, every minute of every day, so rumours wouldn't get spread about her?

'I don't believe that's any of your business, Ma Gamble,' I said to her. 'People should be able to have some sort of personal life here in this town without your commenting about it to everyone you meet. Just because you don't have anything better to do with your time than gossip, doesn't mean that the rest of us deserve to have our lives picked over so that you can feel important. And I don't think I need that bread, either. Have a good meeting, everyone.'

And I slammed out of the shop in exactly the same way that Will had.

His car, or any other sign of him, was long gone. I walked down the High Street quickly with my head held upright. I could almost feel the words that were being spoken back in the Emporium, as a crawling sensation on the back of my neck.

Everything that Lee did, retold and dissected. I'd left Stoneguard because of it, but I hadn't thought about how it would feel even if you weren't a bad twin. Even if you were the successful twin, the one whom everyone loved. No wonder my mother shut herself up in her house when she started losing her reason. No wonder my sister didn't tell anyone she'd broken up with Will, or talk about the job or the relationship she'd given up in Bath. Everyone loved her, everyone trusted her, but who could *she* trust, if it was nearly impossible to keep a secret in Stoneguard?

Not me. She didn't trust me, either, and while that hurt, I couldn't blame her, because I didn't trust her enough to tell her everything, either. All those years when we'd been comparing breakfasts, we'd been ignoring everything else that was going on between us, making the gap wider and wider and wider. Two people with identical DNA and nothing at all in common, except a lack of trust.

I turned into Church Street and up Lee's path. I walked inside the cottage and slammed the door behind me. There – that would give the curtain-twitchers something else to talk about.

And of course with the slammed door I had second thoughts. Not about Ma Gamble; she deserved to be told off at last. But about Lee. I'd let out her secret about Will. I'd made her the talk of Stoneguard, even though that was the very thing she wanted to avoid.

I glanced at the butterflies over the fireplace. 'Looks like I fucked it up again,' I said.

Beetroot and Horseradish

'Lee, it's Edmund Jett for you, on line one.'

I looked up from my sister's sales projection figures at Mouse. It was Friday morning and we were the only two in the office; my delegation of responsibility meant that Jonny Whitehair had abandoned his desk to visit some local customers before he went to Portsmouth on Monday. Apparently visiting local customers was normally my sister's job.

The more I learned about Ice Cream Heaven, the more I was realising that everything was my sister's job. That was obviously one of the side-effects of being a good girl. Ma Gamble's shocked expression the day before had told me that Lee rarely said no when asked to do anything. And the more I looked at Lee's files, the more I saw that all the notes were made in her handwriting, that all the records were kept on her computer, from sales to payroll to production to marketing to accounting to distribution. It was the way my mother had run the company: she didn't just keep a finger in every pie, she kept her whole damn hand in there. Nothing went on in Ice Cream Heaven without her ordering it to happen.

Lee was different from my mother. She was nicer. People liked her better. I'd expected her to be more democratic, more relaxed in running the business. But nothing about my sister's life was quite what I'd expected.

Mouse was actually wearing a suit. True, it was purple, but it was distinctly less frumpy than the flowered dresses I'd seen her in before.

'Is that a new outfit?' I asked her. She blushed.

'They had late-night opening last night in Marlborough,' she said. 'It's not my style, I know, but I thought maybe it looked more, I don't know, professional.'

'It really does,' I told her. 'You look great.'

And she did. She looked less like a harried mother of four and more like an efficient assistant. Incredible what clothes could do for a person.

Though I shouldn't be so surprised about that.

She blushed some more. 'Should I put Edmund Jett through to you?'

'Do you know what it's about?'

'No, he hasn't said. But his assistant rang last week.'

Oh yeah. It seemed so long ago now, but the Post-It was still on the desk somewhere, buried underneath paperwork. 'His assistant rang already, but he's ringing in person now? Do you think I'm in trouble for not returning his call?'

'He sounded perfectly charming.'

I remembered him, all smiles and blond hair that time I'd visited his restaurant with Lee. 'I'd probably better see what he wants.' Mouse nodded and pressed the buttons to transfer the call.

This was the first actual piece of business I'd had to do all week. I crossed my fingers underneath the table as I picked up the receiver. 'Hi, Edmund,' I said, smiling down the line to put warmth into my voice, 'so good to hear from you.'

'Lee, are you well? I'm not sure if you've tried ringing me, my assistant has – flaked out, shall we say, so I'm catching up myself.'

'No, it's my fault, not your assistant's. What can I do to help you?'

'Listen, I've been thinking and thinking about that flavour you mentioned to me the last time we met.'

I racked my brain. The last time he'd met Lee, he'd met me too. The only flavour I could remember mentioning was that joke one I'd said to be silly, something like—

'Beetroot and horseradish,' he continued. 'I can't get it out of my head. I'm thinking grilled steak, an incredible pinot noir reduction, and this fantastic earthy, spicy ice cream to spike the flavour. And the colour must be out of this world. You haven't offered it to anyone else, have you?'

'Er, no, I can guarantee you that I haven't. You are absolutely the only person who's heard about that flavour.' And probably the only one who would even think of wanting it. Purple, hot ice cream. With steak. This guy might have about a million Michelin stars but he was evidently insane.

'Brilliant. I want to start developing the dish as soon as possible. I want it organic, I want it local, I want it in small batches, I want it absolutely exclusive. When can you get me a sample?'

'I –' *have absolutely no idea* '– how about the end of next week?'

'Perfect. Call me on Tuesday. Can't wait to taste it.'

I put down the phone. I had that feeling I only normally got when I'd hit the brakes that split second too late and I wasn't sure whether I was going to stop in time, or hit that enormous brick wall.

'Is something wrong?' Mouse asked me.

'No,' I said. I stood up. My veins were thrumming, my heart beating in my ears. I hadn't felt this good since . . . well, since Sunday, when Will had narrowly missed the tractor. And after that, when he'd kissed me. 'Everything's great. We're

355

going to make a new flavour for Edmund Jett's restaurant.'

Mouse actually clapped her hands. 'A new flavour? Really? Oh my God, that's so exciting! I've always wanted to help make a new flavour! What is it, something amazing? Has it got chocolate in it? I love chocolate so much. And cherries. And vanilla. Well, I like them all, really.'

'You'll be crazy about this one.' I checked my watch. 'I'm going to take an early lunch and check on something. Can you hold the fort?'

'Of course. When will you be back?'

'As soon as I can,' I said. 'I think we have a lot of work to do.'

My mother was sitting in front of *Bargain Hunt* on the telly when I came in. She had an untouched sandwich in front of her and a full glass of milk.

'You're still here,' she greeted me, barely looking up.

'Who do you think I am?'

'You're Elizabeth, of course. You've always been Elizabeth.'

I sat in the chair across from her and turned off the television. 'You're drinking milk?'

'As the glass is full, the obvious conclusion seems to be that I'm not drinking it.'

'Still, I'm surprised the nurse served it to you.'

Her lips compressed. 'She's new.'

'But you've never liked milk. I've never seen you touch it, unless it was made into ice cream first. You only ever had it in the house so that Lee and I could have cereal. Haven't you told her you hate milk?'

'I can't remember. Perhaps I drank it before.'

'You can't just suddenly change the tastes of an entire lifetime, can you?'

She didn't answer for a few moments. She was no longer facing the blank television; she was staring intently at the milk. She'd barely glanced at me since I'd walked in.

'I think I am beginning to unlearn,' she said at last.

'Unlearn? What does that mean?'

Finally, she did look at me, and sharply. 'Where's your sister now?'

'She's still taking a holiday. She rang to say I was a selfish cow, so I'm assuming she's all right.'

'That doesn't sound like Emily.'

'But you don't disagree?'

She raised an eyebrow. As infuriating as my mother could be, I actually welcomed her acidity. It meant she was more nearly herself.

'You are not your sister,' she said.

'No, I'm not. That's why I need you to help me. Can you tell me how you go about creating a new ice-cream flavour?'

'Why do you need to know that?'

'Because I'm going to create a new ice-cream flavour. How do you do it?'

'*You* are going to?'

'Spare me the lecture about how I'm unworthy. Lee went away and left me in charge of Ice Cream Heaven, and unless you want to go down there and start running things yourself again, I'm going to do it. I've got a customer who wants a new flavour, and I'm going to give it to him. I can do it myself, without your help, and probably end up wasting lots of time and materials, or you can tell me how to do it and I can be more efficient. Up to you.'

She actually listened to this whole rant without snorting in derision or tapping her fingers in impatience once.

'Doris will know how,' she said.

'I know she will. Everyone in the factory knows the entire

business upside down and sideways. But I can't ask them, because they all think I'm Lee. Everyone thinks I'm Lee, except for you and— well, except for you. So I'd like you to tell me. Please.'

The last word did something to her. Softened something, not enough to bend, but enough to relax a little bit.

'It's trial and error,' she said. 'After years of experience, you might get the mixture right the first time, but most likely not. Is it a chocolate base?'

'No, a white one. I think.'

'Fruit?'

'Sort of. Yes.'

'Do you want chunks in it?'

'No, I don't think so. I want it to be smooth all the way through.'

'You're not thinking a sorbet, are you?'

'Mother, I may not know much, but I know the difference between an ice cream and a sorbet.'

She nodded once. 'You will want to discover the best form of fruit to use. Which variety? What can you get locally? Do you want it fresh or frozen or preserved? Fresh fruit is often too watery. Will you use a concentrate or a purée? Cooked or raw? Usually you can come up with six to ten different varieties of the fruit itself. And then you have to experiment with amounts. Some fruit is milder and needs a greater proportion for the flavour to come through, but then the mixture freezes differently according to the acidity.'

'I don't think this one is very acidic.'

'Are you only using the one flavour, or are you mixing them together?'

'I've got two flavours. A fruit sort of thing and . . . something else.'

'Trial and error. It's the only way. Make a small batch, taste

358

it yourself, give it to others. Make notes about flavour and texture and colour. Adjust the recipe. Make another small batch. Recruit test tasters to help you, although of course the final judgement is the maker's.'

She could reel all of this off, and yet she couldn't remember if she'd drunk milk yesterday. What an odd thing the brain was.

'How long does all of this take?'

'It varies. Raspberry Rhapsody, for example, we captured perfectly in the first batch. Merry Christmas Pudding took me seven months. It was initially very difficult to find Christmas puddings in spring, and then in the end we had to make our own.'

'I need it done for next week.'

She raised her eyebrows.

'I'm able to work hard, you know,' I told her. 'I've got a pilot's licence and a black belt in jujitsu. I'm certified in six separate stunt skills. Sometimes on a stunt we have to do it a dozen times before we can get it right. I can work extremely hard, if it's something I enjoy.'

'And you suddenly enjoy making ice cream.'

'I enjoy proving that I'm as good as anyone else.'

'You mean as good as your sister.'

'Actually . . .' I began, but then thought the better of it. What good would it do for my mother to know that my sister hadn't introduced a single new flavour since she took charge?

'Whatever,' I said instead. 'Anyway, you should be glad I'm competing with her. God knows you set us up to be rivals from the minute we were born. I've never been able to do anything without being compared to Lee.'

'And she you.'

'Yes, and we both know who you would pick as the winner of all of those comparisons.'

'Yet you love each other.' My mother said it oddly, intently, though she was again looking at the milk instead of my face. 'It's not obligation, is it?'

'I love her more than anyone else in the world,' I said.

'Much more than either of you love me.'

I stood up. 'I've got to get going. I've got ice cream to make. Thanks for the tip.' I headed for the door, and then paused. 'Oh, by the way, you're going to have a visitor on Sunday. Lord Naughton wants to come by and advise you on your roses.'

That made her look up from her milk. 'I do not take visitors.'

'Then send him away. It would be a shame, though. You're not doing yourself any favours stuck in here. Everything I've read about Alzheimer's says that the more you use your brain, the more slowly it deteriorates. Watching *Bargain Hunt* isn't helping you keep those brain cells fit and healthy.'

'I can't have a visitor. There's no place to do it. Look at this room.'

'It's summer, entertain him outside. The fresh air will do you good. And he's the keenest gardener I've ever seen. He'll be in heaven telling you what needs to be done. If you're lucky, you'll have a viscount down on his knees doing the weeding for you.'

'But—'

'I'll come round on Sunday morning and mow the lawn and set up a table and some chairs for you. I'll pick up a cake for you at Ma – in Swindon. All you have to do is put on some shoes and set foot outside. During the daytime.'

'Elizabeth, how many times do I have to tell you? I do not want anybody seeing me this way. I am finished.'

'The thing is, Mum, you're not finished. You're still alive, and it's about time you acted like it every now and then. But even if you don't care about yourself, do it for Lord Naughton.

360

The man's been turfed out of his house, he's living in a barn, and he goes for days on end with nobody to talk to except for his plants. Even you have to be better company.'

'I will not.'

'That's fine, too. I'll come by Sunday anyway. I can't wait to see you locking the door against a viscount.' I went to the door myself, and looked back over my shoulder. 'Thanks for the advice on making ice cream.'

Before I left, I went to the kitchen, where I could hear a radio playing cheerfully. I'd expected to see a new nurse, but Naomi stood at the sink, washing dishes. 'Oh, hello Lee, did you have a good visit with your mum?'

'It was very pleasurable, thanks. Tell me, Naomi, how long have you been looking after Mum?'

She thought. 'It must be nearly sixteen months now. Yes, because I started when my Holly went back to work after having her youngest, and he's two next month. Why?'

'Mum thought you were new.'

'That happens sometimes.'

'I thought she seemed better today, though. She seemed to remember a lot about her old job.'

'Oh, the new memories go first as a rule. I'm not hurt by it or anything.' She laughed.

'Did she tell you that she liked milk?'

'Doesn't she? She asked for it.'

'She hates it.'

'Okey-dokey, then, I'll remember that. Thanks for telling me.'

I closed the door behind me and went through Mum's hole in the hedge, over the hill back towards Ice Cream Heaven. So many things about my mother were exactly the same, and so many had changed. Why would she have asked for milk, for example? If she suddenly did like milk, did that make her a different person?

361

Likes and dislikes help to define a person. I should know that as well as anyone, having carefully and strictly defined my likes and dislikes from a small child, so that they would contrast with my sister's. Lee liked pink, I liked red. Lee liked sweets, I liked savouries. Lee had long hair, I had short hair. My preferences let people know who I was, how I was different and unique.

Maybe, if I hadn't been trying so hard to be different, maybe I could have liked the same things. There could have been some crossover, more for us to share besides DNA and appearance. We could have been more like real sisters, not one good and one bad.

Walking the chalk path I'd forced my mother down last week, I wondered what she would be like once the memories were cleared away from her brain. If I would even recognise her any more, when she didn't recognise me.

Imagine all those years between us, all those fights forgotten. If I came to her with everything erased between us – all her disapproval, all my rebellion. All those hurtful actions gone forever.

Would my mother like me more?

When I got back to Ice Cream Heaven, Mouse jumped up from her chair. 'Oh Lee, I just heard! I'm so so so so sorry.'

Fear squeezed my heart. *Lee*, I thought in a panic, until I realised that Mouse had called me Lee as usual, so she couldn't have got bad news about my sister. But my mother – someone could have called while I was walking from her house. Or Rufus and Tania could have decided to press charges about the car, after all. 'What happened?'

'You and Will breaking up.'

'Oh.' The relief was so strong that I couldn't be bothered

to be irritated. I sat down at my desk. 'Did you go to the Emporium for lunch?'

'Coffee. I'm bringing my own salads for lunch, I'm trying to lose a bit of weight.'

'I'm sure Ma Gamble is having a whale of a time spreading the news to everyone she meets.'

'I didn't talk to Ma, actually, she was on the phone in the back when I got in. Jasbir said he was there last night for a meeting and he saw the two of you and it was clear that you'd fallen out.' She came over to my desk. 'Are you okay? You haven't broken up or anything, have you?'

'We've broken up.'

'Oh no!' Her hand went to her mouth.

'It's okay, really, Annabelle. It's no big deal.'

'Oh Lee, you say that because you're always so cheerful. You never show it when you're upset or anything. But the two of you were perfect together, you must be a little bit . . .' She bit her lip. 'But then it's not any of my business. You probably don't want to talk about it with me anyway.'

Her concern and her instant self-deprecation touched me, and I put my hand on her arm. 'It's not that, Annabelle. If I were upset, you'd be one of the only people in town I would want to talk about it with. I'm honestly not upset about it. Really. It was going to happen sooner or later. We just don't have that much in common.'

'But you do! You're both running your own businesses, and you're both from here, and you're both so smart and good-looking and kind. I always thought you were meant for each other. Everyone did.'

'Well, everyone was wrong. Will isn't meant for me.' He was meant for my sister. And something occurred to me, with all the thinking I'd been doing on my way over here about self-definition and the choices that I'd made. Did I actually fancy Will Naughton *because* he was my sister's man? Because I had to prove I was good enough for him, the same way I had to prove I was good enough to run Ice Cream Heaven?

'I'm really okay about it, Annabelle,' I said. 'It was a mutual decision.'

'Jas said that the two of you looked pretty angry at each other. He said there were practically sparks flying across the Emporium.'

'We might have spoken a few words in anger a couple of nights ago. But it will all blow over, and we'll be friends the same as always.'

Mouse didn't look comforted. 'You'd – you'd tell me if you were unhappy, wouldn't you? I know I can't do anything about it, but I'd want to know.'

'I would,' I said, but I knew as I said it that I was lying. I couldn't tell Mouse my real feelings; if she knew who I really was, she wouldn't care about them anyway. And clearly Lee didn't tell her how she felt, because nobody had known that she and Will were breaking up.

'Anyway,' I said quickly in an effort to dispel my guilt, 'we don't have time to think about that now. We've got to get started on this new ice-cream flavour, and I need you to help me.'

My lie and the distraction made her perk up a bit. 'Oh yes! I can't wait. What do you want me to do?'

'Well, first I need you to get on the phone to our suppliers and ask them to send every version of beetroot they've got. Cooked, raw, pickled, tinned, juice, anything. The more local the better.'

Mouse blinked. She rubbed her ear. Then she rubbed her other one.

'I'm sorry,' she said. 'There must be something wrong with my hearing. I thought you said beetroot.'

As Time Goes By

I caught myself humming as I mowed the lawn on Sunday morning. I was pushing my mother's ancient petrol lawnmower, breathing in the fumes and feeling the early August sun beaming down on my head, and something rose up inside me and came out as music. Not great music, I'll be the first to admit. I can't carry a tune in a bucket.

But nobody was listening, and even if they were, they couldn't hear me, so I started singing it out loud: 'Take Me Home, Country Roads', embarrassingly, by John Denver. I'd done the entire front lawn by the time I got to the second chorus, and moved on to the back.

I felt great. This had nothing to do with pushing the lawnmower and more to do with what I'd done the night before. Saturday night was party night in LA, but here in Stoneguard it was much the same as any other night. There wasn't much excitement for a single girl, unless she wanted to go down to the Druid's Arms for a few games of cribbage. Especially a supposedly newly-single girl.

It wasn't as if I hadn't had invitations. The phone hadn't stopped ringing since Friday afternoon. Candace, Tania, Rebecca Munt, Barbara Raymond, Hazel Whitehair, all having heard about my break-up with Will, all inviting me over for various forms of wine and sympathy. While the wine sounded good, I could do without the pity and the inevitable autopsy of my sister's so-called relationship. So I said no to all of them, told them I was going to have a girly evening in alone, pamper myself a little bit. After saying that several times, I decided I might as well actually do what I'd said I was going to.

Of course, I didn't really know how. The closest I'd ever got to pampering myself was the weeks I spent lying on the couch after my accident in between brutal physical therapy sessions. I'd watched box-set DVDs of every series of *The Sopranos* and *The Wire*, and Jackie Chan and Bond movies ordered on the internet, and called out for food when I got hungry. I'd been crazy with boredom.

Pampering yourself was supposedly more pleasurable than that. I hunted around Lee's house until I'd amassed a quantity of candles, which I arranged around the bathtub. Then I poured myself a glass of wine, put the opened bottle next to the tub, and drew a deep, hot bath. When I remembered the glass phial Candace had given me, I poured the contents of that into the water, and the room instantly filled with the scent of juniper and pine and lavender. I searched Lee's bedside bookshelf for the fattest novel with the cheesiest cover I could find, and settled for one that pictured a man whose ruffled, voluminous shirt was open to expose huge, greasy-looking pectorals. He held a swooning woman who had evidently been practising yoga, because she was in a position no normal human being could ever hold for more than a split second without shouting out in pain. Her tits were nearly as impressive as his, though marginally less greasy, and they were spilling out of the bodice of her flimsy gown. The two of them had been caught in some kind of freak windstorm. *Her Pirate Captor*, it said in curly letters over the top. It was bound to be horrible.

I took this book to the bath with me, lit all the candles and settled in, fully expecting to emerge bored to death within fifteen minutes. Two and a half hours and several top-ups with hot water later, I reluctantly dragged myself out of the high seas of the seventeenth century, got out of the tepid bath, dried my pruny skin and curled up in bed to finish the book. I hadn't even touched my second glass of wine, so I hardly had an excuse for cheering aloud when the heroine Regina D'Arcy grabbed the cutlass of the dashing pirate captain who had abducted her and, instead of fighting the pirate band, started beheading the minions of the evil duke who had ostensibly come to rescue her. I definitely didn't have an excuse for my eyes welling up when Regina finally admitted that she loved her pirate captor, Diego.

Fortunately there had been no one there to see me, and this morning I felt fantastic. Better than I had in ages. I didn't know if was the aromatherapy, or Candace's crystal, or the fact that I'd spent so long immersed in hot water, or even the happy ending of the book, but my back didn't ache at all and my muscles felt relaxed and pain-free. I was going to make it my business to find this aromatherapist, even if she was from Reading, and buy an industrial-sized bottle of her elixir.

In the meantime, I had to get my mother's lawn – and my mother – ready for her to meet with company for the first time in two years.

Before I'd fired up the lawnmower, I'd gone inside the house to see her. I'd given the nurse the afternoon off, and the house was quiet except for the muted babble of the telly. Stoneguard was too small to have its own newspaper, but the *Swindon Chronicle* was delivered every Friday, containing all the Swindon news fit to print, and my mother was sitting in her armchair in front of the television reading it. I could see the headline from here: BOY WINS £50 FOR CATCHING TROUT. She looked up when I entered the room.

'Oh,' she said. 'It's you.'

Incredible how every time she could fit so much into those three little words, none of them more than three letters long. Disappointment. Disapproval.

'I have a list for you.' I put it on top of the newspaper. She picked it up and looked at it.

'Why am I doing this?' she asked.

'Because you're having a visitor. I'll put the cake in the kitchen where you can find it. That's number seven on the list.'

I left her and unpacked my bag in the kitchen. There was a Victoria sponge I'd bought in Marlborough, and the makings for cucumber sandwiches. Then I went out of the back door to get the mower out of the garage.

I fired it up right outside my mother's window, close enough so that the sound would be unmistakable, and I'd seen her curtains twitch. What with that and the list, she was probably fuming. Or at least I hoped she was fuming, because that would mean she was mostly herself today.

I mowed the lawn in neat stripes, or as close to it as I could manage, and then I trimmed the edges, humming the entire time. The garden really was a mess; there were all the brambles out of control near the hedge, and one bed had nearly been taken over by some sort of climbing weed. I was tempted to pull it out, but then I thought of Lord Naughton. Somewhere in his veins ran the blood of Norman conquerors, and he had so little reason to do battle these days. I couldn't deprive him of the pleasure of warring with these weeds.

It ran in his son's blood too. For a moment I recalled Will's eyes blazing with anger in the Emporium. A thousand years ago, he'd have been a Crusader.

The thought turned me on. I snapped the shears shut and replaced them in the garage.

When I went back inside, my mother's room was quiet except for the constant babble of the television. I glanced in and saw that she was sitting in her chair, without her newspaper, but otherwise not having moved an inch. There was no sense getting in an argument before the guest even turned up. With any luck, once Lord Naughton was here it would be enough of a foregone conclusion that my mother would simply give in.

Or maybe she'd fight. And that would be good, too. My mother was no Crusader, but she was a warrior of her own type. Seeing her and Lord Naughton butting heads could be interesting. Anything would be better than growing old and crazy with nothing but the television for company.

But when I stepped inside the kitchen, the first thing I saw was a silver tray, laden with my mother's best tea cups, tea spoons and tea pot, sugar bowl and tongs. The cake had been put on a dish, along with small dishes and forks and a silver cake-cutting thing, and napkins had been carefully folded on the side. The kettle steamed.

Beside it all sat the list I'd written, with step-by-step instructions on how to prepare a tea tray for a Viscount. My mother had done it all herself. All I had to do was make the cucumber sandwiches, and once Lord Naughton arrived, make the tea.

'Hurrah for lists,' I said, grinning.

I began on the sandwiches, something I'd done a thousand times for various business events. Lee and I would do a production line, her buttering bread, me slicing cucumbers. It got done more quickly that way, though sometimes we would work more slowly than we had to, so we could stay in the kitchen together. I remembered the light slanting through the

369

lace curtains at the kitchen window and I could hear Lee's pretty voice lilting a song. 'Whistle While You Work'. She'd try to whistle, too, and she couldn't do it. Nothing came out of her pursed lips but spluttered air and she looked so funny, blowing and puffing with her mouth in a tiny O that I would always laugh, even fuming from an argument with my mother, even one time when I cut my finger on the knife. I'd laugh and I'd do the whistling part for her.

I couldn't fool myself into thinking I was like my sister. I didn't do things just to be kind and make other people feel better. I was forcing my mother to prepare the tea tray herself and to have a visitor because it would be good for her, yes. And because I liked Lord Naughton. But some of my satisfaction today, aside from the acheless muscles, was because for the first time in my entire life I was making my mother do what I wanted her to do. Instead of the other way round.

Except for the night on the hill, when I'd forced her back to the house. But that didn't count. That was physical, that was necessary, that was because she was sick. That had been power, but too much of it, too wrong. She'd been weak, and I'd been strong, and I hated both of us for it.

No, this was more like turning the tables on all those years when my mother dressed me up in a hated frock and demanded good manners. Now it was her turn to mind her manners. Or to choose not to, and bear the consequences.

But I did hope she'd enjoy it. She probably hadn't enjoyed anything in a long time.

I hummed and stacked the sandwiches on a plate, covering them with plastic wrap to keep them fresh. Then I carried the wrought-iron table and chairs from the conservatory onto the newly-mown grass. There were some marguerites growing in one of the corner beds that wasn't too overwhelmed with weeds yet; I picked one or two and brought them into the kitchen to put in a bud vase on the tray. I was still humming when I heard a knock at the door. Wiping my hands on a tea towel, I hurried to get it before my mother could answer and send him away.

Lord Naughton stood on the step. He wore the same corduroy trousers he'd worn the last time I'd seen him, though they were free of dirt and grass stains this time. And instead of a worn waxed jacket he had a shirt and tie and tweed blazer. The uniform of the country-living upper class, even on a hot day. He held a vast bouquet of flowers, roses and lavender and other things I couldn't identify, which put my few meagre marguerites to shame.

'Lee,' he said warmly, 'so lovely to see you.' He gave me a kiss on either cheek, and I could smell tobacco and the flowers in his hand. He'd combed his hair carefully back. When we parted I could see a grey Bentley behind him, parked on the street in front of my mother's house. The Naughtons had expensive taste in cars.

'Thank you so much for coming, Lord Naughton.'

'Thank you for inviting me. Your mother's cherry tree is glorious. I haven't seen that variety in this area before. Wonder if she'd let me have a cutting.'

'I'm sure she would. I've set up a table in the garden, please come round.' I led him around the side of the house. He exclaimed and muttered about the state of the beds and the shrubs all the way to the back garden, when he spotted the rose bushes and let out a sudden cry, of pain or ecstasy I could not tell. He rushed over to inspect them, in his urgency still holding on to the bouquet.

'I'll tell Mum you're here,' I said to his departing back, and went inside. I turned off the television. 'You have a guest. He's waiting outside in the back garden.'

She stood up and smoothed down her skirt, and then ran her hands over her hair to neaten it, though it was perfectly neat already. 'Thank you,' she said, and walked past me out of the door.

No argument? No questions? Was this going to work as well as the list? I followed her out to the hallway, where she hesitated for a moment. 'The garden,' she said softly, and I took a step towards the back part of the house. As soon as I moved in the correct direction she became brisk again, and walked through the corridor to the conservatory and straight out into the garden.

Lord Naughton was still absorbed in the roses when we stepped out. 'Hello,' my mother called in her strong, confident tone and he turned around.

'Mrs Haven,' he said, beaming again. 'How lovely to see you.'

'And you.' She held her hand out to him, and he shook it. 'Thank you for coming to see me.'

'Couldn't resist your daughter's invitation. Heard you were having some trouble with your roses, and I see you are. Oh. These are for you.' He held out the bouquet to her.

'It's very kind of you.' She immediately passed the flowers to me. 'Do sit down. I hope you're well?'

'Oh, healthy as a horse, all of us Naughtons, right up to the day we die. And then we go like that.' He snapped his fingers. 'Father dropped dead of a heart attack at Claridge's, you know. Fifty-eight years old, and just having taken his first sip of port. At least he went happy – he always loved port above anything else – though we all thought it was a pity he never got to finish the glass.'

'How interesting,' my mother said. 'And how is your mother?'

'Ah, my mother was not as lucky with genes. Breast cancer

took her, must be nineteen years ago now. Theodora went of the same thing. My wife, that is. Always thought that was a cruel coincidence. Mother and wife, both carried off the same. Grandmother and mother for Will. It's been seven years since we lost her.'

'It's very sad,' said my mother. Lord Naughton pulled out a chair for her and for me, and then sat across from us. The two of them appeared entirely at ease; Lord Naughton lounged in his casual, aristocratic way, and my mother sat, as usual, poker-straight. Her hands were crossed on her lap and she was nodding and smiling and making all the appropriate expressions and questions for the conversation, slightly bizarre as it was. I stared at her, trying to figure out if she was actually following any of this, or if she was playing along, following his lead as she'd followed mine when she hadn't been able to recall the direction to her own garden.

She seemed almost normal, almost as if she were hosting an afternoon tea that she'd planned herself. Maybe she was playing along to prove something to me. Or maybe Alzheimer's had made her into an actress. Maybe she had no idea who Lord Naughton was, why he was there, and she was improvising because that was easier to do than to admit that the world around her made no sense at all.

She turned to me suddenly. 'Put those flowers in water, will you?' Her voice held all its old authority, and instinctively I bristled against it. Only for a split second, though, before I thought that if this was improvisation, she might not understand what was going on – that she might be floundering in a pool of incoherence, and that giving me orders was a retreat into the safety of habit.

'Of course,' I said. 'And I'll get the tea for you.'

I couldn't find a proper vase in the kitchen, so I looked in the sideboard in the dining room. That room had a window looking out to the back garden, and I stood for a few moments, vase in hand, to watch what was happening out there. Was she faking it? My mother had always been a planner, not an improviser. Although she was studiously polite in company, and entirely professional in her business, she had never once in her life hidden her feelings if you knew how to look. I would have said, before this afternoon, that she was incapable of presenting a deceitful face to the world.

Then again, a few weeks ago I would have thought it was impossible that I could have passed as my sister for more than a few hours.

She smiled, and nodded, and I saw her say something. Lord Naughton stood and they both walked over to the roses together, where he began touching stems and stroking leaves and was clearly explaining something to her.

What was she playing at? And how did I play this myself? If she didn't understand what was going on, surely it was kinder to call her bluff. Ask her outright, get her to admit she didn't remember Lord Naughton, and then tell her what was happening. She wouldn't spend an hour or two being confused and desperately trying to catch up.

But that required me to think of my mother as a victim. And standing there, nodding and listening to Lord Naughton, she didn't look like a victim. She looked quite normal. More friendly, maybe, but there was nothing wrong with that.

The doorbell rang. I put down the vase and went to answer it. It was Ma Gamble, holding a big paper bag and wearing a yellow poncho and Jesus sandals.

'Oh,' I said. 'It's you.'

I sounded exactly like my mother. It was excellent. Ma Gamble's expression, however, didn't change.

'I couldn't help overhearing that Abigail was seeing visitors today,' she said.

374

'She's seeing *a* visitor.'

'So I thought I'd come round and say hello.'

'Ma Gamble,' I said, exasperated, 'I know Will and I were in your shop talking. But as I said the other day – it's none of your business. People can get along quite fine without you spreading their private lives all over the town. And if someone mentions their plans in front of you it doesn't mean you're invited, too.'

'I haven't seen Abigail Haven in nearly two years,' Ma Gamble said. 'I used to see her just about every afternoon. I sell her product in my shop. I can see her house from my kitchen window. I would like to see how she's doing and offer any help that I can. That's what you do when you live in a town like ours.'

'You mean you want to see whether she's totally lost her mind yet, so you can spread the news.'

'Everybody wants to know, because they care.' She held up the bag. 'I brought the milk thistle. It might help her. And some homemade muesli, because it can't be easy staying regular if you're stuck in the house all the time.'

I looked at Ma Gamble. I looked at the bag. She seemed unrepentant about her lifelong rumour-mongering, but on the other hand, the bag had the distinct air of a peace-offering.

'Oh all right then, you might as well join us,' I said. 'They're in the back garden.'

I took her round. Unlike Lord Naughton, she didn't keep up a running commentary the whole way. I suspected she could have, but she was holding back on the gossip after my comments. Mum and Lord Naughton were sitting at the table when we arrived. He stood up.

'Mum, you've got another visitor.' I thought I saw uncertainty flit across her face, so I added, 'Ma Gamble thought she'd come and see how you were doing.'

'Hello,' my mother said.

'Nice to see you at last, Abigail,' Ma Gamble said. She gave my mother's hand a hearty shake.

'Yes,' Mum said. 'You remember my father, David.' She indicated Lord Naughton.

'I do,' Ma Gamble said. She shook Lord Naughton's hand as well.

'Mum, that's not Grandad, it's—'

'Nice to see you, Ma Gamble,' Lord Naughton said. 'Hope you're well.'

'Where's your sister?' my mother asked me.

'She's in London, beating up bad guys for a living.'

'No, that's you. Where's Emily?'

Cripes, my mother could not have picked a worse time to go on about this – in front of Ma Gamble. 'Mum, you know who I am,' I prevaricated. 'What were you talking about with Lord Naughton?'

'Abigail and I were talking about slugs,' he said.

'Broken egg shells,' said Ma Gamble instantly. 'You put them around the base of your plants and the slugs can't get to them.'

'Rubbish,' said Lord Naughton. 'Don't work. The blighters crawl right over 'em. They're like miniature Tiger tanks.'

'Salt kills slugs,' said my mother as if she were imparting the wisdom of the ages.

'But you don't want to kill them.' Ma Gamble pulled out a chair and sat down. It was the chair I'd brought out for myself. 'They're living creatures.'

'They're pests. I lost an entire crop of lettuces in one night. Scissors, they're the only things that work. Cut the nasty little slimeballs right in half.' He made snipping motions with his fingers.

'Salt kills slugs,' said my mother again.

'I'll go and get the tea,' I said, and left them to it.

A lilac bush stood outside the kitchen window, which meant there wasn't as good a view of the back garden as from the dining room, but I could still see bits and pieces through the leaves as I made the tea and added an extra cup and plate. The three of them appeared to be chatting animatedly, possibly about slugs, possibly about something else. Hopefully, not about my sister. I'd never been much of a lip reader, so I couldn't tell.

But I could see my mother's face and hands. I had no idea whether she understood the conversation at all; somewhere around her eyes she looked a little bit lost. Her gaze would wander every now and then, off into the distance, and she would come back only when one of the other two spoke to her directly. Once Ma Gamble had to touch her hand.

But she didn't look defeated. Not like an old woman whose only use was to sit in a chair and watch afternoon quiz shows without knowing any of the answers. Every once in a while she even looked like an old woman who was ready to pour some salt on the slugs and watch them fizz.

I went out to the garden with the tray.

'It was our song,' my mother was saying. 'Harvey and I would listen to it in Paris, before any of this started. Young lovers. And when I saw Sam, I couldn't help it; I asked him to play it for me.'

I began unloading the tray. My mother and father had a song? They'd been young lovers in Paris?

I watched my mother. Her eyes had gone misty. I couldn't picture her as a young girl, wandering the streets holding hands with my father. They'd never been particularly affectionate with each other, as far as I could remember. But of course they had a whole history together, before Lee and I had been born. They'd been married for several years before my mother got pregnant. I'd never thought much about that, all the years that existed before I did.

There must have been some passion at some point. I examined my mother anew. This was a whole new facet of her personality. There was still beauty in her face, though it was austere. As a girl she'd have been softer, prettier. Someone who could be in love in Paris with a man called Harvey.

'That's very romantic,' said Ma Gamble.

'What was the song, Mum?' I asked. I wondered if she'd danced.

'Oh, you know the one. About time.'

'That could be anything. What's the title?'

She wrinkled her brow. 'Time. Something about . . . something about . . .' She trailed off. 'About . . .'

'Try humming it,' I suggested. She hummed, but it was completely tuneless. She was even worse at humming than I was. Or maybe she didn't remember.

'I know the one,' said Lord Naughton.

'Me too,' said Ma Gamble. 'It's a beautiful song.'

'But then I had to leave him at the airport. Right on the runway, with the plane waiting there. It was raining. I wanted to stay with him, but he said I had to join my husband in the Resistance.'

'In the *Resistance*?' I said, but Ma Gamble shook her head at me. I shut up, thinking this all seemed very fishy, yet somehow familiar. It wasn't a story either one of my parents had told to me, I was sure of it. And my father wasn't old enough to have resisted in the war. He wasn't much of a resistor overall, except of course when he'd left us.

'Oh yes,' Mum continued. 'He said if I didn't go, I'd regret it. I'll never forget what he said to me – "Maybe not today, maybe not tomorrow, but soon".'

' "And for the rest of your life",' agreed Ma Gamble.

'Yes.' She looked askance at Ma Gamble. 'Were you there?'

With the final line of the quote, I knew. 'Was the song called "As Time Goes By"?'

'Yes, that's it! Were you there too?'

I sighed. 'Mum, that didn't happen to you. That's the plot of *Casablanca*.'

Someone kicked me under the table. I looked at Lord Naughton to see him staring at me forbiddingly over his aristocratic nose. I moved my leg.

'It's a wonderful story,' Ma Gamble said. 'You're a very lucky woman. Most people don't have anything that exciting happen to them in an entire lifetime.'

'But it didn't—' I began, and Ma Gamble's elbow dug into my ribs.

'And true love,' said Lord Naughton. 'It reminds me of how I met my Theodora. It was very similar. Except we were shooting grouse in Berkshire.'

My mother smiled, a private smile as if she were turning over a precious memory in her mind. Of what – a film she'd seen one afternoon? Or something real this time?

Was there even any difference to her?

'I had a love affair like that once,' Ma Gamble was saying dreamily. 'Me and a dashing young captain in Rio de Janeiro. It couldn't work out, of course. He was Navy.'

'Love is love, wherever you find it.' Lord Naughton took a decisive bite out of his cucumber sandwich.

'Yes, and we all need happy memories.' Ma Gamble gave me a significant glance as she poured more tea into everyone's cups.

'Was it Peachy Keen you wanted?' my mother asked her. 'Or Raspberry Rhapsody? Have you seen any sugar?'

'I'll take both, if you don't mind. People can't get enough

ice cream, especially in the summer. But don't worry, I'm sure Lee will take care of it.' She passed my mother the sugar bowl. My mother didn't appear to notice and kept stirring her tea.

She looked happy. Certainly the happiest I'd seen her in a very long time. The wrinkles in her forehead had smoothed out and a lock of hair escaped her chignon and was blowing softly against her face in the breeze. The clink of her spoon against the side of the cup made a delicate rhythm, the echo of a million cups of tea drunk at parties, in the mornings, in the evenings before bedtime, at work. A sound she'd heard again and again, every day of her life.

Ma Gamble and Lord Naughton talked on, about the town undertaker's affair with some young thing, about Rufus Fanshawe's BMW, the new thatcher and the new aromatherapist and the prospects of rain, deadheading roses and The Grateful Dead, and my mother nodded as they spoke. Every now and then she would add something, more often than not a *non sequitur*, and they accepted it like a tributary into the stream of conversation.

I listened and watched. And thought.

I'd wanted my mother to fight. I still wanted her to. But maybe part of the fighting was going along with the flow. About finding happiness wherever it came. About making sense where there wasn't any because it was kinder, and accepting the new person that my mother was becoming *as* a person, not as a disease.

As time goes by.

The sun sank slowly in the sky, and I fetched a cardigan for my mother and cleared the tea things, and the three older people talked and wandered in the garden until it was time to go. I brought my mother inside and settled her in her chair with another cup of tea, and I went to say goodbye to her guests.

'Thank you for inviting me,' said Lord Naughton, kissing my cheek. 'Done me a world of good.'

'I hope you'll both come again,' I said.

'I'll be here next Sunday afternoon,' promised Ma Gamble. 'Maybe you can get her to come out to the Friends of the Earthworm charity gala on Saturday, it's literally round the corner from here.'

'Um, maybe.'

'Promised Abigail I'd give those roses a good going-over sometime in the next few days,' Lord Naughton put in.

'That would be very nice of you. I've got to warn you, though – she was all right today, but sometimes she can be . . .'

'Not to worry. We all go up and down. I'll come with an extra pair of gloves for her; weeding always helps. Bring her to Naughton Hall one afternoon.'

'Oh.' I shifted on my feet, remembering Will's angry face. 'I'm – I'm not sure how much he's told you, but Will and I aren't exactly the best of friends right now.'

Ma Gamble's ears perked up.

'Nonsense. You must come. My son's a fool – all the Naughton men are when it comes to women. You wouldn't believe what my Theodora had to do to straighten me out. In any case, I'm inviting you myself. So you haven't a choice.' He turned and walked down the path to his Bentley.

Then it was me and Ma Gamble. The woman who'd carried me, at age twelve, all the way up the High Street by the ear. My feet had been literally dragging on the ground. She might look like a dotty old hippy, but in those days at least, she had the muscles of the Army Major that she'd once been.

'It was a good afternoon,' she said.

'Yes. Thank you for coming. I think you did help her.'

'So I was right about that.'

'About that, yes.'

'Where is your sister, did you say?' she asked, rubbing her chin.

'She's working on a film in London.'

She nodded. 'It won't hurt to humour your mother,' she said. 'You might think she needs reminding of reality, but her reality is different, now. Not wrong. Just different.'

'Yeah. It is.' She looked at me for a moment, and I looked at her. If I'd expected an apology for spreading rumours about me, I wasn't going to get it. I gave in. 'What are you going to tell people about Mum?'

'I'll say she's doing as well as can be expected. That she's facing her illness with dignity and strength. That she could probably use some more help from all of us, if she'll take it. I'll also say that you're doing a good job of caring for her.'

Yeah, maybe when I pretended to be my sister. 'She's got nurses, I've hardly had to do anything.'

'Yes, you have. You have to love her through the changes. And that can be the hardest thing. You'll do it, though.'

She turned and walked down the path. I watched her go. Then I went inside to my mother's room.

She was asleep in her chair, her tea growing cold beside her. Her head was tilted back and her mouth was slightly open, like a child who's played too hard and fallen asleep in the middle of a doll's tea party. I considered lifting her up and putting her into her bed, but then I thought, Go with the flow. I took a blanket from her bed and tucked it around her, and put an embroidered cushion from the sofa under her neck. Then I sat down on the other armchair, picked up her discarded newspaper, and waited until she woke up.

A Winged Woman

'Oooh, I feel so naughty.'

Five of them are squished into a rattly old taxi bouncing over the rutted roads of Paros towards to the small capital town of Parikia. Lee is sitting near the window, with the hot dry air blowing her hair around her face. She smiles at Simone, who has just spoken – a smile of complicity.

'I know,' says Monika. Monika was the one who arranged the taxi and orchestrated their escape. 'I'm amazed I lasted this long. I only held out three days in Kerala.'

'I've been dreaming of a big frosty glass of beer for a week now,' says Asmi. 'And a packet of cigarettes. My God.'

'Gin and tonic,' says Ruth, rubbing her hands together.

Simone shakes her head. 'I don't care about anything except steak and chips.'

'You're in Greece,' Asmi says.

'Lamb and chips, then. Chicken. Anything, as long as it used to walk around. One more meal in that place and I was going to turn into a lentil.'

'Mmm, a kebab,' says Monika.

'I'm not even going to think about eating until I've had at least three gins and listened to some rock music,' says Ruth.

Whitewashed houses appear; shops with their jumbles of plastic beach gear; tavernas. Tourists. More people than Lee has seen in two weeks.

'Let's all find a bar first, somewhere near the seafront,' Monika decides.

'Do you think they'll miss us after afternoon meditation?' Simone looks worried.

Lee has been with these four people long enough to get to like them, and also to recognise the archetypes. Monika likes to think of herself as rebellious; she's relishing her role as leader of their Great Escape from the ashram. Ruth and Asmi are enjoying being co-conspirators. Simone, for all her talk of meat, is concerned about breaking the rules. None of them are committed to their roles; Simone will forget about her worries after a couple of beers and her meal, and Monika, Ruth and Asmi will be back concentrating on their *asanas* tomorrow morning, despite their hangovers. They're acting this way because in this situation, someone needs to be the rebel, the followers and the worrier. The expedition wouldn't work otherwise.

'What do you want to do, Lee?' asks Asmi.

'I think I'd like to go to the Archaeological Museum, and to the Church of a Hundred Doors.'

The others stare at her.

'I'll join you in the bar afterwards, though,' she adds.

When the taxi stops near the ferry terminal the others are a bit muted in their exhilaration, and she knows that she's been a damper on their hedonism. She also knows that they'll be talking about her in the bar as soon as she's gone. She doesn't actually care. She's wanted to see the museum and the church since she came through Parikia on first arriving on the ferry, and she might not get another chance. She waves them goodbye and goes through the narrow paved lanes to the museum. The white houses drip with bougainvillaea and azalea, almost too bright to be believed.

The good feeling has crept up on her, almost without her noticing. Maybe it's the meditation, the change of scenery, the healthy diet, the dry heat and the new people around her. The chance to concentrate on her body and its simple needs to be stretched, exercised and rested. She'd thought she'd feel cleansed, but that's not it; she still knows she stole the car, and shoplifted. She knows she's let her mother down, and Ice Cream Heaven, and that she's fought with her sister and concealed things from her, the person she should be closest to in the world. All those are mistakes, and she hasn't washed them away. But she's feeling lighter, and she's feeling as if she's on the edge of understanding why she did them. She's beginning to suspect it's not madness, but instead a small part of her, immensely sane, demanding that she pays attention to Emily Haven for a while.

She can't help checking on Mum, though, which is why yesterday she brought her phone up to the hill again and looked through her messages and missed calls. Nothing about Mum, but there on the top of the list was a number that she hasn't seen or used in a long time.

The Archaeological Museum is cool and quiet. She wanders among marble torsos of gods and heroes. She loves being around old things, the sense of history and human emotion and skill. She used to love that part of working for the auction house – touching something that had been touched by hundreds of other hands, shaped by some and loved by others. All that memory in a single object, whatever it was.

Why is Tim calling her? Why does it matter? Maybe it's just the right time. Away from Stoneguard, and all the responsibilities that made her leave him, she can finally bear to think about what they used to have together. About her own announcement she'd been going to make that Christmas, before Mum brought out her terrifying lists.

It had all seemed so simple and right and perfect. Liza had agreed to come home, and Tim was coming to Stoneguard for Boxing Day. She was going to introduce him to her mother and sister and tell them she was selling the Stoneguard house and moving to Bath with Tim. Then Mum announced her illness, and Liza went away after that awful argument in the street, and Lee was left to hold everything together, keep everything the same, so nothing would fall apart.

Nothing except for her. She buried all those hopes in a dusty box under her bed, along with other things she didn't want to think about, that she couldn't think about because they didn't fit the person she was supposed to be now. Everyone else's idea of Emily Haven – the carer, the coper, the organiser, the good neighbour and dutiful daughter. And she is all of those things, but she's someone else, too, someone more complicated and flawed than that.

Maybe that's why it didn't work out with Will, even though they cared about each other. When he'd come back to town he'd seemed exactly what she needed: someone responsible, someone local. Someone else who'd been away, and who'd come back to take care of his family. And she'd had that huge crush on him all those years ago.

But she failed. She only let Will see her perfect face, not the true person underneath. Or maybe, she failed with Will because she failed Tim first, and those old hopes have never quite gone away.

She can't help but touch the cold marble surface of one of the sculptures. It's a winged woman. Her face has been worn away by time. But every feather on her wings is still perfect, and her footless leg is striding forward. She reads the label: *Gorgo, mid 6th-century* BC, Inv. No. 1285.

Someone clears his throat, and Lee glances over at the attendant sitting on a plastic chair in the corner. He's watching her pointedly. Evidently you're not meant to touch the antiquities. She takes her hand away, but not before she's noticed that the marble is pitted and rough. It wears its ancient scars and it's both beautiful and brave.

Lee leaves the museum, walking out onto the shaded street, and she takes out her phone. She dials a number, she bites her lip, and she thinks of the statue. *Gorgo*. A monster or a queen, or maybe neither.

He answers after one ring. 'Lee?' he says, and her heart lifts.

'Hello, Tim,' she says. 'I've missed you.'

The Perfect Blend

'This one's Red Ace, which Marketa and Ned Richard grow in Clench Green – raw and cooked. Marketa says she hasn't used pesticides on this crop, but the farm hasn't got organic certification. This one's Wodan, grown near Devizes, not organic, raw and cooked. This one's also Wodan, grown in Hampshire, but it's organic and we've got it bottled too.'

I stared down at the little glass dishes of cubed and grated beetroot. Each one of them had a card with a number beside it, and they were all varying shades of dark purple-red except for one. 'What's the orange stuff?'

Mouse checked her clipboard. 'That's Burpee's Golden. The Richards grew that too. Marketta said they were trying to be different.'

'Right. Er . . . now did you cook them?'

'Boiled 'em,' said Doris. 'Except I roasted one batch of Red Ace. If you like it I'll roast the other ones, eh.'

'Right. And – these are the horseradish? With the letter cards?'

'Horseradish was a bit more complicated,' said Mouse. 'We couldn't find anything fresh locally. Ma Gamble sent over a jar of her organic horseradish sauce. We've got a sample from GFA, one of our regular flavour manufacturers. And this is chgg . . . chgg . . .' She made a rough choking noise in her throat.

'Are you okay?' I raised my hand to pat her on the back.

'It's *chrain*,' said Glenys. 'It's Yiddish. My family always ate it at Passover with gefilte fish. I brought it over.'

Mouse set little piles of plastic forks and spoons on the table, and then she passed around photocopied sheets. 'I've made some tasting notes and a checklist. All you have to do is tick off the words that describe each sample next to the number. Or letter, if it's horseradish.'

'Wow,' I said, reading the columns of adjectives. *Earthy. Sweet. Bitter. Tangy. Hot. Warm. Comforting. Nostalgic. New.* 'Did you do all this yourself in just two days?'

'I – I sort of looked at some wine-tasting sites and adapted what I found.'

'Very impressive.' She blushed. I surveyed her and the rest of my tasting team: Doris, Gladys, Brenda, Dennis, Jonny back from Portsmouth. They all looked serious, even with little plastic forks in their hands. 'Okay, this is all great. Remember, though, everyone: we want this ice cream in production by the end of the week. So we need to taste thoroughly, but quickly.' I remembered my shelf-life tasting experience. 'Do you all like beetroot?'

'I've never had it before,' admitted Dennis.

'Well, if you don't like it, just say. I don't want any purple-tinted puking going on. Basically, we want the best-tasting ingredients we can get, in the best combination. So taste the beetroot, taste the horseradish, and taste them together, too. It would be nice to have it all extremely local and organic, but not if that's going to compromise on taste. All right?'

Everyone nodded gravely. I suppressed a bit of a smile. I really didn't need to go through all this palaver. Beetroot was beetroot, and horseradish was weird, and the two of them together in ice cream was quite frankly appalling. I didn't expect the final product to be anything but sick-making, no matter what ingredients we used.

But the customer was a famous chef, and if he wanted beetroot and horseradish ice cream, that was what he would get, and I was going to do it right. And even more than that – Ice Cream Heaven hadn't produced a new or bespoke flavour for two years. This was an occasion. I wasn't going to cut corners.

Nor was I going to deprive the employees of the company of the feeling that they were important and that their jobs mattered.

'Let's get tasting,' I said.

Ninety minutes later, our lips were magenta and everyone was talking at once.

'But the Golden Burpee would make the ice cream orange, not red.'

'We could use the Burpee and add some of the juice from the Red Ace . . .'

'But that would affect the flavour, eh.'

'Let's try them together.'

Silence, as people loaded their forks, chewed, thought.

'Good, but—'

'Sweet.'

'Try the roasted Red Ace with it instead.'

'That's it, there's a sort of smoky . . .'

'He wanted it to go with meat, so . . .'

'But what colour will it be?'

'Only one way to find out. Blender.' Doris took the two samples and left the office with them, leaving us chewing on the pink ends of our forks. Dennis excused himself to go to the toilet.

'Who would have believed that varieties of beetroot could

actually taste so different?' I said contemplatively. I looked at my checklist, which had a good number of ticks on it. And what was more, I could actually remember what each sample tasted like, from looking at the notes. 'I feel like I've entered a whole new world of vegetable appreciation.'

'I don't think I'll ever look at it the same way again,' agreed Jonny.

'Stick out your tongues,' said Mouse, and we all did. They were all bright magenta, as if we'd been chewing on something oddly radioactive. Glenys waggled hers, and we laughed.

'Pheeb's going to think it's so cool that Mummy has a pink tongue,' Mouse said.

'That's not all that's pink,' Dennis said, emerging from the loo.

'It isn't, is it?'

'Really?'

He nodded. 'Looks like Ribena.'

'If that's so, I'm going to leave it so Hazel can find it,' Jonny said. 'She'll scream.'

Doris returned with a single bowl filled with blended beetroot. We dipped spoons in it, tasted and ruminated. It was earthy, but clean-tasting. Sweet and smoky and savoury.

'Nice,' Mouse said. Jonny nodded, and so did Doris. Glenys and Dennis took another taste, and then they nodded too.

'I think this is it,' I said. 'But I'd like to make sure. Do you mind roasting the other varieties of red ones, Doris, and blending with the Golden? We can have a final taste-test this afternoon.'

'No problem. That will give us some extra to choose from, too, eh, if this turns out the wrong consistency to freeze well.'

'Exactly what I was thinking,' I agreed.

'Is it time to try it with the horseradish now?' asked Dennis, and he sounded eager. To my surprise, I was eager too. Even more eager than I was to check my pee for purple, and that was saying something. We all pushed the rejected samples aside and began dipping spoons into the horseradishes. It was notably quieter this time.

'I'm not sure,' said Glenys, at last.

'I don't think any of them are quite right,' I said. 'The essence is too strong, and the sauce is too weak. It tastes more like mustard. And the . . .'

'*Chrain.*'

'. . . *chrain* is too, I don't know . . .' I fluttered my fingers.

'Bottled-tasting,' supplied Doris.

'Yes.'

'It's very good on gefilte fish,' said Glenys sadly.

'But not right for this.' I sighed. 'I thought we were really close.'

'Once we've found the perfect beetroot mix, I can make up some test ice-cream batches with the flavouring,' Doris said. 'Might taste different cold.'

'Maybe,' said Dennis.

'I'd really hoped we could get this sorted out this morning,' I said.

'Chin up,' said Jonny. 'Some just take longer than others, that's all. Remember Christmas Pudding?'

Everyone but Mouse and me agreed, but I could tell they were as disappointed as I was. All the excitement and enthusiasm hadn't come to anything. Not yet, anyway. And we were on a tight schedule.

'Tell you what,' I said, 'I think we've all earned a pub lunch. On me. Let's go freak everyone out at the Druid's Arms with our purple mouths.'

That brightened everyone up. 'Can we sit next to the loos?' asked Dennis as we headed for the door.

Memory and Ashes

I didn't even have to look at the clock this time; I knew as soon as the phone rang that it was three in the morning.

'She's out again?' I said as a greeting into the receiver.

'I have no idea how this keeps on happening. I've double-checked all the locks . . .'

I swung my feet out of bed. 'It's fine. I'll go and get her.'

At least it wasn't raining. I got dressed quickly and headed out with my torch.

In my interrupted dream, I'd been fighting somebody. Not stunt fighting for the camera; this was real. But it wasn't working. The person was dressed in black and I couldn't get a focus on their face, and every time I tried to land a punch or a kick, they parried me. It was as if they could read my mind, had trained in the same places, had the same experiences and instincts. It was like fighting myself. We were exactly matched, neither one able to win, or to lose, and no way to end the battle.

I shook it off as I hurried through the dark, shoving my hair back into an elastic band as I went. The moon was waning, and there were thousands of stars tonight. I knew the path well enough so that I didn't have to use my torch.

How was she getting out? The doors were locked, the keys

were hidden, and I'd fixed that window. I had to hand it to my mother – she was one determined woman. And probably just as desperate to escape that house as I'd been as a kid. Though I knew better than to expect her to be hanging around the school playground with holidaymakers' sons.

I trotted across the empty car park and up the path, and sure enough, there she was, on her way up the hill again. 'I hope she's in a less stubborn mood tonight,' I muttered to myself as I climbed.

She climbed steadily, slowly, and her feet were bare again. 'Mum!' I called, and at the same time my foot landed on a loose stone and my ankle twisted. I stumbled a few steps and by the time I was walking properly again, Mum was quite a ways up the path. I ran after her, not pleased that I was beginning to get out of breath. I was seriously going to have to get back into a regime when all of this was finished.

'Mum!' I called again, but again she didn't seem to have heard me. I caught up with her and put my hand on her shoulder. 'Mum, it's me. It's time to go home now.'

She didn't pause, just kept on walking. Like the last time.

'Come on, Mum. It's the middle of the night and I really don't fancy picking you up again.'

No response. Her eyes were focused upward, where the stones loomed against the star-studded sky. The path went up in steps now, and she negotiated each one without looking. Her bare feet landed exactly in the middle of each step, as if she knew the path so well she could walk it in her sleep. Which was pretty much what she was doing. But to my knowledge, she'd never come up here in all the years I'd lived in the same house as her, and certainly not for the past year or two. Except during the middle of the night.

'Mum, you'll catch cold. You'll hurt your feet. You'll twist your ankle.'

She paid no attention. I climbed after her.

'This is getting really boring, you know. And you're not the only one with problems. I've got lots of problems, too.'

She kept on climbing, apparently deaf.

'I haven't got a job any more, and it looks like I never will. Apparently directors don't like to hire people who trash expensive cars and lose their nerve. I've got the hots for my sister's boyfriend, I can't tell anybody who I really am, I've got chronic backache when it's rainy which is almost always in this country, and there's no decent horseradish in Wiltshire.'

No response. Just climbing.

'I could be fast asleep in a nice warm bed. So could you. Doesn't that sound good? A nice warm bed? I'll even make you some cocoa, and believe me, I've never made cocoa for anyone. I'm not even sure how to do it. But I will, if you'll turn around yourself, now, and come back home.' I sighed. 'Mum?'

It wasn't working. Nothing was going to work. I was going to have to put her in a hold again and carry her back down. Suddenly, fiercely, I longed for my mother as she used to be. Infuriating, domineering, inflexible, logical, sane. I even wanted to argue with her and have her argue with me back.

You have to love her through the changes, Ma Gamble had said. But how did you love someone through the changes if you weren't sure how much you loved them in the first place? How did you learn to love someone you didn't even recognise?

I remembered what I'd been thinking on Sunday, how maybe it was kinder, sometimes, not to fight.

'Fine,' I said. 'You win. Let's go up to the stones.'

She kept walking, as if she hadn't heard me, which she probably hadn't. I walked alongside her, looking out for stray rocks or anything else that might hurt her feet. We climbed and climbed and then the ground levelled out and we were at the entrance to the stone circle.

In the darkness, the stones were patches of pitch black. But that doesn't quite describe them, because they were more than black. They had volume and weight. As we walked past the taller guardian stone and past the other monoliths to the centre of the circle, I could feel them. I wasn't sure why. It wasn't as if they were warmer or colder than the air around them, and it wasn't a feeling like hot or cold anyway. It was something more basic and permanent. The stones were big and solid and there. Among them, my mother and I were much smaller. Damselflies or wisps of paper.

She walked us into the centre of the circle and then on to the other side. It was difficult to make out the exact shapes of the stones, but here two of them were quite close together, and I knew which ones they were. The jigsaw puzzle stones, I'd always called them in my head, because one was slightly irregular on its right side, jutting out on the top, and the one next to it was slightly irregular on its left. It reminded me of how South America looked like it could fit into the side of Africa, if they weren't two continents rooted to the ocean floor. My mother slipped between them, and then she walked five or so more steps, and then she stopped.

'What's up here, Mum?' I asked her, and I followed her gaze and I knew. From this place, the hill gave a view directly over to Ice Cream Heaven. I could see the shape of the factory barn and beyond it, the white walls of what used to be her family home. 'Are you thinking about work?'

'They're all dead,' she said.

The vehemence, the sadness in her voice made me blink. 'What?'

'All of them. I killed them myself. They're over there, can't you see?' She pointed. It looked like an empty field.

'I can't see anything, Mum,' I said carefully. 'It's too dark.'

'It's the smoke. It makes everything dark. But you have to burn them, otherwise it will spread.'

I had to check again, because she was speaking with so much conviction. It was too dark to see properly, but I certainly couldn't see any bodies. 'Is this a memory, Mum, or are you making up things again?' Maybe the nurse had been letting her watch horror movies on TV. I'd have to have a word.

'Can't you smell it? It's everywhere. It's on my hands.' She raised her hands to her face and sniffed them, then shook her head hard. 'Burning and skin and hair and grass. And that disinfectant, it smells blue. Can't you smell it? Can't you?' Her voice raised to a plea, nearly a screech.

Horror movies didn't have smells. Memories did. I could still smell the oil and heat from the wrecked Ferrari, when I let myself. 'Yes, Mum. I can smell it too.'

That seemed to calm her a bit. My mother held the skirt of her nightgown in one hand and she sat down on the ground. She bent her legs, her ankles tucked together, and gathered her skirt around her legs, as if she were wearing a demure dress instead of a flannelette nightie. I sat beside her on the grass.

'Right over there,' she said. 'From here you can see it all. It's everything we own, you know.'

'I know. Yes.'

'The legs are the worst. The calf legs like burning sticks. There's nothing left. What are we going to do now? What are we going to do?'

She sounded near tears. I touched her hand. It was cold, so I took it and put it between my knees. To warm it up. 'Maybe we should go back down to the house.'

'We can't. The smell, it's everywhere.' She pointed again to the dark fields with the hand I wasn't holding. Her wrist was thin and her hand was shaking. For a moment I could imagine a picture, like something off the television, of calf legs blackened and sticking up in the air, though I didn't know where it came from in my head.

'I killed the calves myself,' she said. 'The vet said he'd do it but I wanted to know they wouldn't suffer. I turned them around so they'd never know. But they're burning now and I did that. They're dead, they're dead, they're dead, their legs and their feet and that smell . . .'

She was crying. I put my arms around her because there was nothing else to do and nobody could see us. I wasn't sure if she saw me, either, because her face was still turned to her memory, the burning field of calves beyond the barn that was now the factory and the house that belonged to tourists. She cried without relaxing, permitting my embrace but not giving in to it, but the sobs were deep and I'd never heard this sound from my mother before.

I can't cry when other people cry. I held her and felt her lungs straining for air beneath her brittle ribs. I smelled her cold cream and toothpaste and a faint smell underneath that, of age. When you hold your own mother in your arms you should feel something but I felt nothing, or maybe I felt so much that I couldn't tell what it was.

She was mourning calves. Not her parents, or her marriage, or her own sickness, or even Lee and me. She was mourning calves and with that thought I felt the old familiar anger, though it was floating somewhere around my head, detached, as if someone not me had said, 'Liza is angry now.'

I held her as gently as I could. I looked at the parting in her hair, which gleamed white in the darkness. From photographs I knew that she had parted her hair in this same straight way since she was a child. Eventually her sobs quieted, and then calmed. For a moment I kept her in my arms, and then she wiped her nose and eyes with the palm of one hand.

I don't know what it was about that gesture, her wiping

398

her face without a handkerchief or a tissue, but as soon as she did it, I wasn't angry any more. My anger melted away, even the little detached voice telling me about it. I was just here, with my mother, on a hill next to some rocks, and she needed my help.

She wiped her hand on her nightgown and sat up straight. 'Let's go home, Mum,' I said. I took my trainers and socks off and I put them on her bare feet, brushing the dirt off her soles and rolling the socks up over her bony ankles and tying the laces of the trainers tight. We wore the same size, all three Haven women. Then I helped her stand up. She went with me, without protest or words, away from the vista of her memories and back through the stone circle to the path on the other side.

We had gone down the steps and were following the chalk trail downward, my attention taken by guiding her and also watching out for my own bare feet, when she spoke again.

'I never told any of them that I love them,' she said. 'That's what I feel sorry for.'

I'd thought the anger was wiped away, but it tapped me on the shoulder again. 'Who, Mum? The calves?'

'No,' she said. 'Not the calves. You don't love calves, silly girl. Did you get the post?'

'Yes, I got the post.'

'Did you turn off the gas?'

'Yes. It's all safe. Who didn't you tell them that you love them?'

She paused. We walked. I waited for her to answer. I knew at that moment, with my feet dented by small rocks and gritty with dust, that I'd been waiting for this answer, my whole life.

'Did you get the post?' she asked.

The View From Here

'Wow, look at that colour!'

It was a scoop of magenta in a white bowl. Doris had placed it right in the middle of my desk, and now, with a flourish, she handed me a spoon.

My eyes ached from exhaustion and my mouth tasted of the coffee I'd been swigging all day to keep myself awake. I'd spent most of my working hours staring at the same piece of paper, except for a few minutes looking something up on the internet. My thoughts were going round and round in circles: my mother pointing at a dark field, talking about a memory as if she were still in it, and her final, maddening statement dissolving into endless questions about trivialities. I'd tried to sleep after bringing her home and mostly failed, and today my brain kept on worrying at it, as if it was trying to figure it out but hadn't found the time and space yet.

Still, I put on a bright smile for Doris and for the other Ice Cream Heaven employees who came crowding around my desk.

'It's the roasted Red Ace, with some Golden Burpee juice and the GFA flavour,' Doris said.

'Numbers Five and Nine mixed with B,' supplied Annabelle.

400

'Right, well then, this is the moment of truth.' I took a sip from the glass of water on my desk, to clear my palate. Then I cleared my throat, dug a semi-circular bite out of the soft-frozen magenta, and put it in my mouth.

Cold. And then *hot*. Hot enough to scour out my nasal passages and rip a strip off my tongue.

'Mrrrrrr,' I said, and I swallowed the lump as soon as I could and then grabbed the glass of water to douse the fire on my tongue. 'Um – that's a bit spicy.'

'I hardly put any in,' Doris said sadly. 'It's powerful stuff, eh.'

'You can say that again. We could market it as a cold remedy, the way it blasts through your sinuses.' I finished the glass of water. 'I'll give Edmund Jett a ring and ask him, but I think we might be going for a more subtle flavour than that.'

'I'll try it with less.' She picked up the bowl and left the room. There was dejection in her shoulders.

I got up and ran after her. 'Doris,' I called, and she turned around. 'I'm sorry, that wasn't exactly tactful, was it?'

She shrugged. 'Fair enough, eh, it would take the paint off the side of the barn.'

'But you're doing your best, and I've put you and everyone else under a lot of pressure. The least I can do is to be nice to you about it.'

A smile twitched the corner of her mouth. 'Don't you worry, there. I worked for your mother for nigh-on forty years, I'm not going to curl up and die if you speak a harsh word.'

'But I'm not my mother. And compared to you I don't know anything about making ice cream.'

'You're a Haven, and that's enough for me.' She settled her hairnet more firmly on her head, then turned around and went into the factory.

401

I sighed, rubbed my eyes and sat down on the stone wall. I'd flubbed that one, and good. And what was I doing, trying to make stupid ice cream with horseradish? I was fooling myself thinking I could do something that Lee couldn't. I was wasting everyone's time. It was only because I was a Haven that any of these people were going along with this at all.

'Are you all right, Lee?' I opened my eyes to see Mouse hovering nearby.

'Just failing to extract my foot from my mouth,' I said. 'I really might as well not be here today. I'm useless.'

'No, you're not!'

'You're just being nice, Annabelle. Let's face it, I don't know what I'm doing here. And Doris is doing her best, it's not her fault that the horseradish packs the punch of a blowtorch.'

Mouse sat down on the wall beside me. 'Lee, you're not useless. You're doing a great job with the company. And everybody's having lots of fun with the new flavour. Just because it's not working out now, that doesn't mean anything. We'll have to figure out a new recipe, that's all. It's a challenge.'

I looked at her. This was the woman who not long ago had looked absolutely terrified when I'd sat her on this wall and given her more responsibility?

'You sound like you're actually excited about having a challenge.'

'Do you know what? I am.' She blushed, and chewed her lip for a moment before she said anything. 'Can I tell you something, Lee? Don't get offended.'

'Of course I won't get offended.'

'Up until last week, I thought you hired me out of pity.'

'Pity?'

'Well, maybe that's a little strong. Sympathy, maybe? I

mean, you offered me the job after I'd been spending all that time moaning that I never did anything but chase after the kids and I didn't feel like I had any kind of a life other than being a mum. And then when I started working here, you didn't seem to need me for anything. You're so good at taking care of everything, and of course I didn't know how to do anything. It was like – I felt like I didn't really have any part in the company, you know? I was only here because you felt sorry for me and you wanted to get me out of the house a bit.'

I remembered how when I'd first walked into Ice Cream Heaven, I'd thought that very thing: that she was one of Lee's charity cases. 'Annabelle, you do a great job here. Look at the way you pulled together all those ingredients for us. Not to mention how you've kept everything going so smoothly in the past couple of weeks. You're totally my right-hand woman.'

And she definitely wasn't Mouse any more. Not even in my head.

'Thanks.' She ducked her head with the compliment. 'I do feel that I've been doing a good job, you know – that I'm useful. It's funny, but things have been easier at home too, somehow. Like every time Pheebs has a potty-training accident, it doesn't feel like the end of the world any more. I just feel like I'm an okay person and that hey, she'll stop having accidents eventually, and even if it takes a while, I'm still a good mum.'

'Well, I don't know anything about potty training, to be honest. But I'm sure you're a good mum.'

'The thing is, I don't always feel it. But I've surprised myself with how well I've done here. I'm actually proud of myself. And that's all down to you trusting me. So I'd say you definitely know what you're doing.'

I bit my lip. I was nearly tearing up. Must be lack of sleep.

Or maybe, just maybe, praise from Annabelle meant something to me. When had that happened?

'Thanks,' I said. My throat was rough.

'No, thank *you*.' She smiled at me. 'Want some more coffee?'

'I think I need some.'

She got up and went inside. I sat there for a moment longer, and then I stood to follow her. It was only then that I realised that today, for the first time since I was a child, I had actually eaten ice cream.

It was the tail-end of the day and the tourists were beginning to pack up and head for their cars and coaches. I passed several groups of them coming down on my way up to the stone circle. 'Well, you can't even touch the rocks at Stonehenge,' a man wearing a Union Jack T-shirt was saying loudly to the five hefty ladies beside him as they puffed down the path, 'but you'd think they'd make it a little bit easier here.'

'You can drive right up to the Grand Canyon,' one of his companions agreed as they went by. They were followed by a man and a woman both entirely dressed in purple and carrying dowsing rods. '*Completely* destroying the aura,' muttered the woman. Three children thundered past them all, gleefully yelling, 'Baa!' They clattered down the path, setting small pebbles rolling afterwards. Several steps later, I encountered their father, wearing a floppy hat, a red face and a baby in a backpack. 'Kayleigh, Sonya, Keenan!' he shouted, lumbering behind them. If I was any judge, the whole family would be in the ice-cream parlour in the next twenty minutes, being bribed to stay quiet on the ride home.

I stood aside to allow a tour group through, led by a whippet-thin man in an anorak, and then I was back in the stone circle, about fifteen hours after the last time I'd been here. In daylight, I could see the stones properly, but they seemed smaller rather than bigger. I nodded at a couple who were circumnavigating the stones, touching each one as they went. Lots of people did that up here; I didn't know whether it was supposed to create some magical effect, or if the perfect circularity of it all just brought out innate obsessive-compulsive behaviour. Anyway, they seemed to be enjoying themselves. I slipped through the gap between the jigsaw puzzle stones and sat down with my back against the Africa one. The rock was warm from the sun and it felt good between my shoulder-blades.

It wasn't quite where I'd sat with my mother last night, but nearly. I could see Ice Cream Heaven, which I'd left not long ago, and the whitewashed house where my mother and my grandparents had used to live. And the field she'd pointed to, which was smooth and unmarked.

Time and space. I leaned my head back, letting my muscles relax. I could hear a faint breeze and the murmur of other people, the brushing of their feet through the grass. It wasn't as irritating as I'd have thought it would be; for the moment, at least, the stone circle was big enough for me and all the tourists too. I let my gaze wander over the fields and the hills, the sparse cottages and houses, a single road visible winding between stone walls. So many different colours, all of them green.

Los Angeles was full of people, crammed to the gills with everyone looking for the same kind of dream. And that was one reason why I'd chosen to live there, to gain a certain kind of anonymity. But Wiltshire was full in a different way. Not with people, traffic, signs and hurrying; but with the long weight of the past, layered over the landscape. Feet treading on paths, soil cropped and tilled. Stones dug up and hauled miles for a reason lost in mysterious time.

And the charred circle of my mother's bonfire of cattle, which years had covered with smooth green grass.

I'd looked it up this morning on the net. My mother had started Ice Cream Heaven in 1968, when she was twenty-eight years old, and had been working on her father's dairy farm since she was old enough to carry a pail. In 1967, a foot and mouth epidemic caused the slaughter of nearly half a million animals across the country. They were burned, supposedly to stop the infection spreading. In California, it had been the Summer of Love. In Wiltshire, my mother had killed her family's calves.

I thought I'd seen the image of the calf legs before; it turned out I had, on television, when foot and mouth hit the country again in 2001. I'd been in London, far away from the carnage, and it had registered, but only dimly. I had my own life to think about. The burning cattle wasn't my own memory, it was someone else's. I hadn't known then that it had anything to do with me.

And I'd never really thought about why my mother had turned the dairy farm into an ice-cream factory. She'd been doing it for a dozen years before Lee and I were even born; as far as I'd been concerned, she'd been doing it forever.

'But when was the Bronze Age? Isn't that when these rocks are from?' The voice was close enough for me to jump, but when I looked around it was someone walking on the other side of the stones, inside the circle. 'Was it before the Ice Age, or after the Stone Age?'

'I think it was after the dinosaurs some time,' answered someone else vaguely, and their conversation faded out as they walked away.

Ancient history. Yet to my mother last night, it had been as if it was actually happening that moment. I stared out at the smooth grassy field and tried to understand. She'd been the only child of a farming family, a last daughter in a long line of sons. By 1967 she was an adult, unmarried, and if I knew my mother, she was probably practically running the farm by herself. And then in one fell swoop, it was all gone.

What will we do? she'd asked last night, of the empty air.

Her parents wouldn't know anything but dairy farming. It would have been my mother's idea to start afresh with ice cream. She would've looked around at the tourists – there must have been tourists in 1967, and probably a lot of long-haired truth-seekers too – and realised she had a built-in market. She perfected her recipe for ice cream and began selling it, first in vans, then in her own parlour, then in outlets all over the country, until the profits overshadowed those of the original dairy. Ice-cream success story. She started with the ashes of sick animals and the death of my grandfather's dreams, and she turned it into sweet transient pleasure.

While the publicity materials for Ice Cream Heaven stressed the long history of the family and the local provenance of all the ingredients, they didn't mention the fact that the company had been founded in order to save the family from financial ruin. Desperation and images of burning corpses didn't sell ice cream. And it turned out my mother was very, very good at selling ice cream.

She had to be. There was nothing else left.

I shifted my back against the stone, feeling its warmth penetrate the scars there. I knew what it was like to have everything taken away. Hadn't I been putting myself through hell, torturing my body for months, fighting to make sure that I wouldn't lose my job and my life and my identity?

Every time my mother sold an ice cream, that was one more step away from the burning field. She must have looked at those flames in her memory thousands of times. It would

407

have taken guts and strength and a lot of fighting to do.

I frowned and rubbed my eyes, still tired from last night. It was getting late. The shadows were lengthening, and the sky was turning the orange of embers. What was I doing, anyway? I already understood my mother. Whatever had happened in her past, she'd had enough time in her life to make up for it. But she hadn't. She cared about Ice Cream Heaven more than she cared about my father and me and even my sister. Why did it matter *why* she cared so much about her company? It didn't make her a better mother.

But maybe it could help me forgive her for it.

'I don't want to forgive her,' I said out loud. 'If I stop fighting her, what am I going to be?'

As soon as I said it, I realised how pathetic it was. I was a grown woman. I didn't need to define myself in relation to my mother. Or to my home town, or to my twin. Except, of course, that was exactly what I'd been doing for the past weeks, and maybe for my entire life.

I flopped sideways onto the grass with a sigh of frustration. On the intake of breath, I smelled a familiar scent – appropriately for my thoughts, it was of burning, but not flesh and hair. It was resiny, herby, and instantly identifiable. Someone was up in the stone circle, not far from where I sat, smoking a spliff and probably contemplating the mysteries of the universe.

Good. I hoped they were happier about what they were coming up with than I was. This was why I'd always wanted to keep on working, keep on going. Keep on driving fast. If you were moving, you never had to stay still and think about things. Like how the powerful figure of your mother was not only becoming vulnerable with age, but had been vulnerable all along. And how maybe I'd never understood this because I didn't want to. And how I only really started thinking about who I really was when I was spending all my time pretending to be someone else.

'It's all completely fucked up,' I said to the sky and the shadows and the sunset. But I gritted my teeth and I thought about the last thing my mother had said last night. Well, the last thing before she'd become concerned with the post.

I never told any of them that I love them. That's what I feel sorry for.

It was the closest to an apology I'd ever heard from Abigail Haven. And the closest I'd ever come to her telling me that she loved me. Drawn out of her muddled brain that sometimes believed that she was living inside *Casablanca*, and sometimes that her parents were still alive.

The corners of my eyes stung. I wiped them and came away with moisture.

'Hey, what's up?'

It was a new voice, low and drawling. I lay still, expecting the person to pass by like the others had. I heard a soft rush of exhaling breath and the marijuana smell got a lot stronger.

'Hey, you all right there, Lee?'

I sat up. It was Rock Hamlin. He was leaning against South America, wearing black jeans and a black T-shirt, his spliff dangling from between his fingers.

'Oh hi, Rock.'

'You okay?'

'Yeah, yeah, sure, fine.'

'All right. Good. I thought maybe you were in some sort of trance.'

'No, I was just thinking.'

'What about?'

Love and death and who the hell I am. 'Horseradish,' I said.

'Huh.'

'I'm done now, I guess.'

'Oh. Okay. Mind if I join you?'

'Why not.'

He sat down beside me on the grass, crossing his boot-clad feet and offering me his joint. 'Want some?'

I shook my head. I wondered if it was the first time someone had offered my sister pot. 'What are you up to, Rock?'

'Oh, I come up here a lot after work.' He put out his spliff, carefully, against the ground and then tucked it away in his back pocket.

'Why's that? To watch the sunset?'

'No, I'm waiting for them.'

Who is *them*? I was about to ask, but then I remembered what he'd said at the dance. The aliens.

'It was about this time of day they came before,' he said. 'But that was in the winter, and it's hard to know if they're going by actual clock time, or more time of day. Sunset happens at about five o'clock in the winter, but it's pretty crowded up here at five o'clock in the summer. So I reckon it's sunset, because why would they be following human clocks anyway? And I like it better up here at sunset, and who knows if they're coming, so I might as well please myself, right? But maybe they don't even care about human time at all, or they have different time. Maybe in their time, they haven't even come here at all yet, like maybe they go backwards or something.'

'It's possible,' I said.

'Later on I'll do a sign for them.'

'What, you're going to paint a big board or a sheet with *Welcome Aliens*?'

'Something like that. Nice sunset, though.'

We weren't facing west, but the orange light echoed and

spread across the sky and tinged all the clouds. 'Yeah, it is. So do you come up here most nights, Rock?'

'Sometimes. I go some other places too – there's loads to do. Why were you thinking about horseradish?'

I sighed. 'Do you know how hard it is to find good horseradish?'

'What do you consider good?'

'Strong, but not too strong. Just with the right bite, you know? Fresh. Locally grown.'

'Right. Yeah, I get it.' He looked contemplatively into the distance.

'Why do you ask?'

'I like plants, especially wild ones.'

I nodded. 'Do you happen to know anywhere I can find horseradish?'

'I might.'

'Really?' I said, sitting up straighter. I pictured Doris and Annabelle and the others, and how happy they'd be if I suddenly came in with exactly the right ingredients tomorrow morning.

'Yeah. But it's a bit . . .' He wobbled his hand back and forth like a see-saw. 'Dodgy. We can't get caught.'

'Not a problem.' I stood up. 'Can you show me it now?'

'I can show you it later. But I'm going to need you to help me to do something in return.'

'I'll do anything for the right horseradish,' I said, and then suddenly thought that Rock might be referring to sexual favours. 'Almost.'

'Don't worry,' he said, and he sounded amused. He got to his feet too and pushed his wild hair out of his face. 'Meet me at the north corner of the Hendersons' field at half past midnight. On the footpath, near the stile. Don't drive, wear dark clothes, and don't have anything in your pockets that can fall out. Bring a bag. And be careful with your torch, don't wave it about.'

Now my curiosity was as strong as my desire for horseradish. 'Why?'

'You'll see.' He began to walk away, with a distinct loose gait. 'You'd better try to get some sleep before then,' he said back over his shoulder as he left. 'It's going to be a long night.'

Going Round In Circles

When I got to the stile that night, Rock was waiting for me. He was a slim shadowy form, barely visible from a distance except for a blaze of white on his chest.

'You didn't use a torch,' he said when I reached him, approval in his hushed voice.

'I'm getting used to walking around in the middle of the night.' I could see he'd pulled his hair back into a black baseball cap, and that his black T-shirt had a white stylised alien head on it. At least he had a sense of humour about his beliefs. He zipped up his black sweatshirt, covering up the white before we set off. Between the beard and the hat and all the dark clothes, he was nearly invisible. We went past the stile and climbed over the metal gate into a different field. It was planted with something low, maybe potatoes; I wasn't very up on agriculture and I couldn't see the plants clearly anyway. Rock led me down the path along the side of the planting.

'So how do you know so much about horseradish?' I asked him.

'I like plants. They're pretty peaceful and they have good auras.'

'Are you still growing marijuana? My – sister used to buy

it off your brother sometimes.' I couldn't smell it on him tonight, though.

'Personal use only.'

We went along two sides of the field, and then, when we were in the far corner, diagonal from where we'd entered it, Rock stopped and dropped into a crouch. 'Here it is.'

I crouched beside him. He was pointing to a clump of leaves. I couldn't make out their precise shape, but they looked vaguely ruffly and a bit like broader versions of the dock I'd used to rub on my nettle stings from running wild around the countryside. 'How'd you know this was here?'

'I like to walk around fields. You get to see a lot of interesting things.'

'Like aliens?'

'I saw the aliens at the circle.'

'Oh yeah, that's right, I'm sorry.'

'Mostly in the fields you see fairies. Things like that. They don't like to be seen though so you have to be pretty quiet.'

'Oh. Of course.' I touched the cool horseradish leaves. 'Is this a planting?' I asked.

'It's wild. It might have escaped from a planting. It's a nuisance plant.'

'If it's a nuisance, why did we have to come here at night?'

'Because Henderson hates people in his fields, and he's got a gun.'

'Oh.'

Rock dug into the pockets of his combats and produced a small trowel. 'Got your bag? How much do you need?'

I shrugged off my backpack, which I'd lined with a plastic bag. 'Not a lot; we're testing a recipe. If it's the right stuff, I can offer to buy it off Henderson.'

'You've got money, he'll be interested.'

414

'Though I fancy the description "Night-stolen Horseradish" on a list of ingredients, don't you?'

He grunted an assent and dug the trowel into the soil in the middle of the clump. 'Digging it up cuts up the roots and spreads it more. He wouldn't be pleased to know we were doing it.'

'You sound strangely satisfied about that proposition.'

'Henderson stole one of our dogs and tried to sell it back to us last year. I don't mind spreading his weeds.'

'Even better. "Night-stolen Horseradish of Revenge". I might not pay Henderson for it, after all.'

I heard and watched him rummaging around in the dirt with his hands. Considering it was the middle of the night and he was digging up a big long root, he was surprisingly quiet and gentle. I waited, listening for irate gun-toting farmers. After a few minutes Rock straightened up again. He was holding a long root, sort of like a big parsnip, connected to a plume of leaves. I took it from him and put it in my backpack.

'Thanks.' The root was nicely heavy in my pack. 'Everyone at Ice Cream Heaven is going to be really excited.'

'No problem. I hope it's what you need.' He brushed himself off and put the trowel back in his pocket. I helped him rearrange the leaves of the remaining plants so it wasn't apparent that someone had been digging around in there.

'We'll only know once we've tried it. Where to now?'

'I left my gear about half a mile from here, just off the bridleway.' We went back around the field to the gate, climbed over and started down the path. In the distance, a sheep baaed sleepily.

'What do fairies look like?' I asked. I figured he'd helped me out; I might as well play along with his beliefs.

415

'Oh, you know. They sort of look like children. Only really old. And sometimes they look like trees.'

'Have you talked to any?'

'Well, I have, but they haven't talked back.'

'Did the aliens talk to you? When you were in their spaceship?'

'They don't have to talk, they can put sort of pictures in your head. It's a little bit like TV.'

'I see.'

He climbed over a stile, and waited for me on the other side. 'Path's diagonal through the meadow here. Can you see it?'

'Yes, no problem. Do we still have to worry about Henderson and his gun?'

'No, we're off his land now. This used to belong to your grandparents.'

'Oh.'

The path was narrow, between pliant walls of long grass, and I followed Rock. I wondered if my mother had played in this field as a child. If it was the one where they'd burned the cows. If so, there were no traces left. It just felt like a field, in the middle of the night.

'You must believe in ghosts, huh?' I asked Rock.

'Not really, no. I mean, why would somebody bother to come back after they're dead? It doesn't make any sense to me. But each to his own, right?'

'Right. Candace keeps on giving me crystals, for example.'

'I don't believe in the crystals. Seems to me they'd lose their power when they were taken out of the earth. It's better to lie down on the ground for a little while, you know? Energy's strongest closest to its source. But like I said, each to his own. There's a lot of power in the mind.'

We reached the end of the field and went over another

stile, across another field and through a gap in a hedge into a copse. The trees blocked out the starlight and waning moonlight, reducing everything to flat shadow. I should have known where we were – we were evidently somewhere within half a mile of the factory – but between the darkness and the many fields I was disoriented. We could have been anywhere in the English countryside. We could have been in fairyland.

'What's it like to be in an alien spaceship?' I asked Rock.

'It wasn't even fast. They don't go fast when they're near living creatures, they don't want to hurt anything. But it was so smooth, and they had this thing where the side of their ship melts away and all you can see is this faint outline, and it's like you're flying yourself. And that's not the best thing. I think the best thing really was that I felt so peaceful, you know? So much like I belonged there, right there, with them at that moment. No past, no future. Just now.'

We stepped out of the copse onto a wide bridleway. It ran by an open field with a low hedge, and in comparison to the copse, it was almost bright. My heart thumped as I saw a tall figure standing next to a gate, holding something long and straight. Henderson with his rifle, I thought immediately, and then I thought that having a gun pointed at you on a film set was all very well and good, but it didn't really compare with having a gun pointed at you by an angry farmer in the middle of the night with no witnesses.

Then the figure stepped forward, and I didn't have to see his face. I recognised him by his stride, though I wouldn't have known I could have done that before.

It was Will.

'I see you brought a guest, Rock,' he said dryly, in the same hushed tones we'd been using. 'I wondered about the third board.'

'Lee needed some horseradish and I thought we could use a hand.'

'Is it Lee Haven?'

He knew it wasn't. I gritted my teeth. 'It's me, Will.'

'Welcome.' He turned to Rock. 'I've got the equipment, shall we go?'

'We'd better if we're going to be finished before dawn.' Rock picked up a bag from the ground and what looked like several long thin poles. He slung the bag over his shoulder and tucked the poles under his arm. The two men started down the bridleway and I went with them. I could see, now, that Will wasn't carrying a gun but some wooden planks. They had rope wound around them and they didn't even remotely resemble a gun. He carried a backpack, too.

'I'm surprised to see you here,' he said to me.

'It really is a small town.'

'Have you done this before?'

'I have no idea what we're doing, so I can't really tell you.'

'I should have known if there was trouble you'd be in the middle of it.'

'Are we doing something illegal?'

'I like to think of it as above the law,' said Rock.

'I'm surprised you're involved, then,' I said to Will.

'I owe Rock a few favours.'

'And he makes good coffee,' Rock said. 'This one here.' He stooped and pushed aside some branches in the hedge, and then disappeared through it, pushing his planks ahead of him.

'After you,' said Will.

'Good thing it's dark, or I'd suspect you wanted me to go first so you could stare at my arse.'

He didn't reply. I shrugged, took off my backpack, pushed

it through the hedge first, and followed. I stood up in a field of something, wheat or barley, which stood in a smooth wall at nearly chest height. It rustled faintly in the small breeze. Rock was walking down the perimeter of the crop, evidently looking for something.

I heard a rattle, and saw the planks coming through the hole. I bent down and pulled them out. Will's backpack came next, and then him. 'What are we doing?' I asked him. 'It's not a human sacrifice or anything, is it? Because I hate to tell you, but if you were thinking of using me as a victim, I'm definitely not a virgin.'

'Are you always obsessed with sex, or is it being near me?'

He was right; I was using the smart remarks because he was near me. Because my heart was beating and my palms were sweating and I sort of felt the way Rock had on the spaceship, except without any of the peacefulness. More like nearly missing the tractor in the Aston Martin.

This man made me feel as if he were dangerous, and I liked that way too much. And I wanted him to be offguard, too.

'How's the Portman ceiling?' I asked, instead of answering him.

'The preservation work is going as expected, thank you.'

'Have they improved it at all?'

'No, it's still extremely ugly.'

'And your father?'

'He's very well. He tells me he's planning on visiting your mother again this weekend. This is a very civil conversation, isn't it?'

'Well, I'd probably beat you in hand-to-hand combat, so I thought I'd give you a sporting chance with something you're good at.'

Ahead of us, Rock had found a tractor line through the crop and he was following it. We fell into step behind him, the stalks of the crop brushing our sides. After a few minutes' walking, Rock stopped and looked up into the sky.

'What are we doing?' I asked again. This time I was close enough to Rock so that he could hear me.

'We're making that sign I was telling you about,' he answered. 'This is where we start.' He stuck a pole into the ground. The tip was painted white. Then he took some folded pieces of paper from his back pocket, unfolded them, and held them up close to his face.

'How far?' Will asked him. He put down his planks, leaned over the crop and took something from Rock's bag. It was a disk, like a can of film.

'Seventy-two eleven for the first one,' Rock answered.

'Clockwise, or anticlockwise?'

Rock considered. 'Clockwise,' he said finally. He pulled a length of something like string from the disk and held on to it, standing by the pole he'd planted.

Will walked back down the tram line the way that we'd come, spooling out the white string behind him. I touched it; it was a measuring tape of some sort. Rock held it taut and still, watching it. Finally Will stopped, I was assuming nearly seventy-three feet away. He was a distant shadow, but I could see the white filament of the tape stretching out to him. He moved to the right, into the crop, and I heard a distant rustling sound as he walked sideways through it slowly.

'You're making a crop circle,' I said.

'Well, more like a spiral actually.'

'Well, fuck me sideways.' I shook my head. 'It's to call the aliens?'

'It's hard to know if it will work. I mean, they've put

420

pictures in my head so it seems like they could pick up on my wanting them to be here. But it can't hurt.'

'You've done this before, haven't you?'

'A few times every summer.'

'And do they come for it?'

'No. But that's not to say it can't help. I reckon it's like a sign on a motorway for services. It wouldn't make you stop if you didn't want to, but if you happened to be tired or hungry or needed a pee, you'd see the sign and you'd pull off, wouldn't you?'

'So you're trying to catch aliens who might need a pee.'

He giggled.

Will was still walking around, only visible from the waist up. I could see that the tape served as the radius of the circle. Presumably his side-stepping was trampling down the crop to make the outline of the pattern.

'So do you know who makes the other crop circles?' They were a semi-permanent feature of the Wiltshire landscape, appearing like wildflowers every spring into the summer. Maureen Lilly and her husband had a big map on their shop wall, with pins stuck into the places the circles appeared. Rock could never manage all of them himself. There were coach tours to visit them and every year they held a conference about them somewhere and all the circle-seekers came into Stoneguard and ate ice cream and bought dowsing rods and talked about how the circles converged around Stoneguard because of the ancient energies there.

'No clue,' Rock said.

'How'd you learn?'

'Some old guy in a pub.' He was revolving, slowly, as Will circumscribed the pattern with his feet.

'Does Will always help you?'

'Only since he's come back.'

'Why?'

'For fun, I think. He's good at making the circles. I don't think he believes in the aliens, like you don't.'

I didn't quite know how to respond to that, since it was true although it sounded very rude, so I shut up and watched. Rock had turned away from me by now, anyway. He spun and Will trod until Will appeared in the tractor line again where he'd begun. He waved and beckoned.

'The next one is eighty-three ten,' Rock told me. I went to join Will, following the tractor trail and the white measuring tape.

'How far?' he asked me. I told him. He stepped back the correct amount and then beckoned me to him again.

'Your turn,' he told me.

'Had enough walking?'

'It's not easy, walking sideways like that. You need to drag the following foot a bit to flatten down the stalks. Keep the tape taut, or you'll mess up Rock's measurements. It's best to wind it round your hand.'

'No problem.' I took the disk from him. It was warm from where he'd gripped it. I wound the tape around at the correct measurement and got ready to sidestep off the path.

'Have you heard from Lee? Is she okay?'

That stopped me. 'Yes. She's fine. She's having a holiday, like I said.'

'You were wrong,' he said. 'I do care about her.'

'Funny way of showing it,' I said, but I didn't move.

'I care about her enough that I didn't want to believe it was really you instead. Even though I could tell the difference. I've been thinking about it, and I could tell the difference from the minute I saw you again.'

'Well, that's reassuring.'

'But I was denying it to myself. I wanted to think that if Lee

422

had changed, or my feelings for her had changed, maybe we could make a go of it.'

'But you got me instead. Too bad. Oh well, don't worry. She'll be back soon, and I'll be gone.'

I began to step sideways away from him. I expected him to follow me on the trail I was making, but he stayed in the tractor line. Even though I was facing Rock, I felt Will watching me. But I kept on moving around, getting farther and farther from him. By the time I met the tram line halfway round the circumference, Will had gone back to where he'd dropped his bags and planks.

I did my best to conquer my disappointment. I didn't want Will to come after me. I didn't want him to watch me, either. He was off-limits, an arrogant righteous man who thought I was no better than the dirt on his shoe. My sarcasm had been purposely designed to shove him away.

But his admission that he cared about my sister twisted around in my head. I could understand why he wouldn't want to know that I wasn't who I was pretending to be. Hadn't I spent this afternoon wishing I didn't know the truth about my mother's history and her motivations for putting the business above her family? My resentment was a familiar friend, and it was easier to hold on to it than to empathise with her.

The thing was, I liked Will for liking my sister. For wanting to make it work out with her and taking any opening to make it happen. His motivations for denying the truth were probably a lot purer than mine. It made him the better person. Which made his righteousness justifiable. Which made me not deserve him at all.

Which was fair enough, because although he might be attracted to me, he didn't care about me like he cared about Lee. So the reason I liked him more was the exact same reason why I should stay clear.

Talk about going round in circles. I kept on walking and dragging and flattening and pulling. My legs were getting sore. Rock and Will were far away, barely visible. Not visible at all, in fact. If I hadn't known Rock was at the other end of this tape, I'd think I was out alone in this field in the middle of the night. Going nowhere. I wiped a bit of sweat from my forehead and kept going, the swish of trampled crops in my ears.

Step to the side. Step to the side. I told Will I'd leave as soon as Lee got back, but where was I going to go? I could return to LA and beg for work. I could spend some more time in London and beg for work. Wherever I went, there was going to be some begging involved. And I hated begging, goddammit.

And meanwhile Lee would be back, and she and Will would—

I collided side-on with something warm and big. Its arm went around me to steady me and I knew from the scent and feel that it was Will. 'Careful,' he said.

'Sorry.' I stood straight, away from him. I'd reached the tractor line again, which was what he was standing in.

'It's not as easy as it looks, is it? Have some coffee and a rest.'

He pressed a Thermos top into my hand and I took it. 'Thanks,' I said. He kept looking at me. This close, I could see his face perfectly well.

'What?' I said.

'The tape?'

'Oh, yeah.' I unwound it, feeling blood returning to my fingers. There were dents in my skin where I'd held it. Will took it and we both went back to where Rock was sitting next to his pole, studying his sheets of paper. He jumped up, took the tape from Will and measured several distances, marking each with another pole. Despite the darkness, he moved with complete assurance. Will held the centre while Rock trod down what looked like semicircles of different diameters. Then I walked a few, and then he gave me the tape to hold while Will walked. It was a long, slow, careful process, with Rock checking his paper frequently.

'You're making a spiral of some sort?' I asked Rock, when he passed me a bottle of water.

'That's right.'

'The lines are pretty thin,' I said. 'Do the aliens have good eyes?'

'We'll flatten it out properly in a minute,' he said. 'We've got plenty of time before dawn.'

Will came back to us, the tape in loops in his hands; he sat down next to Rock and we shared the Thermos between us. The coffee was good, strong and rich. Like the man who'd made it.

No, wait. He wasn't rich any more. He was an average working Joe, like the rest of us. Making crop circles on his free evenings for fun.

He was just strong and good.

'Nice night for it,' I said at last. Everything was quiet around us except for the faint whisper of a breeze through the crop and an occasional bleat of sheep. A distant car's engine. The breathing of the two men next to me. We spoke in hushed tones, still.

'It's easier when it's dry,' Rock said. 'Stone says you like your Mini.'

'Yes, thank him for me when you talk to him.'

'So how's your mother doing anyway?'

'She's about—' I stopped myself from saying 'the same'. Because it wasn't, and had never been, the truth.

'She does well sometimes, and sometimes it's horrible. She's changing every day. She looks like the same person I've always

425

known, but she's not any more. Maybe she never was. It's a lot of adjustment.'

Rock nodded. 'How's your twin sister?'

'Can you keep a secret?' I asked him.

'As long as it's someone else's. I'm not very good at keeping my own.'

'I'm my twin sister. I'm really Liza. I'm pretending to be Lee.'

Rock nodded again. 'Okay.'

'Will knows already. It's why he's giving me such a hard time.'

'One of the reasons,' said Will.

'He thinks I should be honest about it. And I probably should be. So I'm telling you first, because you helped me with the horseradish and you told me about the aliens.'

'Okay. That's cool.'

'But I can't tell anyone else yet, because I'm right in the middle of this project at Ice Cream Heaven. And I don't want to upset anyone until it's finished, because they care about how it turns out. And so do I.'

'Fair enough,' said Rock. 'Do you like being your sister?'

'Sometimes,' I said. I felt Will looking at me, waiting for me to dig myself into a hole.

Then again, how much more of a hole could I dig? 'I like how people react to my sister. I like how they respect her and ask her for help. I like – feeling at home.'

'I haven't felt at home for a while,' Rock said. 'But maybe this will cure all that, eh?' He drank some more coffee and then stood up. 'Better get going, though; these crops don't flatten themselves. I think.'

'It's all caused by glowing balls and vortices,' Will said. 'That's what they say on the paranormal websites, and down at the pub.'

426

'In this field, it's my good old stomping boards. I'll get started, and you guys can catch up when you're done with your coffee. You can do the outer perimeter first.' Rock picked up one of the planks and loped the couple of steps over to where he'd started the spiral. I heard some rustling, starting there and moving away from us. It was the only sound.

'You must be used to doing foolish things in the middle of the night,' Will said.

'Are you referring to the stunts, or have you suddenly become the sex-obsessed one?'

'The stunts.' I heard the ghost of a smile in his voice.

'You're not berating me. Can I take this as a truce?'

'Yes, it's a truce. We've got to work together, after all. At least for the next couple of hours.'

'And also I've appeased you by telling Rock the truth.'

'Maybe a bit.'

I sighed. 'Tell you what,' I said. 'If my sister doesn't come back by next week, I'll tell everyone myself and all the gossips can have a field day. But I really do want to finish this project first. If this horseradish works out, it'll be next Tuesday at latest. How does that sound?'

'I have no idea what the horseradish is about, but otherwise, it sounds like the best you're willing to do.' He stood up. 'Ready to get to work?'

'Just tell me what to do.'

'Considering how many people think this is done by UFOs, it's remarkably low-tech.' He picked up the two remaining planks from the ground and handed me one. It was a plain board, with a hole drilled through either end. A rope had been passed through and tied, so that it formed a loop with plenty of slack. He took me to the beginning of the spiral; the crop here had already been flattened down. There was a nested whorl in the very centre, with a few stalks folded over

427

themselves to form a little knob, like an outie belly button. Then the crop lay flat, all pointing the same way, in a path curving outward towards where we could hear Rock working. We followed the tractor line to the first two circles we'd trampled.

'The only difficult part is making sure you're keeping the width even and straight so we get a precise line with no wobbles. But we've got the foot lines to guide us, so we just flatten inside of them.' He put his board down on the ground in the tractor line and pulled up the rope so that he held the loop at about waist height. Then he lifted the board up under his foot, so it was several inches up onto the side of the crop, and then stepped down on it with a double step. The stalks underneath bowed and flattened under his weight, all pointing in the same direction. Then he did it again.

I followed suit, going slightly behind him. It was a very simple manoeuvre, repetitive. Lift step-step. Lift step-step. The stalks bent and bits of straw flew up around and into my nose. I was fairly close behind Will and could see his shoulders and legs working in the same rhythm as mine.

'Do you want a shock?' I asked. Rock was far away out of hearing.

'All right. Thrill me.'

'I'm sorry I lied to you,' I said. 'If it helps, I was trying to avoid you because I didn't want to mess up my sister's relationship, or have to do something she wouldn't want me to do.'

'I wonder why she didn't tell me she was leaving?'

'Well, you had split up.'

'But we're still friends. We were still friends.'

'If you want to stay friends with her, maybe you'd better keep that kiss we had to yourself.'

He snorted. 'Now you've got me keeping secrets, too.'

'Suit yourself. I thought you'd want to spare her feelings and keep yourself out of trouble, especially as you didn't mean to kiss me in the first place. It's not as if we're going to be kissing any more, so I thought you could do without the grief for having made a simple mistake. But if you want to tell everyone, go ahead. I'm used to being the bad girl.'

He was quiet for a minute as we stepped. 'I said to you that everyone would hate you when they found out the truth. I don't think that will happen.'

'Nobody liked me before anyway. So I haven't lost anything, right?'

'I don't think you mean that.'

He wasn't looking at me, so I could afford to think about it. I pictured Annabelle, Jonny, Doris, everyone at Ice Cream Heaven looking at me with betrayal in their eyes.

'No, I didn't mean it,' I said quietly. 'I don't want people to hate me.'

Swish, swish went the seed heads as we flattened down the stalks.

'What's it like, looking exactly like someone else?' Will asked me.

'What's it like, *not* looking exactly like someone else?' I countered. 'It's been that way all my life. I can't imagine it any other way.'

'You didn't used to look alike.'

'No. You know what's funny, we started looking more like each other when we hadn't seen each other for a year and a half. We grew our hair the same way.'

'Maybe you didn't feel you had to choose to be different from each other.'

'We are different. And we don't really look alike when you look closely.'

He didn't answer this; I thought he was probably feeling guilty. So I kept on talking.

'Maybe we chose to be different at the beginning, maybe we both needed to carve out our own niche when we were children. But you make one choice, it leads to another, and then another, and then you're a different person than you would have been if you'd chosen to do other things. And then people react to you because of your choices, and that makes you different too. You can't tell me that people here would have welcomed me with open arms if they'd known who I really was.'

'They might have.'

'I seriously doubt it.'

'Listen, Liza. I think you're over-analysing this, and I think you're not giving people a chance. I know there were some people who felt that I'd turned my back on my father and the town when I chose to live in London and work for a record company. But when I came back and it was clear that I was doing something that would contribute to the town, people did welcome me with open arms.'

'You're different. You're the only son of the local toff. Everybody thinks you're rich as sin. You could have been off running a brothel somewhere or in jail for tax evasion and people would still treat you like the golden boy.'

'Maybe it's the class I was born into. But I doubt it. Everyone in Stoneguard is always talking about how unique the community is, but I think that it's like anywhere. There are some people who are open-minded and accepting, and some who like to hold on to their prejudices. But most of them are willing to revise their opinions when they're offered new evidence.'

'So basically, you're saying that people are good at heart. Sounds like the moral of a Disney movie.'

'Whereas you prefer the movies where people get blown up.'

'Precisely.'

We reached the tractor line and stopped to rest. I wiped sweat off my forehead.

'Where is Lee, anyway?' he asked.

'She's doing yoga in Greece.'

'And she just went off there without telling anybody – not even the people at work?'

'That's right. Nobody knows except for you and me and my mother. And Rock now.'

'That doesn't sound like her. She's so conscientious.'

I hesitated. On the one hand, Will did care about her, and he knew her. On the other, revealing my sister's weaknesses seemed like a betrayal. 'I think she sort of suddenly felt like she needed a break.'

'You said the other day that her life was a stone drag.'

'I . . .' Will was starting to flatten the crop again, and I watched his strong shoulders, his sure step. Lee hadn't trusted him. But she hadn't trusted anybody. Just like I hadn't.

It wasn't an easy way to live.

'I should have known she wasn't happy,' he said. 'She was tense. On the surface, she was the same as always, sunny Lee. I asked her out in the first place because I'd always liked her so much. I enjoy her company. But she didn't relax. It was one reason why we broke up, but now that I think of it, maybe it was because we were breaking up.'

Two hours ago, I would've shot back something about the world not revolving around him. But now, working with him even on something so useless as a crop circle, still thinking about his admission that he cared about my sister, I could see his concern differently.

'Breaking up might have made it worse,' I said, 'but I think it was hard anyway. Lee expects herself to be perfect; she always has. She works too much. I don't think she's taken a holiday for the whole time she's been in charge of the business. And then our mother's not well, and she's been shouldering all that herself. I think she's felt trapped. And I haven't been helping.'

'Lee has never said a word against you.'

'No, she wouldn't. But she doesn't need to. I can see it from being in her shoes for a few days.' I flattened along with Will. 'It's like a big circular fence. If you're inside it, you're hemmed in and can't get out, not without breaking something. If you're outside it, there's no entrance point for you. I've been outside it for my whole life, and I thought that everything was easier inside. But it's not.'

'Lee's an incredible person.'

'I know,' I said, and I felt the familiar mixture of envy for my sister and pride for her, so close together that it was impossible to tell either of them apart.

'And you haven't been outside the circle for your whole life.'

I laughed suddenly and hard enough to drop my rope. 'What planet have you been on?'

'You've always been part of Stoneguard. You lived right inside the town, and you went to the school. Your family's been here for generations and your mother's business is the biggest success story of the town. And you've got a twin sister.'

'None of that means anything. It's all circumstance.'

'Well, it was circumstances that I didn't have, for example. We were in that huge house, only the three of us and the servants, and I got sent away to school.'

'You're a Naughton. You own this town.'

'Owned. And owning something doesn't make you belong

to it. Even as a child I got this bloody – deference. As if it still mattered that one of my ancestors did some favours for Henry VIII. Even if people didn't like what you were doing, at least they were treating you as an equal.'

He'd got ahead of me in the field. I picked up my rope and began stomping again. 'Treating me as an equal? You really have been on another planet. Remember that Christmas pageant, for example, when you were Joseph and I was a sheep.'

'And you set the stage on fire.'

'People still talk about that, you know. Horrible Liza Haven. Exhibit A.'

He laughed. 'That's Exhibit A, but not for what you think. It's because you made that pageant into something nobody could ever forget. You're part of the town mythology now. The person people tell stories about, because you were alive and different and wanted to be paid attention to. If that's not acceptance, I don't know what is.'

I grunted in a way meant to convey scepticism. 'You must remember things differently than I do.'

'I have a lot of memories of you,' he said. 'For example, every summer when I came home from school, I didn't know anybody any more. I'd ride my bike round and round, over and over. You'd be in the schoolyard with a group of boys, tourists all of them. Smoking cigarettes and laughing.'

'You remember that?'

'Of course I do. I fancied you like crazy.'

I stopped again. 'You what?'

'I always have. I wanted to punch all those boys for even talking with you.'

'Why didn't you?'

'You wouldn't have let me. Lee was always nice to me, but you didn't even talk to me.'

'I thought you were the biggest snob in the universe,' I said, and resumed stomping so that I didn't have to look at him. 'Plus, Lee always had a crush on you so I wasn't allowed to like you.'

The crop swished.

'Do you think you would've liked me if not for Lee?'

I remembered Will as a teenager, tall and messy-haired and always riding by. Had I stared after him? Did it even matter? It was bad enough that I was attracted to him now. 'I don't take what's hers.'

'So what you're doing now is just borrowing for a little while?'

'That's right. Holding her place for her.'

'But why would you even do such a thing? Don't you have a career of your own? Lee said you're always fantastically busy, doing one film after another. Seems like you're successful enough not to care what anybody from your past thinks about you.'

'I don't,' I said quickly, probably too quickly, because Will looked over at me, but I kept stepping and abruptly we were at a place that had already been flattened down. Rock was standing there, waiting for us, his board in hand.

'This is the last part to fill in,' he said to us. I started without pausing, and I heard the two of them working as well. We flattened in silence now. I stomped and stomped, thinking about why I'd opened up to Will. Was it the darkness? Because he asked? Or simply because I was ready to?

I followed the line until I reached the end, and then I looked around. The other two had finished too. There was a broad path behind us, narrowing in front of us, and then some parts that were still standing. I couldn't see the pattern here from the ground.

'Did we get it right?' I asked Rock.

'Seems to be.' We walked together through the flattened wheat to where we'd left our stuff. Will picked up the Thermos and held it out to me. I reached for it, and then thought about the possibility of brushing fingers with him, and shook my head. He gave it to Rock instead.

'So what do we do now?' I asked.

'Pick up all the poles, make sure we haven't left anything, and go home. We're not too far off sunrise.'

By the time we were back through the hedge and in the bridleway again, the sky was beginning to lighten. It was almost imperceptible, but once it had started morning would come quickly, so we hurried in silence down the bridleway and footpaths back towards Stoneguard. My shoulders and legs and backside ached, though this was hardly surprising, as making crop circles seemed to be a rural equivalent of a cross-training machine. I felt as if the three of us had been working together for days, rather than hours.

The path we were on fed into Dog Shit Lane, so without thinking I said, 'We're near Lee's house. Do you want to come in for a wash and some more coffee?'

'We shouldn't be seen together in daylight this early,' Rock said. 'People would suspect something. Besides, I've got to stash the equipment.'

'I've got to go home and catch a couple of hours' sleep before some meetings,' said Will.

We reached the place where the lane met Church Street. The sky was very definitely lighter. I knew I should hurry up and get home, before the morning's dog walkers came out. I couldn't work out why I was reluctant to leave. Maybe it was the odd sense of camaraderie; the truce I'd made with Will; the way Rock had responded to my true identity. The memories Will had told me. I felt like it was a glimpse into another world, all of it.

'Well,' I said. 'It was definitely a new perspective. Thanks.'

'No problem,' said Rock. 'I'll be up at the stones most of the day if you want to wait with me.'

'I've got something urgent to do at Ice Cream Heaven. But maybe later. Can you see the design we made from the hill?'

'We should be able to see most of it. Not as well as from the air, though.'

'Too bad we don't have an aeroplane,' said Will.

I smiled. 'Now that, I can help with.'

This Is It ✳

I didn't think I'd be able to sleep when I got home, but exhaustion must have been waiting in the wings because the minute my head touched the pillow I was out. I awoke a couple of hours later, wide awake and energised and excited, and only paused to have a quick shower to wash the dirt, sweat and bits of crop off before I pulled on my trainers and ran to Ice Cream Heaven. Even with the nap, I arrived before anyone else. I didn't bother to unlock the office, but went straight to the barn, put on a hairnet, took my backpack to the prep kitchen sink and got out the horseradish. It was bigger than I remembered, dirty and hairy with rootlings. I put it in the sink and began to wash it off. Underneath the soil, it was a creamy white.

'If you're no good, I don't know what I'll do,' I said to it.

'Who you talking to, eh, the little elves at the bottom of the plughole?'

'Doris!' I said, turning around. 'I've got some new stuff for us to try.'

She joined me at the sink and gazed down at the scrubbed root. 'Ooh, that looks good.'

'I hope it is, because I promised Edmund Jett a sample of

the ice cream by tomorrow. What do we use on it? A grater?'
I began opening cupboards.

'Calm down, we'll use the food processor. And you'd better wear these.' Doris opened a drawer and pulled out a couple of pairs of swimming goggles and surgical masks.

'Why?'

'If you think this here root is bad to eat in ice cream, you've never been in the room with it fresh. Practically gouge your eyes out, it will. Volatile as anything. That's why it needs vinegar, to fix it. Better wear gloves, too.'

Thus kitted up, I took a knife from Doris and cut a section off the root, peeled it and fed it into the food processor. She was waiting to add vinegar and we put it in a glass bowl, looking at it through our goggles.

'Think this is it?' she asked.

'Maybe. Do we need to roast some more beetroot?'

'I've got it all ready. Want to mix it up yourself?' It was hard to see Doris's expression through her goggles and her face mask, but I could swear I saw her eyes twinkle.

'You do it, Doris. And you tell me what to do to help.'

It was a test batch, so we used the smaller machine. Doris siphoned the proper amount of pasteurised milk, cream and sugar mixture from the big tanks for me and I poured the puréed flavourings in by hand and stirred it into glorious liquid magenta. Doris said the flavours should settle in together so I waited, pacing the floor, while the team got started making today's batch of Cappuccino Cloud. The air smelled enough of coffee that I felt as if someone had injected me with caffeine.

When I wasn't sleeping or stomping down wheat or making ice cream, I could think about what Will had said last night. For example, about my being part of the town mythology. About everyone talking about me not because I was wrong but because I was interesting and alive. About how he, the town golden boy, had looked at my life from the outside and wanted to be in it.

He's only saying that because he fancies me and he wants to get into my pants, I thought, but that didn't ring true. We both knew that mistaken kiss would be our last. He hadn't even come round for coffee this morning.

But he'd said he'd had a thing about me for years. Me, myself.

The thought gave me a warm feeling in my stomach that I had no right to have. I'd meant what I'd said: *I don't take what's hers*. It was the unwritten rule of our whole lives; we split the world down the middle and if she happened to have what I wanted too, well tough luck, because Lee deserved it more.

Though maybe, now that I thought about it, I might have looked at Will a little bit more than I should have when we were teenagers. Might have had a dream or two, quickly squashed. Otherwise, why would I remember exactly what his hair used to look like, and have noticed him on the edge of things, always too special to touch?

I heard a sound coming from deep inside me, floating to the top like a delicious bubble, and I clapped my hand to my mouth. It was a giggle. An honest-to-goodness giggle, of the sort emanating from the mouths of silly schoolgirls who found out that their crush fancied them back.

I looked around the floor. Everyone was absorbed in their work, and the noise of the machinery was loud enough so that it was improbable that anyone had heard me. Still, I went outside in case. The morning had been fine but it was beginning to drizzle now. My back nagged but I didn't much care.

I'd just giggled because of Will Naughton?

'Get a grip, Elizabeth April Haven,' I said. 'You've never

giggled over the opposite sex before and now is not the time to start.'

I ran my hands through my hair, realised I was still wearing a hairnet, took it off and stuffed it into my pocket and went inside to talk to Annabelle about potty training or to Jonny about Hazel's embroidery. Anything that didn't involve Lord Naughton's son.

Annabelle and Jonny both looked up expectantly as I came in. 'It's not ready yet,' I told them, and they went back to their work with resignation. I spent some time tidying Lee's desk and flipping through her emails. The tension was worse in here; we were all like fathers waiting for their baby to be born. I took my mobile from my handbag and went outside to make some calls.

I'd just finished the call to the airfield and was looking at my phone, wiping the damp off the screen and wondering if I could go back inside and get Will's number and ring him, and what would happen if I did, when it rang in my hand. It showed Lee's number.

Guilt feels awful, like something crawling into your stomach and immediately starting to eat its way out. I quickly looked away, as if Lee could see me through the screen, and I turned off the phone. Which was stupid, because I hadn't done anything to feel guilty about. Or anything more than I'd already done. Aside from trespassing, maybe, and some wilful plant damage, but Lee wasn't going to be angry about that.

But I still didn't want to talk to her.

The barn door opened and Doris came out, followed closely by Dennis and Gladys. I shoved my phone into my pocket and ran to them.

'Is it ready? Can I pour it into the pump?'

'Yep.' I pulled on my hairnet and went with them to the

small pump. Dennis had already prepared a funnel and the 500-millilitre tubs emblazoned with the Ice Cream Heaven logo. I poured the purple mixture in and we stood there, listening and watching as the machine whipped the mixture with enough air to give it the right consistency, and froze it soft. It came out the other end in bright peaks, swirling into the tubs. I grabbed the first one to be filled and we all hurried through the door into the office. Annabelle and Jonny jumped out of their chairs. Doris put the tub down on my desk and Gladys put a glass bowl next to it while Brenda reached for the ice-cream scoop. 'Don't worry about that,' I said. 'Everyone just get a spoon and dig in.'

A clatter, and then reaching and scooping, and I put my spoonful in my mouth at the same time as everyone else. Heat, mixed with cold. Earthiness, mixed with sweetness and a tang of vinegar, and some spice too. I rolled the melting mouthful on my tongue and tasted dark starry nights and the Wiltshire countryside. I swallowed and my tongue and palate tingled.

Nobody said anything. I realised my eyes were closed. I opened them and looked around at the team. Annabelle and Brenda were smiling, Jonny was nodding, Dennis had his eyes closed too and Doris and Gladys were holding hands.

'This is it, isn't it?' Annabelle said.

'It really, really is,' I replied, and for the second time since I'd walked through the gate to Ice Cream Heaven an unexpected noise came out of me because I whooped in triumph.

'We did it!' Dennis cheered, and Jonny was the first to hug me and say softly into my ear, 'Well done, sweetheart,' and then it was all hugs, all cheering and laughter and triumph.

'Who would have thought it, eh,' said Doris, shaking her head. 'I don't mind saying I thought you were mad as a box of frogs for even trying it.'

'Well, it's never going to be a favourite with the summer

crowd,' I said, 'but it's good. It's really good. Edmund Jett is going to be impressed as hell.'

'I never knew that making ice cream would be so dramatic,' Annabelle beamed. 'Or so interesting. What do you think we're going to make next? Something wild and crazy, too?'

'There's someone down in Dorset who makes chilli,' Dennis said. 'And that bald bloke off the telly who makes egg and bacon.'

'I always fancied green tea myself,' Gladys said. 'Or lavender, that would be nice. Lavender and nasturtium.'

'Peanut butter and jelly,' Jonny said. 'Or jam. Like the American sandwiches.'

'Make a list,' I said. 'You all deserve to pick the next flavour.'

'What are we going to call it?' asked Annabelle. 'We need an Ice Cream Heavenly sort of name.'

'Beet It,' said Dennis.

'Horsing Around.'

'Beeting a Dead Horse, eh,' said Doris dryly.

'No,' I said. 'Beatitude. As in beet-attitude.'

'Beatitude,' said Jonny. 'Spot-on.'

'So is it ready to send to Edmund Jett?' Annabelle asked. 'Do you want me to call him?'

'I'll call him myself,' I said. 'But not yet. I have one more opinion to get first.'

I used one of the cut-crystal ice-cream dishes. A porcelain dish below it, to catch any drips, a linen napkin, a silver spoon. I cut a sprig of mint from the garden and put it on the side of the perfect scoop of magenta. And then I sat on my hands, biting my lip, while my mother examined what I'd given her.

'What is it?' she asked, although I'd told her.

'A new flavour. Edmund Jett asked for it. He's a Michelin-starred chef in London.'

'What's the flavour?'

'Beetroot and horseradish.'

Her mouth turned down at the corners.

'It's all local ingredients. The horseradish comes from about half a mile from here.' I crossed my fingers underneath my thigh. 'We're calling it Beatitude.'

'And you made this?'

'Me and Doris and Glenys and Brenda and Dennis and Annabelle and Jonny and everyone else. The whole team.'

'It's a savoury ice cream?'

'Yes. Well, beetroot is quite sweet, but it's meant to be eaten as part of a main meal, yes.'

'What's this mint for, then? You don't put mint on savoury.' She picked out the offending sprig.

I didn't mention lamb and mint sauce. 'It's to show off the colour.'

'The colour.'

She stared at it, her gaze travelling over it as if she were reading. The scoop was starting to go soft around the edges in the warm room. Suddenly it looked far, far too bright. *What about the colour?* I wanted to ask, I wanted to scream, but I was beginning to get used to the new Abigail Haven. If she was thinking, she would say it. If she had drifted off to her own world, asking wouldn't do any good.

Patience. Something I had never been good at. But I bit my lip and I watched her and I waited.

After a million lifetimes, she picked up the spoon. She cut a delicate semi-circle out of the scoop and she paused for about eighty more years. Then she lifted it to her mouth.

She'd tasted more ice cream than I could imagine. All the flavours Ice Cream Heaven had ever sold, and all the ones she'd rejected. It was her life and it had never been mine. I could see the small workings of her cheeks and jaw and lips as

443

she moved the morsel in her mouth, testing texture and flavour and a dozen other things I probably had never heard of.

I held my breath. She swallowed. I saw her eyes narrow slightly and I knew she was registering the residual tingle of the horseradish.

'You made this?' she said at last.

'Yes.' I didn't mention Doris and all the rest this time because although they were part of the ice cream, they weren't part of this moment. This moment was between my mother and me.

When was the last time I had asked for her approval rather than her disdain? Twenty years ago? The Horrid Christmas, less than two years ago?

I kept still in my seat. I had been asking for it, whether I'd known it or not, every single day of my life.

She dug her spoon into the scoop again. The tasting, this time, was even more agonisingly slow. What did this mean? It was a positive sign that she took a second taste, right? But surely she'd know right away if it was any good? We'd only taken one taste at the office before we knew.

I didn't say a thing. If she starts talking nonsense, I thought, I will scream.

'I didn't think you would,' she said, at last. 'Not you.'

I didn't quite scream. But I did explode. All I wanted to know was whether the ice cream was all right, and here she was, going into the same old argument.

'I know you don't think I'm good enough to work in the business,' I said. 'You've made it very clear. I don't need to know about that. I just came here to find out what you thought about the flavour. As a matter of courtesy, and – I was thinking, silly me – respect. If you don't want to tell me, that's fine. I trust my own judgement and the judgement of everyone at Ice Cream Heaven. I'll send it off myself.'

I stood up and reached for the crystal dish, though there was no reason for me to take it.

'You're too brave,' she said. 'Always too brave. I couldn't hold you here, I couldn't make you stay, it would have been such a waste.'

I paused. This wasn't quite the same argument, or not the same words. 'A waste of what?' I said.

'A waste of you.'

I sat down again, in the armchair across from her.

'What do you mean?'

She waved her hands slightly, as if searching for words she could no longer grasp. 'Emily was always safe, she is happy looking after people. I couldn't make you do that, not for me. Not for anybody. You're too . . . the word is . . .' She tried to pluck the word out of the air. 'Like pandas.'

Something was happening here; she was trying to tell me something that I couldn't quite comprehend or believe. 'Black and white?' I tried.

'No.'

'Cute?'

'No. It's . . .' Her gaze wandered to the ice cream. 'The colour, that's not the colour of anything else. It couldn't be anything else. Some people use it for strawberry, but it's not. It's itself.'

'Is it good, Mum?' I asked gently. 'Do you like the ice cream?'

'Of course I do. Anybody would.'

I remembered *Casablanca*. 'You mean this ice cream, here? Have another taste, to make sure.'

'I never forget a flavour.' But she took another spoonful. 'Yes. It's good. I've already said that, haven't I?'

'No,' I said. My eyes were stinging as if I were grating a thousand horseradish roots. 'No, you never have, before.'

Flying High

I tapped my foot on the damp ground and looked at my watch. It was nearly half past six already, and there was no sign of Will or Rock. I'd been late myself. I'd had to walk back to Ice Cream Heaven, call Archie off his ice-cream rounds and get him to drive the batch of Beatitude to Edmund Jett in London. Jonny gave me a lift to Lee's to pick up documents and change clothes, and then he brought me here to the airfield. My time had been so full, in fact, that I hadn't been able to grab a moment to look up 'pandas' on the internet to try to puzzle out the meaning of what my mother had said. So I stood here, in a waterproof and boots, running it through my head.

She'd called me brave – incredibly, she'd called me not foolish, not reckless, but brave. And like a panda. But pandas weren't brave. They sat in one place and ate bamboo. Maybe, with her problems with speech, she meant something other than pandas. She'd been grasping, as if she couldn't catch her real meaning. What sounded like panda? I ran through rhymes in my mind. Sander, dander, Uganda. Unlikely. Maybe she meant another bear. I could resemble a grizzly after too much drinking.

Pandas were endangered, they lived in China, they were difficult to breed. My mother had said I would be wasted staying here, looking after her. Not that I would waste time, or money, or love. That it would be a waste of *me*. As if she believed I was meant for something different, something almost better. Something my own.

It can't be anything but itself, she'd said. And pandas were endangered, they were a bear, rhymed with rare.

I shoved my hands in my pockets. The drizzle had accumulated in my hair, enough to be running down the side of my face, but I wasn't feeling it.

Rare.

Surely not?

Then I heard the approaching roar of an engine and saw Will's Aston Martin coming up the airfield's drive. I waved to him and he pulled up and parked in the space next to where I stood. He opened the door and stepped out, and I had to swallow hard to tamp down the giggle that wanted to come out because he was gorgeous and when he met my gaze a hot shiver of attraction ran between us.

He joined me on the pavement outside the airfield office. 'Sorry I'm late,' he said. His eyes said more than that. Last night I hadn't been able to see him properly but I'd felt him working side by side with me and he hadn't been out of my thoughts since.

'No problem,' I said, 'there's plenty of daylight left. Or whatever passes for it in Wiltshire. Rock's not here yet anyway.'

'No. That's why I'm late. I'd arranged to pick him up – he said he'd be waiting in the circle car park, but he wasn't there. I searched the whole hill but I couldn't find a trace of him.'

'He's probably sleeping it off somewhere,' I said.

'That's what I thought, so I went to his place, but he wasn't there either. Stone said he was in the kitchen this morning packing an enormous lunch, but nobody's seen him since. He hasn't been in the Heavenly Scoop, either.'

'Maybe the aliens picked him up.'

Will smiled, but didn't laugh.

'It's too bad,' I said. 'I think he would have enjoyed this. On the bright side, Larry says the wind's going to pick up soon, and it saves a second trip.'

'A second trip?' I'd waved to Larry in the office to let him know we were off, and now we were walking along the tarmac to where the planes stood in a row.

'I could only get a microlight, two people max.'

'I've never been in a microlight. So we'll take turns going up with the pilot?'

'I'm the pilot.'

He didn't say anything. I checked his face for excitement, fear, pleasure, but he only showed that aristocratic calm.

'Scared?' I said.

'You know how to fly?'

'It's part of my job.'

'Of course it is. Yes.'

'Don't worry, it's an enclosed one. You won't get wet.' He still didn't say anything, so I asked, 'How has your day been?'

'A bit of an anticlimax after last night. Still, it looks as if we'll be able to open the Hall to the public by next month.'

'That must be a relief.'

'It is. I hope they're right, because we've started taking bookings for the studio on the strength of it.'

'Is your father proud of you?' I asked.

That cracked the calm a bit; he seemed surprised. 'Yes. I think so.'

'How do you know? Does he say it, or do you have to figure it out yourself from things that he says?'

'I think I just know.'

'I've never even suspected that my mother might be proud of me. I'm not sure whether she is now.'

'Do you *feel* that she's proud of you?'

I thought about it. The way I'd felt. The way I'd cared.

'Yes, I do,' I said. 'I made a new ice cream. And I never thought I'd like doing it, but I did. She said it was good. And I'd always thought that she didn't want me to help take care of her and the business because she didn't think I was good enough. But today she said something like she'd known I wouldn't be happy here. And when I think back on it, she never actually said I wasn't good enough to stay. That was just what I thought she meant.'

We reached the plane, a three-axis microlight that looked like a white dragonfly, and I opened his door for him. But he wasn't looking at the plane; he was looking at me.

'What?' I said.

'You are a continual surprise.'

His gaze was intense and made my fingers tingle. 'You didn't answer my first question,' I said. 'Are you scared?'

He climbed in his side of the tiny plane, reached for his seatbelt, and buckled in before he answered me. 'I have complete confidence in your ability to fly this plane. It's you who scares me.'

This time I saw the sparkle in his eyes. 'Contrary to my reputation, I'm completely harmless,' I said.

'Not to me.' He shut his door.

I walked round the tail of the aircraft so that Will wouldn't be able to see me giggling. Then I got in and buckled myself in. I checked; I didn't feel nervous in the least. Maybe it was because this was a plane, not a car. Maybe it was Will. Maybe it was just the way I felt today. *Rare.*

'Ready?'

'Yes.'

'Good.' I taxied to the strip, hit the throttle and within seconds we were rising up into the air. I always loved that moment, when you lifted and felt the ground dropping away from you like a weight you never needed. Below us, the fields spread out in a carpet of different greens and golds.

I couldn't hear anything over the engine, and conversation was out of the question, but I glanced at Will. He was gazing out over the landscape below us, his hands relaxed on his thighs. I couldn't see his face, but I knew from his posture that I didn't have to worry about him being a nervous flier. Not that I would have expected it anyway, after the way he handled a fast car in a pinch, but some people couldn't handle heights.

Will Naughton looked like he could handle just about anything.

I approached the field from the south, over the village. From here Stoneguard was a collection of grey and thatched roofs, tidy walls and the bright Pointillism of flower gardens. Funny how something that was so important in my childhood imagination, and had been taking up so much of my thought and energy over the past weeks, was so small from this viewpoint. The hill was dotted with sheep and the stone circle was clotted with tourists. They wore coloured jackets and carried umbrellas. From up here, you could see how perfect the circle was, despite its age, despite the fact that a handful of people had probably made it with only the most primitive of tools.

The field where we'd made our own circle was only a quarter of a mile away. The wheat was a ripe golden colour. I spotted it as a foreshortened oval, a dent in the wheat. I deliberately looked away as we approached it. I wanted to see it all at once.

Then Will put his hand on my leg and he pointed, and I looked down.

Rock had said it was a spiral, but it wasn't a simple spiral, like a spring. It was a double spiral. Two halves intertwined around each other, curled and joined. One spiral was the wheat we hadn't touched. It curved pristine and pure and cradled the other spiral, which was flattened into beaten gold.

Wow. We'd done this, with a few planks and some strong coffee?

I banked and came around again, lower. Staring at it, it almost made an optical illusion. First one spiral was more important and the other was a shadow; then perspective shifted and the other spiral came to the front. Together, they made a whole. A perfect circle. Alike and opposite all at once, each one necessary.

I knew the plane was buzzing and the wind was rushing, but I didn't hear or feel them. I was remembering.

One day long ago, Lee and I had run across a field like this one. Maybe it *was* this one. We must have been about seven, or eight maybe; too early for me to remember why we were there, but late enough for me to recall the senses, the smell of late summer and the halo of sun in my hair. The buzz of small insects in my ears. At first it had been her idea to run, but I had caught up with her and my sandals had slapped against the earth. I ran ahead, and then she ran ahead, laughing, and then one of us grabbed the other's hand, I'm not sure which one of us it was, maybe it was both at once.

Our fingers had twined together like this circle.

For the second time today, my eyes stung with tears wanting to be shed.

Then Will's hand tightened on my leg, and when I looked at him, he was pointing, but not at our circle any more. I followed his finger.

'Holy shit,' I said, though nobody could hear me.

It stretched across the entire neighbouring field to the one we'd spent last night in. Long, leggy, a series of graduated circles of flattened wheat linked by lines and flanked by vaguely familiar-looking symbols and arcs. It sprawled with an odd symmetry, like a strange lizard or an unfamiliar tree.

I looked at Will. He was looking back at me, surprise clear on his features.

'Did you hear anything last night?' I shouted. He shook his head, and shrugged his shoulders, and looked back down at the second huge crop circle. Which had been made in the field adjoining the one we'd been in all night, without us having the least suspicion of it.

It dwarfed ours. I flew around it. Last night we'd made a giant symbol of unity, and someone, something else had made a even more giant question mark.

I felt Will's hand on the back of mine. He ran his thumb down the inside of my wrist and I caught his eyes and the two of us began to laugh. I wasn't even sure why. Maybe because the world seemed suddenly so big, so inexplicable, so wonderful that laughing was the only thing to do.

At that moment a spatter of rain hit the windscreen and a gust of wind buffeted the rudder. I turned the fragile aircraft back in the direction of the airfield and Will took his hand off mine, but I still felt him there beside me as I flew us the short distance back and landed us on the strip.

There had been times when returning to earth had been a disappointment, a slow anticlimax after the adrenaline rush of flying, especially flying for the camera. This time, it felt more like a well-deserved rest. A pause before I discovered what would happen next. I taxied to where we'd found the aircraft and switched off the engine. In the sudden silence, past noise ringing in my ears, I turned to Will.

'How'd they do it?' I asked him.

'I don't know.'

'Where do you think Rock is?'

He shook his head. 'He couldn't have made that. Not in the daylight and alone.'

We sat for another moment. 'I don't believe I'm seriously contemplating whether he's been picked up by aliens.'

'It's a mad world,' he said. 'As Tears for Fears said.'

That giggle came up again, pure exhilaration and wonder, and I couldn't help letting it out. Will winked at me and climbed out of the plane.

It was really blowing now, gusts that made me glad we'd landed. I got out and pulled up my jacket collar. The rain had picked up with the wind and it hit the back of my head and jacket like little bullets. I went into the office, signed the log book for Larry, and then met Will outside again.

'Well,' I said. For two people who liked to shoot their mouths off, we were both being amazingly quiet.

'Thanks for that,' Will said. 'It was extraordinary.'

'It was. I'm sorry Rock couldn't see it.'

'Maybe he has.'

We stood there getting wet. I kept my hands in my pockets, holding my phone and keys. Lee's keys.

'Do you need a lift home?' Will asked.

'That would be great.'

He went round and opened the Aston's door for me, and I climbed into the leather seat and waited while he got in and started the car. It was quiet compared to the plane. Without another word he pulled out of the car park, while I looked out of the window at the countryside and the rain.

It all felt like too much to process. Making the ice cream, and my mother maybe proud of me, at least for however long her memory of it would last. The idea that maybe she'd never banned me from the business and from her life, that maybe she'd known I'd feel trapped here. Which showed that in some ways, at least, she understood me better than she understood my sister, who actually had been trapped.

I knew my mother. I knew her pride, and her hatred of being a burden. She'd thought she was sparing me. It was fucked-up reasoning, but I got it. Probably because I'd felt the same way about not telling her or my sister about my accident. Of all the reasons for hiding my hurt and my failure, sparing my loved ones was the best. And the worst. It meant they couldn't help me. It drove a wedge in the cracks between us, forced them wider.

And yet that crop circle, the one I'd helped to make. Two opposites twined together to make a whole. Was geometry the only place where that actually worked?

I glanced at Will, who was watching the road. For a moment, I thought about a different world. Where I'd noticed Will before my sister, and somehow staked a claim. It would have been okay to like him, to admire him, to get closer to him. Right now we could be on our way to Naughton Hall, or to a hotel, or even to an empty by-road somewhere that we could park and touch each other and kiss and laugh and touch some more.

I folded my arms across my body. What was I thinking? That was total fantasy. Even if I'd got to Will first, I certainly wouldn't be with him now. I'd never had a relationship that lasted longer than a week or two, a few months at most. I was too busy working, travelling around the globe, training. Protecting myself.

I could only remember a few of their names now, the men I'd shared a bed with, had a laugh with, whose calls I'd ignored. Benjamin, one was called. He could beat anyone alive at poker. Sanjay, who learned diving as a child looking for pearls. Kurt, homesick and clever. Allen, who'd saved my life.

'*I never told any of them that I love them,*' my mother said in my memory. '*That's what I feel sorry for.*'

Maybe I was more like my mother than I'd ever thought; maybe I was worse, because I hadn't even let myself love any of them. In truth, it wasn't Lee's claim that was stopping me, that had always stopped me, from being with Will. It was me, the wall I'd built round myself to keep everyone out.

I blinked hard. It was probably the lack of sleep that was making me so emotional. I hadn't eaten properly either, or even stretched out. I was riding high on caffeine, adrenaline, victory and feeling. All I needed was a good meal and ten hours' sleep and I'd be more like myself again.

The car stopped, and though I'd been looking out of the window the whole time, I was surprised to see we were on Church Street, outside my sister's house. Will cleared his throat. 'Here we are.'

'Thanks,' I said. 'Er, would you . . .'

'I need to go.' His hands were still on the wheel, the engine was still running.

'Oh, yeah, me too. I'm expecting a call.' I touched the door handle, but couldn't quite open it yet. I was waiting for something. But what? You couldn't change who you were by wishing for it.

He cleared his throat again. 'You're going to tell everyone who you are next week, is that the plan?'

'Er, yes. Okay. Sure.'

He nodded, and put the car in gear. I couldn't seem to leave him, and he was eager to get away.

'Thanks for the lift,' I said. 'I'll see you soon, I'm sure. Small town and all that.'

'Yes. Goodbye, Liza.'

I got out of the car and watched as he drove off down Church Street and turned right onto the High Street. I'd spent far too much time with Will Naughton already in the past twenty-four hours and distance would only be a good thing. I'd forget what he sounded like when he laughed and how the rain clung in drops to his dark hair. The small tired lines around his eyes and the smell of his sweat in the starlight.

And he'd reminded me of my promise to tell the truth. I had to wait for Edmund Jett to call and say whether he'd liked the ice cream, and then I'd go straight to Ma Gamble and tell her I was Liza. I wasn't going to be the most popular person when that happened. Maybe they'd even ask me to leave town. So there was very little chance I was going to spend any more than a few minutes with Will Naughton again. I might as well get used to it.

I turned on the path and the heavens suddenly opened. I ran to the door as the rain dumped down, and fumbled with wet fingers for the keys. By the time I got inside, I was dripping and I was grateful for it, actually, because it gave me something immediate to do, something that would stop me from noticing that the house was empty and that I was the wrong person in it. I had to strip, and hang up my wet clothes, and then maybe take a hot shower, and then get dressed again and find something to eat and then go to bed. Busy, busy, busy. Hopefully Edmund Jett would call. Maybe my sister would ring again. Maybe my mother would wander up to the stone circle at 3 a.m. I had plenty to think about.

Instead of doing any of that, I went into the living room and looked at the pinned butterflies up on the wall, the beautiful and rare things trapped forever, never able to escape or to change.

'I'm sorry, Lee,' I said to them. 'I'm sorry I wasn't here to help you. I'm sorry I made it harder for you.'

Nobody answered. I kept the words in my head, for when I needed to say them again.

I was at the top of the stairs when the doorbell rang. By now I was looking forward to having a shower so much that I considered not opening it. But then it occurred to me that it might be Rock, so I turned around and went back down and opened the door.

It wasn't Rock. It was Will. Tall, and out of breath from running in the rain, with water dripping from his hair and his shoulders. My heart made a great leap.

'I couldn't stay away,' he said.

I stepped backwards to let him in, out of the wet. He closed the door behind him. We stood there, gazing at each other, not saying anything. As if we couldn't bear to break the final barrier between us.

Am I afraid? I asked myself. The hammering of my heart and the blood hot in my veins answered for me.

Oh, yes. I was terrified.

On that thought, I stepped forward and so did Will and we kissed each other.

He felt and tasted familiar, as if our last kiss had been residing right in the front of my memory this whole time, waiting to be revived. He was hot and sweet, and his chin was slightly rough. And last time he'd kissed me it had been the best kiss of my life and this one was even better, because this time he knew he was kissing me.

I went from sodden and chilly to too-hot and desperate within a racing heartbeat. Our mouths attacked each other, too urgent for breath. I grabbed his wet hair with one hand and with the other I hung on to the front of his jacket, as if for life. He had my hips and was holding me against him hard enough so I could feel the length of his thighs and the thud of his heart even through all our clothes.

And the clothes had to go. Every little bit of my body was screaming out for the feel of his naked skin. I fumbled with his shirt, without stopping kissing him. My cold and clumsy fingers couldn't work the wet buttons, and I made a noise of frustration in my throat.

'Upstairs,' he said, and I nodded and pulled him after me, up the flight of stairs. I was so eager I nearly tripped. His hands stayed on my hips and I could feel his fingers resting low on my stomach.

And then we were at the top and I was nearly panting with anticipation, and I didn't hesitate at all. The barrier had already been broken between us. I wasn't sure what had done it, the kiss or the fact we were upstairs together. More probably, the fact that he'd come after me.

We both knew what we were going to do, and we knew all the reasons we shouldn't do it but we were going to anyway, because that was the kind of people we both were. It was why we were perfect together and why we were wrong, why we wanted each other so badly, because we both wanted this moment, right now, and forget about the past or the future.

I pulled him into the spare room. Without taking my eyes off Will, I swept my arm along the spare bed, throwing all the papers and folders to the floor. The rain spattered on the window. With Will in it, the room seemed smaller and the bed seemed tiny.

'I've never been in here,' he said.

'That's the point.' I reached for his shirt buttons once again. They wouldn't fit through the tiny damp holes. I managed two, but had to stop for a moment while he lifted my top up over my head. He put his hands on my breasts and I gasped and redoubled my efforts with his buttons.

'You're very wet,' I complained.

'I parked in the circle car park and ran here.' He bent and began to kiss my neck and the slopes of my breasts. Through the lace of my bra, he plucked and rubbed at my nipples.

'Oh, fuck it.' I grabbed either side of his shirt and pulled, hard. I heard a ripping sound and several tiny plinks as buttons hit the hardwood floor.

'I thought I was supposed to do the bodice-ripping.' His voice was slightly muffled against my skin, amused and sexy as anything.

'You can do whatever you want, as long as I get to touch you.' I spread my hands out on his chest. Muscles, smooth skin, rough hair. I tweaked both of his nipples in imitation of what he was doing to me and he let out a growl and grabbed me and threw me on the bed.

It was a small bed, a single, but all the better to touch Will on. He fell down beside me, our bodies pressed together all the way from head to foot, and kissing every inch we could reach, we worked at removing each other's clothes. He had a thick brown leather belt, soft from wearing with a heavy iron buckle. I undid it about the same time as he unfastened my bra and the feeling of his hands on my bare breasts was good enough to make me cry out against his collarbone, which was what I happened to be kissing at the time. I redoubled my efforts at his flies and somehow, using hands and mouths and legs and feet, we shed our shoes and jeans and underwear.

You can imagine being naked with someone as much as you like (and I'd imagined being naked with Will quite often in the past several days) but it doesn't match up to the reality. There are surprises about a person. They're someone of their own. Not a memory or a dream, but a living breathing body, full of complex desires and pleasures. Will felt bigger than I'd imagined and remembered him, more real. His hands enveloped and surrounded me, held on to me and stroked me and I wrapped my legs around his and pushed myself against him. I kissed him, hard, on the lips, sucked his tongue into my mouth and felt him squeezing my buttocks with his big hands, enough to almost deliciously hurt, and then he grabbed the hair on the back of my head, wound it around his fingers and pulled my head back so he could kiss my neck. The other hand travelled up my skin, tracing the inward curve of my back and around my hips, and I felt his teeth nipping at my skin and I sighed and pulled him still closer to me with my legs.

And then he stopped.

'Liza? What's this, sweetheart?'

I noticed the endearment before I noticed where he was touching. And then I remembered, and for a moment I closed my eyes because I couldn't believe that I'd forgotten about the something that had been with me every day for months, that I'd tried not to see every time I was naked near a mirror.

I couldn't believe that Will had made me forget I wasn't whole.

I opened my eyes. He'd propped himself up on his elbow, and the fingers of his other hand were touching my right thigh. The corrugated skin there, silvery and pink.

'What happened to you?' Will asked me. He brushed his fingertips up and down my scars. I knew the skin there was slightly cooler, unnaturally smooth or pitted. I touched it myself, in the dark, when I couldn't help remembering. He moved upward, smoothing the long scar across my belly with his thumb.

I leaned up on my own elbow. The bed was small enough so that our faces were only inches apart. The rain pattered and I could feel his soft breathing on my face. He wasn't looking at my thigh or my belly; he was looking at my eyes.

'I had a car crash,' I said. 'No, strike that – I crashed a car because I was being bloody stupid.'

'You must have crashed a lot of cars.'

'Yes, but this one wasn't on purpose. I wasn't listening to

my stunt coordinator and I was too cocky. I took the wrong risk and I chose to do it.'

'What happened?'

'I wrote off the car, for a start.'

'What happened to you?' His voice was so gentle, nearly as gentle as his fingers.

'I got trapped in the car and it exploded. To use a technical term. It crushed around me. If my friend hadn't got there in time to pull me out, I would have died right there.'

'And what happened to you?' he repeated.

I swallowed. I hadn't catalogued my injuries out loud before. But the list had run through my head in all its completeness. 'Injuries are part of the job. For example, Jackie Chan has broken every bone in his body at least once.'

'What happened to you, Liza?'

'I broke both my legs in several places. Shattered my left foot. I crushed two vertebrae. The doctor said that half a centimetre's difference would have paralysed me for life. I had third-degree burns over my thigh and hip where the fire ate through my clothes. They took skin grafts from my back. The scar on my stomach is where I had to have my spleen removed. It ruptured and I nearly bled to death.'

'When did this happen?'

'The first of April. My birthday.'

'How long were you in hospital?'

'Less time than you'd think. The physical therapy lasted much longer.'

'Lee didn't tell me about it.'

'Lee didn't know. Nobody here knows. I didn't tell them.'

This time, he didn't ask another question. Instead he knelt on the bed near the middle of my body. I watched as he ran his thumb and fingers over the curving scar on my stomach again, slowly, carefully, as if he were learning it. He found the burn marks and smoothed them with his palms. I held my breath. Gently, he turned me over and though I could only see the flowered pillowcase, I felt his eyes on me. Felt his curious, tender fingertips on the ridges of my spine, on the stripes where the skin had been taken. He could see it better than I ever could. Softly, he pressed his lips there.

'You're thinking about how much it hurt,' I said to the pillowcase, 'but that doesn't really matter. You get hurt as a stuntwoman. Everyone gets hurt. Scars are a badge of honour. But these aren't. These ones are a badge of how stupid I was. I was more attracted to the risk than the job. I didn't listen and I didn't care and both of those are dangerous. Every one of those scars is my own fault and that's why I don't have a job any more.'

He didn't stop kissing me. Along my side and up the curve of my healed and hidden spine, to the back of my neck, along my shoulders. His breath was another caress.

'And I didn't tell my sister and my mother because I didn't want to worry them, but that was only the smallest part. It was mostly because I was ashamed. I crashed a car and I made a mistake and I lost my job and it confirms absolutely everything that everyone here expected of me, that I'd never turn out to be anything. That I'm a fuck-up. It's— I couldn't show them that weakness.'

He turned me over and started at my forehead, brushed my hair back and kissed me over and over on my face. I could feel his legs against mine. He didn't look into my eyes, and that made it easier to talk.

'And the thing is, I think I might have actually wanted to crash that car. Because it was easier to prove everybody right.'

He kissed me once, softly, on the lips. Then he did look into my eyes.

'Did you want to hurt yourself?' he asked.

'I think – I might have. I think . . . sometimes I think I wasn't careful because I didn't feel like I deserved to be safe. I had a lot of near-misses before that day. I told myself it was because I was pushing everything to be better. But I'm not sure that's the truth. I just didn't care enough.'

He nodded slightly. 'Is that all?'

'Yes, I think I've spilled my guts enough for the time being, thank you.'

The side of his mouth creased.

'You can get on with what you're doing,' I said.

'Thank you so much for your permission.'

'Unless you pity me because of my scars and because of what I've just told you. If you pity me, you can put your clothes back on and go out into the rain.'

'I don't pity you,' he said, and he kissed me again, his hands on either side of my head holding me still for him, the length of his body pressed against mine. I tasted desire and tenderness, maybe even a little bit of impatience.

I didn't taste any pity.

He kissed my lips and then my chin, and then continued downward. Between my breasts, with his hair brushing the side of my left one. Down to my navel, which he dipped into briefly with his tongue. And then around my hip, over the scar there, touching every bit of the flesh, once-hurting and whole alike. The nerve endings in my burns felt different from the rest of my skin; not less sensitive, not more, but different, as if the skin was grasping for sensation.

I lay there, my eyes open, watching him. I saw the way his hair curled from the damp and I saw the precise movements of his hands. I saw the long line of his back and shoulders, the way his eyelashes made a fringe against the skin of his cheek when his eyes were lowered. In a sudden moment of clarity, I understood that this wasn't a fuck but something else, something dizzying and dangerous and scarier than I'd suspected and yet something I'd wanted so very much without even knowing that I did. Then he parted my legs and licked me, and past pain disappeared into present pleasure and I whispered, 'Will.' I wound my fingers in his wet hair, felt it tangled around me like an embrace.

And then all I could do was to breathe and to feel. The rain pattered outside and Will licked and kissed and sucked at me so gently and thoroughly, until I hitched my breath with impatience – no, not impatience, with desire for more, always more – and he began to speed up, he slipped a finger inside me and I couldn't tell the individual strokes any more, just a building wave of pleasure that grew and grew and I threw back my head on the pillow and saw the orgasm that contracted to a single point of stillness and then exploded outward.

I think I shouted. I know I bucked on the bed and kicked the wall and hardly felt it. I tugged on Will's hair and pulled his face up to my level and kissed his heated lips, full of the taste of me, deep and long as his body lay atop mine, pressing me into the quilt and the mattress.

Our long kiss turned into little kisses. I could feel his erection long and hard against my belly. 'Thank you,' I said to him.

'Anytime.'

'I don't only mean for making me come. Thank you for asking me the questions.'

'Again, anytime.' I felt him smile. 'Can I ask two more?'

'All right.'

'You said you didn't listen and you didn't care. Do you still not care?'

I didn't know what I'd been expecting him to ask, but this wasn't it. My throat suddenly got tight, like it had in Allen's Porsche 911. This time, I breathed through it.

'I do care now,' I whispered.

'Okay.' More small kisses, as if we were sipping from each other. I closed my eyes to feel him better and waited for the next question. He'll ask me what I care about, I thought, and that made my heart thump again, a tiny curl of dread in my stomach.

'The second question,' he said against my lips, 'is how do you want me? Because I want to fuck you so badly I'm about to go insane if we don't do it now.'

Dread dissolved. I laughed and pushed him over onto his side, towards the wall. There was barely enough room for us both on the bed. I wrapped my leg around his hip and guided him into me.

It was perfect and shocking at the same time. Dangerous and right. He gasped in a ragged breath and his hands tightened on my hips. 'You feel incredible,' he said to me.

'You feel better than incredible,' I told him, and I began to move on him, with him.

We couldn't keep it slow. We managed three or four long, sensual strokes and then he groaned and rolled us over with him on his back and me on top of him, and my knee was wedged between the mattress and the wall but I didn't care. He put one hand on my breast and the other on my hip and I bucked and came again and he thrust upward, frantic now, a look on his face as if he were in so much bliss that it hurt. I reared back to get him in deeper, further, harder, and he roared and I cried out and his body arched off the bed and lifted me, up as far as I could go.

Then I fell on top of him, our hearts racing each other.

The Morning After

We were both asleep before the sweat cooled off our bodies. When I woke up again it was dark outside and Will's face was so close to mine that I barely had to move to kiss him. He was already hard when I reached for him and we made love for the second time, more slowly, like a dream. Then he rolled us both up in the quilt and we slept together like spoons, his breath in my hair and the rain falling so far away.

In the morning the sun shone through the window. I saw it and felt it before I opened my eyes, as a glow through my eyelids and warmth on my face. Will stirred and kissed me on the back of my neck.

'Good day, sunshine,' he murmured.

I knew he was smiling. I turned over in bed to face him. 'That was fantastic,' I said.

'Mmm. It was.' I liked his smile and his sleepy eyes. The roughness of his chin. He looked the exact opposite of a stuffy aristocrat.

'Will you promise me something?' I asked.

'Anything. Especially if you give me coffee afterwards.' He pulled me closer.

'You might laugh, but this isn't an idle promise. It could change your life. So think deeply before you agree.'

He stroked lazily up my spine. 'Anything. Absolutely anything.'

'Promise me that you will never, ever again wear a jumper draped around your shoulders.'

'Done.'

'Are you sure? Because I can tell you, William Naughton, you're a good-looking man, but I will never be seen in public with you if you dress like that.'

He raised his eyebrows slightly. 'Are you planning on being seen with me in public?'

I realised what I'd said. Still, an ultimatum about a wardrobe error wasn't exactly a declaration of commitment. 'Let's just worry about the jumper problem for now, shall we?'

'Mm. Tell you what. I'll keep the jumpers off my shoulders if you'll start wearing your own clothes.'

'I'm wearing all my own clothes now.'

He ran both his hands up my sides. 'It's a start.'

His fingers were nicely near my breasts and I expected, from the evidence of the past twelve hours, that he'd continue where he'd left off earlier. Instead, his hands didn't move.

'We need to talk about it, you know,' he said.

I didn't pretend to think he meant clothes. 'We could just have sex again.'

'We can. I'd like to. But it's up to you. You need to know, first, that Lee and I have slept together.'

'I know,' I said, and of course I did. It didn't stop jealousy from searing my guts as soon as he said it.

'Do you – want to know about it?'

'No,' I said immediately, and then, 'Yes. Well, just one thing. Are we . . . different?'

'Very. Extremely.'

'You say that like you've been thinking it through.'

He sighed and gazed at the ceiling. 'Liza, I think you can appreciate that I'm in a situation here where I can't win. If I say you're different, you'll think I'm comparing you. If I say you're not, you'll think I believe you're interchangeable.'

I sat up. The quilt fell down, baring my breasts. 'I wish I hadn't asked. We could be having sex again now. Instead, I'm pissed off.'

'I can understand that,' he said carefully, 'but if you think about it for a minute you'll probably see that it's not fair to be angry at me for having sex with the woman I was dating before I even really met you, and while you were in a different country.'

'No. But logic has never kept me from being angry before. I've spent most of my life being angry, I'm used to it.'

'Do you want to be angry?'

I looked down at my hands. 'Not really. Not any more. It's tiring.'

'If it helps, I feel guilty as hell about this whole thing, even though Lee and I most definitely broke up before she left. I feel bad about mistaking you for her. But you broadsided me; I couldn't work out what was happening and how I felt. I jumped to the most obvious conclusion. And this feels like it's behind her back.'

'So you're guilty and I'm angry.'

'Yes.'

'Well, that just sucks.'

'It's not the sexiest post-coital conversation I've ever had.' He propped himself up on his elbow. 'Unlike the sex, which was.'

'Was what?'

'The sexiest.'

Despite myself, I laughed. 'Sexiest sex. Boy, that expensive education built your vocabulary to an almost unbelievable degree.'

'Here, I'll use some different words. It was superb, Liza. It was astounding and earth-shaking. It was exceedingly marvellous.'

'Now you sound like a thesaurus.'

'I've got one up my sleeve. See?' He held up his naked arm, and then used it to pull me down to lie beside him. 'I loved doing it with you, Elizabeth Haven, and I want to do it again.'

'Mmm.' I wriggled against him, all warm maleness. Somehow, lying beside him on sheets smelling of sex, with his leg twined around mine and him looking at me like that, the anger and guilt melted away. Or at least it was easy to forget. 'Sweettalk like that might get you just what you want.'

'And coffee afterwards. Don't forget.'

I pulled up the quilt over my head and began to kiss down his chest. 'By the time I'm finished with you,' I said, 'you're not going to remember what coffee is.'

Some time later, I left Will recovering in the bath and went, finally, to make the coffee. Every inch of my body felt fulfilled, used and tingling in the best possible way, and I considered wandering around the house naked to revel in the sensuality of it but then remembered the tourists strolling past the windows, to say nothing of the good people of Stoneguard. So, mindful of my promise to Will, after splashing about in the bath with him, I pulled on a little T-shirt and a pair of lacy pants, both of them my own, and I went down the stairs.

I hummed as I filled the coffee-maker. I should be hungry, not having eaten since lunchtime yesterday, but it seemed that plenty of sleep and sex had sated all other requirements. I should also probably not feel great, given that I'd just slept with my sister's boyfriend in her house.

But I did. I felt wonderful. I felt all cocooned in a special bubble of *now*-ness. I didn't have to think about the future, or no more of the future than making this coffee and bringing it upstairs to Will. Sooner or later, I'd have to think things through, go back to that conversation we'd had and puzzle and pick it apart to try to work out how I felt about it. But not now.

Now was for living.

'Where's my coffee, woman?' yelled down Will from upstairs. The house was small enough that I could hear him, and faintly, the splash of his bath.

'It's coming,' I called, coming to the bottom of the stairs. 'How do you take it?'

'Come up here and I'll show you.'

'I meant the coffee, and stop it with the horrible cheesy jokes, you pathetic toff.'

He laughed; in my mind I could see him throwing his head back and resting it on the side of the tub. I had the feeling my mind was going to be full of him for a long time to come. I didn't know what I thought of that, and I didn't need to know, yet.

'Milk, no sugar,' he called. I went back to the kitchen and phoned Ice Cream Heaven to leave a message for Annabelle saying I wouldn't be in today. Then I poured two big mugs of steaming coffee. I did a little dance while I stirred, and then, humming again, went back towards the staircase. We'd drink coffee in the bath, and then maybe I'd convince Will he needed to let me drive the Aston Martin for a little while, maybe to somewhere isolated where we could steam up the windows for a bit.

A rattling sound, a familiar turning rattling sound, and I

froze, a drop of Will's white coffee slopping over the edge of his mug and landing on my bare foot. I stood, staring at the front door, because that sound was a key in the lock.

The door opened and my twin sister stepped into her house.

The Homecoming

'Hi, Liza,' she said. 'I'm back home.' I stared at her as she put her keys in the basket on the small table near the door, the place where she'd obviously put her keys a million times, because she belonged here and I didn't.

I stared at her and waited for her to do something. Normally, at this point, she'd come and hug and kiss me. But she didn't. She was looking at me, really looking at me, staring as if we hadn't seen each other for years and had forgotten what the other one looked like. It was the same way that I was looking at her, and for a second I imagined someone watching us and seeing the same girl, twice, both with the same expression, except one was wearing a little T-shirt with no bra and a pair of skimpy pants, and one was wearing white linen trousers, a blue tunic and sandals.

'You look great,' I said, because she did. Sun-kissed and slim, with her clothes rumpled from travel but her eyes clear and bright. 'Your skin is beautiful.'

'Thank you. It's been lots of good food and good exercise. Greece is gorgeous.' She put down her canvas bag and her handbag.

'That – sounds great.'

Neither one of us had moved closer to the other. I worked

on this film once, a science-fiction film, as the double for the lead actress, who was supposed to be some cyborg. The premise was that she was positively charged, and the other cyborg, her enemy, was also positively charged, and no matter how they wanted to get close to each other, their magnetic fields repulsed each other. We had to do this elaborate pantomime of leaping and twirling around each other without ever touching.

I don't know what would have happened if the two cyborgs had managed to touch. I guess they'd be destroyed. It never happened in the film, so I never found out.

'How are you?' I asked lamely. 'I didn't know you were coming back today.'

'Yes, I felt that I'd had enough time away. I tried to ring you yesterday to tell you.' She tilted her head slightly and narrowed her eyes, and this was weird, because though we'd been sharing the same expression a moment ago, I'd have said this expression she had now was 100 per cent mine. 'You know what's funny, though. I ran into all kinds of people on my way from the station, and none of them seemed to know I'd been away.'

'No?' I said. I shifted from one foot to the other.

'No. In fact, they seemed to think I'd been here the whole time. I saw Candace and she complimented me on my fake tan and asked how I liked the aromatherapy oil she'd given me last Thursday.'

'Ah.'

'And then I saw Lord Naughton.'

'Ah,' I said again.

'And I was quite surprised because he doesn't usually come into town, but he said Ma Gamble had got him helping with the earthworms, and he thanked me for inviting him round to Mum's and said he'd be around again on Sunday.'

'Well,' I said, 'that. I can actually explain.'

'I never invited Lord Naughton round to Mum's. She doesn't want any visitors.'

'Yes. Well, as I said—'

'I thought at first that they thought I was you, but no, they were using my name. I have to admit, I was puzzled. I thought at least somebody would have noticed that I'd been gone. Especially if there have been changes, like having visitors for Mum even though she's specifically forbidden that to happen, ever. I thought people would be asking me about my holiday. I wondered if someone might even mention Rufus's car. But nobody seems to have noticed I've been gone for three weeks.'

'So how was your holiday, anyway?'

'Liza, please tell me something,' she said, and her voice was patient, though her face was not. 'Have you been pretending to be me this whole time?'

'The thing is, Lee, you have to go right back to the beginning. It wasn't what I meant to do, but people just assumed, and it was easier—'

I heard, from upstairs, the unmistakable sound of a plug coming out of the bath and the water running down the drain. I probably should have kept talking, to provide a distraction, but I stopped at the sound, dread filling me, and Lee looked up the stairs and frowned.

'Who's here?' she asked.

'Actually, that's another thing where you have to go back to the beginning. Come on into the kitchen and I can explain.' I was backing away, trying to get her to come with me, so she wouldn't go upstairs and find Will naked. Maybe, if I was lucky and if I was fast, I could keep her in the kitchen while Will made his escape.

'It sounds like there's somebody in my bath.'

474

'It does, doesn't it? The plumbing in this place is pretty crazy. Come into the kitchen, I've just made some coffee.'

'Hello, Lee.'

My stomach sank. There was Will, at the top of the stairs and coming down. His hair was damp, he had stubble on his face, and he'd put on his clothes, which looked every inch as if they'd spent the night wet on the bedroom floor.

'Will?' My sister stood completely motionless while Will reached the bottom of the stairs and went to her and gave her a kiss on the cheek, one of his hands on her shoulder, the other on her waist. Like old friends, or lovers.

'I'm glad you're back,' he said to her. 'I was a little worried.'

My hands clenched on the mugs as I stood there, outside of Will's embrace while my sister was in it.

'What are you doing here?' she asked.

'It's a bit of a long story,' he said.

Lee looked from him, to me, and back again. I saw her taking in his dishevelled appearance, his wet hair, his unshaven chin. And my tiny T-shirt, thin enough to show my nipples through it, my underwear, my bare feet, my bed-rumpled hair and smudged make-up. The two mugs of coffee in my hands.

'Oh my God,' my sister said.

'It's not as bad as it looks,' I said, though I had no idea why I said it, because actually, it was much worse. From the evidence, Will could have come over to use the bath because the plumbing had gone at Naughton Hall, and I could have misplaced my dressing-gown. There was nothing about our appearance that definitively stated that we'd made love four times and slept in each other's arms in between. In her house.

She stepped away from Will, so he wasn't touching her any more. 'What's going on? Do you think that she's me, because she— no, you can't, you just said . . .' She'd been half-talking to Will, but now she turned wholly to me. 'What have you done, Liza?'

The pain in her voice cut me like a red-hot knife. 'Lee, I haven't been trying to hurt you, I've only been trying to help.'

'Help? *Help* me? What have you done? Pretending to be me, taking over my life, living in my house and sleeping with my boy . . .' She choked on the words. Her cheeks were blazing.

Suddenly I could see it all from her perspective. How crazy everything I'd done could look, how it would appear that I'd been trying to mess things up on purpose. I opened my mouth to deny it.

'Lee,' said Will, 'I am so sorry.'

I snapped my mouth shut. Will was apologising for me.

I wouldn't be apologised for. I wouldn't be pitied, and I wouldn't be called a mistake and I would not be the subject of someone else's apology and blame, cut out by someone I'd confided in, someone I'd been naked with and who I'd shown my scars.

I would much rather fight. If you fought and you lost, at least you lost on your own terms.

'Will, this is between me and my twin,' I said, my voice loud in my ears, loud enough to be a shout. 'Your precious guilt isn't important right now, and neither are your apologies. It's about us, not you, and you need to leave. Right now.'

Anger flared in his eyes, too, and for a moment I thought he was going to argue with me. But then the veneer of polite calm descended once again.

'Is that how you feel about it too, Lee?' he asked, and I gripped the mug handles so hard I thought they might break.

Either that, or I'd fling them both at his head for asking her first, for not fighting with me.

'I need to sort this out with Liza,' she said.

'Right. I'll go. You know where to find me.' He looked at her for what seemed like forever, and then shot me a glance, so quick I couldn't read what it could possibly mean, if anything. And then he went out of the door, shutting it gently behind him, and I and my twin sister were alone.

'Well,' I said. 'Here we are. Together at last.'

She ran her hands through her hair, which swung back into place immediately like a curtain of silk. 'Liza, I need to know what you've done.'

Her voice was accusatory, as if I were on trial. My blood ran hotter. 'You've figured it out already. Yes, I've been pretending to be you. I've been working at Ice Cream Heaven, going to your yoga classes, visiting Mum, all the time wearing your clothes and answering to your name. I've lived in your house and I've fucked your boyfriend. Well, your ex-boyfriend, but I suppose that doesn't matter much in the scheme of things.'

'Why?' It came out hoarse, in direct contrast with her perfect appearance.

'I kept on telling myself it was because it was the easiest way to take care of things while you were gone. That nobody would listen to Liza Haven but they would always be happy to see Lee. I told myself that you wouldn't really care and it would be easier for you to come back if nobody knew you'd been gone. But that wasn't why, not really. Really I pretended to be you because I wanted to have your life.'

She stared at me. 'You want my life?'

'Of course I do. I always have.'

'But—'

'So I thought I'd steal it. That's what I do, right? Take what

I want, without caring about who I hurt. I'm the bad twin. I was born that way. No point trying to be anything else.'

I raised my chin and looked at her along the line of my nose. The way our mother looked when she was laying down a decree. Maybe Lee saw the resemblance, because she said, 'You made Mum have visitors?'

'I didn't give her a choice. I bullied her into it.'

'And why— I didn't even think you liked Will.'

At his name my anger flared again. 'You know what? Seeing him again reminded me that I'd wanted him all along, too. Since we were kids.'

My remark was meant to cause hurt and confusion, but it was too plain on my sister's face to bear.

'I'm getting rid of this damn coffee,' I said, and turned around and marched to the kitchen. I poured the coffee into the sink and watched it go down the drain. My black coffee, Will's white, swirled and mixed together in their race to oblivion.

What was the point? I'd ended right exactly where I'd begun. As the wrong one, the wanting one, the dark shadow.

I could hear Lee following me. Her sandals made whispering thumps on the hardwood floor. I took long breaths that failed to calm me, and looked down into the sink.

'Liza,' Lee said behind me, and I knew she was standing in the door of the kitchen, 'I'm trying to understand all of this. We spoke on the phone so many times, and you never mentioned any of this. I thought we were— I thought we were getting closer, finally, again. I thought you sympathised with how I was feeling about being stuck here, I thought you agreed it was time for me to have a break . . . Oh my God, hold on, did you encourage me to stay away because you wanted to carry on living my life for me?'

478

I shrugged without turning to face her. 'If that's what you want to think, go right ahead.'

'Liza, don't do this. You always do this. I can't take it this time.'

'You don't have to,' I said, turning around, and at that moment the telephone rang on the kitchen wall. Out of habit, I reached for it, but Lee was closer. And it was hers. Of course.

'Hello?' she said into it, still looking at me, frowning slightly at the voice on the other end. 'Yes, this is Lee.' She paused, listening, and then her frown got deeper, though her voice stayed sunny. 'Well, that's wonderful. I'm so glad.' She listened some more. 'Yes, of course. I'll sort that out on Monday, I'll make it my first priority. Fine. Thank you so much, I appreciate it. Goodbye.'

She kept hold of the phone, even though the call was over. 'That was Edmund Jett,' she said slowly. 'He called to say he loves the new ice cream.'

'Oh.'

'Did you make Edmund Jett an ice cream while I was gone?'

'Yes. I did that, too. Because I knew you'd never made a new flavour before. You've been treading water, Lee. You haven't changed a single thing here since you took charge. No wonder you've felt trapped.'

I saw that her hand was shaking. Her hand was gripping the phone so hard that her fingers had gone white and the rest of her hand had gone red.

'You fucking bitch,' she said, each word clear, her voice high and more angry than I'd ever heard it, ever – even the time I'd ruined her favourite doll, even the time we'd fought and lost each other. 'You fucking bitch. You stole my life. And then you *lived it better than I do*.'

I stepped backwards. Her anger was like a wave, a blow, a revelation. It blasted me and it blew away all my own rage so suddenly I didn't even realise it was going until it was gone and I was left there, empty.

I had never been empty before. Without anger, without fight, without desire or hunger or euphoria or adrenaline. It felt . . . horrible.

It felt alone.

'I didn't live it better than you do,' I said. 'I didn't. And I never meant to hurt you. But I did. And I'm sorry.'

I reached out my hand to touch her, on the shoulder or on the cheek, to welcome her back to her life in the way I should have done as soon as she walked in the door. She stepped back and flattened herself against the wall.

I'd encouraged her to get angry. To be more flawed and selfish, like me. And this was the result.

'I'll go,' I said. 'I don't belong here and you do. You really do, Lee. Everyone here loves you. And that makes up for a lot.'

I walked past her, out of the kitchen. I heard her sharp intake of breath.

'What happened to your leg?' she whispered.

Oh. I touched my burn scars with my hand. Of course my knickers didn't cover them up. And I'd forgotten, because Will, with his kisses and his loving and his questions and his laughter, had given me the illusion that I was whole.

The thought didn't make me feel worse. I couldn't feel worse. It just sat there, bleak and static, in the emptiness.

'I got in an accident at work,' I said without turning to face her. 'I crashed a car and I nearly died. It was my fault, which is why I don't have a job any more.'

'And you didn't tell me.'

'You kept things from me, too,' I said dully, looking down

the corridor at the door beyond. 'Like how difficult you were finding it, how bad Mum had got. That you'd broken up with Will and that you still thought about Tim. That you felt trapped and unhappy.'

'That doesn't compare. This was – you nearly died.'

'I think it does compare. We're completely different in most every way that counts, but when it comes to hiding the truth about ourselves, I think we're exactly the same.'

'Didn't you even think I'd care?'

'I knew you'd care. And I knew you'd look down on me for screwing up. You'd feel sorry for me. So I didn't tell you, even though I knew it would hurt you not to know.' I drew in a long breath which failed to fill me, and then I let it out. 'But I'm not going to argue about it. I don't feel like arguing any more. I'm going upstairs to pack my things, and then I'm going to leave.'

I went up the stairs. I found my suitcase, next to the rumpled bed where I'd made love with Will, and shoved whatever of my clothes I could find into it. I pulled on a pair of jeans, some socks and trainers. I stripped the bed and threw the sheets and duvet cover in a heap on the floor. It felt like I was stripping away all the memories I'd made there, but at least it meant that Lee wouldn't have to look at it.

When I came downstairs, Lee was sitting on her white couch. Her hands were in fists on her lap. She saw my suitcase in my hand and her cheeks flushed.

'I thought I was going to get home and things were going to be better,' she said. 'I thought you and I maybe had sorted some things out. But you've undermined absolutely everything I've done with the business and with Mum. And then . . . Will.'

'You broke up with Will.'

'It doesn't matter,' she said, and I saw tears in her eyes.

'He's still part of my life, not yours. You never wanted him until you thought that I did. Is that why you talked about ruining what I wanted? Did you want me to find you that way, together like that in my house? Was it in my bed?'

I'd thought I was empty but I wasn't, quite yet, because that question scraped more away.

'You really do believe I'm that bad, don't you?' I said.

'Go. I want you to go.'

There wasn't even a *please* this time. I went out of the door and shut it behind me.

I left my suitcase outside my mother's door and went inside without knocking. The last time I left Stoneguard I hadn't said goodbye to her. But this time we had shared something. I wasn't exactly sure what yet. Maybe something as simple and as difficult as asking and receiving, telling and listening.

She was sitting in that chair, the same leather chair. The television wasn't on. She was wearing a tweed skirt and her house slippers. She looked up when I came in.

'Oh, it's you,' she said.

'Yes, Mum. It's me.' I knelt beside her on the floor, close enough to speak with her, far enough away so that she had to look down into my face.

'What are you doing?' she asked.

'We're just alike, aren't we? We're both fighters. We're both stubborn bitches. We both won't let anyone help us except on our own terms and we don't give a damn about what anyone else thinks. I never saw that until recently. I'd thank you for it, if it didn't make me completely miserable.'

Her eyebrows frowned.

'Lee's come back home. You need to be good to her, Mum. The ice-cream factory is your dream. It's not hers. She loves you, God knows she probably loves you more than anyone, and she'll do anything for you but you have to let that go, Mum. You have to let her do it the way she can.'

'The way she can,' she repeated.

'That's right. Please try to remember. No, wait, I know you won't remember. I'll write it down for you.' I found a piece of paper and a pen and wrote, and then I folded it up and put it in her hand. Her fingers were warm and fragile and still strong. 'And thank you, Mum. For taking me up on the hill. And seeing who I was when nobody else did.'

I pressed a kiss into the back of her hand. For a moment I breathed in tweed and cold cream and my mother who, like me, was beginning to unlearn.

'Bye, Mum. I won't leave it so long before I see you again. I promise.'

I put her hand back in her lap and I stood up. She looked up at me.

'Who are you?' she asked.

Clearing The Air *

The thing is, Liza probably hasn't even noticed that the house is a mess. Dust has collected in the corners of the floors. There's a coat of lily pollen on the table in the living room. When Lee goes upstairs to put her bag in her room, the bed there is unmade, and the guest bedroom is a tip, with papers all over the floor and bedlinen wadded in the corner. Liza has left her toothbrush on the side of the sink and there's a wet towel hung over the shower rail.

Will had wet hair. She doesn't let herself think about that.

Downstairs in the kitchen, she makes herself her first cup of proper tea in nearly three weeks and sees the dirty dishes in the sink. She fills the sink with soapy water and washes up and thinks about every single time she's cleaned up after her sister.

She told me to get angry. She told me to be more selfish.

The nerve.

Lee dries her hand on a fresh tea-towel taken from the drawer – the one hanging up was the same one she'd left there – and looks around at the other changes in the kitchen. The plants haven't been watered. The compost jar looks empty; she bets Liza hasn't put a single teabag in there the whole time she's stayed. A folder and some papers litter the worktop.

Actually, she recognises the folder. She picks it up. It's the paperwork she's kept from when she was working with Tim. Liza's brought it downstairs. Poking into her stuff, of course. His card is on top, with his phone number.

Did Liza call him? Is that why Tim rang the other day? The thought disgusts her; another thing she thought was going to change for the better, another thing that's no longer completely hers. She shoves the folder and the card under the breadbin.

The next day, Saturday, she goes to Rufus and Tania Fanshawe's house to set things right. They're in matching bathrobes, sitting in their breakfast nook having coffee and croissants. They offer her a coffee, which she refuses.

She's been gearing herself up for this for hours now. Days. She takes a deep breath and says, 'Rufus, I'm really sorry. But I stole your car.'

She's not sure what she's been expecting. The world to explode, the two of them to start screaming, police sirens to ring out. She doesn't expect silence, or Rufus and Tania to exchange a look.

'Lee,' says Tania, 'are you all right?'

'I'm fine. Well, I'm working on making myself fine. But you've got to believe me, this is really important. I'm the one who took your car. I don't know why I did it, well, yes, I do – I needed to get away fast because I was feeling too much pressure and I felt really unhappy. But that's no excuse; it was wrong and it hurt you and I'm very sorry. I'll go to the police and confess, but I wanted to tell you first.'

'Well,' Rufus says slowly, exchanging another look with his wife, 'that's very conscientious of you, Lee, but we agreed when you asked us last week that we wouldn't press charges.'

'For your sister Liza stealing the car,' added Tania.

485

'So there's really no problem.'

It's Lee's turn to stare. 'You think Liza stole it?'

'Yes, don't you remember? You came over last week.'

'That wasn't me,' she says, shaking her head. 'That must have been my sister. She must have told you that she stole the car, when she didn't. It was me.'

Rufus and Tania exchanged another look, this one even longer.

'Do you want us to call someone for you?' Tania asks kindly.

'Good morning, Lee!' says Ma Gamble. She pours boiling water on a Fair Trade organic tea bag and adds sugar. 'Have you heard about Marian Tarr? Got herself engaged to someone off the internet. Candace was in this morning and says she's going to feng shui their wedding. And that new aromatherapist, did you know she used to be a private detective, of all things?'

'I'd like green tea, actually, Ma.'

'Oh. Oh yes, that's fine.' Ma Gamble puts the tea aside and selects a green tea bag, equally Fair Trade and organic, for a new cup of water. 'How's your mother?'

'I think she's about the same.'

'She was in fine form last week, I'm looking forward to seeing her tomorrow. I still think you should bring her to the Friends of the Earthworm this afternoon. Has Liza left, then?'

She passes the cup over the counter. Lee takes it. She stares at Ma Gamble.

'You knew that Liza was here?'

'Goodness, yes. She's been keeping up your side while you've been gone. And infuriating the young Naughton.'

'Did she tell you who she was?'

486

'Oh no, I worked it out on my own. She's not much of a liar, never has been. Even when she was a child, you could see when she'd done something wrong by the look on her face. Speaking of Will Naughton, his father, by the way – now *that's* the big gossip of the town. Did you know he's lost all his money? He told me yesterday morning, while we were testing the compost for this afternoon.'

Lee puts down the cup of green tea. 'How many people know about this?'

'About Lord Naughton? Just about everyone by now. I asked if he minded, and he said no, it was about time everyone knew. He said Will wanted to clear the air anyway.'

'About my sister being here. Pretending to be me.'

Ma Gamble scratches her head under her beanie. 'Now that's a question. Your mother did – Will too, I should think. I have a feeling one or two people know at Ice Cream Heaven, but you know Doris, she doesn't open her mouth unless there's a spoon coming at it.'

'*You* don't know who knows?'

Ma Gamble shrugs and sips the tea she's made for Lee. 'Your sister had quite the little outburst on me about spreading rumours. I thought she'd prefer it to be on a need-to-know basis. Anyway, will you be there for the Friends of the Earthworm? Two o'clock in the marquee, on the green by the car park.'

'Maybe,' says Lee. She drops some money on the counter for her green tea and leaves the shop, not too steady on her feet. She's greeted by Fenella Dearborn, Jasbir Singh, Derek Hunter with his terriers sniffing at her sandals, Rock Hamlin cleaning the window of the ice-cream parlour and whistling cheerfully through his beard. Even a tourist or two, buoyed by the sunny day, offers her a smile. She turns the corner up to her mother's house.

Mum's sitting in her chair by the open window. There's a cup of tea beside her, but it's gone cold; she's asleep, her head leaning on the back of her chair, her face tilted towards the sun. Lee kisses her warm cheek but she barely stirs. She's about to go and find the nurse to talk about how Mum has been, when she spots a piece of paper in her mother's hand. It's been unfolded, and it hangs loose in her fingers. Lee gently takes it out.

It's a list, in Liza's handwriting. Messy and bold.

1) *Keep making lists.*
2) *Wear slippers to bed.*
3) *Let Lee follow her own dreams.*

Halves and Wholes

'Are you going to Florida for business, or pleasure?'

The woman sitting next to me in the gate waiting area was American, with a poodle perm and trousers printed with tiny turtles. She had a thick book, with her finger keeping her place in it, but she was evidently in the mood for a little conversation.

'Neither,' I said. 'I'm changing planes in Miami for Bolivia. I'm going llama trekking.'

'Oh, that's interesting. And is this something that you've always wanted to do?'

'Not particularly. But my sister hates me, my mother doesn't remember me, my lover is ashamed of me, I don't have a job and if I go back to my own apartment, I'll probably end up jumping out of the window.'

The woman stood up. 'Excuse me, I'm going to use the restroom before we board.'

I watched her scurry away, toting her book and her carry-on. I didn't blame her. The gate waiting area was full, without any other vacant seats. I got up, so that when she came back, she wouldn't have to worry about sitting next to me again. She'd been brave sitting next to me in the first place; I probably looked exactly like what I was, which was a woman who'd spent the night in an airport waiting for the first flight that would take her llama-ward. I wandered to the window and looked out at the plane that was going to take me away from the colossal mess I'd made.

My phone was off. If I'd learned one lesson from Lee's holiday it was that if you don't want to be contacted, turn off your phone. If Lee was acting true to form, she'd be trying to get in touch with me, to apologise for getting angry or some ridiculousness like that. Talking with her wasn't going to make any difference. Our phone calls hadn't sorted anything out while she was gone, and we hadn't sorted anything out before that, when I was gone. The telephone made it too easy to hide.

And I couldn't call Will even if I wanted to, because I didn't have his number. Lee did, but I wasn't Lee any more, and that was irrelevant anyway. There was no point phoning Will. I'd been wrong to get angry with him and to send him away. But he hadn't cared enough to fight me about it. So that was that.

I'd go to La Paz. There wasn't anything for me there, but there wasn't anything for me anywhere. I'd try to hook up with a guide and some animals. It was bound to be slow and smelly going, but maybe the scenery would be spectacular enough so that I'd forget about Stoneguard. Maybe in the mountains on the back of a llama, spending the last of the balance on my credit card, I'd find out who I was really supposed to be.

Or maybe not.

And when I got back, I'd . . .

I put my forehead on the glass. I could call Allen, maybe. Call him and apologise properly. I owed lots of people apologies, and he should have got one a long time ago. Maybe he'd repeat his offer of setting me up with some teaching work. By then, I might be ready to try team-building again. After all, it hadn't worked so badly with the Ice Cream Heaven team.

Except, of course, that I'd been deceiving the entire team. I sighed, and my breath fogged the glass between me and the plane.

'Two, six, nine, ten, GO!'

It was close enough and loud enough so that I looked down to see where it had come from. A small boy launched himself off the low windowsill beside me and hit the floor running. He sped through the waiting passengers, yelling 'Brrrmmmmm!' twisting an imaginary steering wheel, dodging legs and bags and disappearing behind a group of teenagers wearing yellow sweatshirts.

Funny that they called them toddlers when they were so damn fast. I wondered if Annabelle's Pheebs liked pretending to race. I'd probably never get to see Annabelle's kids now. She probably wouldn't want to talk with me once she found out I was really the twin who'd always called her Mouse.

I remembered what I'd said to Will, out in the starlit field trampling wheat into a double spiral. *Nobody liked me before anyway. So I haven't lost anything, right?*

Too bad it felt like I'd lost everything.

The little boy climbed back onto the windowsill. It was only about four inches high, but he had to concentrate to get his little trainers lined up on it perfectly. While he was doing it, a second little boy appeared out of the crowd, wearing the same striped T-shirt, the same jeans with a hole in the left knee, the same body and face and hair. He climbed onto the windowsill with the same fierce concentration as his twin. They stood side by side looking ahead together at their imaginary racetrack.

They opened their mouths in tandem. 'One, four, seven,

ten, GO!' they both yelled and jumped off at exactly the same time. 'Brrrrmmmmm!' yelled one with his steering wheel. 'Vrrrrrooooom!' yelled the other, his hands outstretched to make wings. They ran together, missing obstacles and each other, both with identical joy on their faces. They left a wave of smiles behind them, and myself, staring.

'Good afternoon, ladies and gentlemen, we would like to begin boarding of Flight 147 to Miami International Airport.'

Usually I tried to be either first or last boarding planes, to avoid the crowd. This time I shuffled dully to the gate entrance carrying my small suitcase, along with all of the other passengers, working my way into one of the chaotic queues. I found myself directly behind the poodle-permed American, who glanced at me briefly before transferring her gaze quickly away.

The twins and their parents were in the queue next to us. When they were standing close together, I could see one had a cowlick, and the other had the fidgets. They had a Buzz Lightyear backpack which was too big for them and had been made for an older child; each boy was holding a strap and every time the queue moved forward, they dragged it behind them in tandem.

'They're so adorable,' said the American woman to their mother. 'They must be a real handful.'

'Oh, they're not too bad,' their mother said. We all edged forward with the queue. The boys grunted with the effort of dragging their backpack, which looked heavy. Who knew what was inside it – toys, snacks, their rock collection. Clearly it was precious, and clearly neither one of them would have been able to handle it by himself.

'How can you tell them apart?' the American asked.

'It's not so hard really, once you know them. They're quite

492

different.' The mother had a vague smile on her face, and she exchanged a quick glance with her husband. I could tell that she'd answered these questions or similar ones a million times, probably from the moment the boys were born. I could sympathise. We were near the front now, and the father gave the family's boarding passes to the airline employee.

'They're so cute,' persisted the American. 'Just as alike as two buttons. They look like two halves of the same person.'

The mother shook her head. 'No, nothing like that. They're not two halves, they're two wholes. Come on, boys, it's our turn to get on the plane.' The whole family trooped forward through the gate. The Buzz Lightyear bag dragged behind them.

I waited in the queue holding my own passport, my own boarding pass, my own suitcase. Leaving home, as I'd done dozens of times before. Something was turning in my mind. Something about two halves.

Or two wholes.

The American woman gave her boarding pass to the attendant. 'I'm so glad to be going home,' she said. Then she was through the gate, and it was my turn. But I didn't step forward.

Lee already belonged in Stoneguard. But maybe, by being there, I'd started to make some room for myself too.

And come to think of it, llamas weren't much more than giant sheep, and I hated sheep. Why would I want to sit on the back of one? Why would I want to run away, when I could stay and fight?

I didn't have anything left to lose. I might as well take my chances in Stoneguard, helping to run the business and taking care of Mum. Taking some risks. Getting my nerve back. Going home.

Becoming whole.

'Excuse me, madam? Your boarding pass?'

The airline employee was looking at me, expectant and a little bit annoyed, one plucked eyebrow raised in impatience. I handed over my boarding pass. But not my passport.

'I've changed my mind,' I said. 'I'm not taking the flight.'

Five minutes later, I was running down the concourse. Inside my head, I yelled 'Brrrrrmmmmm!'

'Is that really all you've got?'

'It's been a busy day,' said the bored teenager in the polyester car-rental uniform. 'Anyway, this is a very popular model, our most economical. I think you'll find it gets you from A to Z.'

'It's a one-litre diesel hatchback. With automatic transmission.'

'My sister drives one of them,' he added. 'It's actually pretty zippy.'

'Pretty. Zippy.'

'Yes. You'll probably like it.'

I checked my watch. It had taken me three hours to get to Heathrow via public transport from Stoneguard yesterday; even driving a one-litre hatchback would be quicker. 'Fine. I'll take it.'

Outside in the car lot, I found the car I'd agreed to drive. It was square and yellow. It smelled of plastic. It was plastic. When I turned the key in the ignition, the engine chirped to life like a moderately disgruntled budgie.

'Pretty zippy,' I muttered, and pressed the accelerator. After a short delay, the car started forward. It went over the bump at the exit, jarring my tailbone in the plastic seat, and then I was in the adrenaline-inducing stretch of road known as the Northern Perimeter, heading for the M4 and home.

I'd faced so many of my fears in the past forty-eight hours

that I was nearly at Slough before I realised that for the first time in five months, I was driving a car.

The budgie farted and buzzed, dithering between gears and reaching a dizzying speed of sixty-six on the motorway. I turned up the radio as loud as it would go and did my very best not to think of what was waiting for me in Stoneguard. Trying not to remember those movies where the whole town bands together against the monster or the bad guy, waving torches and pitchforks. Trying, instead, to think about what I'd say to Lee.

Even dawdling behind tractors and the Saturday tourist traffic, it was the fastest journey I'd ever done. I pulled up in front of Lee's house and went up the path to her door. I hadn't decided on what to say to Lee. I would have to wing it. What else was new.

I knocked. And waited. There wasn't an answer.

I chewed on my lip. Maybe I should have chosen the Bolivia option, after all.

'Don't be a coward, Liza,' I muttered to myself, and I turned the doorknob. The door was unlocked, and it swung open. The was a good sign, then. Maybe.

'Hello?' I called, stepping into the entranceway. And there it was: vanilla, clean clothes, something warmer. The scent of Lee, as if she'd just stepped out of the room. This was her house again, and here I was in the same place I'd been weeks ago when I'd first walked in, looking for her and not finding her. Her keys were in the basket, her shoes were lined up neatly near the door. She'd probably hung up the spare set of keys underneath the bird table. Tidied away all traces of my ever being here.

How was I going to find my own space in her life?

I looked into the living room, which was empty and clean.

And then paused, because something was different. The wall above the fireplace was blank yellow, with only a single nail remaining where the framed and pinned butterflies used to be. She'd taken them down.

'Lee? Where are you?' Frowning, I went through into the kitchen. Clean, bright, sunny. No dishes on the draining board, clean tea towel perfectly straight on its rail. One chair was pulled out slightly, as if Lee had just stood up from where she'd been sitting. On the table nearby lay Timothy Clifton's business card. And the back door to the garden was ajar.

I pushed it open, and I saw my twin. She had her back to me, hanging washing up on the line. Her hair was pulled back into a neat plait and she was reaching up, pinning a sheet. Maybe one I'd slept on. Maybe with Will.

I stepped backwards, and that's when Lee turned around. Her eyes met mine and she didn't smile but right away at that moment I knew.

She stepped forward and I did too and without a word, we were in each other's arms. I held her tight to me and felt her holding me, too.

'I'm sorry,' I whispered into her hair, into the smell of vanilla and flowers.

'I'm sorry too.'

'I was only trying to help. But I should have told you.'

She leaned back enough so we could see each other's faces. 'Do you remember Mum's Chinese vase?' she said. 'I was thinking about it. Do you remember I broke it when I was taking off my winter coat? You told her you broke it. I'd forgotten all about it until now. You took the blame for me. Remember?'

I shook my head. 'Lee, I've just come back practically from Bolivia, and you're talking about a Chinese vase?'

'You're the one who said that when we were talking about the past, we were really talking about now.'

'What did you have for breakfast?'

'Nothing.'

'Me too.' I began to laugh. She held me again, and I hugged her back. It was a natural thing to do, once you were used to it.

'You did help me,' she said. 'Everything you said to me on the phone was true. I never would have been able to come back here, if not for you. I was shocked when I got back, that's all. And I wish—'

'I should have trusted you. I should have told you. I know.'

'But I didn't tell you everything either.'

'I didn't ask.' A strand of her hair, loose from her plait, fluttered across her face and I brushed it back. 'I'm not going to leave it all to you any more, Lee. I'll be here. I don't care what anybody in the village thinks of me, if they don't like me, because I want to work together with you. I don't want to take over, I don't want your life for myself. I just want to help. If – if that's all right with you.'

She nodded. 'That would be good.' Her hand squeezed mine.

'And I'm sorry about Will,' I said. 'I'm not sorry I slept with him, but I'm sorry you found out that way. It wasn't on purpose. Neither of us wanted to hurt you.'

'I know.' Her eyes widened. 'Oh my God. Will.'

'What? Is he all right?'

'He left here twenty minutes ago. He's on his way to Heathrow.'

'Fucking hell, I just came from there. I didn't pass him. I couldn't have, I wouldn't have missed his car. Why's he going there?'

'I gave him your address. He's got a flight to Los Angeles. Maybe – maybe he went to Naughton Hall first.'

'He's going after me?'

'Maybe you can catch him.'

She hadn't finished the sentence before I was running, through the house and out the other side, back to the yellow budgie car. I pulled on my seatbelt with one hand and turned the key in the ignition with the other. Then I did a three-point turn in the middle of the road and headed down Church Street.

Even with this car, even with the Saturday summer tourists and the traffic, I could be at Naughton Hall in under ten minutes. If I was lucky, he'd still be there. If I was even luckier, he'd be—

There, in the gap in traffic. British Racing Green, sleek and low, like a genteel crouching panther. It crossed over the junction of Church Street and the High Street, heading straight east on the far side of the road, and I was close enough to see Will's profile as he drove.

I hit the horn as hard as I could and the car responded with a feeble *brip*.

There was nothing for it. I'd have to try to catch up with him. I gunned the throttle and the car downshifted, robbing me of power. It stuttered to the corner and I could see the back of the Aston Martin before the westward traffic passed in front of me, blocking my way out of Church Street. I craned forward and saw the long line of cars coming my way. And then the unmistakable white blob of the Ice Cream Heaven van coming eastward, tinkling its music, following in its merry way behind the DBS.

'Damn!' At this rate, it would be five minutes before I could pull out onto the High Street, and even if I did, I'd be stuck behind Archie and the van. Once Will was out of town, I wouldn't have a chance in hell of overtaking him in this car.

I made a split-second decision, checked my mirrors, and threw the car into reverse. Backed up onto the pavement, and whipped the wheel round to head in the other direction, up Church Street as fast as I could go. This car wasn't powerful, but it was small. Maybe even small enough.

When Church Street curved right, I kept on going, into the dark gap of Dog Shit Lane. The tyres bounced in a pothole and my head nearly banged the top of the car, but I twisted the wheel and slid round the corner on the narrow strip of gravel between the hedge and the churchyard wall.

'Please, no dogs,' I muttered and floored the accelerator, hoping for a kickdown.

Gravel and rocks spat behind me and the hedge scraped the yellow side of the car. Dog Shit Lane had not been designed for cars. I'd never even been foolish enough to try it when I was joyriding. I splashed through a puddle and God only knew how much dog crap, years' worth, probably, and heard the crack as I ran over a fallen branch and a snap as the wing mirror broke off against the wall.

'Come on, come on, come on,' I told the car, and it buzzed down the tunnel-like lane, my hands dry on the wheel, my heart racing. The lane opened out into the sudden car park and I hit the horn and the handbrake, scattering pedestrians as I weaved between parked cars towards the exit. If I was lucky, I'd beaten Will to the end of the High Street and I could cut him off at the pass. If I could get a gap in traffic. If I could . . .

A fat silver bus sat in the exit, crammed full of tourists, blocking the road. I twisted the wheel to the right, around the gate to the green. If it was clear I could drive on the grass and get onto the High Street in seconds.

I slammed on the brakes, which screeched and fishtailed

the car to a stop. The seatbelt grabbed me and dug into my chest.

'Will!' I cried out, in despair.

There wasn't a green. It was covered by a big white marquee tent emblazoned with a banner. *SAVE THE GIANT PALOUSE EARTHWORM*. Underneath it, in a pair of tie-dyed dungarees, stood Ma Gamble.

Our eyes met. I reached for the gear stick, to put the budgie into reverse. But it would be too late.

Ma Gamble bent down and lifted the side of the marquee, opening it up. She stood up straight, threw her chest out, and even above the buzz of my engine I could hear her hollering in her Army Officer voice.

'ALL CLEAR! CAR COMING THROUGH!'

It was instantaneous. Every single one of the Friends of the Earthworm jumped into action, falling back out of the way, carrying chairs and tables and boxes with them. At the far end of the marquee, Jasbir Singh pulled open the canvas.

I had a clear shot to the High Street.

The tyres of the budgie spun and caught on the gravel, and I accelerated through the marquee in a blur. I had just enough time to see that Maureen Lilly had stepped into the westbound lane, waving down the traffic, before I jumped off the kerb and skidded to a halt neatly blocking the road, with the front of the budgie car about an inch and a half away from the bumper of Will's Aston Martin.

I kicked my car door open. Will stepped out of the DBS.

'What the hell are you doing, Liza?' he asked me.

'One of the things I do best,' I said. 'The other one is this.'

I grabbed him and kissed him.

He met me halfway and pulled me up into his arms, my feet off the ground. From somewhere, there was a catcall. And a car horn beeping. And applause.

500

Will broke his lips away from mine. 'Are you staying?' he asked.

'I'm staying.'

'Are you sure?'

'Do you want me to?'

'Yes.' Will smiled at me and held me tighter. 'They're going to be talking about this for years, you know.'

'Let them talk,' I said, and kissed him again. And this kiss, definitively, was the best one of my life.

Except for the next one. And the next.

Acknowledgements

Every book is a journey, but this book was an especially long and inspiring one. I'm very fortunate to have had a lot of help on the way.

Getting Away With It would not exist without my agent, Teresa Chris, nor my editor, Sherise Hobbs of Headline. Their belief in me is quite stunning and humbling, and I am lucky to work with these amazing women.

Anna Louise Lucia and Brigid Coady helped with brainstorming and drafts and keeping me marginally sane. Kathy Love, Ruth Ng, Lizi Owens, Michelle Manson, Valerie Debord, Monika Mann, Asmi Desai, Simone Comley and Marketa McFadyen all listened to me going on incessantly about the ice-cream twins, and put up with me doing things like interrupting a child's birthday party to demonstrate various scenes from the book using a toy Ferrari Enzo. Thanks to the Reading Writers and to the Romantic Novelists' Association, particularly the Reading chapter. All of the *Sweet Valley High* references in this novel are dedicated to Cat Cobain, as an inadequate token of my debt to her.

Stunt women Kelly Jane Dent and Abbi Collins helped me with the life of a stunt woman, and told me everything I wanted to know about crashing cars, stuffing chicken fillets into your bra, and risking your life on a daily basis. My brother Matthew Cohen MD helped me with injury plans and recovery times.

Hazel Hartle of Purbeck Ice Cream in Dorset answered all my questions about running a family ice-cream business and was very generous with her time. I was thrilled to have a tour of Gifford's Ice Cream in Skowhegan, Maine; thanks to the Gifford family and especially to production manager Joel Violette. Thanks too to Gloria Minghella of Minghella's Ice Cream on the Isle of Wight who spoke with me about her passion for her product.

Thanks to John Lundberg of *www.circlemakers.org* for his expertise in crop circles and for designing a schematic for this book. Thanks, and apologies, to the farmer in All Cannings, Wiltshire into whose rapeseed field I trespassed last May, to examine one of the first crop circles of the 2009 season.

Thanks to the twins and parents of twins and multiples who talked with me over the past year and a half. And to all of the pairs of identical twins at whom I unashamedly stared in public, trying to learn – I'm sorry if I came across as pretty weird.

I owe a debt of gratitude, too, to my brave friends who cope with their loved ones' dementia. Kim Wilmott helped me in both instances.

And thank you, always and forever thank you, to my parents and to my son and to my husband, and to both my grandmothers, who will never be forgotten.